Disney

DONALD and MICKEY

The Magic Kingdom Collection

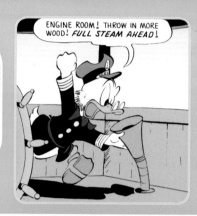

Fantastic River Race

From *Uncle Scrooge Goes to Disneyland* #1, 1957
Writer and Artist: Carl Barks
Colorists: Scott Rockwell and Jamison Services
Letterer: Garé Barks

ENGINE ROOM! THROW IN MORE WOOD! FULL STEAM AHEAD!

C'MON, YOU GUYS... IT'S NOT FAR TO THE WATER!
YEAH, BUT THE TRAIN IS ZOOMING ALONG!

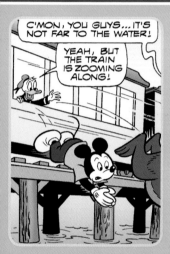

Donald and Mickey in Frontierland

From *Walt Disney Comics Digest* #32, 1971
Artist: Pete Alvarado
Colorists: Digikore Studios with David Gerstein and Erik Rosengarte

AYE! AND WHAT A TREASURE HUNT! PITY WE'VE KIND OF EXHAUSTED THE REAL WORLD'S SUPPLY! WHAT I'D GIVE FOR ANOTHER PROFITABLE ADVENTURE...

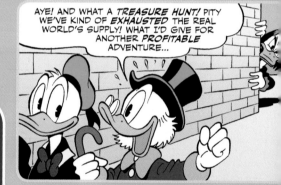

Red Rogue's Treasure

From Danish *Anders And & C:o* #9/1992
Writers: Paul Halas and Unn Printz-Påhlson
Artist: Victor "Vicar" Arriagada Ríos
Colorist: Digikore Studios
Letterers: Travis and Nicole Seitler
Translation and Dialogue: Thad Komorowski

Goofy in Fantasyland

From *Donald Duck in Disneyland* #1, 1955
Writer: Don R. Christensen
Artist: Al Hubbard
Colorists: Digikore Studios with David Gerstein

For international rights, contact licensing@idwpublishing.com

Special thanks to Daniel Saeva, Julie Dorris, Manny Mederos, Roberto Santillo, Camilla Vedove, Stefano Ambrosio, and Carlotta Quattrocolo

ISBN: 978-1-63140-796-3

20 19 18 17 2 3 4 5

IDW®
www.IDWPUBLISHING.com

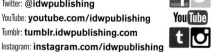

Ted Adams, CEO & Publisher
Greg Goldstein, President & COO
Robbie Robbins, EVP/Sr. Graphic Artist
Chris Ryall, Chief Creative Officer
David Hedgecock, Editor-in-Chief
Laurie Windrow, Senior VP of Sales & Marketing
Matthew Ruzicka, CPA, Chief Financial Officer
Dirk Wood, VP of Marketing
Lorelei Bunjes, VP of Digital Services
Jeff Webber, VP of Licensing, Digital and Subsidiary Rights
Jerry Bennington, VP of New Product Development

Facebook: **facebook.com/idwpublishing**
Twitter: **@idwpublishing**
YouTube: **youtube.com/idwpublishing**
Tumblr: **tumblr.idwpublishing.com**
Instagram: **instagram.com/idwpublishing**

Originally published as DISNEY MAGIC KINGDOM COMICS issues #1–2.

Plunkett's Emporium

From Danish *Anders And & C:o* #21/1992
Writers: Paul Halas and Jack Sutter
Artist: Victor "Vicar" Arriagada Ríos
Colorists: Anthony Tollin, Jamison Services, and Digikore Studios
Letterer: Gaspar Saladino
Dialogue: John Blair Moore

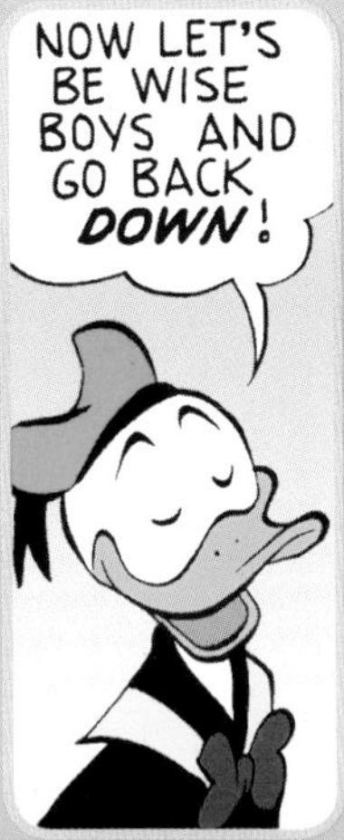
NOW LET'S BE WISE BOYS AND GO BACK *DOWN*!

Mastering the Matterhorn

From "Vacation in Disneyland" *Four Color* #1025, 1959
Artist: Carl Barks
Colorists: Susan Daigle-Leach and Jamison Services
Letterer: Garé Barks

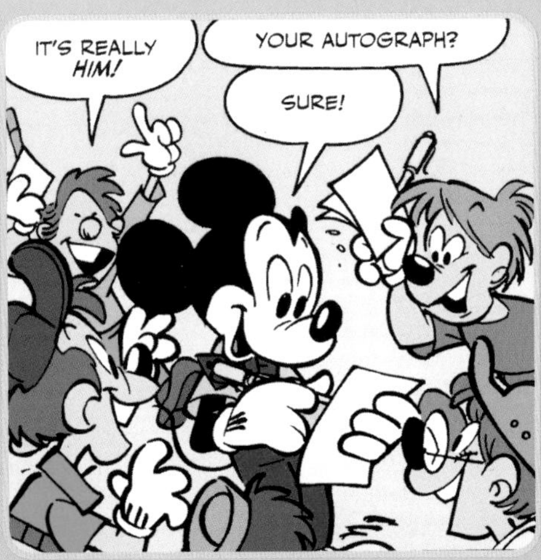
IT'S REALLY *HIM!*
YOUR AUTOGRAPH?
SURE!

Incredible Disneyland Adventure

From Italian *Topolino* #1552, 1985
Writer: Angelo Palmas
Artist: Giorgio Cavazzano
Colorists: Digikore Studios with David Gerstein
Letterers: Travis and Nicole Seitler
Translation and Dialogue: Jim Fanning

Series Editor: Sarah Gaydos
Archival Editor: David Gerstein

Cover Artist: Massimo Fecchi
Cover Colorist: Marco Colletti
Collection Editors: Justin Eisinger & Alonzo Simon
Collection Designer: Clyde Grapa
Publisher: Ted Adams

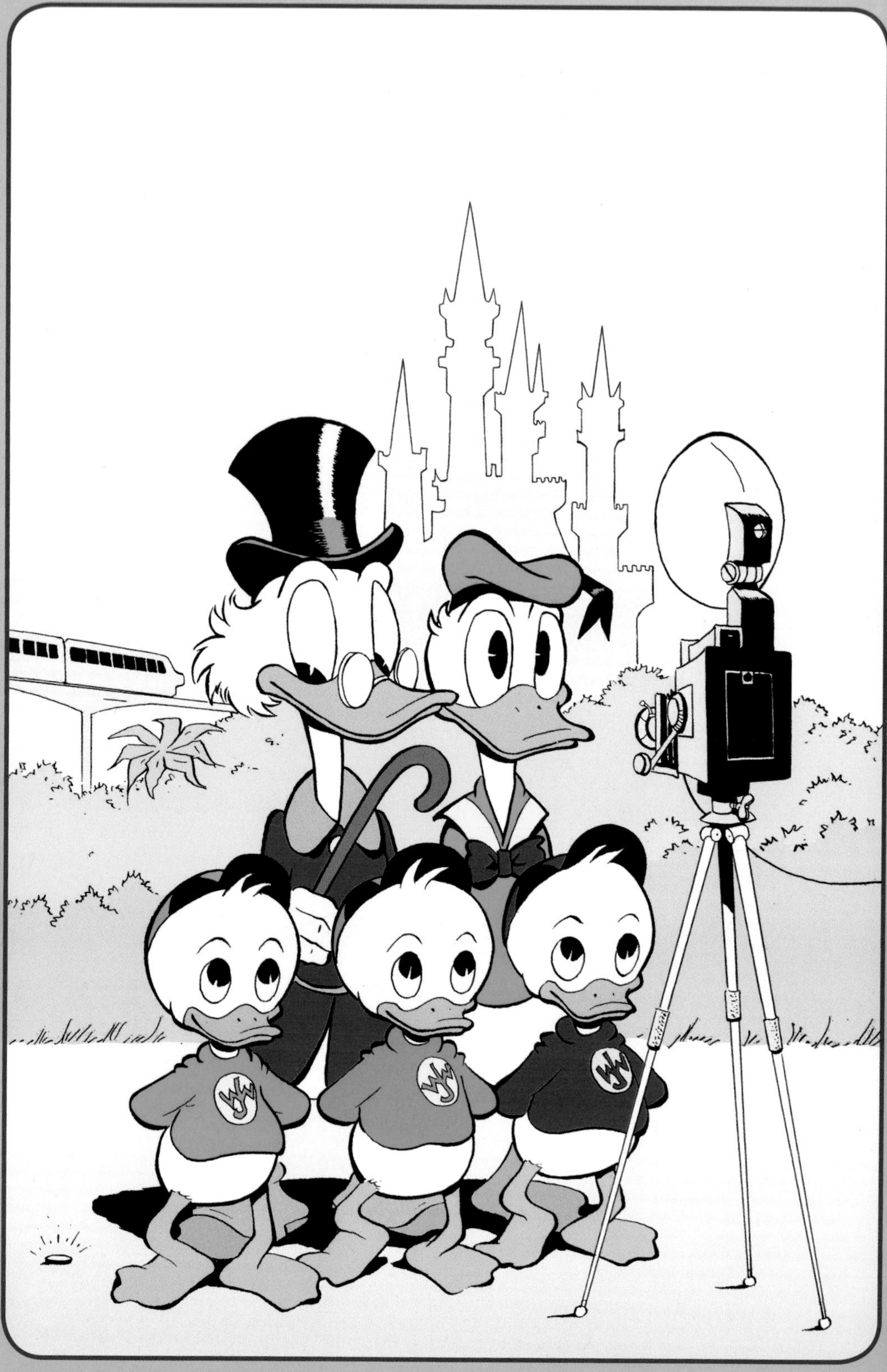

Art by Carl Barks, Colors by David Gerstein and Erik Rosengarten

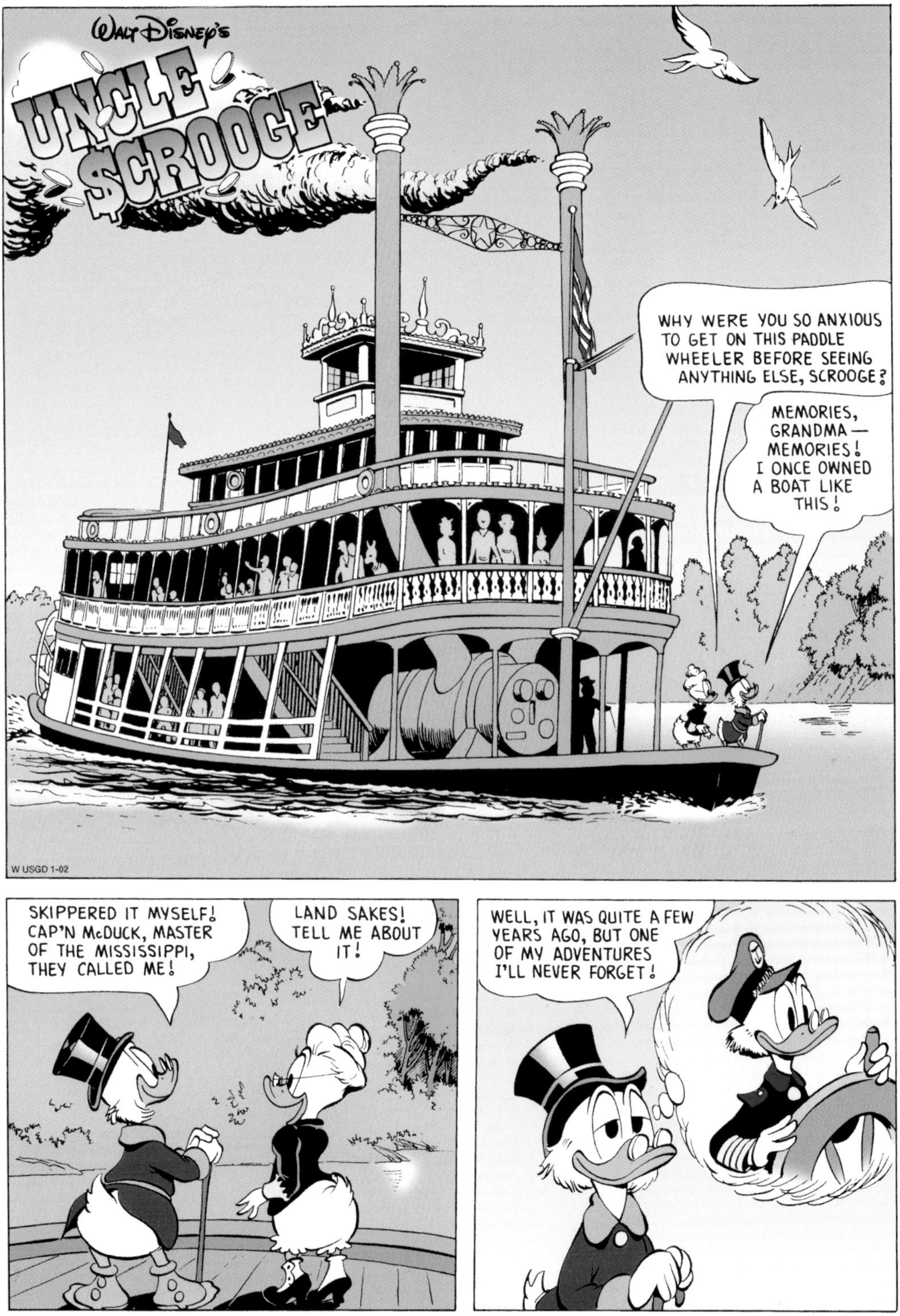
Walt Disney's
Uncle $crooge
WHY WERE YOU SO ANXIOUS TO GET ON THIS PADDLE WHEELER BEFORE SEEING ANYTHING ELSE, SCROOGE?
MEMORIES, GRANDMA — MEMORIES! I ONCE OWNED A BOAT LIKE THIS!
W USGD 1-02
SKIPPERED IT MYSELF! CAP'N McDUCK, MASTER OF THE MISSISSIPPI, THEY CALLED ME!
LAND SAKES! TELL ME ABOUT IT!
WELL, IT WAS QUITE A FEW YEARS AGO, BUT ONE OF MY ADVENTURES I'LL NEVER FORGET!

Originally published in *Uncle Scrooge Goes to Disneyland* #1 (USA, 1957)

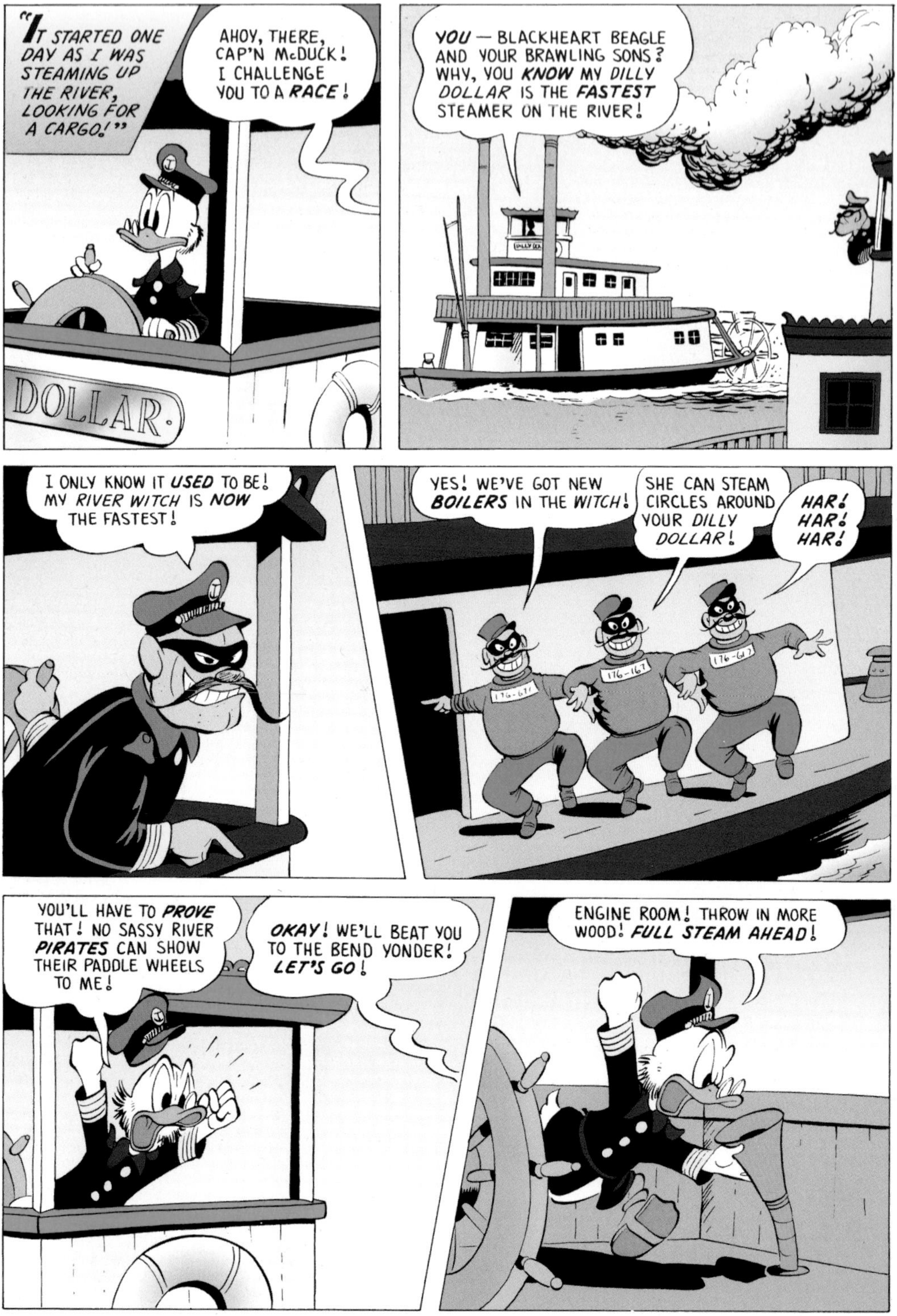
"IT STARTED ONE DAY AS I WAS STEAMING UP THE RIVER, LOOKING FOR A CARGO!"
AHOY, THERE, CAP'N McDUCK! I CHALLENGE YOU TO A RACE!
DOLLAR
YOU — BLACKHEART BEAGLE AND YOUR BRAWLING SONS? WHY, YOU KNOW MY DILLY DOLLAR IS THE FASTEST STEAMER ON THE RIVER!
I ONLY KNOW IT USED TO BE! MY RIVER WITCH IS NOW THE FASTEST!
YES! WE'VE GOT NEW BOILERS IN THE WITCH!
SHE CAN STEAM CIRCLES AROUND YOUR DILLY DOLLAR!
HAR! HAR! HAR!
176-167
YOU'LL HAVE TO PROVE THAT! NO SASSY RIVER PIRATES CAN SHOW THEIR PADDLE WHEELS TO ME!
OKAY! WE'LL BEAT YOU TO THE BEND YONDER! LET'S GO!
ENGINE ROOM! THROW IN MORE WOOD! FULL STEAM AHEAD!

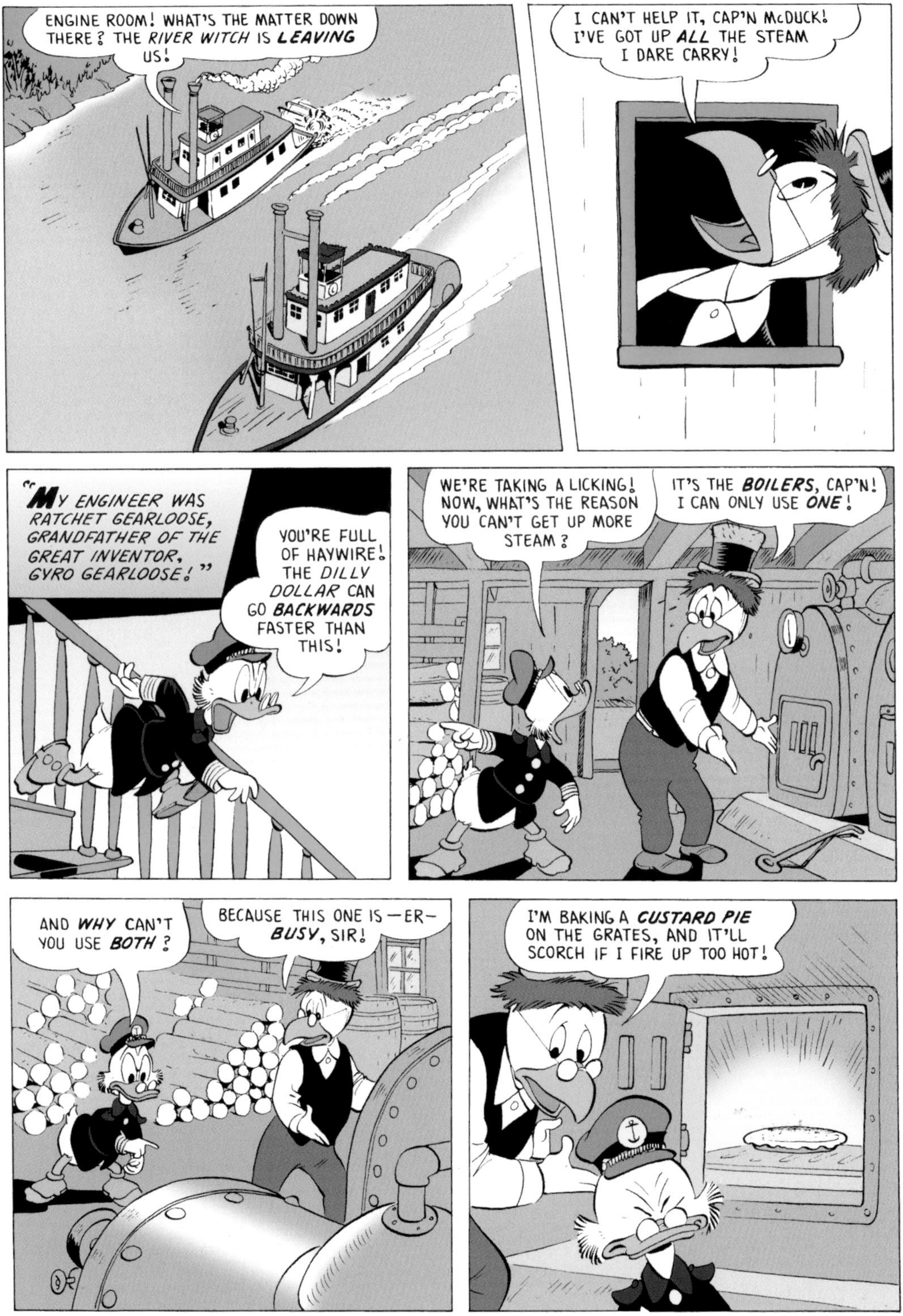
ENGINE ROOM! WHAT'S THE MATTER DOWN THERE? THE RIVER WITCH IS LEAVING US!
I CAN'T HELP IT, CAP'N McDUCK! I'VE GOT UP ALL THE STEAM I DARE CARRY!
"MY ENGINEER WAS RATCHET GEARLOOSE, GRANDFATHER OF THE GREAT INVENTOR, GYRO GEARLOOSE!"
YOU'RE FULL OF HAYWIRE! THE DILLY DOLLAR CAN GO BACKWARDS FASTER THAN THIS!
WE'RE TAKING A LICKING! NOW, WHAT'S THE REASON YOU CAN'T GET UP MORE STEAM?
IT'S THE BOILERS, CAP'N! I CAN ONLY USE ONE!
AND WHY CAN'T YOU USE BOTH?
BECAUSE THIS ONE IS—ER—BUSY, SIR!
I'M BAKING A CUSTARD PIE ON THE GRATES, AND IT'LL SCORCH IF I FIRE UP TOO HOT!

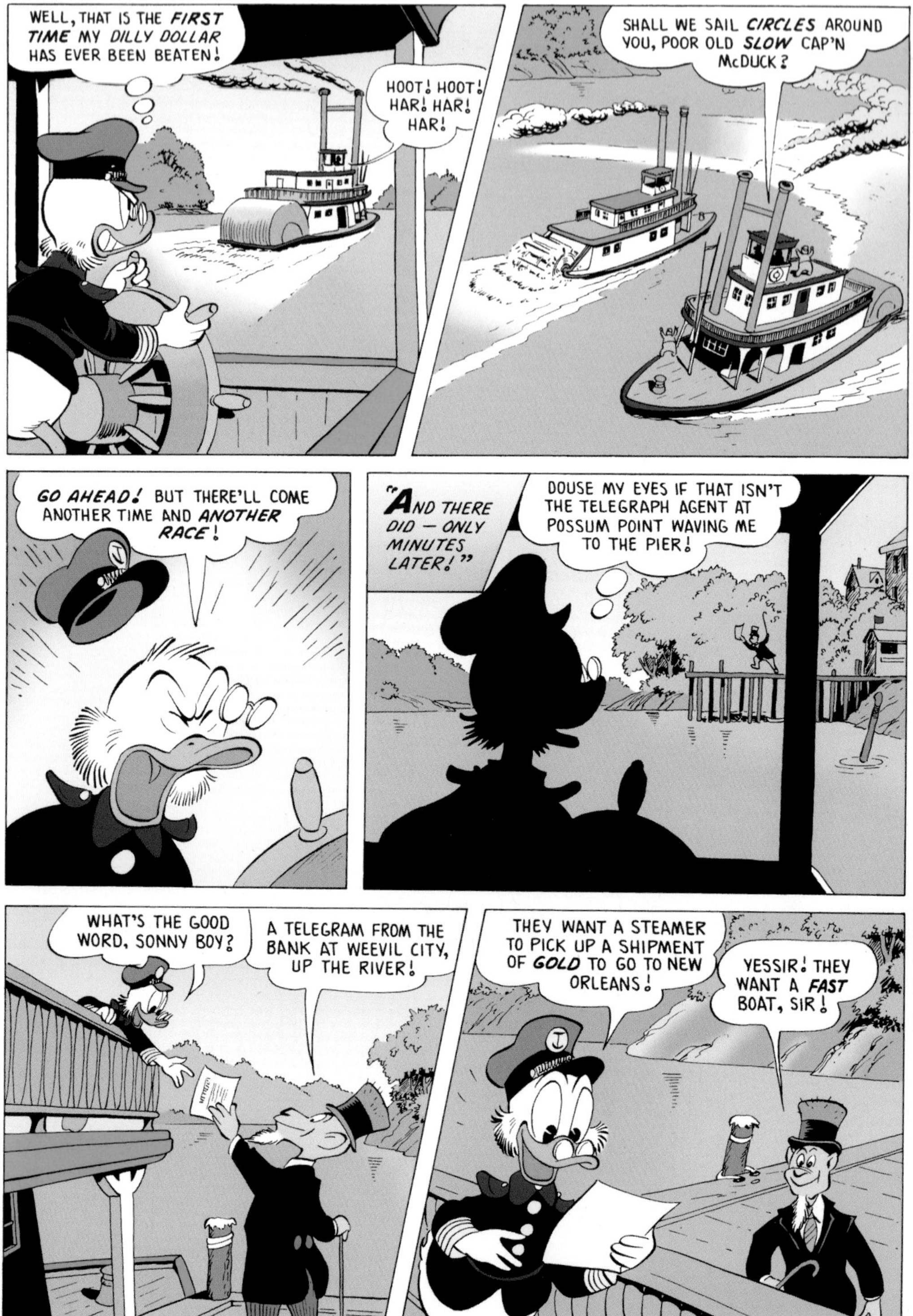
WELL, THAT IS THE *FIRST TIME* MY *DILLY DOLLAR* HAS EVER BEEN BEATEN!
HOOT! HOOT! HAR! HAR! HAR!
SHALL WE SAIL *CIRCLES* AROUND YOU, POOR OLD *SLOW* CAP'N McDUCK?
GO AHEAD! BUT THERE'LL COME ANOTHER TIME AND *ANOTHER RACE*!
"*AND THERE DID — ONLY MINUTES LATER!*"
DOUSE MY EYES IF THAT ISN'T THE TELEGRAPH AGENT AT POSSUM POINT WAVING ME TO THE PIER!
WHAT'S THE GOOD WORD, SONNY BOY?
A TELEGRAM FROM THE BANK AT WEEVIL CITY, UP THE RIVER!
THEY WANT A STEAMER TO PICK UP A SHIPMENT OF *GOLD* TO GO TO NEW ORLEANS!
YESSIR! THEY WANT A *FAST* BOAT, SIR!

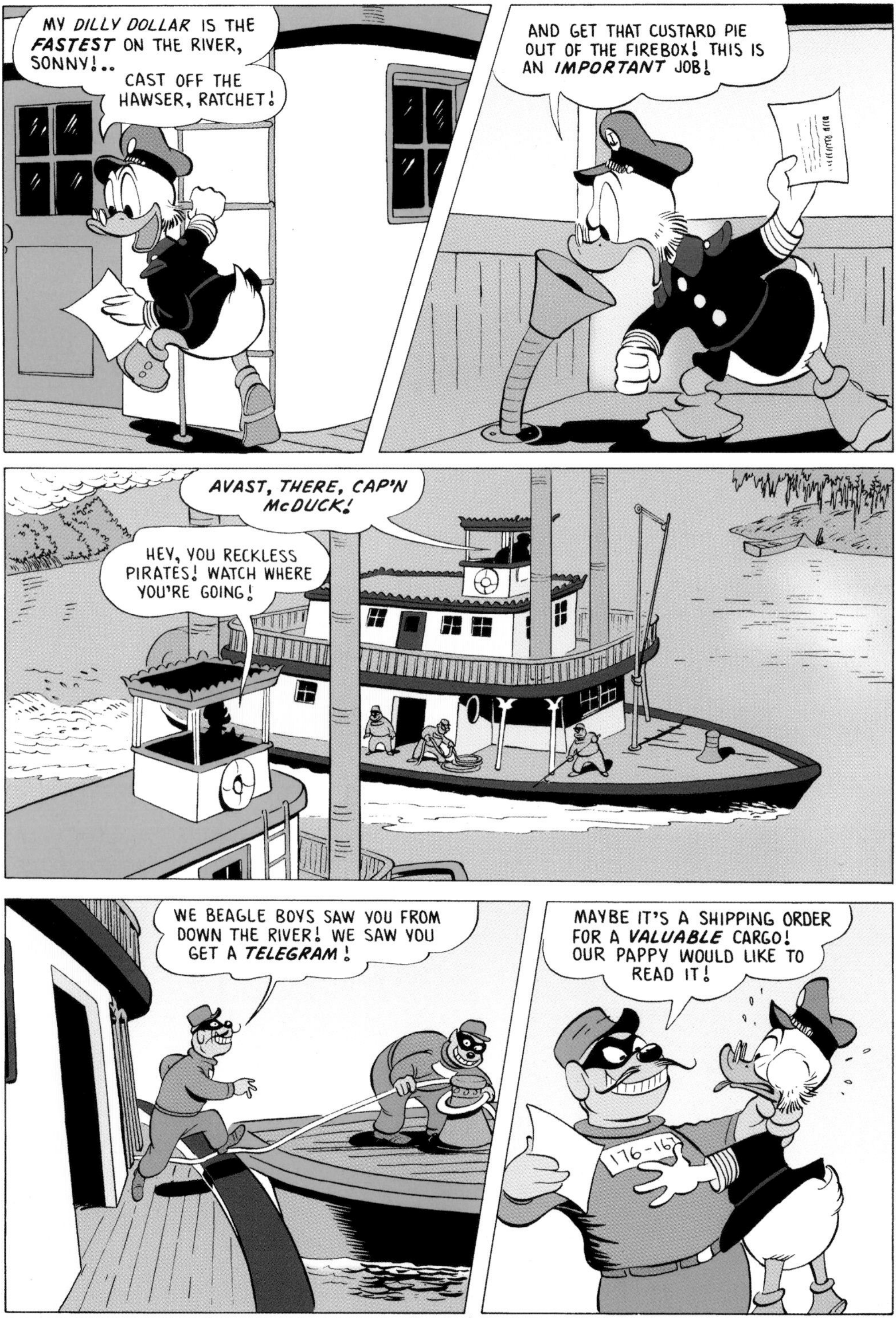
MY DILLY DOLLAR IS THE FASTEST ON THE RIVER, SONNY!..
CAST OFF THE HAWSER, RATCHET!
AND GET THAT CUSTARD PIE OUT OF THE FIREBOX! THIS IS AN IMPORTANT JOB!
AVAST, THERE, CAP'N McDUCK!
HEY, YOU RECKLESS PIRATES! WATCH WHERE YOU'RE GOING!
WE BEAGLE BOYS SAW YOU FROM DOWN THE RIVER! WE SAW YOU GET A TELEGRAM!
MAYBE IT'S A SHIPPING ORDER FOR A VALUABLE CARGO! OUR PAPPY WOULD LIKE TO READ IT!

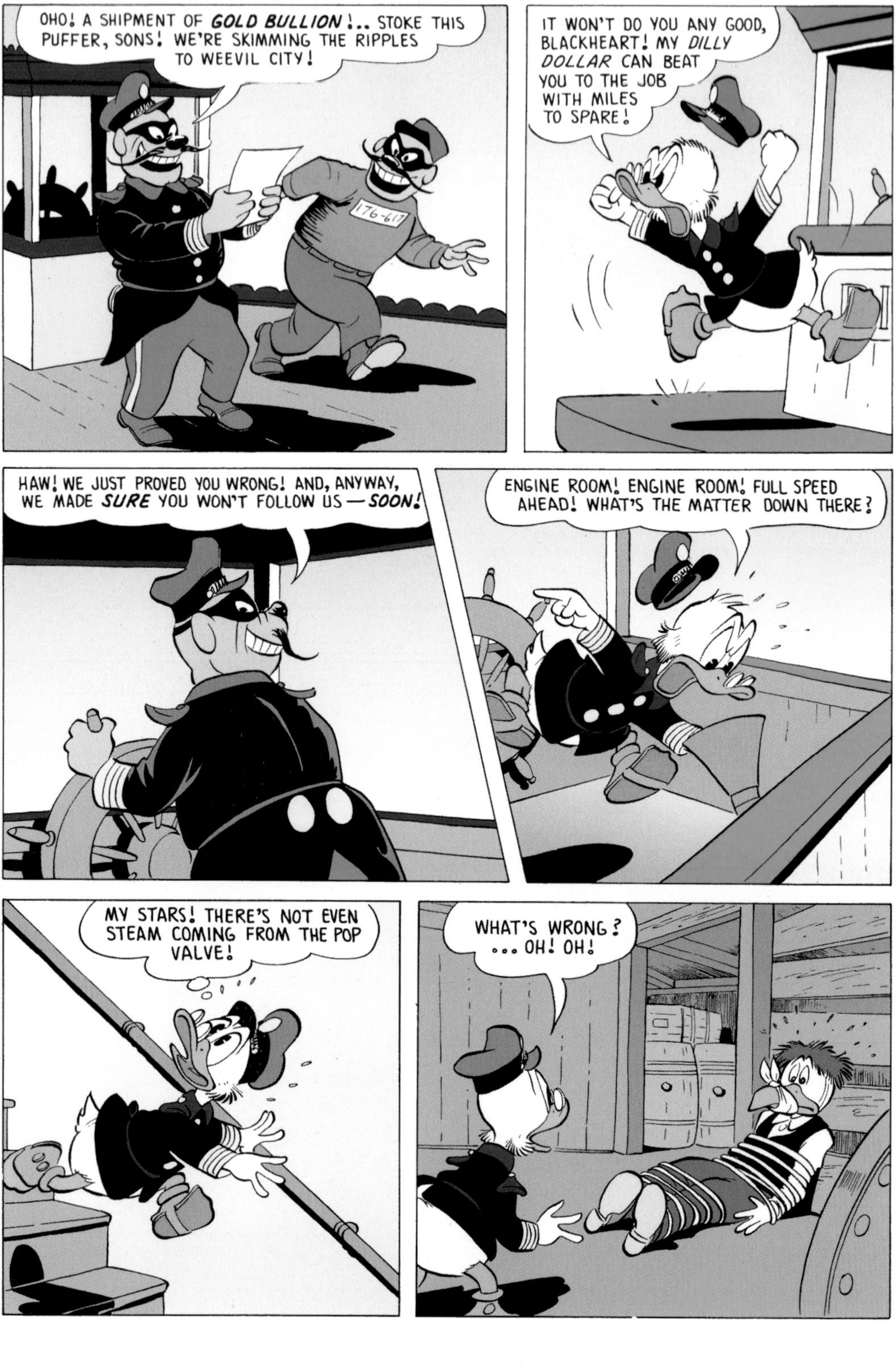
OHO! A SHIPMENT OF GOLD BULLION!.. STOKE THIS PUFFER, SONS! WE'RE SKIMMING THE RIPPLES TO WEEVIL CITY!
176-617
IT WON'T DO YOU ANY GOOD, BLACKHEART! MY DILLY DOLLAR CAN BEAT YOU TO THE JOB WITH MILES TO SPARE!
HAW! WE JUST PROVED YOU WRONG! AND, ANYWAY, WE MADE SURE YOU WON'T FOLLOW US — SOON!
ENGINE ROOM! ENGINE ROOM! FULL SPEED AHEAD! WHAT'S THE MATTER DOWN THERE?
MY STARS! THERE'S NOT EVEN STEAM COMING FROM THE POP VALVE!
WHAT'S WRONG? ... OH! OH!

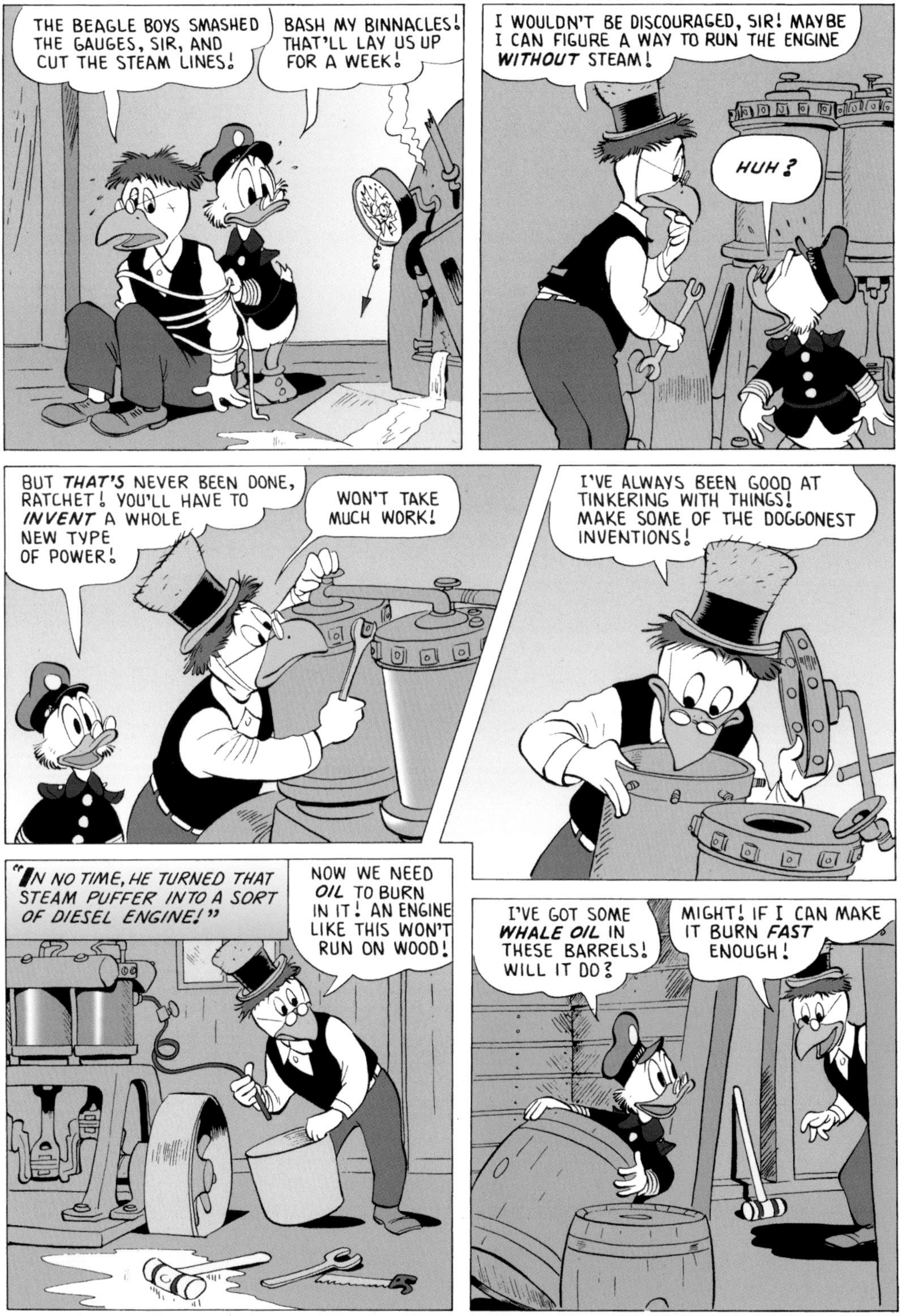
THE BEAGLE BOYS SMASHED THE GAUGES, SIR, AND CUT THE STEAM LINES!
BASH MY BINNACLES! THAT'LL LAY US UP FOR A WEEK!
I WOULDN'T BE DISCOURAGED, SIR! MAYBE I CAN FIGURE A WAY TO RUN THE ENGINE *WITHOUT* STEAM!
HUH?
BUT *THAT'S* NEVER BEEN DONE, RATCHET! YOU'LL HAVE TO *INVENT* A WHOLE NEW TYPE OF POWER!
WON'T TAKE MUCH WORK!
I'VE ALWAYS BEEN GOOD AT TINKERING WITH THINGS! MAKE SOME OF THE DOGGONEST INVENTIONS!
"IN NO TIME, HE TURNED THAT STEAM PUFFER INTO A SORT OF DIESEL ENGINE!"
NOW WE NEED *OIL* TO BURN IN IT! AN ENGINE LIKE THIS WON'T RUN ON WOOD!
I'VE GOT SOME *WHALE OIL* IN THESE BARRELS! WILL IT DO?
MIGHT! IF I CAN MAKE IT BURN *FAST* ENOUGH!

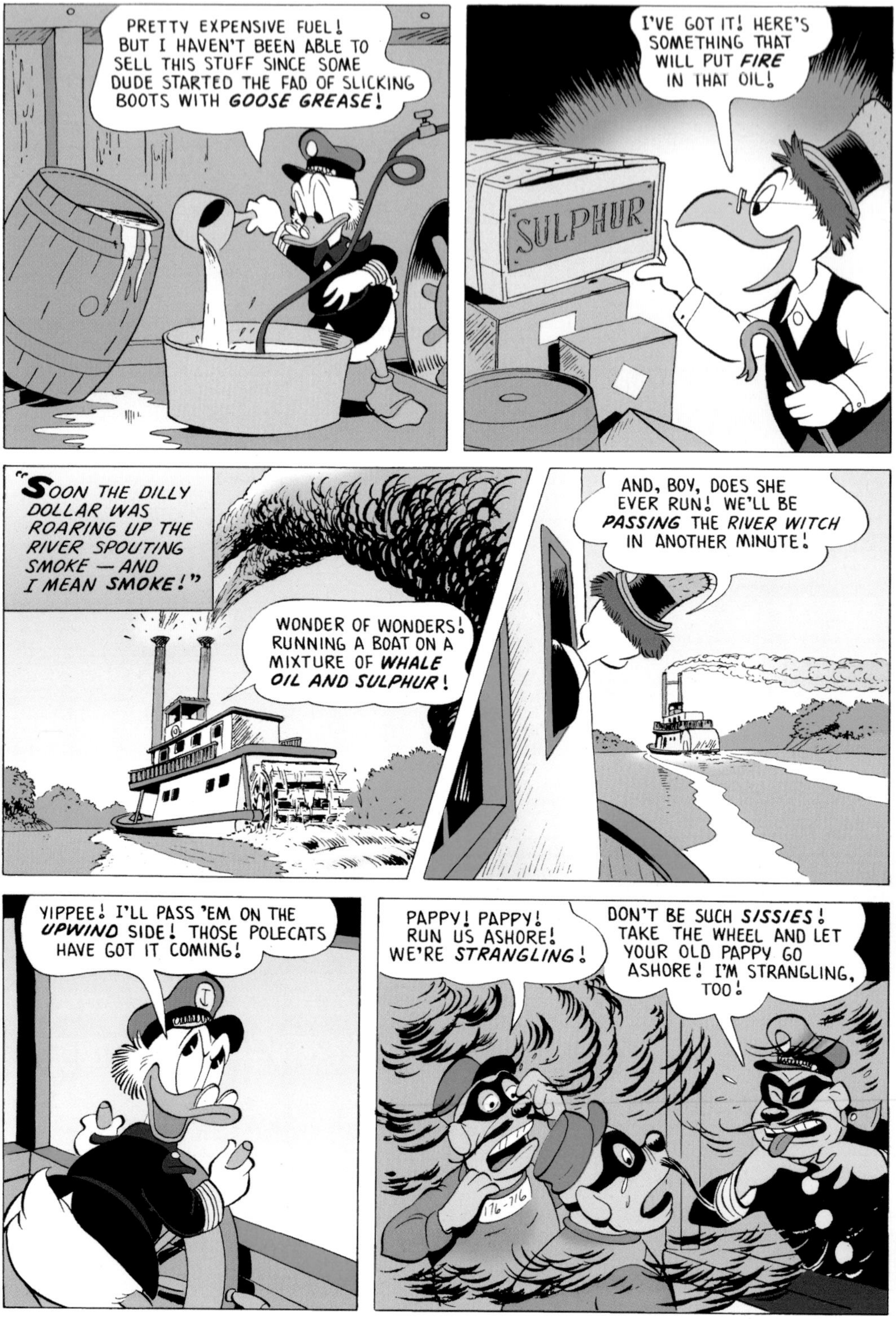
PRETTY EXPENSIVE FUEL! BUT I HAVEN'T BEEN ABLE TO SELL THIS STUFF SINCE SOME DUDE STARTED THE FAD OF SLICKING BOOTS WITH GOOSE GREASE!
I'VE GOT IT! HERE'S SOMETHING THAT WILL PUT FIRE IN THAT OIL!
SULPHUR
"SOON THE DILLY DOLLAR WAS ROARING UP THE RIVER SPOUTING SMOKE — AND I MEAN SMOKE!"
WONDER OF WONDERS! RUNNING A BOAT ON A MIXTURE OF WHALE OIL AND SULPHUR!
AND, BOY, DOES SHE EVER RUN! WE'LL BE PASSING THE RIVER WITCH IN ANOTHER MINUTE!
YIPPEE! I'LL PASS 'EM ON THE UPWIND SIDE! THOSE POLECATS HAVE GOT IT COMING!
PAPPY! PAPPY! RUN US ASHORE! WE'RE STRANGLING!
DON'T BE SUCH SISSIES! TAKE THE WHEEL AND LET YOUR OLD PAPPY GO ASHORE! I'M STRANGLING, TOO!
176-716

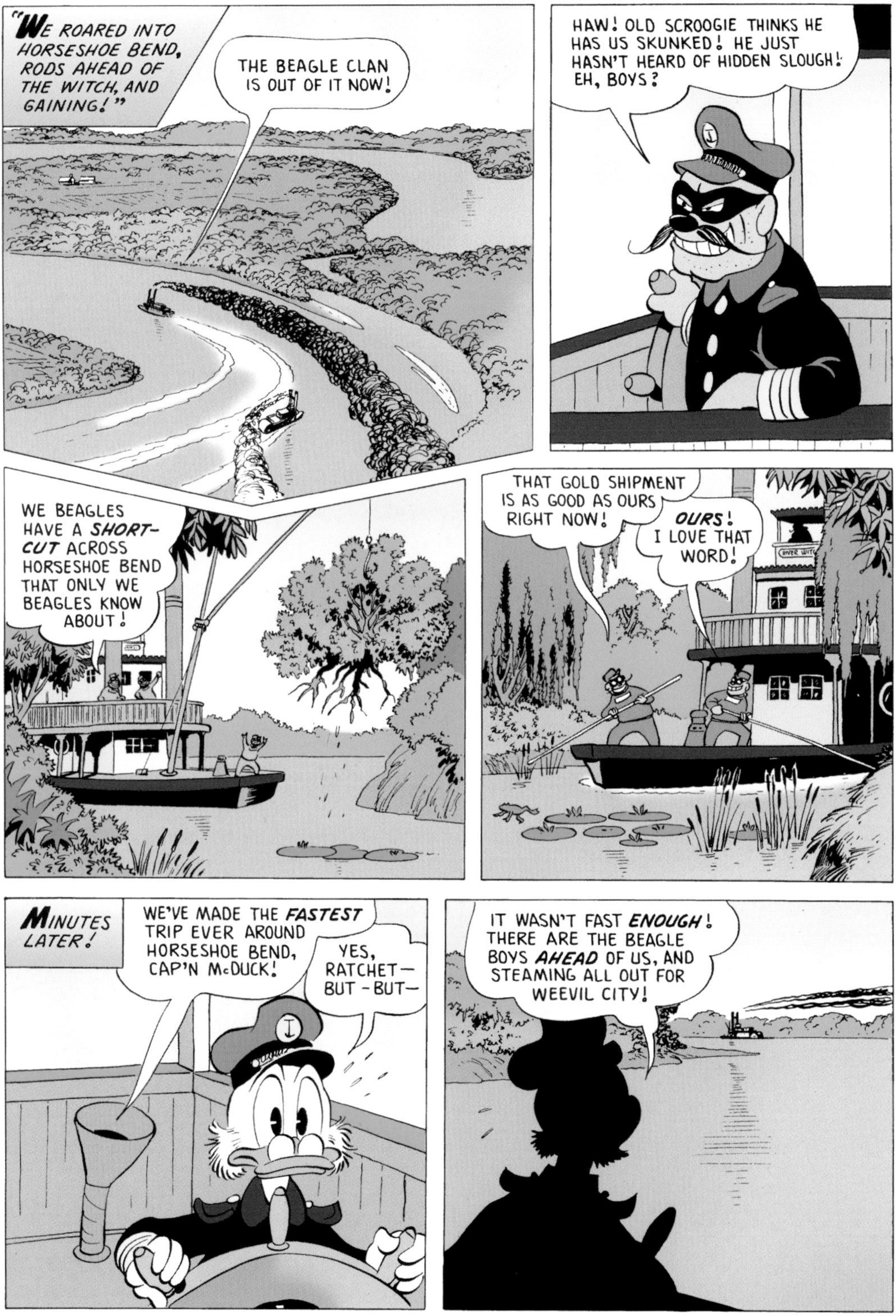
"WE ROARED INTO HORSESHOE BEND, RODS AHEAD OF THE WITCH, AND GAINING!"
THE BEAGLE CLAN IS OUT OF IT NOW!
HAW! OLD SCROOGIE THINKS HE HAS US SKUNKED! HE JUST HASN'T HEARD OF HIDDEN SLOUGH! EH, BOYS?
WE BEAGLES HAVE A SHORT-CUT ACROSS HORSESHOE BEND THAT ONLY WE BEAGLES KNOW ABOUT!
THAT GOLD SHIPMENT IS AS GOOD AS OURS RIGHT NOW!
OURS! I LOVE THAT WORD!
MINUTES LATER!
WE'VE MADE THE FASTEST TRIP EVER AROUND HORSESHOE BEND, CAP'N McDUCK!
YES, RATCHET— BUT - BUT—
IT WASN'T FAST ENOUGH! THERE ARE THE BEAGLE BOYS AHEAD OF US, AND STEAMING ALL OUT FOR WEEVIL CITY!

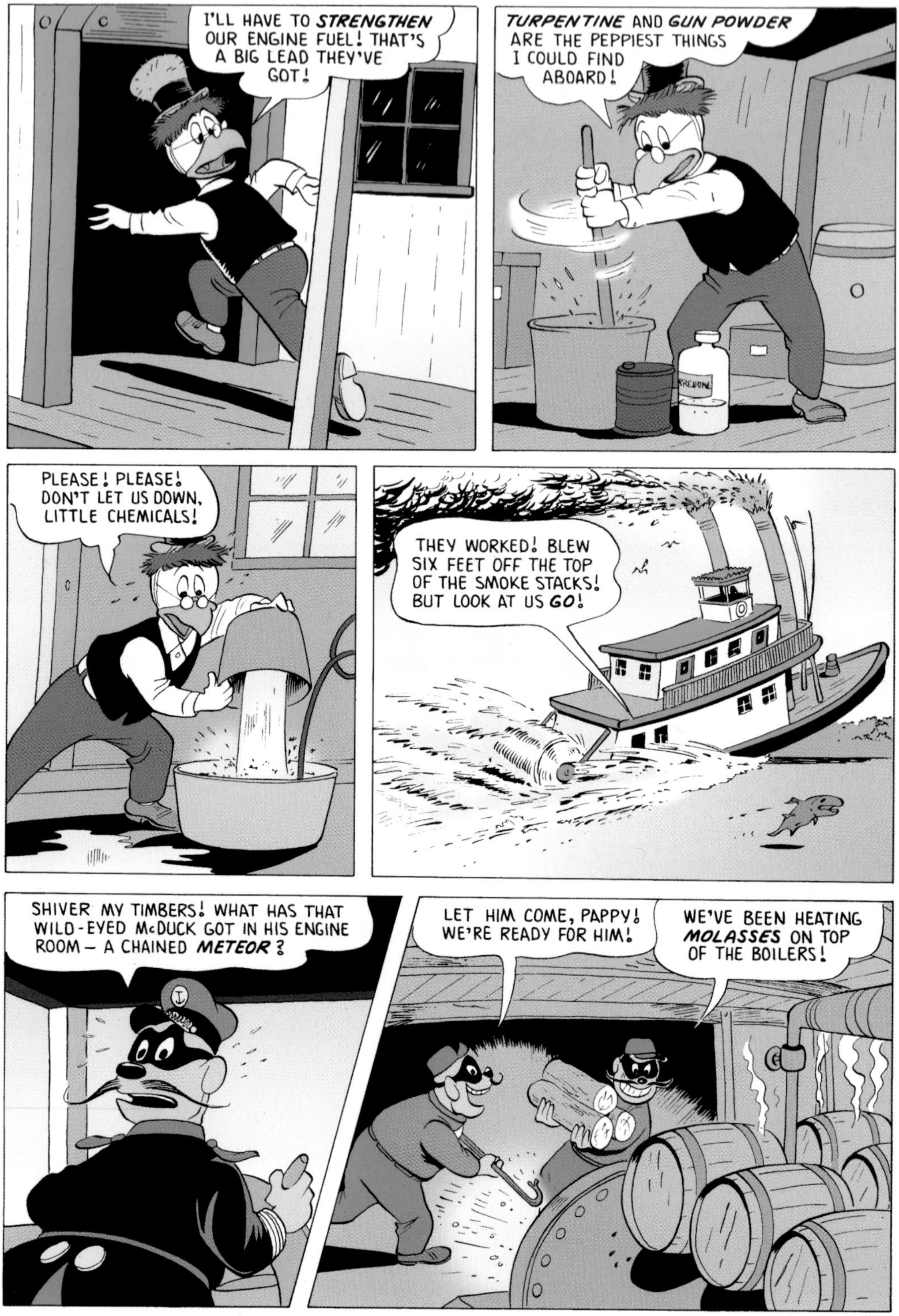

I'LL HAVE TO STRENGTHEN OUR ENGINE FUEL! THAT'S A BIG LEAD THEY'VE GOT!
TURPENTINE AND GUN POWDER ARE THE PEPPIEST THINGS I COULD FIND ABOARD!
PLEASE! PLEASE! DON'T LET US DOWN, LITTLE CHEMICALS!
THEY WORKED! BLEW SIX FEET OFF THE TOP OF THE SMOKE STACKS! BUT LOOK AT US GO!
SHIVER MY TIMBERS! WHAT HAS THAT WILD-EYED McDUCK GOT IN HIS ENGINE ROOM — A CHAINED METEOR?
LET HIM COME, PAPPY! WE'RE READY FOR HIM!
WE'VE BEEN HEATING MOLASSES ON TOP OF THE BOILERS!

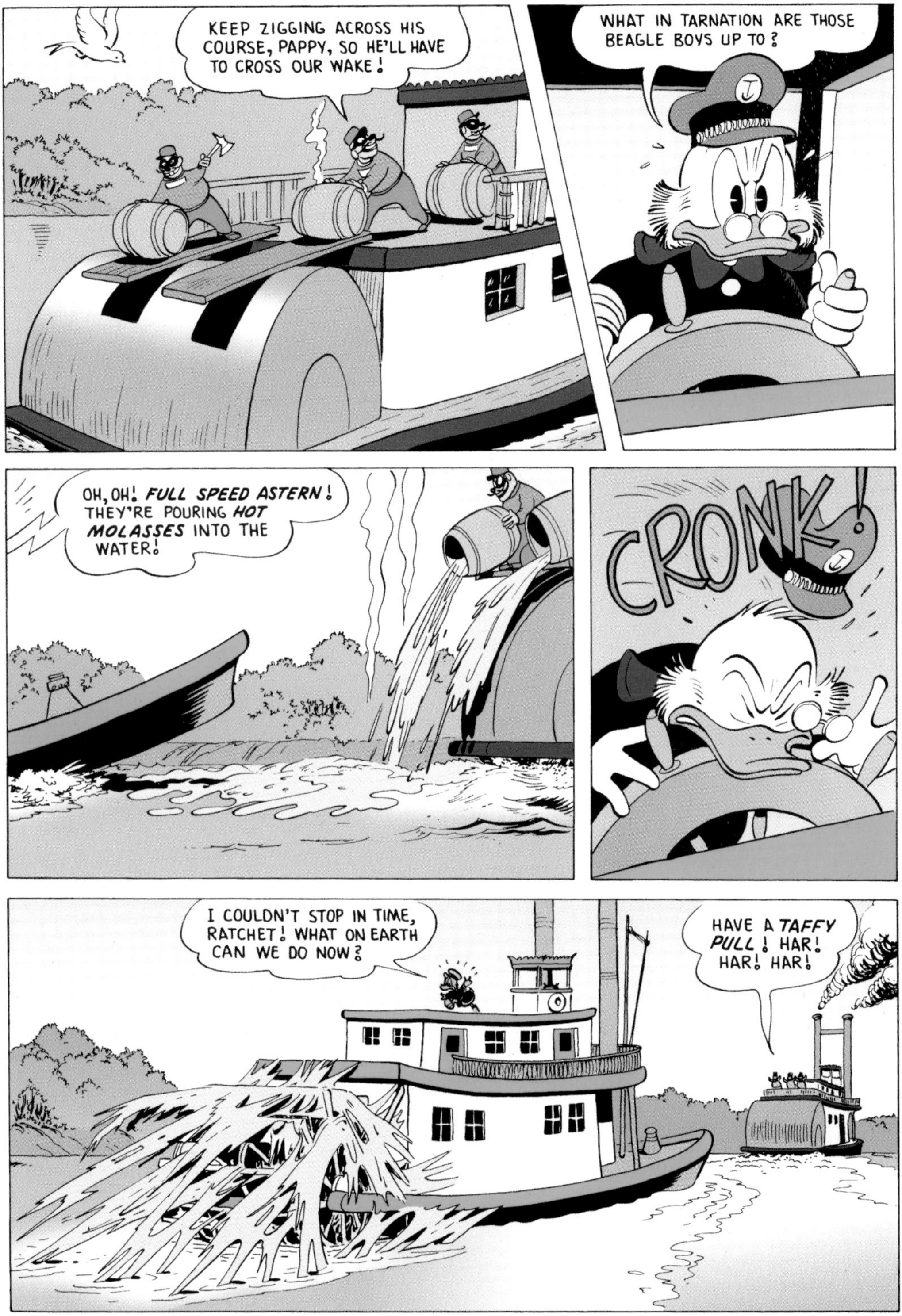
KEEP ZIGGING ACROSS HIS COURSE, PAPPY, SO HE'LL HAVE TO CROSS OUR WAKE!
WHAT IN TARNATION ARE THOSE BEAGLE BOYS UP TO?
OH, OH! FULL SPEED ASTERN! THEY'RE POURING HOT MOLASSES INTO THE WATER!
CRONK!
I COULDN'T STOP IN TIME, RATCHET! WHAT ON EARTH CAN WE DO NOW?
HAVE A TAFFY PULL! HAR! HAR! HAR!

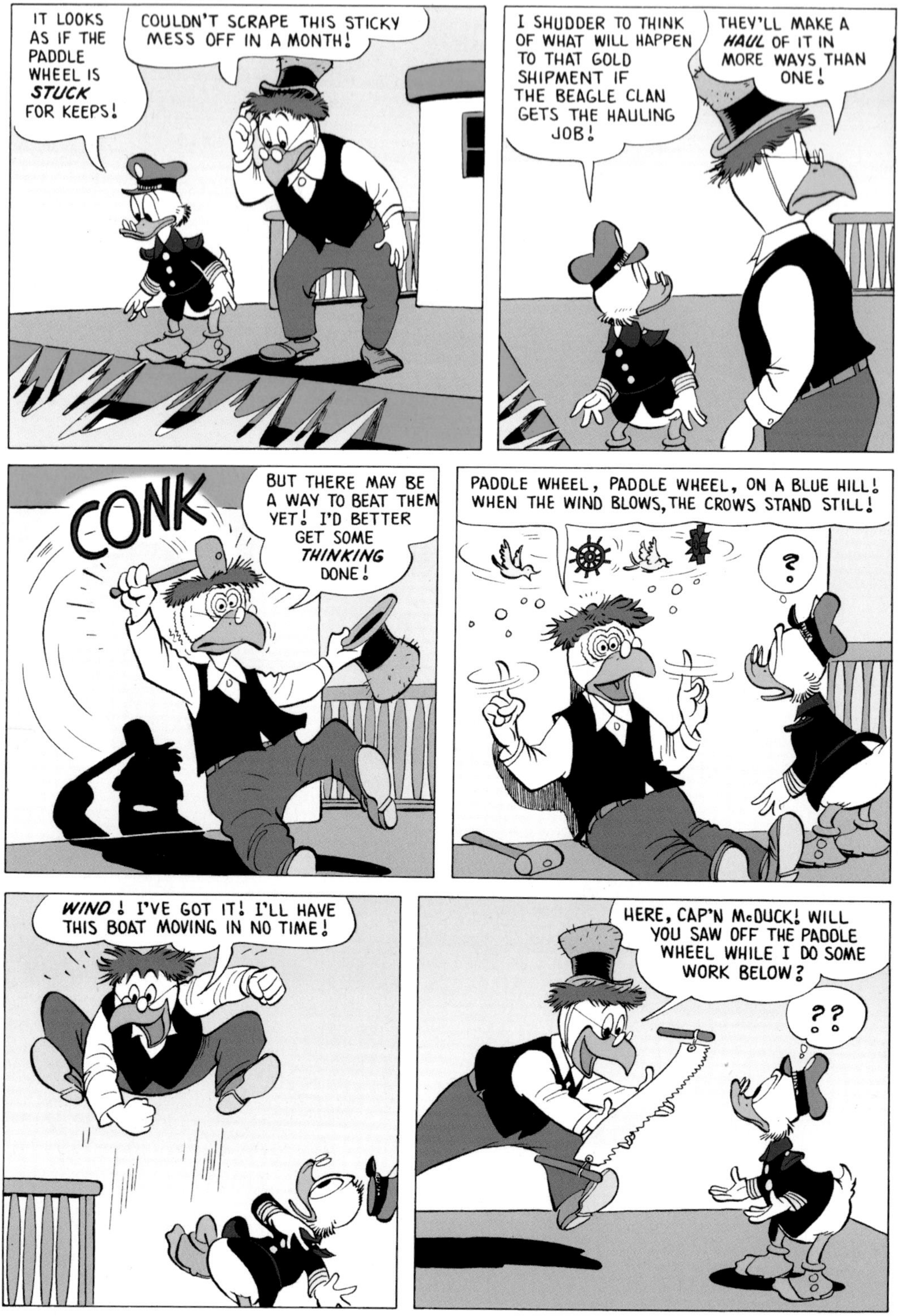
IT LOOKS AS IF THE PADDLE WHEEL IS STUCK FOR KEEPS!
COULDN'T SCRAPE THIS STICKY MESS OFF IN A MONTH!
I SHUDDER TO THINK OF WHAT WILL HAPPEN TO THAT GOLD SHIPMENT IF THE BEAGLE CLAN GETS THE HAULING JOB!
THEY'LL MAKE A HAUL OF IT IN MORE WAYS THAN ONE!
CONK
BUT THERE MAY BE A WAY TO BEAT THEM YET! I'D BETTER GET SOME THINKING DONE!
PADDLE WHEEL, PADDLE WHEEL, ON A BLUE HILL! WHEN THE WIND BLOWS, THE CROWS STAND STILL!
?
WIND! I'VE GOT IT! I'LL HAVE THIS BOAT MOVING IN NO TIME!
HERE, CAP'N McDUCK! WILL YOU SAW OFF THE PADDLE WHEEL WHILE I DO SOME WORK BELOW?
??

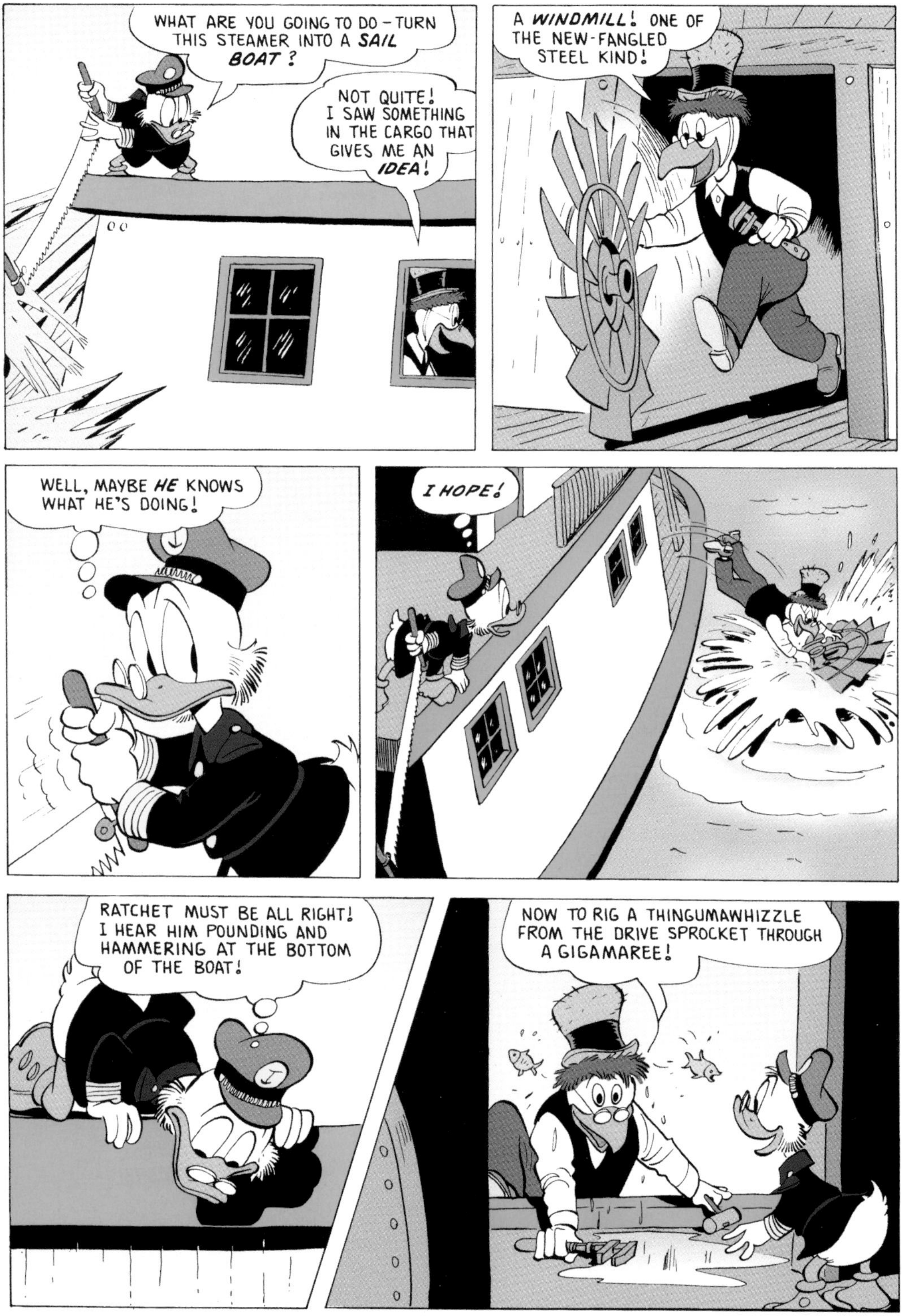
WHAT ARE YOU GOING TO DO – TURN THIS STEAMER INTO A *SAIL BOAT* ?
NOT QUITE! I SAW SOMETHING IN THE CARGO THAT GIVES ME AN *IDEA*!
A *WINDMILL*! ONE OF THE NEW-FANGLED STEEL KIND!
WELL, MAYBE *HE* KNOWS WHAT HE'S DOING!
I HOPE!
RATCHET MUST BE ALL RIGHT! I HEAR HIM POUNDING AND HAMMERING AT THE BOTTOM OF THE BOAT!
NOW TO RIG A THINGUMAWHIZZLE FROM THE DRIVE SPROCKET THROUGH A GIGAMAREE!

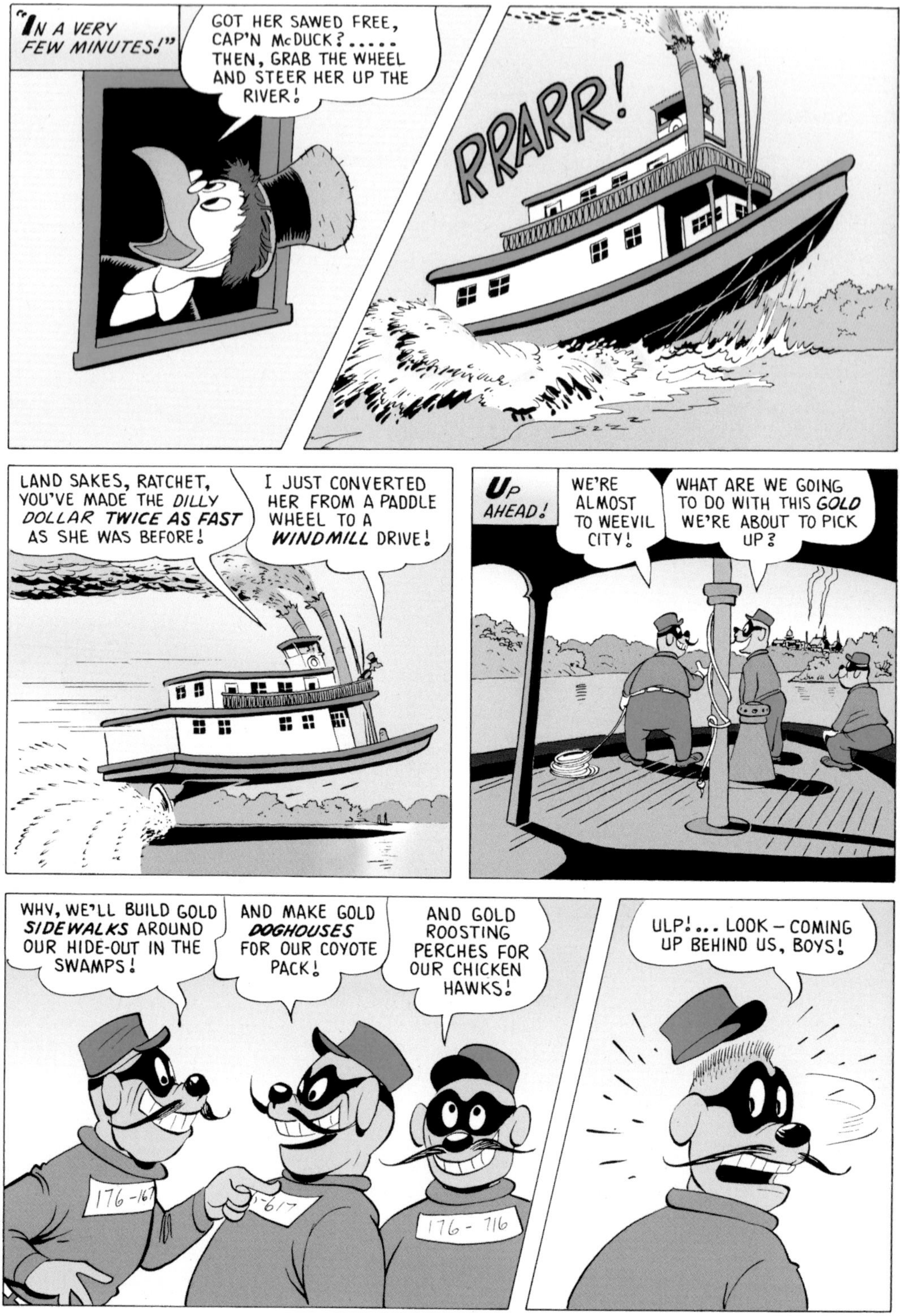
"IN A VERY FEW MINUTES!"
GOT HER SAWED FREE, CAP'N McDUCK?..... THEN, GRAB THE WHEEL AND STEER HER UP THE RIVER!
RRARR!
LAND SAKES, RATCHET, YOU'VE MADE THE DILLY DOLLAR TWICE AS FAST AS SHE WAS BEFORE!
I JUST CONVERTED HER FROM A PADDLE WHEEL TO A WINDMILL DRIVE!
UP AHEAD!
WE'RE ALMOST TO WEEVIL CITY!
WHAT ARE WE GOING TO DO WITH THIS GOLD WE'RE ABOUT TO PICK UP?
WHY, WE'LL BUILD GOLD SIDEWALKS AROUND OUR HIDE-OUT IN THE SWAMPS!
AND MAKE GOLD DOGHOUSES FOR OUR COYOTE PACK!
AND GOLD ROOSTING PERCHES FOR OUR CHICKEN HAWKS!
176-167
176-716
ULP!... LOOK – COMING UP BEHIND US, BOYS!

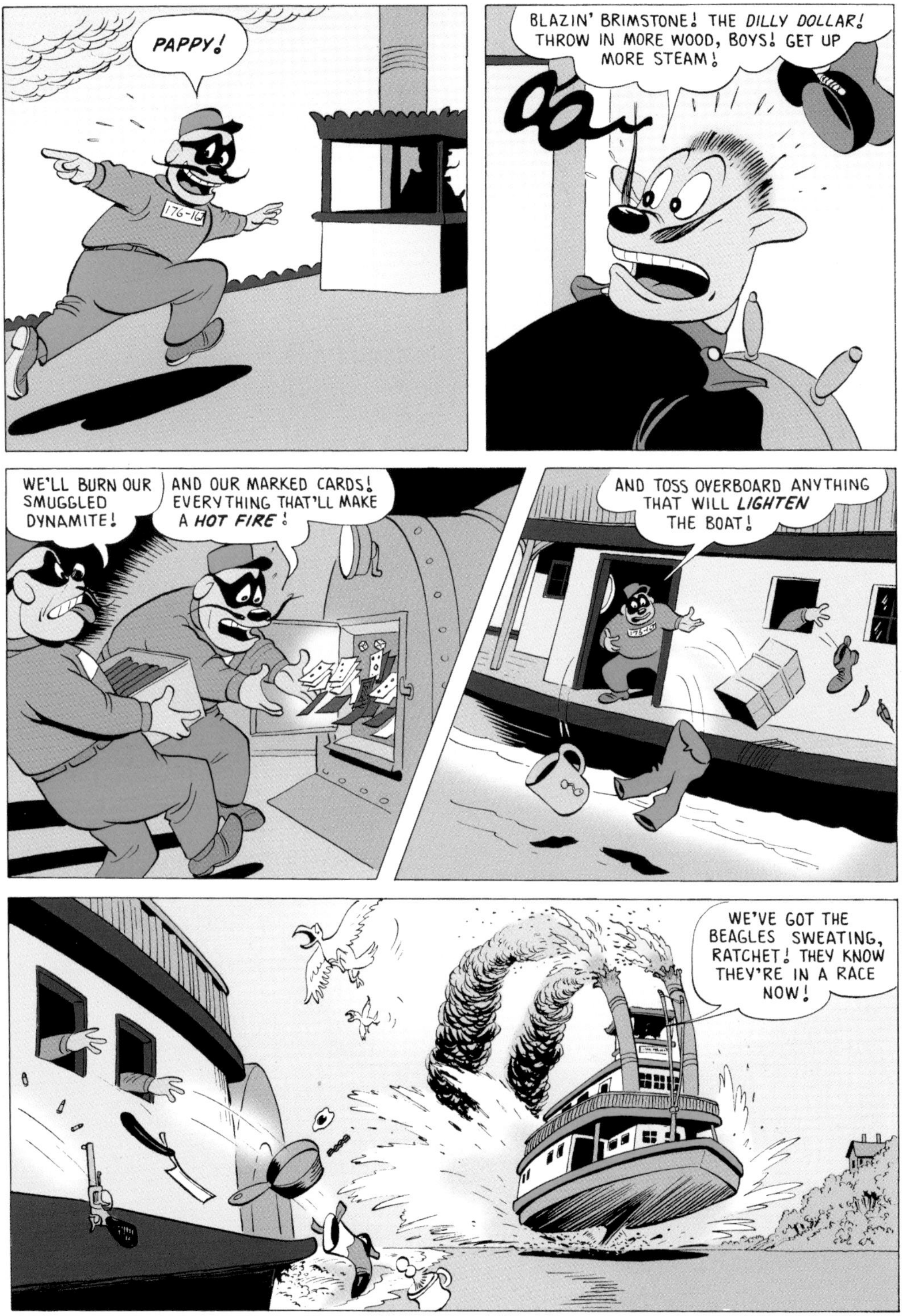
PAPPY!
BLAZIN' BRIMSTONE! THE DILLY DOLLAR! THROW IN MORE WOOD, BOYS! GET UP MORE STEAM!
WE'LL BURN OUR SMUGGLED DYNAMITE!
AND OUR MARKED CARDS! EVERYTHING THAT'LL MAKE A HOT FIRE!
AND TOSS OVERBOARD ANYTHING THAT WILL LIGHTEN THE BOAT!
WE'VE GOT THE BEAGLES SWEATING, RATCHET! THEY KNOW THEY'RE IN A RACE NOW!

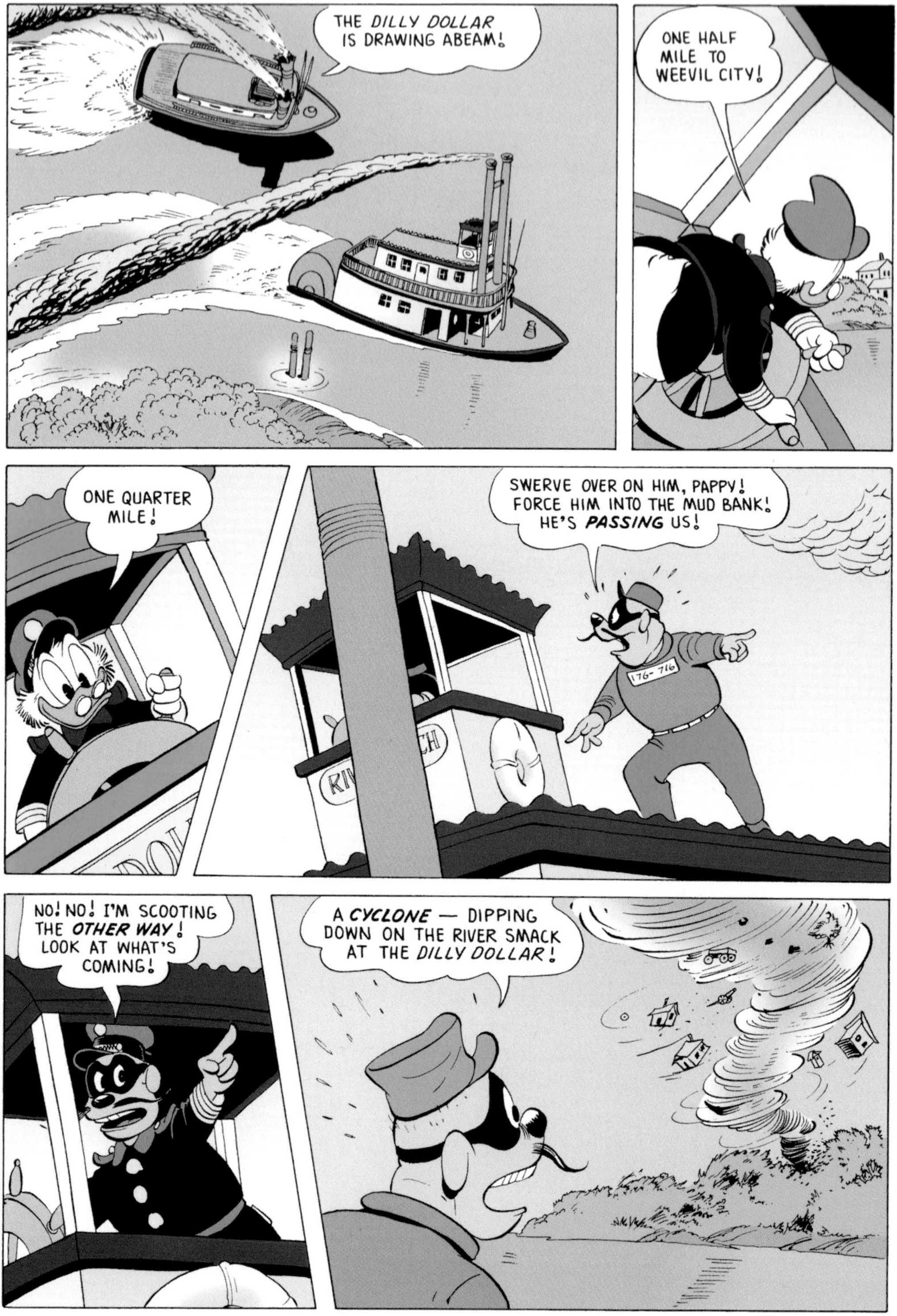
THE DILLY DOLLAR IS DRAWING ABEAM!
ONE HALF MILE TO WEEVIL CITY!
ONE QUARTER MILE!
SWERVE OVER ON HIM, PAPPY! FORCE HIM INTO THE MUD BANK! HE'S PASSING US!
176-716
NO! NO! I'M SCOOTING THE OTHER WAY! LOOK AT WHAT'S COMING!
A CYCLONE — DIPPING DOWN ON THE RIVER SMACK AT THE DILLY DOLLAR!

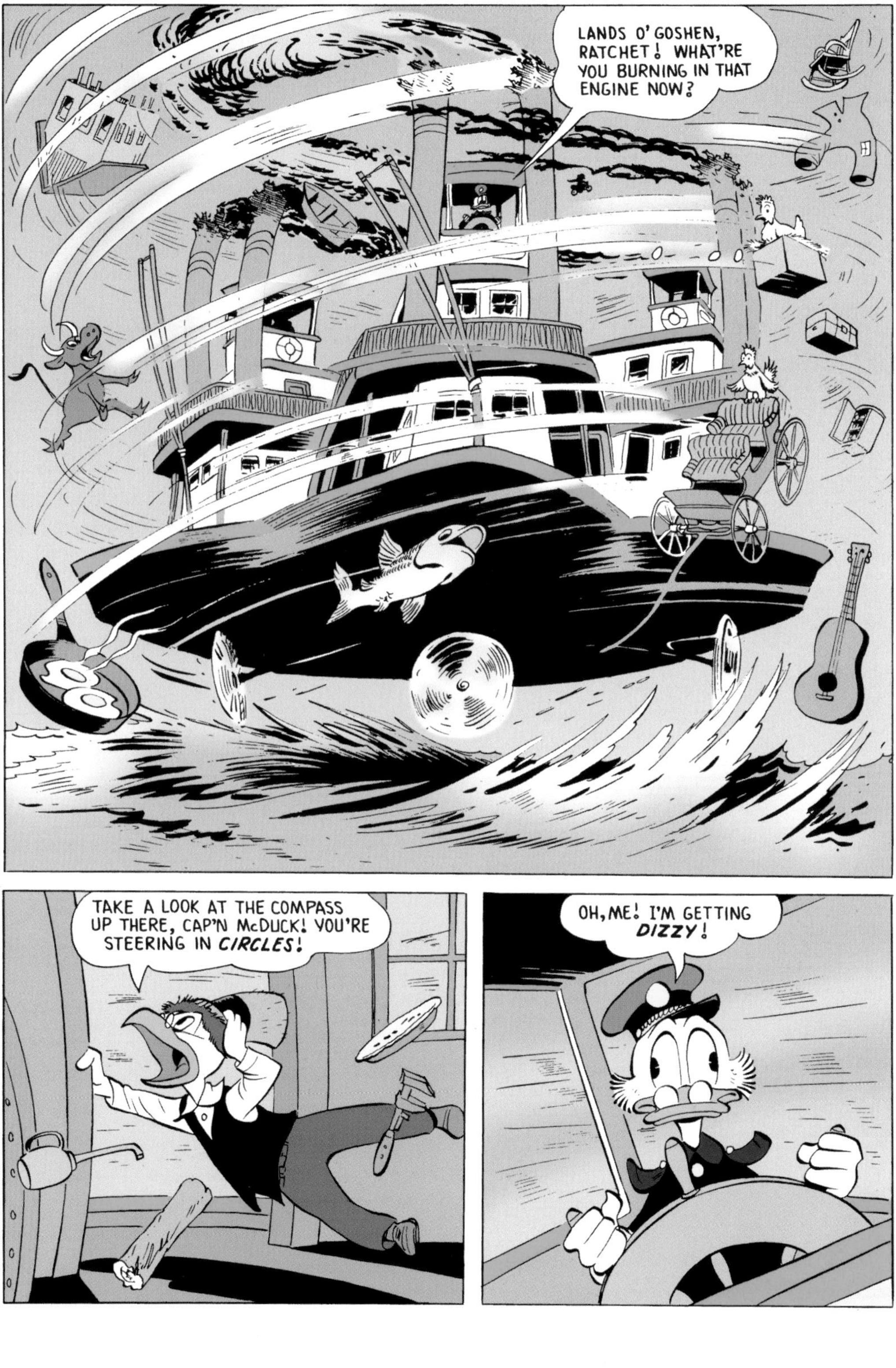
LANDS O' GOSHEN, RATCHET! WHAT'RE YOU BURNING IN THAT ENGINE NOW?
TAKE A LOOK AT THE COMPASS UP THERE, CAP'N McDUCK! YOU'RE STEERING IN CIRCLES!
OH, ME! I'M GETTING DIZZY!

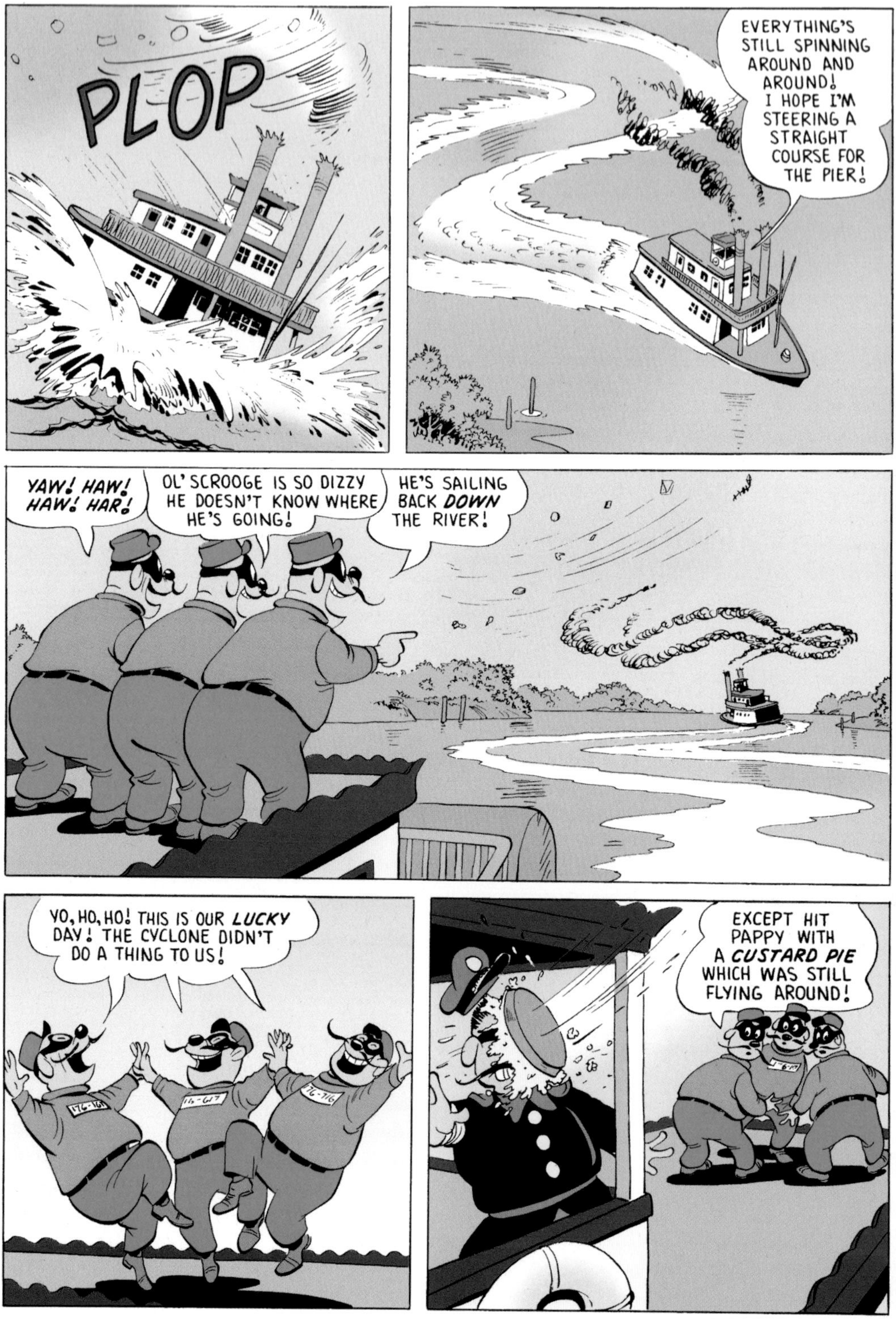
PLOP
EVERYTHING'S STILL SPINNING AROUND AND AROUND! I HOPE I'M STEERING A STRAIGHT COURSE FOR THE PIER!
YAW! HAW! HAW! HAR!
OL' SCROOGE IS SO DIZZY HE DOESN'T KNOW WHERE HE'S GOING!
HE'S SAILING BACK *DOWN* THE RIVER!
YO, HO, HO! THIS IS OUR *LUCKY* DAY! THE CYCLONE DIDN'T DO A THING TO US!
EXCEPT HIT PAPPY WITH A *CUSTARD PIE* WHICH WAS STILL FLYING AROUND!

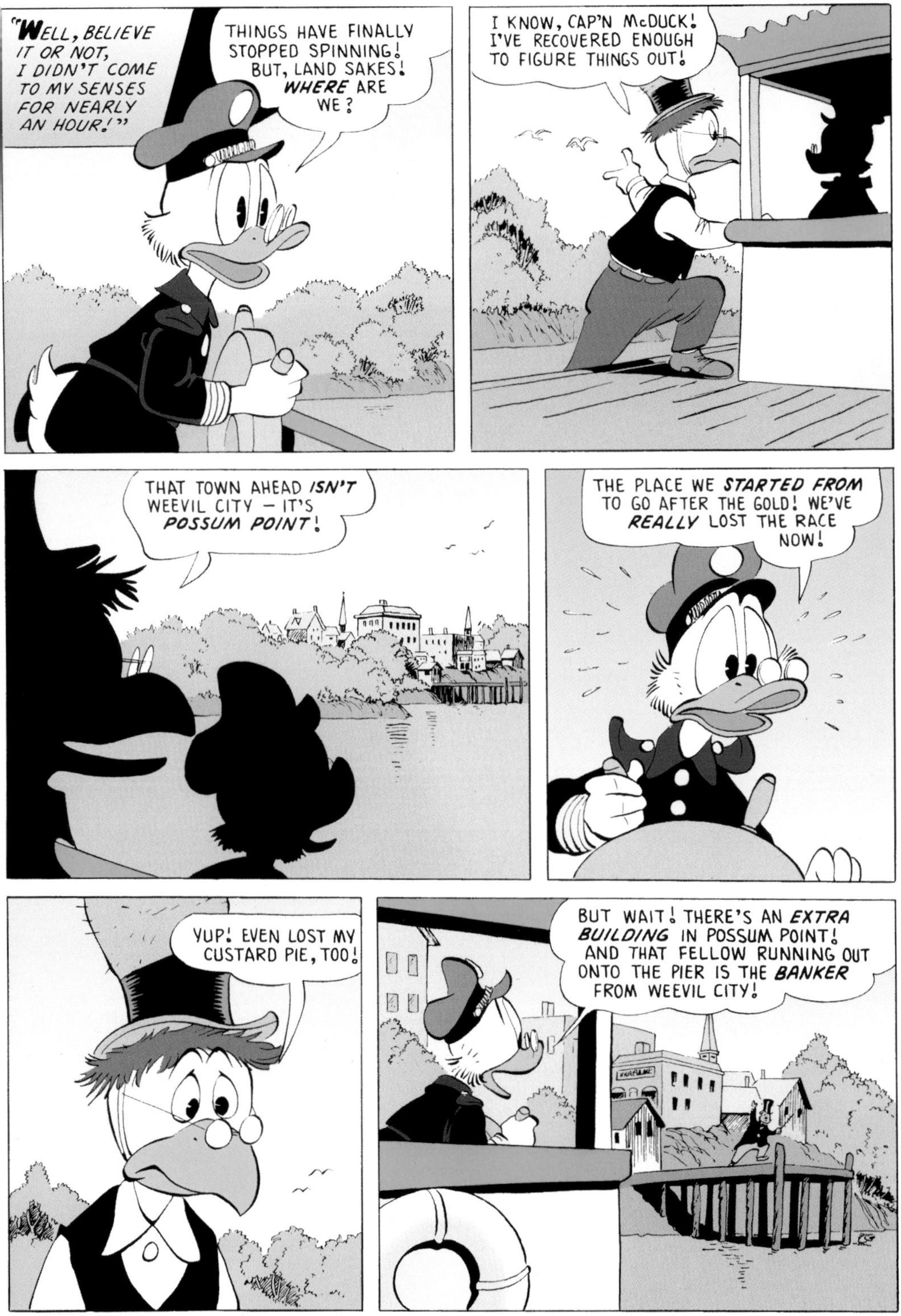

"WELL, BELIEVE IT OR NOT, I DIDN'T COME TO MY SENSES FOR NEARLY AN HOUR!"
THINGS HAVE FINALLY STOPPED SPINNING! BUT, LAND SAKES! WHERE ARE WE?
I KNOW, CAP'N McDUCK! I'VE RECOVERED ENOUGH TO FIGURE THINGS OUT!
THAT TOWN AHEAD ISN'T WEEVIL CITY — IT'S POSSUM POINT!
THE PLACE WE STARTED FROM TO GO AFTER THE GOLD! WE'VE REALLY LOST THE RACE NOW!
YUP! EVEN LOST MY CUSTARD PIE, TOO!
BUT WAIT! THERE'S AN EXTRA BUILDING IN POSSUM POINT! AND THAT FELLOW RUNNING OUT ONTO THE PIER IS THE BANKER FROM WEEVIL CITY!

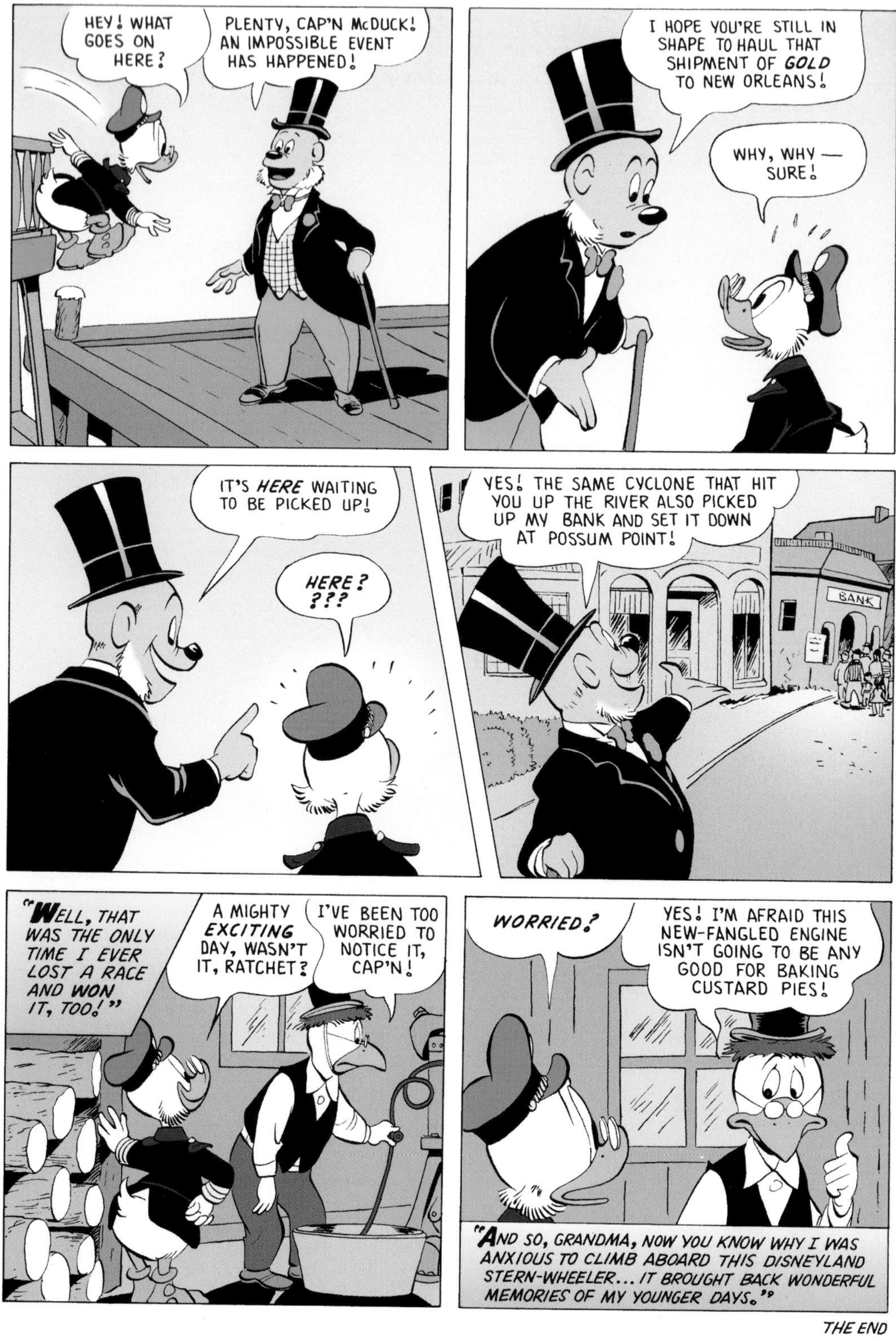
HEY! WHAT GOES ON HERE?
PLENTY, CAP'N McDUCK! AN IMPOSSIBLE EVENT HAS HAPPENED!
I HOPE YOU'RE STILL IN SHAPE TO HAUL THAT SHIPMENT OF GOLD TO NEW ORLEANS!
WHY, WHY — SURE!
IT'S HERE WAITING TO BE PICKED UP!
HERE? ???
YES! THE SAME CYCLONE THAT HIT YOU UP THE RIVER ALSO PICKED UP MY BANK AND SET IT DOWN AT POSSUM POINT!
BANK
"WELL, THAT WAS THE ONLY TIME I EVER LOST A RACE AND WON IT, TOO!"
A MIGHTY EXCITING DAY, WASN'T IT, RATCHET?
I'VE BEEN TOO WORRIED TO NOTICE IT, CAP'N!
WORRIED?
YES! I'M AFRAID THIS NEW-FANGLED ENGINE ISN'T GOING TO BE ANY GOOD FOR BAKING CUSTARD PIES!
"AND SO, GRANDMA, NOW YOU KNOW WHY I WAS ANXIOUS TO CLIMB ABOARD THIS DISNEYLAND STERN-WHEELER... IT BROUGHT BACK WONDERFUL MEMORIES OF MY YOUNGER DAYS."

THE END

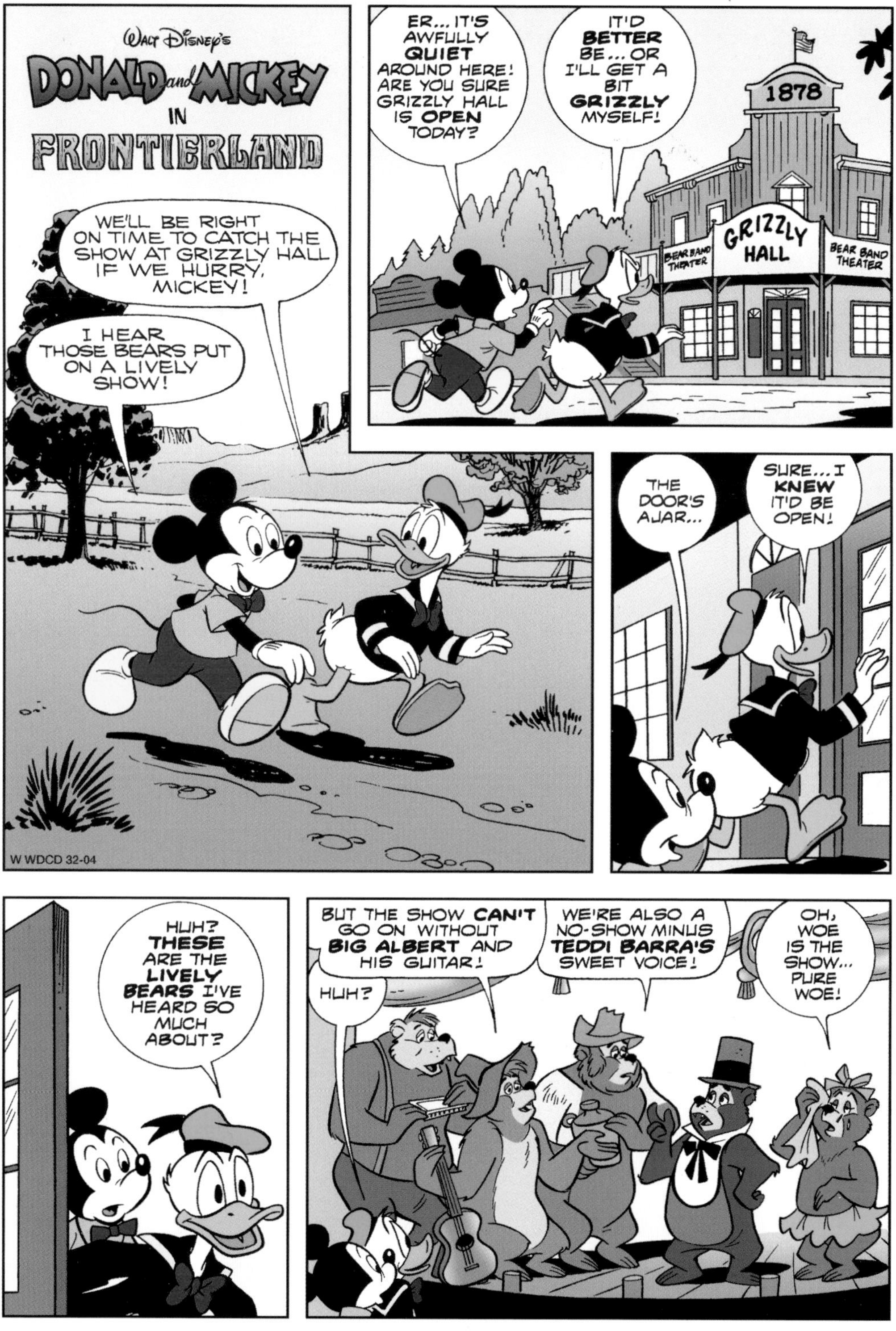
WALT DISNEY'S
DONALD and MICKEY IN FRONTIERLAND
WE'LL BE RIGHT ON TIME TO CATCH THE SHOW AT GRIZZLY HALL IF WE HURRY, MICKEY!
I HEAR THOSE BEARS PUT ON A LIVELY SHOW!
W WDCD 32-04
ER... IT'S AWFULLY QUIET AROUND HERE! ARE YOU SURE GRIZZLY HALL IS OPEN TODAY?
IT'D BETTER BE... OR I'LL GET A BIT GRIZZLY MYSELF!
1878
BEAR BAND THEATER
GRIZZLY HALL
BEAR BAND THEATER
THE DOOR'S AJAR...
SURE... I KNEW IT'D BE OPEN!
HUH? THESE ARE THE LIVELY BEARS I'VE HEARD SO MUCH ABOUT?
BUT THE SHOW CAN'T GO ON WITHOUT BIG ALBERT AND HIS GUITAR!
HUH?
WE'RE ALSO A NO-SHOW MINUS TEDDI BARRA'S SWEET VOICE!
OH, WOE IS THE SHOW... PURE WOE!

Originally published in *Walt Disney Comics Digest* #32 (USA, 1971)

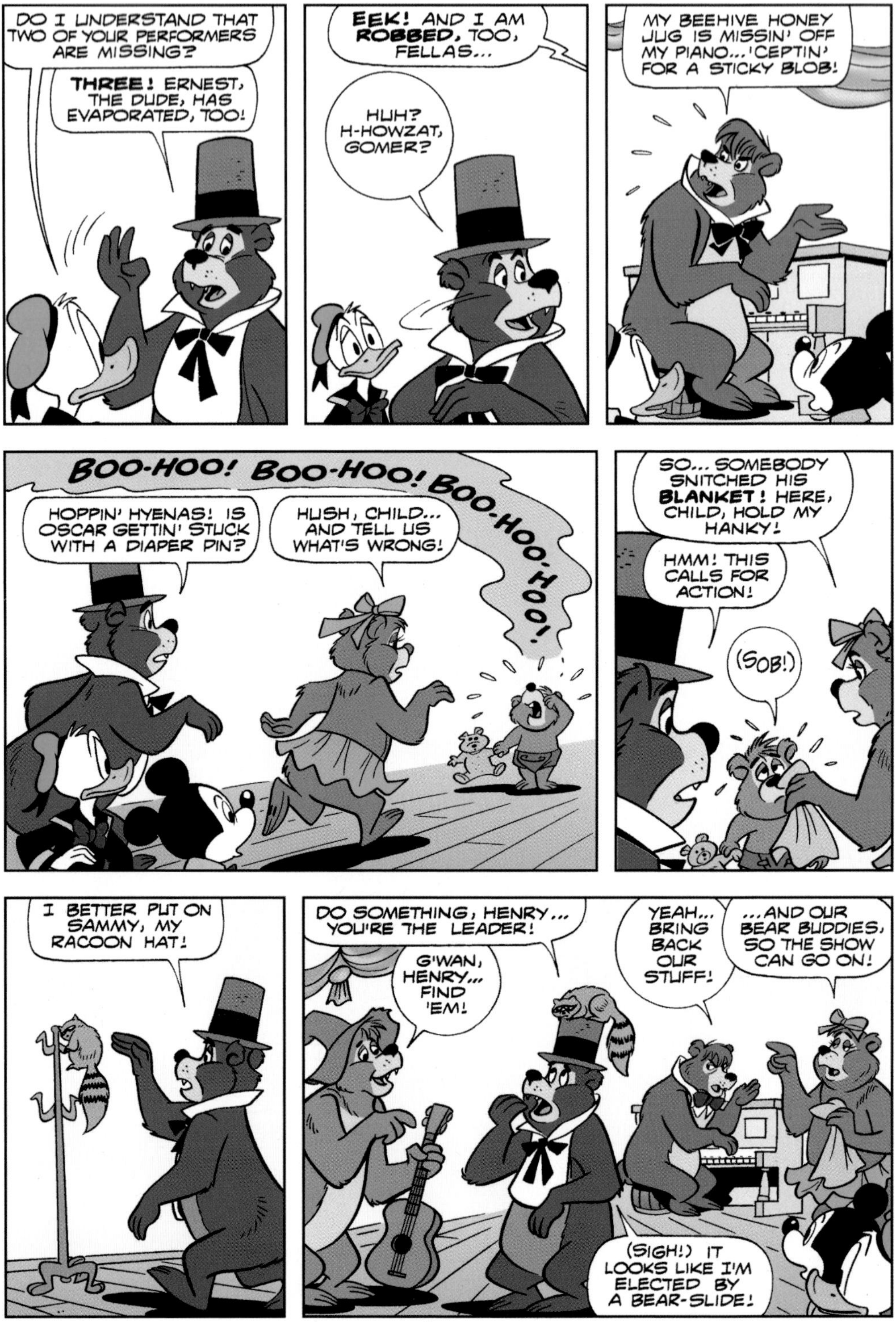
DO I UNDERSTAND THAT TWO OF YOUR PERFORMERS ARE MISSING?
THREE! ERNEST, THE DUDE, HAS EVAPORATED, TOO!
EEK! AND I AM ROBBED, TOO, FELLAS...
HUH? H-HOWZAT, GOMER?
MY BEEHIVE HONEY JUG IS MISSIN' OFF MY PIANO...'CEPTIN' FOR A STICKY BLOB!
BOO-HOO! BOO-HOO! BOO-HOO-HOO!
HOPPIN' HYENAS! IS OSCAR GETTIN' STUCK WITH A DIAPER PIN?
HUSH, CHILD... AND TELL US WHAT'S WRONG!
SO... SOMEBODY SNITCHED HIS BLANKET! HERE, CHILD, HOLD MY HANKY!
HMM! THIS CALLS FOR ACTION!
(SOB!)
I BETTER PUT ON SAMMY, MY RACOON HAT!
DO SOMETHING, HENRY... YOU'RE THE LEADER!
G'WAN, HENRY... FIND 'EM!
YEAH... BRING BACK OUR STUFF!
...AND OUR BEAR BUDDIES, SO THE SHOW CAN GO ON!
(SIGH!) IT LOOKS LIKE I'M ELECTED BY A BEAR-SLIDE!

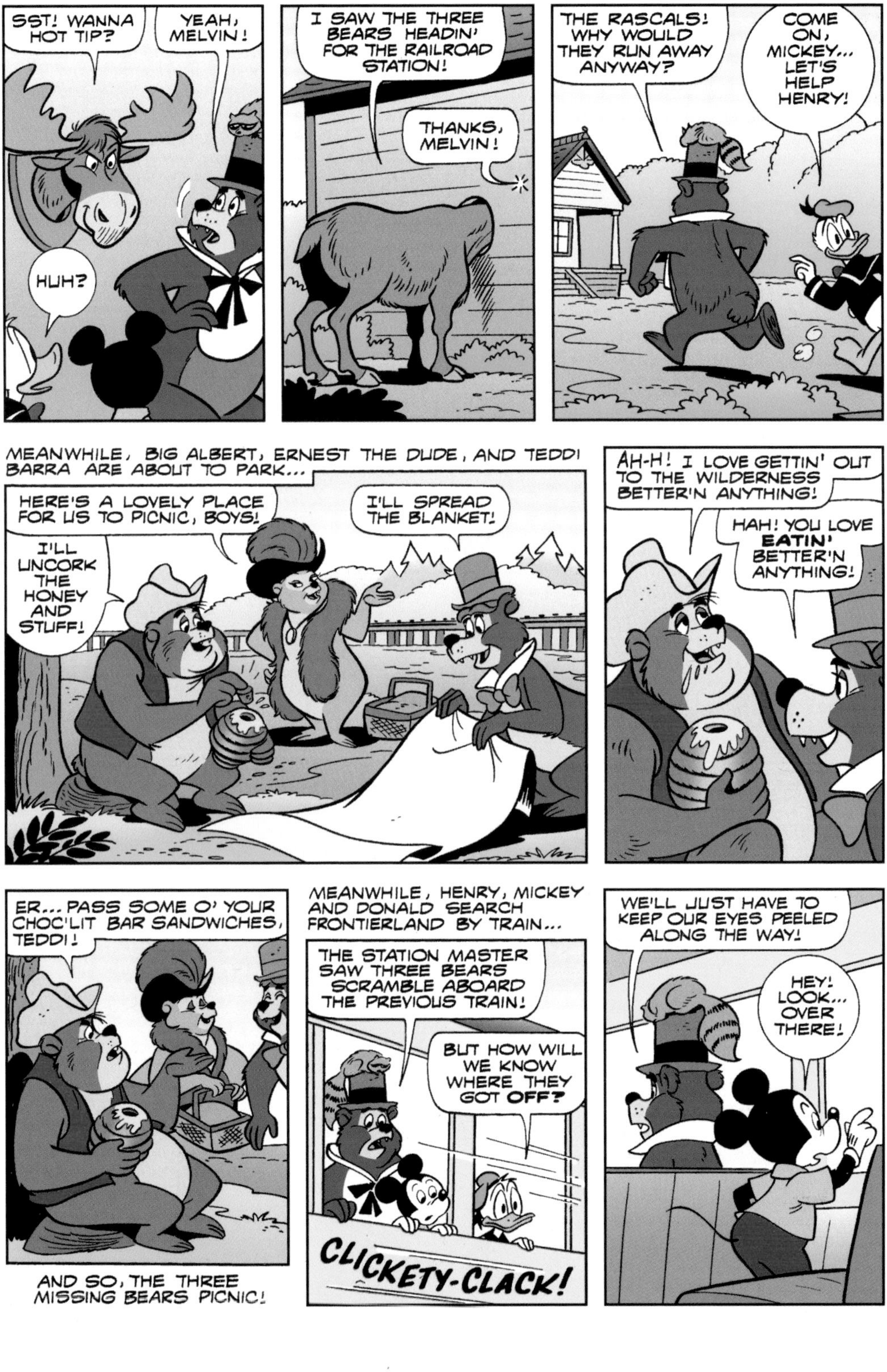
SST! WANNA HOT TIP?
YEAH, MELVIN!
HUH?
I SAW THE THREE BEARS HEADIN' FOR THE RAILROAD STATION!
THANKS, MELVIN!
THE RASCALS! WHY WOULD THEY RUN AWAY ANYWAY?
COME ON, MICKEY... LET'S HELP HENRY!
MEANWHILE, BIG ALBERT, ERNEST THE DUDE, AND TEDDI BARRA ARE ABOUT TO PARK...
HERE'S A LOVELY PLACE FOR US TO PICNIC, BOYS!
I'LL SPREAD THE BLANKET!
I'LL UNCORK THE HONEY AND STUFF!
AH-H! I LOVE GETTIN' OUT TO THE WILDERNESS BETTER'N ANYTHING!
HAH! YOU LOVE **EATIN'** BETTER'N ANYTHING!
ER... PASS SOME O' YOUR CHOC'LIT BAR SANDWICHES, TEDDI!
AND SO, THE THREE MISSING BEARS PICNIC!
MEANWHILE, HENRY, MICKEY AND DONALD SEARCH FRONTIERLAND BY TRAIN...
THE STATION MASTER SAW THREE BEARS SCRAMBLE ABOARD THE PREVIOUS TRAIN!
BUT HOW WILL WE KNOW WHERE THEY GOT **OFF?**
CLICKETY-CLACK!
WE'LL JUST HAVE TO KEEP OUR EYES PEELED ALONG THE WAY!
HEY! LOOK... OVER THERE!

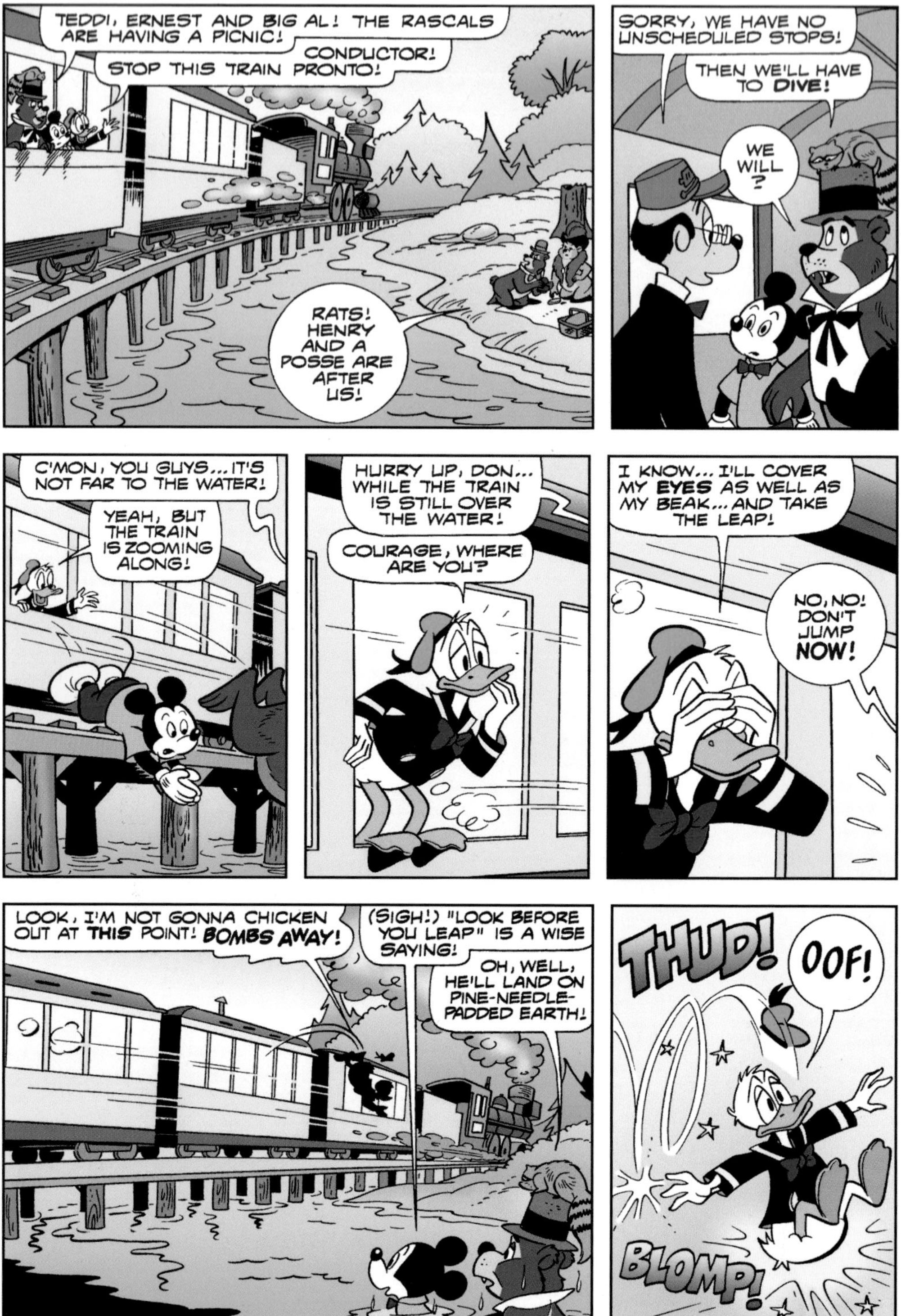

TEDDI, ERNEST AND BIG AL! THE RASCALS ARE HAVING A PICNIC!
CONDUCTOR! STOP THIS TRAIN PRONTO!
RATS! HENRY AND A POSSE ARE AFTER US!
SORRY, WE HAVE NO UNSCHEDULED STOPS!
THEN WE'LL HAVE TO DIVE!
WE WILL ?
C'MON, YOU GUYS... IT'S NOT FAR TO THE WATER!
YEAH, BUT THE TRAIN IS ZOOMING ALONG!
HURRY UP, DON... WHILE THE TRAIN IS STILL OVER THE WATER!
COURAGE, WHERE ARE YOU?
I KNOW... I'LL COVER MY EYES AS WELL AS MY BEAK... AND TAKE THE LEAP!
NO, NO! DON'T JUMP NOW!
LOOK, I'M NOT GONNA CHICKEN OUT AT THIS POINT! BOMBS AWAY!
(SIGH!) "LOOK BEFORE YOU LEAP" IS A WISE SAYING!
OH, WELL, HE'LL LAND ON PINE-NEEDLE-PADDED EARTH!
THUD!
OOF!
BLOMP!

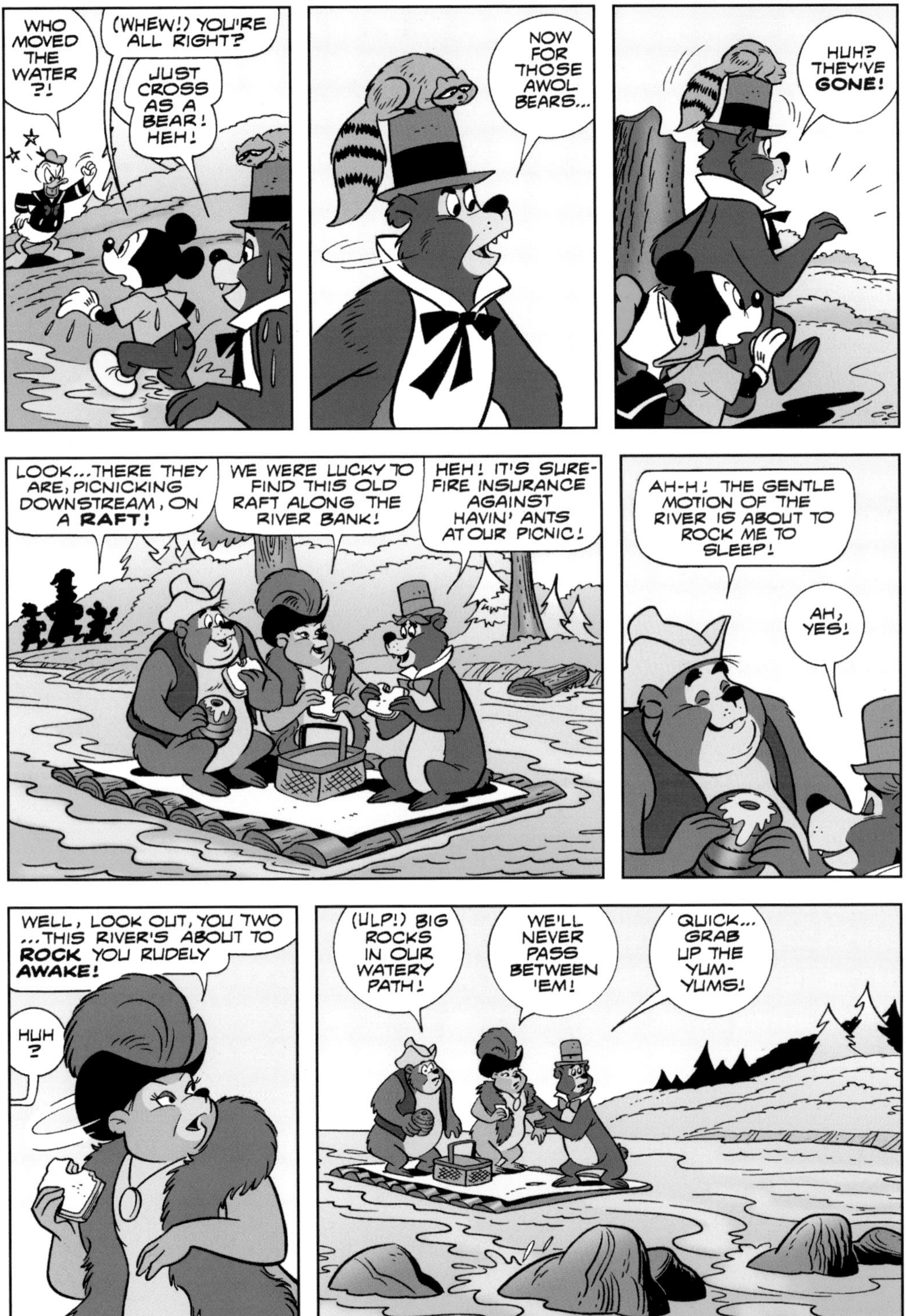
WHO MOVED THE WATER ?!
(WHEW!) YOU'RE ALL RIGHT?
JUST CROSS AS A BEAR! HEH!
NOW FOR THOSE AWOL BEARS...
HUH? THEY'VE GONE!
LOOK...THERE THEY ARE, PICNICKING DOWNSTREAM, ON A RAFT!
WE WERE LUCKY TO FIND THIS OLD RAFT ALONG THE RIVER BANK!
HEH! IT'S SURE-FIRE INSURANCE AGAINST HAVIN' ANTS AT OUR PICNIC!
AH-H! THE GENTLE MOTION OF THE RIVER IS ABOUT TO ROCK ME TO SLEEP!
AH, YES!
WELL, LOOK OUT, YOU TWO ...THIS RIVER'S ABOUT TO ROCK YOU RUDELY AWAKE!
HUH?
(ULP!) BIG ROCKS IN OUR WATERY PATH!
WE'LL NEVER PASS BETWEEN 'EM!
QUICK... GRAB UP THE YUM-YUMS!

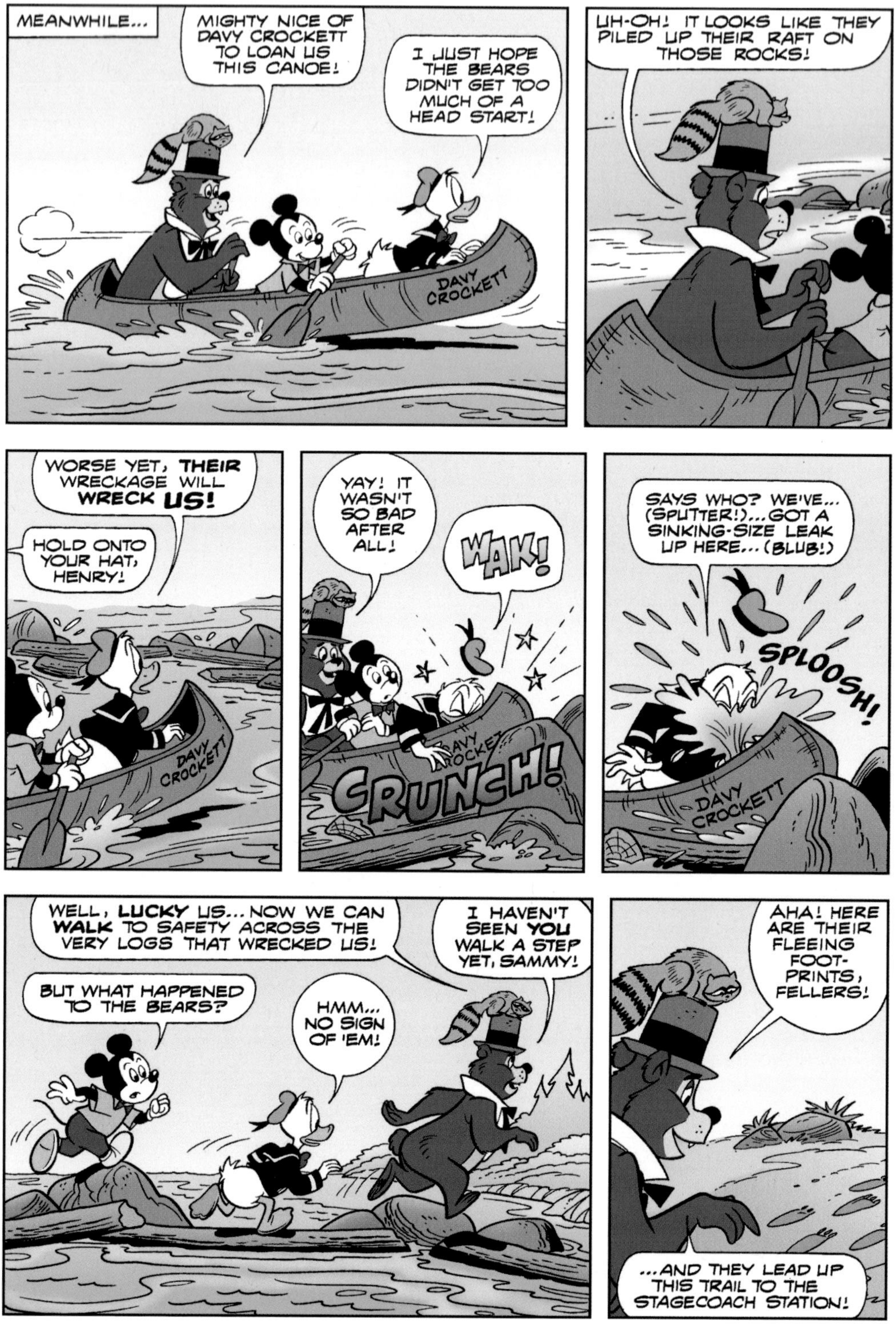
MEANWHILE...
MIGHTY NICE OF DAVY CROCKETT TO LOAN US THIS CANOE!
I JUST HOPE THE BEARS DIDN'T GET TOO MUCH OF A HEAD START!
DAVY CROCKETT
UH-OH! IT LOOKS LIKE THEY PILED UP THEIR RAFT ON THOSE ROCKS!
WORSE YET, THEIR WRECKAGE WILL WRECK US!
HOLD ONTO YOUR HAT, HENRY!
DAVY CROCKETT
YAY! IT WASN'T SO BAD AFTER ALL!
WAK!
CRUNCH!
SAYS WHO? WE'VE... (SPUTTER!)... GOT A SINKING-SIZE LEAK UP HERE... (BLUB!)
SPLOOSH!
DAVY CROCKETT
WELL, LUCKY US... NOW WE CAN WALK TO SAFETY ACROSS THE VERY LOGS THAT WRECKED US!
I HAVEN'T SEEN YOU WALK A STEP YET, SAMMY!
BUT WHAT HAPPENED TO THE BEARS?
HMM... NO SIGN OF 'EM!
AHA! HERE ARE THEIR FLEEING FOOT-PRINTS, FELLERS!
...AND THEY LEAD UP THIS TRAIL TO THE STAGECOACH STATION!

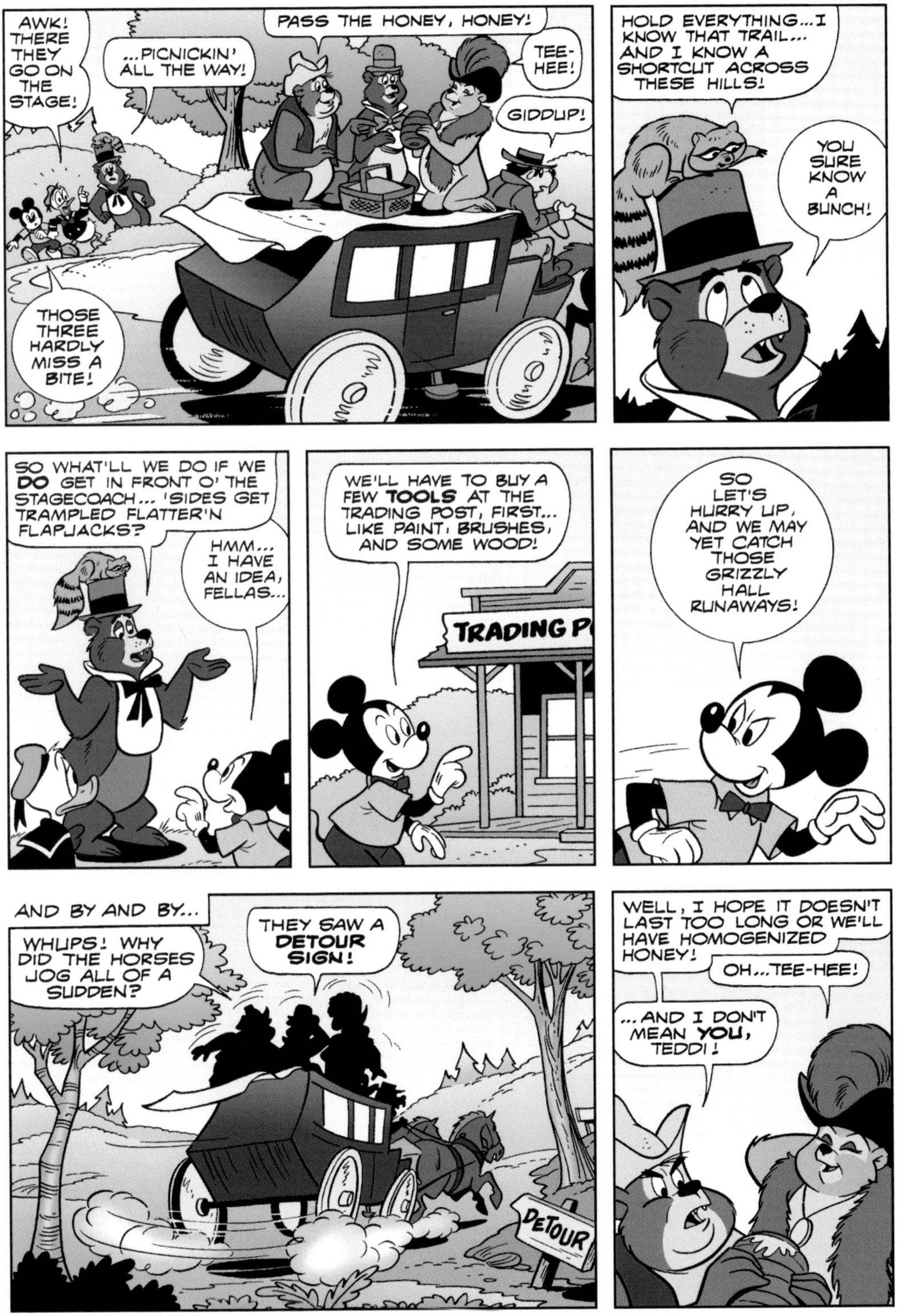
AWK! THERE THEY GO ON THE STAGE!
...PICNICKIN' ALL THE WAY!
PASS THE HONEY, HONEY!
TEE-HEE!
GIDDUP!
THOSE THREE HARDLY MISS A BITE!
HOLD EVERYTHING...I KNOW THAT TRAIL... AND I KNOW A SHORTCUT ACROSS THESE HILLS!
YOU SURE KNOW A BUNCH!
SO WHAT'LL WE DO IF WE DO GET IN FRONT O' THE STAGECOACH... 'SIDES GET TRAMPLED FLATTER'N FLAPJACKS?
HMM... I HAVE AN IDEA, FELLAS...
WE'LL HAVE TO BUY A FEW TOOLS AT THE TRADING POST, FIRST... LIKE PAINT, BRUSHES, AND SOME WOOD!
TRADING P
SO LET'S HURRY UP, AND WE MAY YET CATCH THOSE GRIZZLY HALL RUNAWAYS!
AND BY AND BY...
WHUPS! WHY DID THE HORSES JOG ALL OF A SUDDEN?
THEY SAW A DETOUR SIGN!
DETOUR
WELL, I HOPE IT DOESN'T LAST TOO LONG OR WE'LL HAVE HOMOGENIZED HONEY!
OH...TEE-HEE!
...AND I DON'T MEAN YOU, TEDDI!

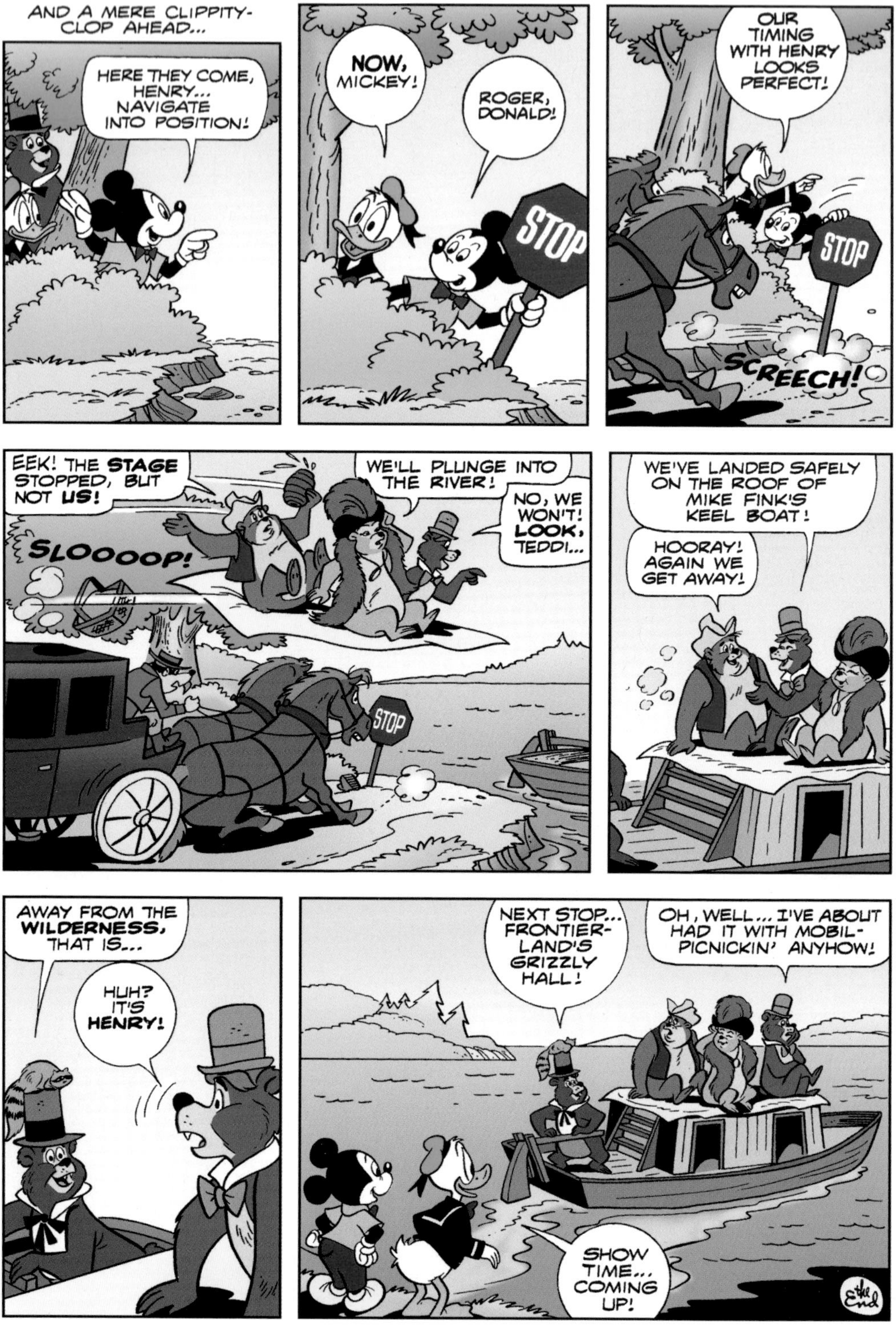

AND A MERE CLIPPITY-CLOP AHEAD...
HERE THEY COME, HENRY... NAVIGATE INTO POSITION!
NOW, MICKEY!
ROGER, DONALD!
STOP
OUR TIMING WITH HENRY LOOKS PERFECT!
STOP
SCREECH!
EEK! THE STAGE STOPPED, BUT NOT US!
SLOOOOP!
WE'LL PLUNGE INTO THE RIVER!
NO, WE WON'T! LOOK, TEDDI...
STOP
WE'VE LANDED SAFELY ON THE ROOF OF MIKE FINK'S KEEL BOAT!
HOORAY! AGAIN WE GET AWAY!
AWAY FROM THE WILDERNESS, THAT IS...
HUH? IT'S HENRY!
NEXT STOP... FRONTIER-LAND'S GRIZZLY HALL!
OH, WELL... I'VE ABOUT HAD IT WITH MOBIL-PICNICKIN' ANYHOW!
SHOW TIME... COMING UP!
the End

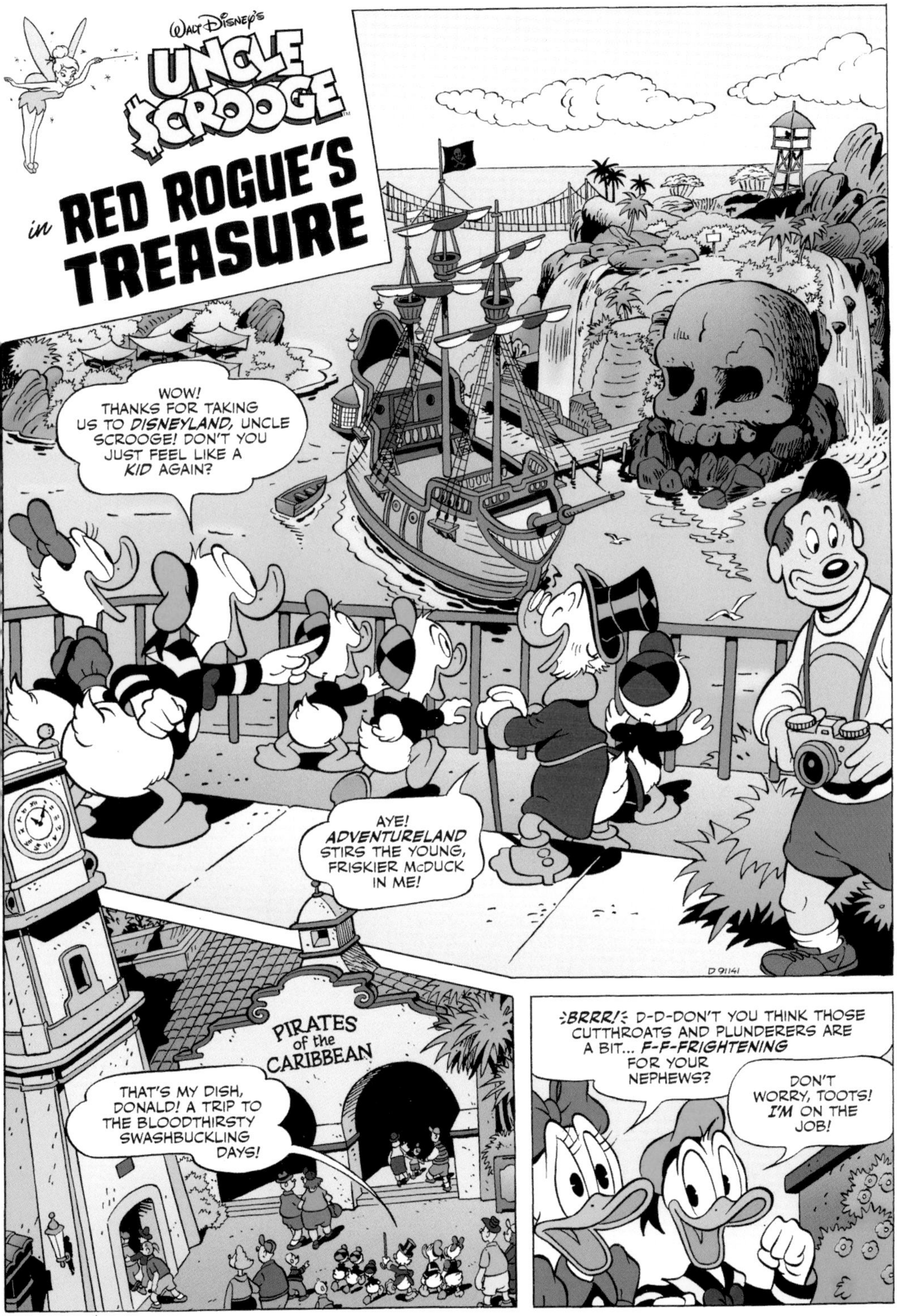
Walt Disney's
UNCLE $CROOGE
in RED ROGUE'S TREASURE
WOW! THANKS FOR TAKING US TO DISNEYLAND, UNCLE SCROOGE! DON'T YOU JUST FEEL LIKE A KID AGAIN?
AYE! ADVENTURELAND STIRS THE YOUNG, FRISKIER McDUCK IN ME!
D 91141
PIRATES of the CARIBBEAN
THAT'S MY DISH, DONALD! A TRIP TO THE BLOODTHIRSTY SWASHBUCKLING DAYS!
BRRR! D-D-DON'T YOU THINK THOSE CUTTHROATS AND PLUNDERERS ARE A BIT... F-F-FRIGHTENING FOR YOUR NEPHEWS?
DON'T WORRY, TOOTS! I'M ON THE JOB!

Originally published in *Anders And & C:o* #9/1992 (Denmark, 1992)

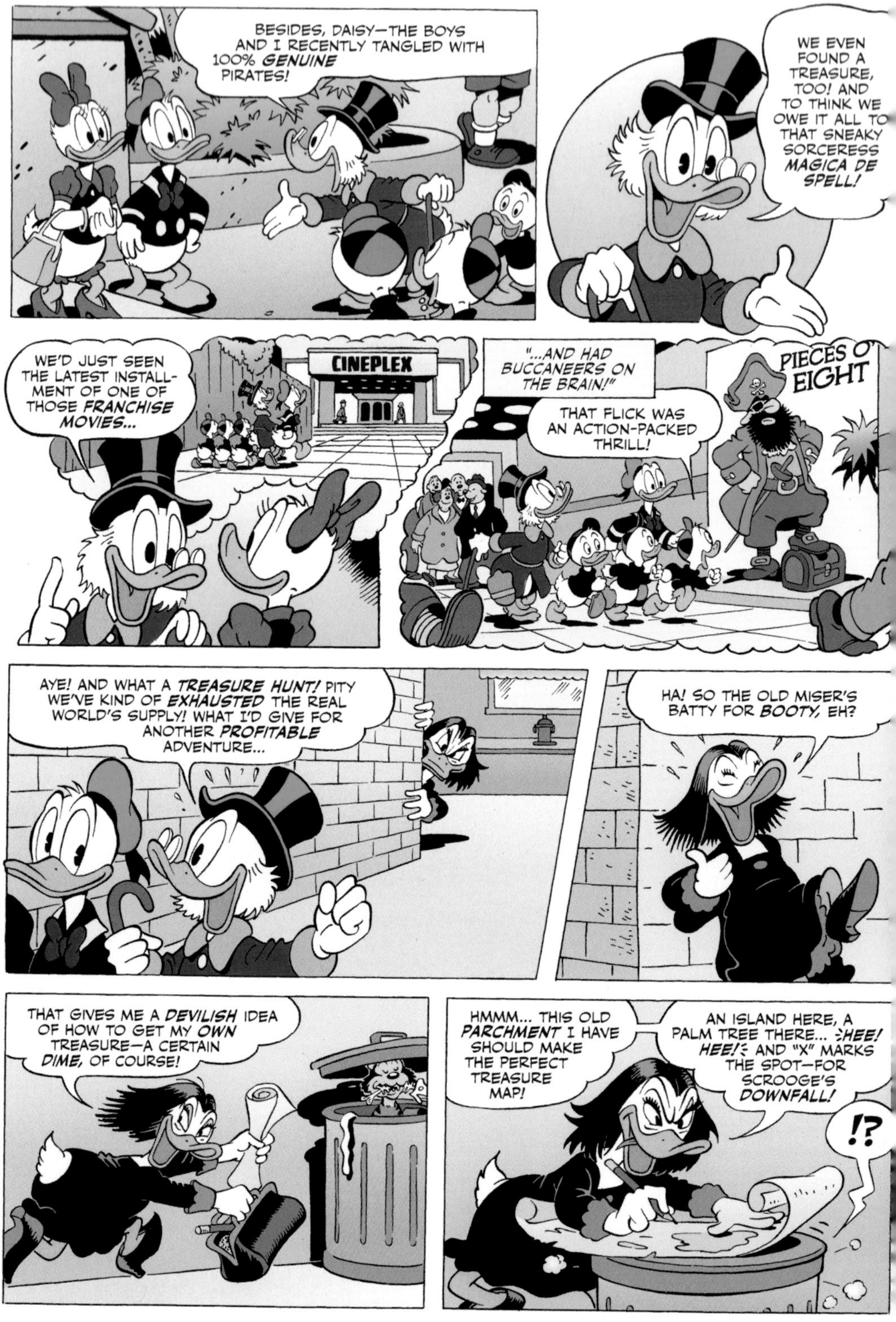
BESIDES, DAISY—THE BOYS AND I RECENTLY TANGLED WITH 100% GENUINE PIRATES!
WE EVEN FOUND A TREASURE, TOO! AND TO THINK WE OWE IT ALL TO THAT SNEAKY SORCERESS MAGICA DE SPELL!
WE'D JUST SEEN THE LATEST INSTALLMENT OF ONE OF THOSE FRANCHISE MOVIES...
CINEPLEX
"...AND HAD BUCCANEERS ON THE BRAIN!"
THAT FLICK WAS AN ACTION-PACKED THRILL!
PIECES O' EIGHT
AYE! AND WHAT A TREASURE HUNT! PITY WE'VE KIND OF EXHAUSTED THE REAL WORLD'S SUPPLY! WHAT I'D GIVE FOR ANOTHER PROFITABLE ADVENTURE...
HA! SO THE OLD MISER'S BATTY FOR BOOTY, EH?
THAT GIVES ME A DEVILISH IDEA OF HOW TO GET MY OWN TREASURE—A CERTAIN DIME, OF COURSE!
HMMM... THIS OLD PARCHMENT I HAVE SHOULD MAKE THE PERFECT TREASURE MAP!
AN ISLAND HERE, A PALM TREE THERE... HEE! HEE! AND "X" MARKS THE SPOT—FOR SCROOGE'S DOWNFALL!
!?

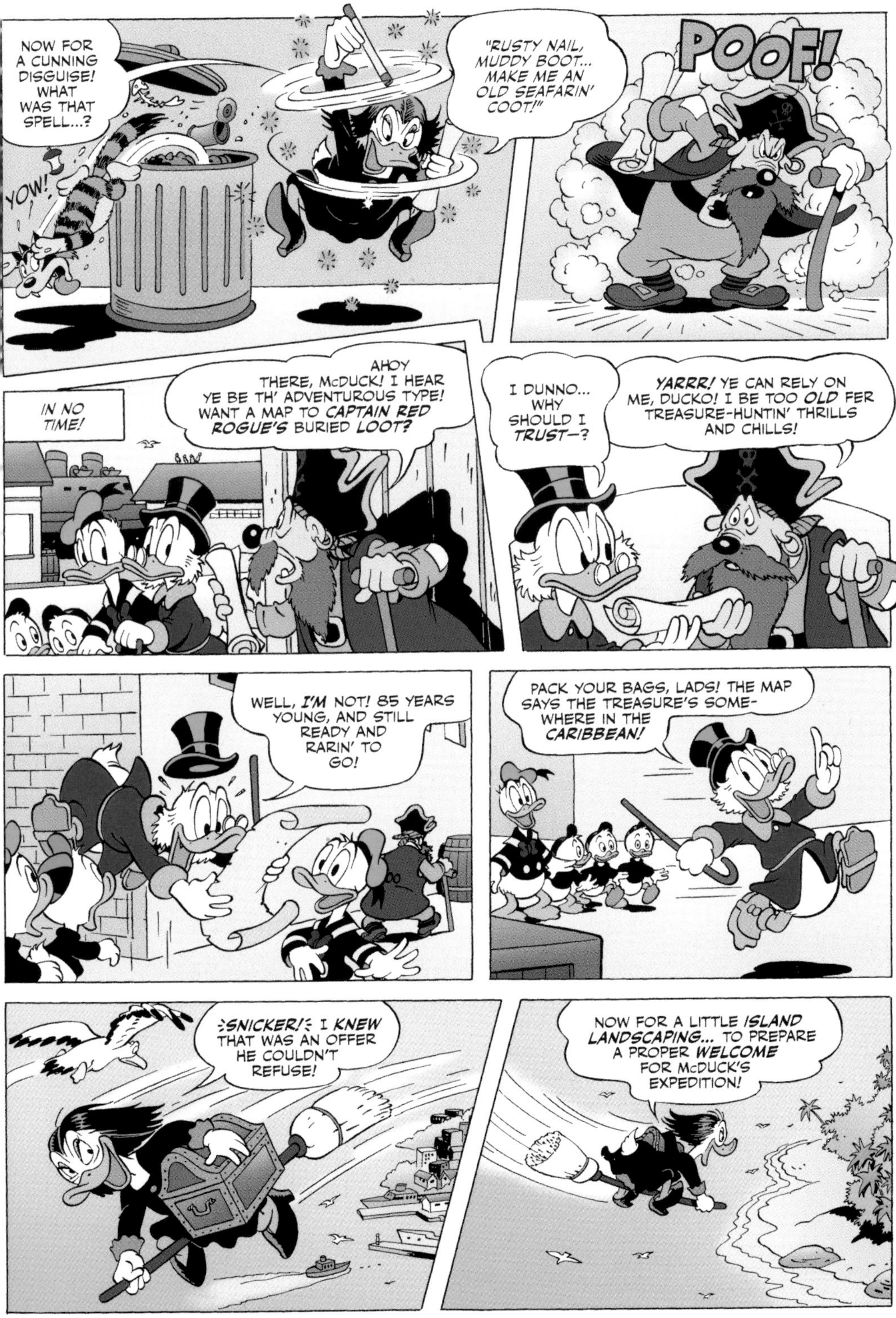
NOW FOR A CUNNING DISGUISE! WHAT WAS THAT SPELL...?
YOW!
"RUSTY NAIL, MUDDY BOOT... MAKE ME AN OLD SEAFARIN' COOT!"
POOF!
IN NO TIME!
AHOY THERE, McDUCK! I HEAR YE BE TH' ADVENTUROUS TYPE! WANT A MAP TO CAPTAIN RED ROGUE'S BURIED LOOT?
I DUNNO... WHY SHOULD I TRUST—?
YARRR! YE CAN RELY ON ME, DUCKO! I BE TOO OLD FER TREASURE-HUNTIN' THRILLS AND CHILLS!
WELL, I'M NOT! 85 YEARS YOUNG, AND STILL READY AND RARIN' TO GO!
PACK YOUR BAGS, LADS! THE MAP SAYS THE TREASURE'S SOMEWHERE IN THE CARIBBEAN!
SNICKER! I KNEW THAT WAS AN OFFER HE COULDN'T REFUSE!
NOW FOR A LITTLE ISLAND LANDSCAPING... TO PREPARE A PROPER WELCOME FOR McDUCK'S EXPEDITION!

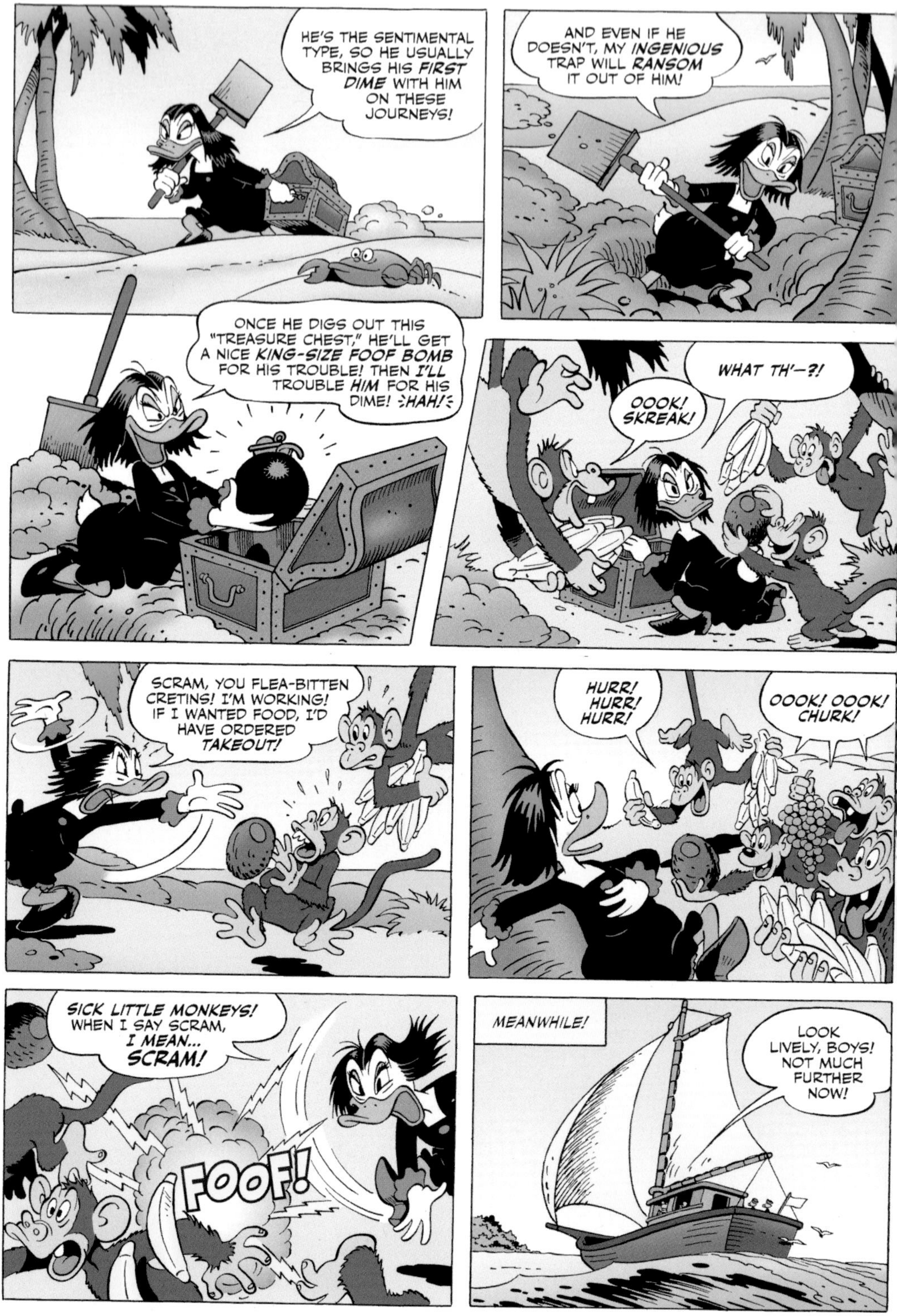
HE'S THE SENTIMENTAL TYPE, SO HE USUALLY BRINGS HIS FIRST DIME WITH HIM ON THESE JOURNEYS!
AND EVEN IF HE DOESN'T, MY INGENIOUS TRAP WILL RANSOM IT OUT OF HIM!
ONCE HE DIGS OUT THIS "TREASURE CHEST," HE'LL GET A NICE KING-SIZE FOOF BOMB FOR HIS TROUBLE! THEN I'LL TROUBLE HIM FOR HIS DIME! HAH!
WHAT TH'—?!
OOOK! SKREAK!
SCRAM, YOU FLEA-BITTEN CRETINS! I'M WORKING! IF I WANTED FOOD, I'D HAVE ORDERED TAKEOUT!
HURR! HURR! HURR!
OOOK! OOOK! CHURK!
SICK LITTLE MONKEYS! WHEN I SAY SCRAM, I MEAN... SCRAM!
FOOF!
MEANWHILE!
LOOK LIVELY, BOYS! NOT MUCH FURTHER NOW!

WE'D BE THERE SOONER IF IT WEREN'T *THRIFTY* AND *AUTHENTIC* TO SEEK PIRATE GOLD BY *BOAT!* ⚡SNORT!⚡

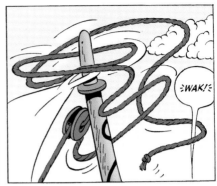

⚡WAK!⚡

SAILING ON UNCLE SCROOGE'S OLD VESSEL MEANS NO *FUEL* TO *BUY...* AND AS WE WELL KNOW, HE ISN'T *MADE* OF MONEY!

IF YOU CAN USE YOUR *UNDERPAID NEPHEWS* FOR A CREW, SO MUCH THE BETTER, RIGHT? ⚡GRUNT!⚡

⚡YOICKS!⚡

RRRR RRRIPPPP!

YOU DUNDERHEAD! THAT SAIL ONLY HAD 134 YEARS ON IT! NOW WE'VE GOTTA STOP AND BUY A *NEW* ONE!

"BUY," YOU SAY? SURE YOU CAN *AFFORD* IT?

YOU BET! IT'LL BE COMING OUT OF *YOUR* WAGES!

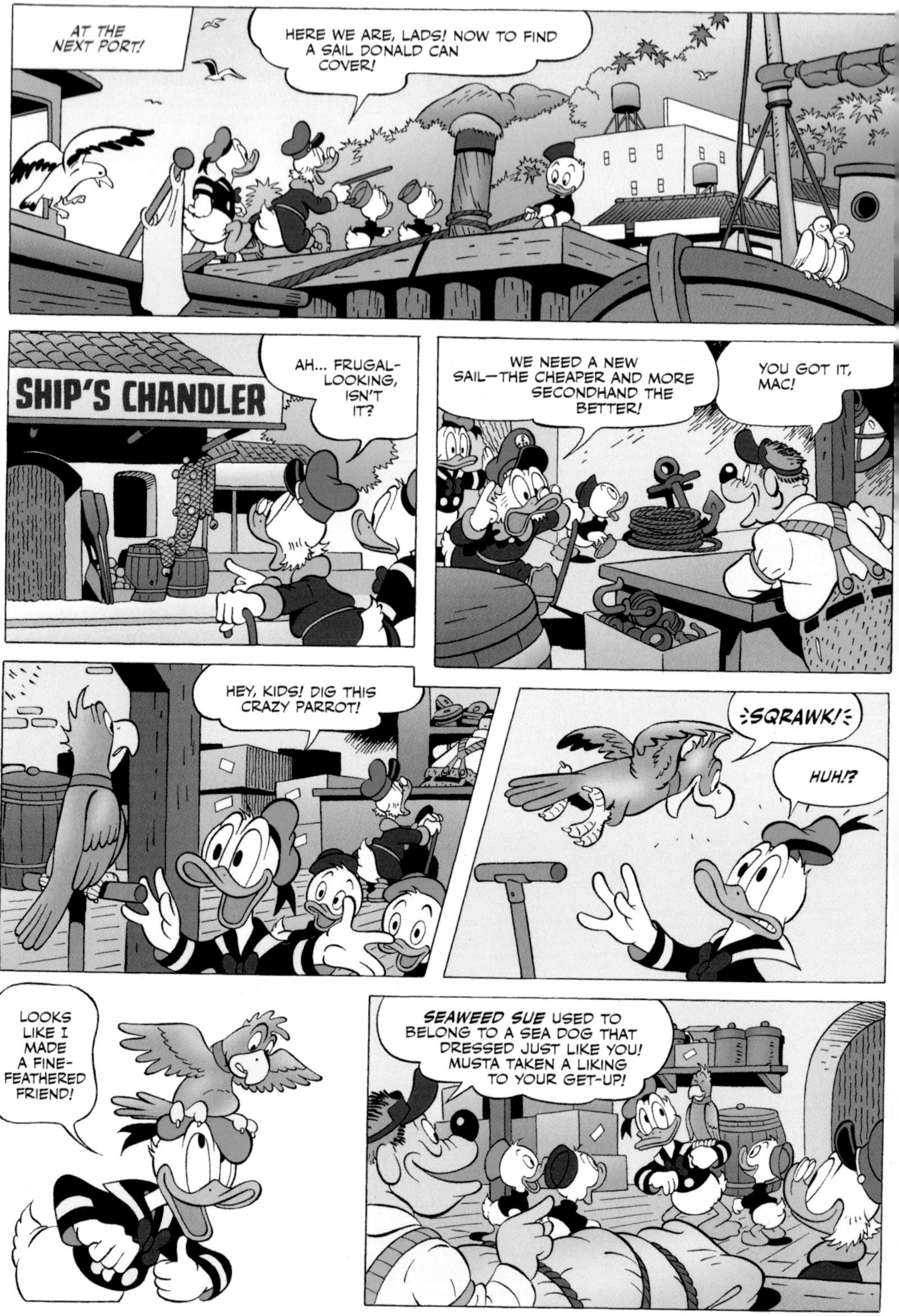
AT THE NEXT PORT!
HERE WE ARE, LADS! NOW TO FIND A SAIL DONALD CAN COVER!
SHIP'S CHANDLER
AH... FRUGAL-LOOKING, ISN'T IT?
WE NEED A NEW SAIL—THE CHEAPER AND MORE SECONDHAND THE BETTER!
YOU GOT IT, MAC!
HEY, KIDS! DIG THIS CRAZY PARROT!
SQRAWK!
HUH!?
LOOKS LIKE I MADE A FINE-FEATHERED FRIEND!
SEAWEED SUE USED TO BELONG TO A SEA DOG THAT DRESSED JUST LIKE YOU! MUSTA TAKEN A LIKING TO YOUR GET-UP!

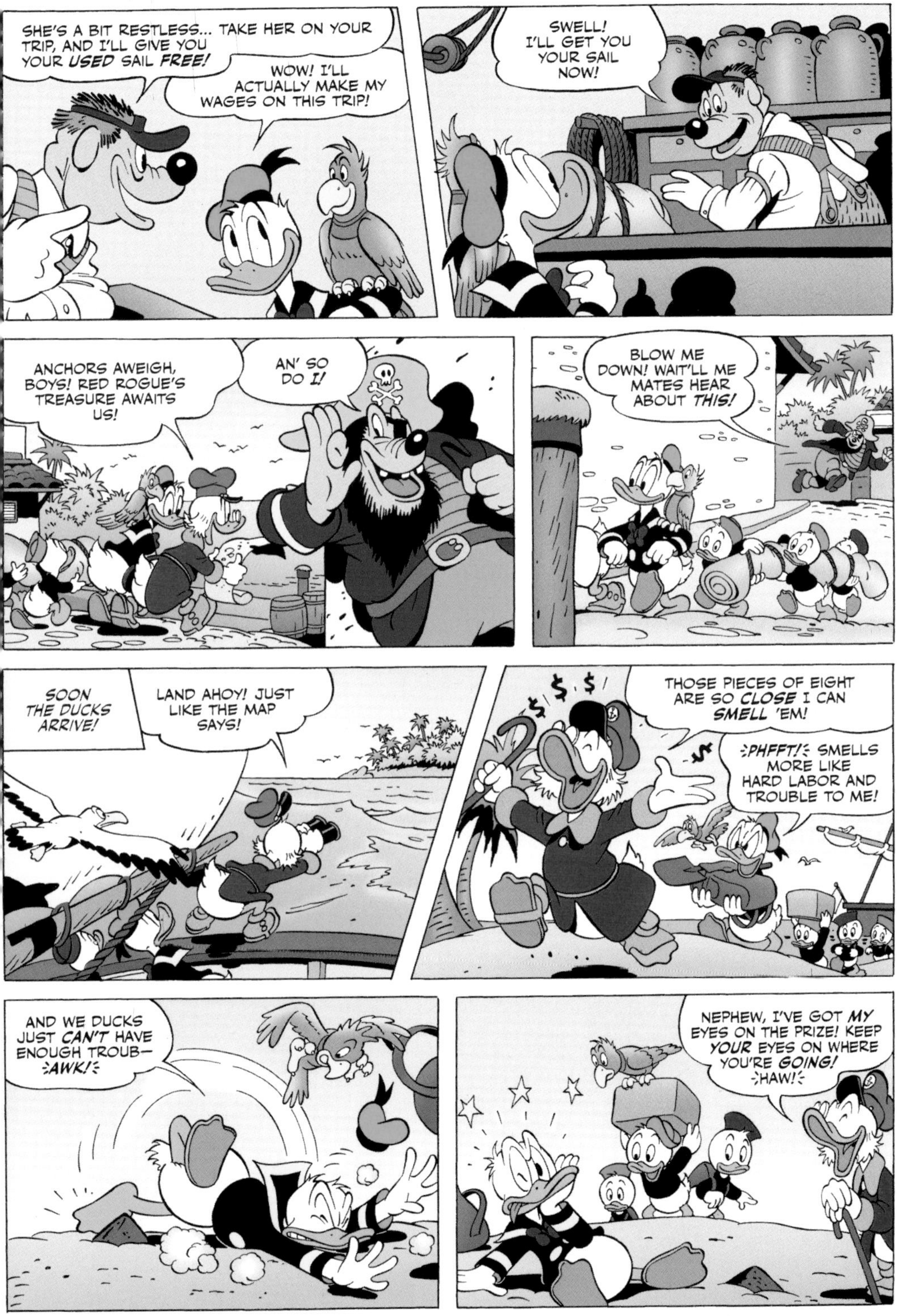
SHE'S A BIT RESTLESS... TAKE HER ON YOUR TRIP, AND I'LL GIVE YOU YOUR USED SAIL FREE!
WOW! I'LL ACTUALLY MAKE MY WAGES ON THIS TRIP!
SWELL! I'LL GET YOU YOUR SAIL NOW!
ANCHORS AWEIGH, BOYS! RED ROGUE'S TREASURE AWAITS US!
AN' SO DO I!
BLOW ME DOWN! WAIT'LL ME MATES HEAR ABOUT THIS!
SOON THE DUCKS ARRIVE!
LAND AHOY! JUST LIKE THE MAP SAYS!
THOSE PIECES OF EIGHT ARE SO CLOSE I CAN SMELL 'EM!
PHFFT! SMELLS MORE LIKE HARD LABOR AND TROUBLE TO ME!
AND WE DUCKS JUST CAN'T HAVE ENOUGH TROUB— AWK!
NEPHEW, I'VE GOT MY EYES ON THE PRIZE! KEEP YOUR EYES ON WHERE YOU'RE GOING! HAW!

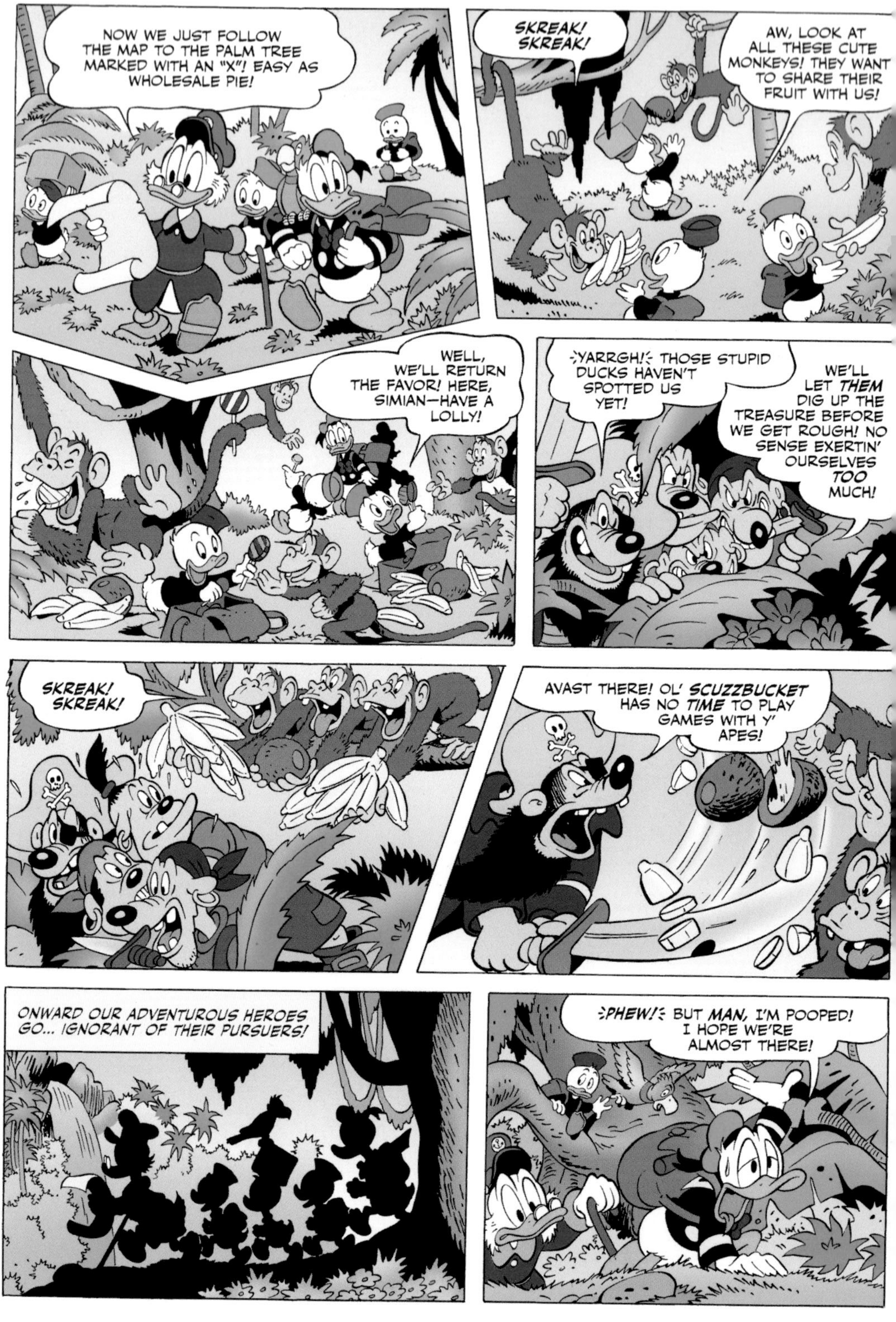
NOW WE JUST FOLLOW THE MAP TO THE PALM TREE MARKED WITH AN "X"! EASY AS WHOLESALE PIE!
SKREAK! SKREAK!
AW, LOOK AT ALL THESE CUTE MONKEYS! THEY WANT TO SHARE THEIR FRUIT WITH US!
WELL, WE'LL RETURN THE FAVOR! HERE, SIMIAN—HAVE A LOLLY!
YARRGH! THOSE STUPID DUCKS HAVEN'T SPOTTED US YET!
WE'LL LET THEM DIG UP THE TREASURE BEFORE WE GET ROUGH! NO SENSE EXERTIN' OURSELVES TOO MUCH!
SKREAK! SKREAK!
AVAST THERE! OL' SCUZZBUCKET HAS NO TIME TO PLAY GAMES WITH Y' APES!
ONWARD OUR ADVENTUROUS HEROES GO... IGNORANT OF THEIR PURSUERS!
PHEW! BUT MAN, I'M POOPED! I HOPE WE'RE ALMOST THERE!

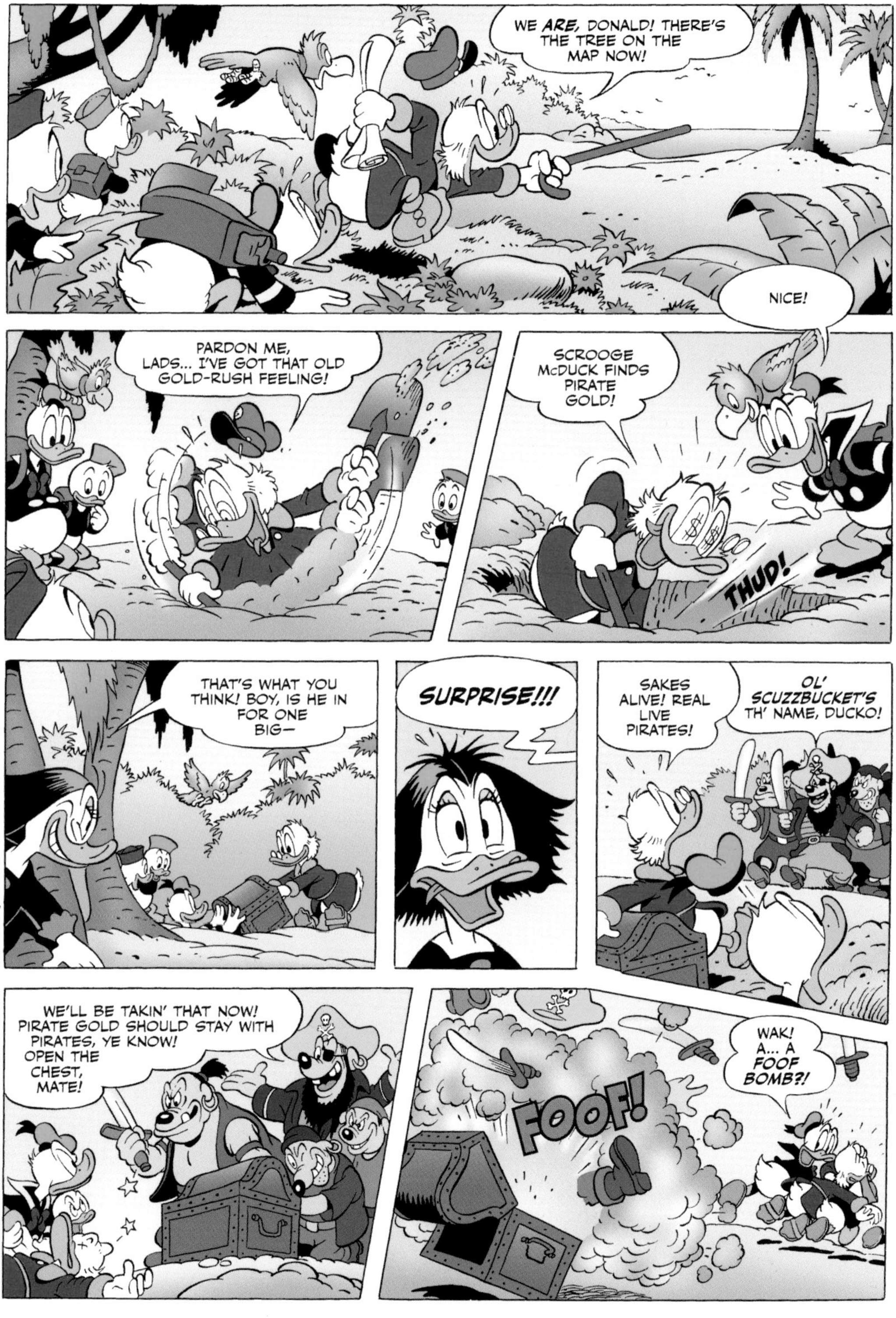
WE ARE, DONALD! THERE'S THE TREE ON THE MAP NOW!
NICE!
PARDON ME, LADS... I'VE GOT THAT OLD GOLD-RUSH FEELING!
SCROOGE McDUCK FINDS PIRATE GOLD!
THUD!
THAT'S WHAT YOU THINK! BOY, IS HE IN FOR ONE BIG—
SURPRISE!!!
SAKES ALIVE! REAL LIVE PIRATES!
OL' SCUZZBUCKET'S TH' NAME, DUCKO!
WE'LL BE TAKIN' THAT NOW! PIRATE GOLD SHOULD STAY WITH PIRATES, YE KNOW! OPEN THE CHEST, MATE!
FOOF!
WAK! A... A FOOF BOMB?!

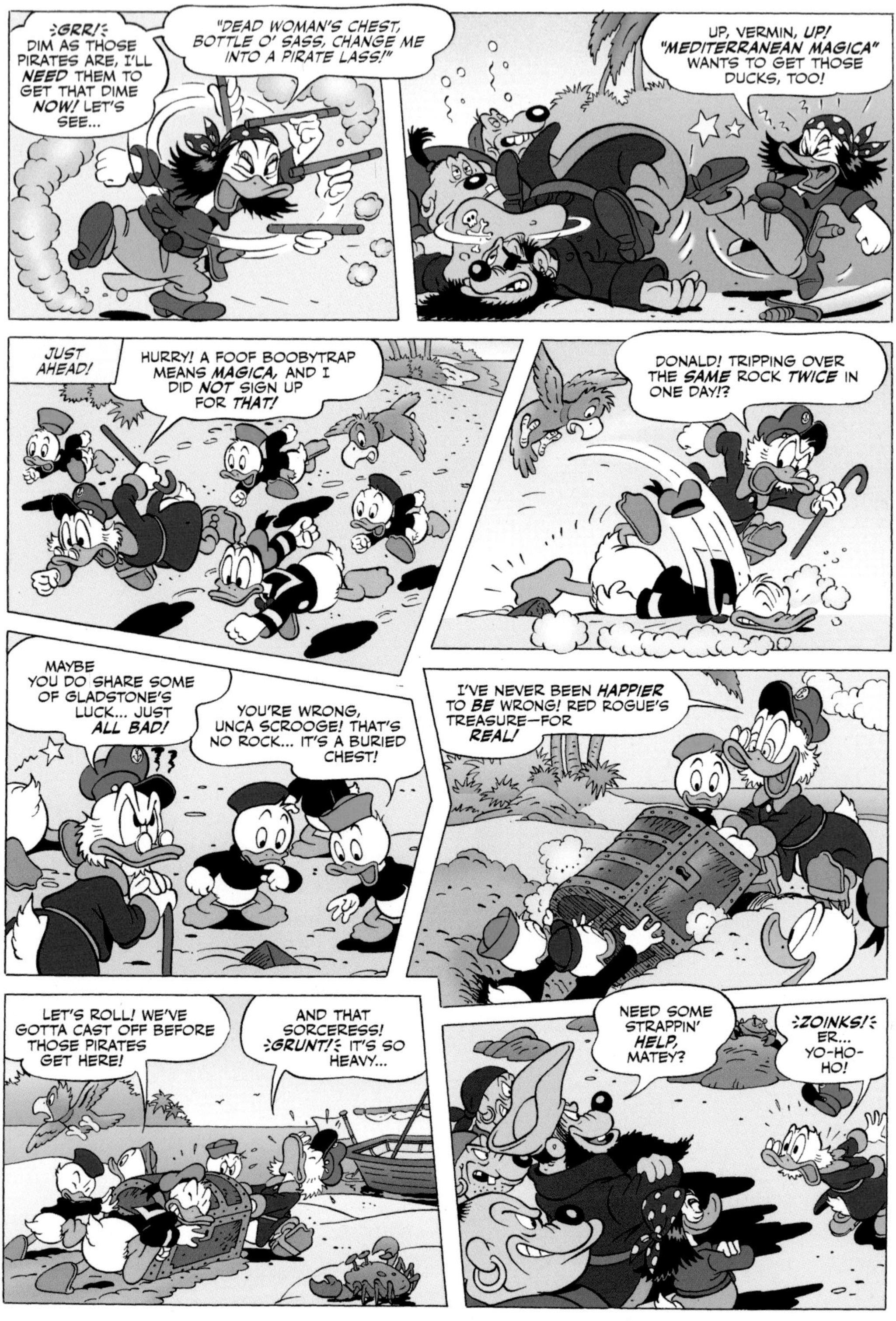
:GRR!: DIM AS THOSE PIRATES ARE, I'LL NEED THEM TO GET THAT DIME NOW! LET'S SEE...
"DEAD WOMAN'S CHEST, BOTTLE O' SASS, CHANGE ME INTO A PIRATE LASS!"
UP, VERMIN, UP! "MEDITERRANEAN MAGICA" WANTS TO GET THOSE DUCKS, TOO!
JUST AHEAD!
HURRY! A FOOF BOOBYTRAP MEANS MAGICA, AND I DID NOT SIGN UP FOR THAT!
DONALD! TRIPPING OVER THE SAME ROCK TWICE IN ONE DAY!?
MAYBE YOU DO SHARE SOME OF GLADSTONE'S LUCK... JUST ALL BAD!
YOU'RE WRONG, UNCA SCROOGE! THAT'S NO ROCK... IT'S A BURIED CHEST!
I'VE NEVER BEEN HAPPIER TO BE WRONG! RED ROGUE'S TREASURE—FOR REAL!
LET'S ROLL! WE'VE GOTTA CAST OFF BEFORE THOSE PIRATES GET HERE!
AND THAT SORCERESS! :GRUNT!: IT'S SO HEAVY...
NEED SOME STRAPPIN' HELP, MATEY?
:ZOINKS!: ER... YO-HO-HO!

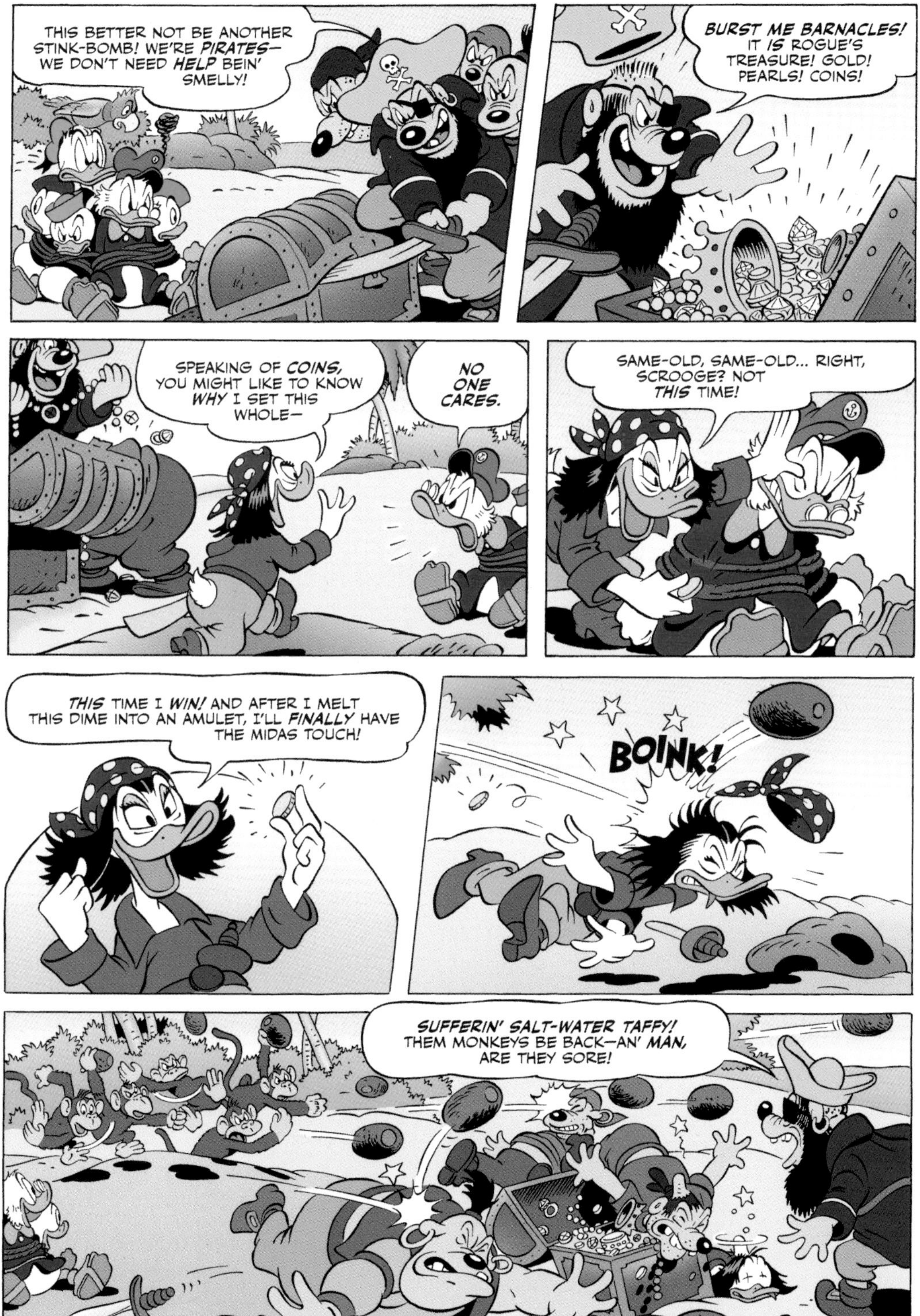
THIS BETTER NOT BE ANOTHER STINK-BOMB! WE'RE *PIRATES*— WE DON'T NEED *HELP* BEIN' SMELLY!
BURST ME BARNACLES! IT *IS* ROGUE'S TREASURE! GOLD! PEARLS! COINS!
SPEAKING OF *COINS,* YOU MIGHT LIKE TO KNOW *WHY* I SET THIS WHOLE—
NO ONE CARES.
SAME-OLD, SAME-OLD... RIGHT, SCROOGE? NOT *THIS* TIME!
THIS TIME I *WIN!* AND AFTER I MELT THIS DIME INTO AN AMULET, I'LL *FINALLY* HAVE THE MIDAS TOUCH!
BOINK!
SUFFERIN' SALT-WATER TAFFY! THEM MONKEYS BE BACK—AN' *MAN,* ARE THEY SORE!

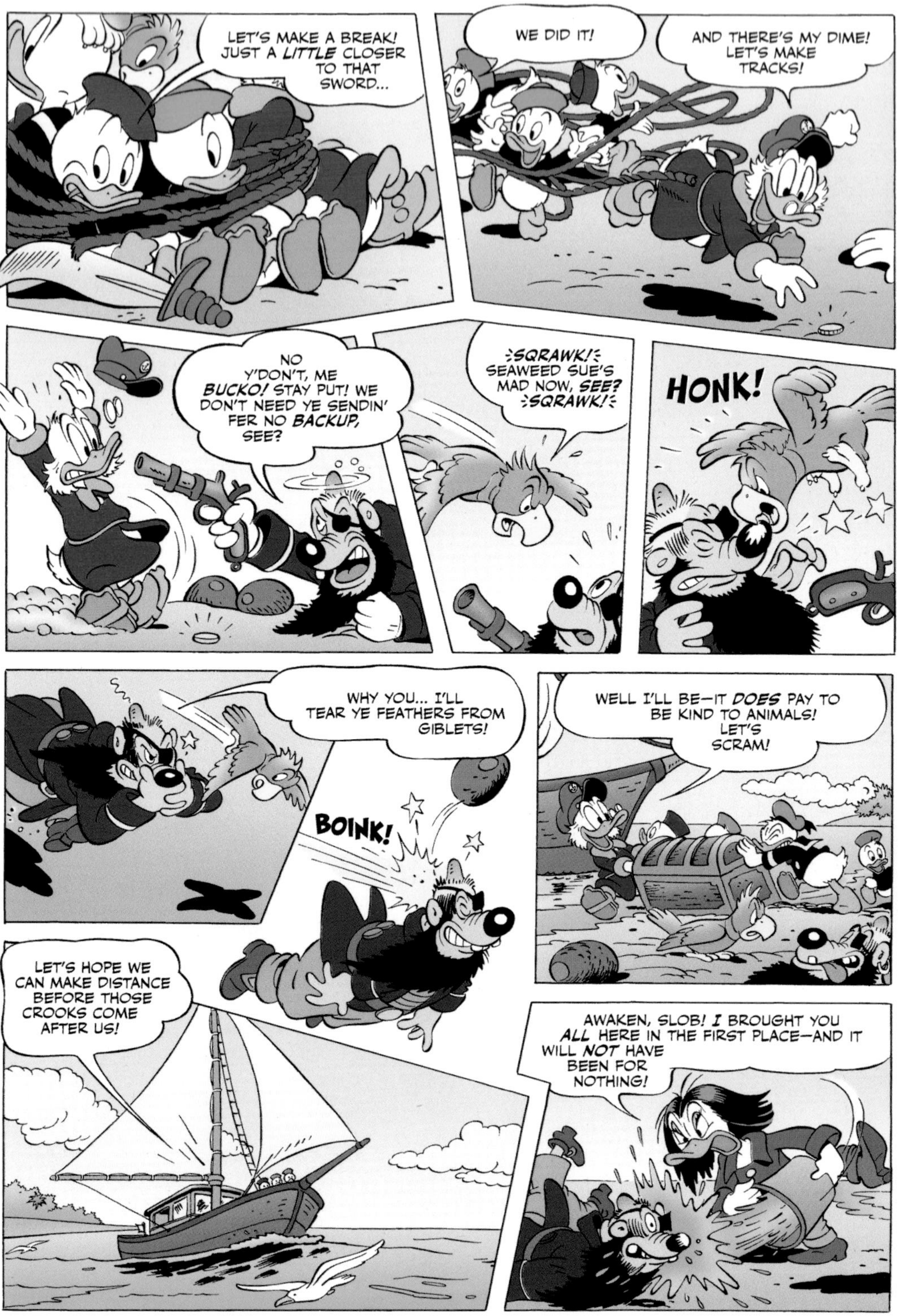
LET'S MAKE A BREAK! JUST A LITTLE CLOSER TO THAT SWORD...
WE DID IT!
AND THERE'S MY DIME! LET'S MAKE TRACKS!
NO Y'DON'T, ME BUCKO! STAY PUT! WE DON'T NEED YE SENDIN' FER NO BACKUP, SEE?
SQRAWK! SEAWEED SUE'S MAD NOW, SEE? SQRAWK!
HONK!
WHY YOU... I'LL TEAR YE FEATHERS FROM GIBLETS!
BOINK!
WELL I'LL BE—IT DOES PAY TO BE KIND TO ANIMALS! LET'S SCRAM!
LET'S HOPE WE CAN MAKE DISTANCE BEFORE THOSE CROOKS COME AFTER US!
AWAKEN, SLOB! I BROUGHT YOU ALL HERE IN THE FIRST PLACE—AND IT WILL NOT HAVE BEEN FOR NOTHING!

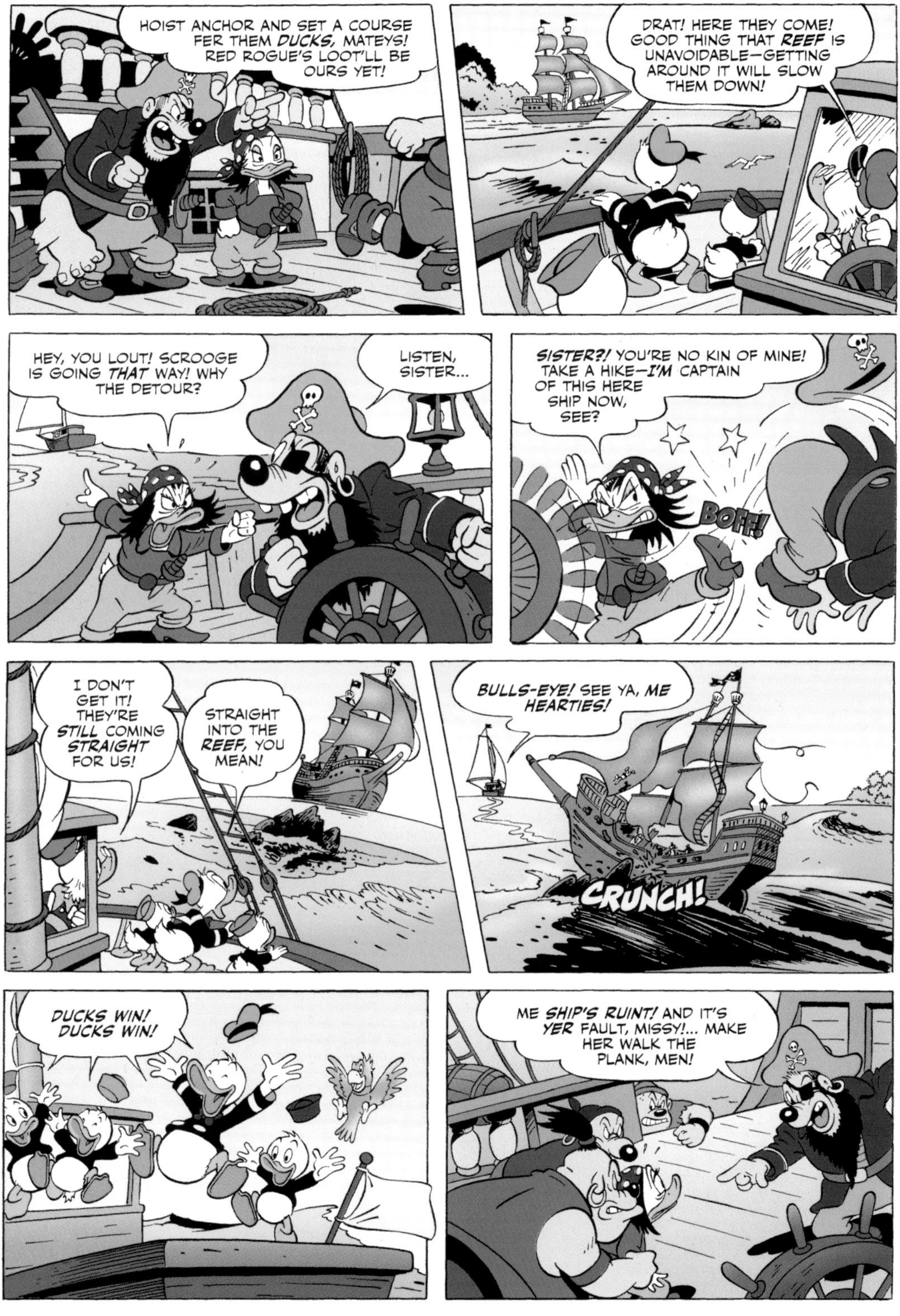
HOIST ANCHOR AND SET A COURSE FER THEM DUCKS, MATEYS! RED ROGUE'S LOOT'LL BE OURS YET!
DRAT! HERE THEY COME! GOOD THING THAT REEF IS UNAVOIDABLE—GETTING AROUND IT WILL SLOW THEM DOWN!
HEY, YOU LOUT! SCROOGE IS GOING THAT WAY! WHY THE DETOUR?
LISTEN, SISTER...
SISTER?! YOU'RE NO KIN OF MINE! TAKE A HIKE—I'M CAPTAIN OF THIS HERE SHIP NOW, SEE?
BOFF!
I DON'T GET IT! THEY'RE STILL COMING STRAIGHT FOR US!
STRAIGHT INTO THE REEF, YOU MEAN!
BULLS-EYE! SEE YA, ME HEARTIES!
CRUNCH!
DUCKS WIN! DUCKS WIN!
ME SHIP'S RUINT! AND IT'S YER FAULT, MISSY!... MAKE HER WALK THE PLANK, MEN!

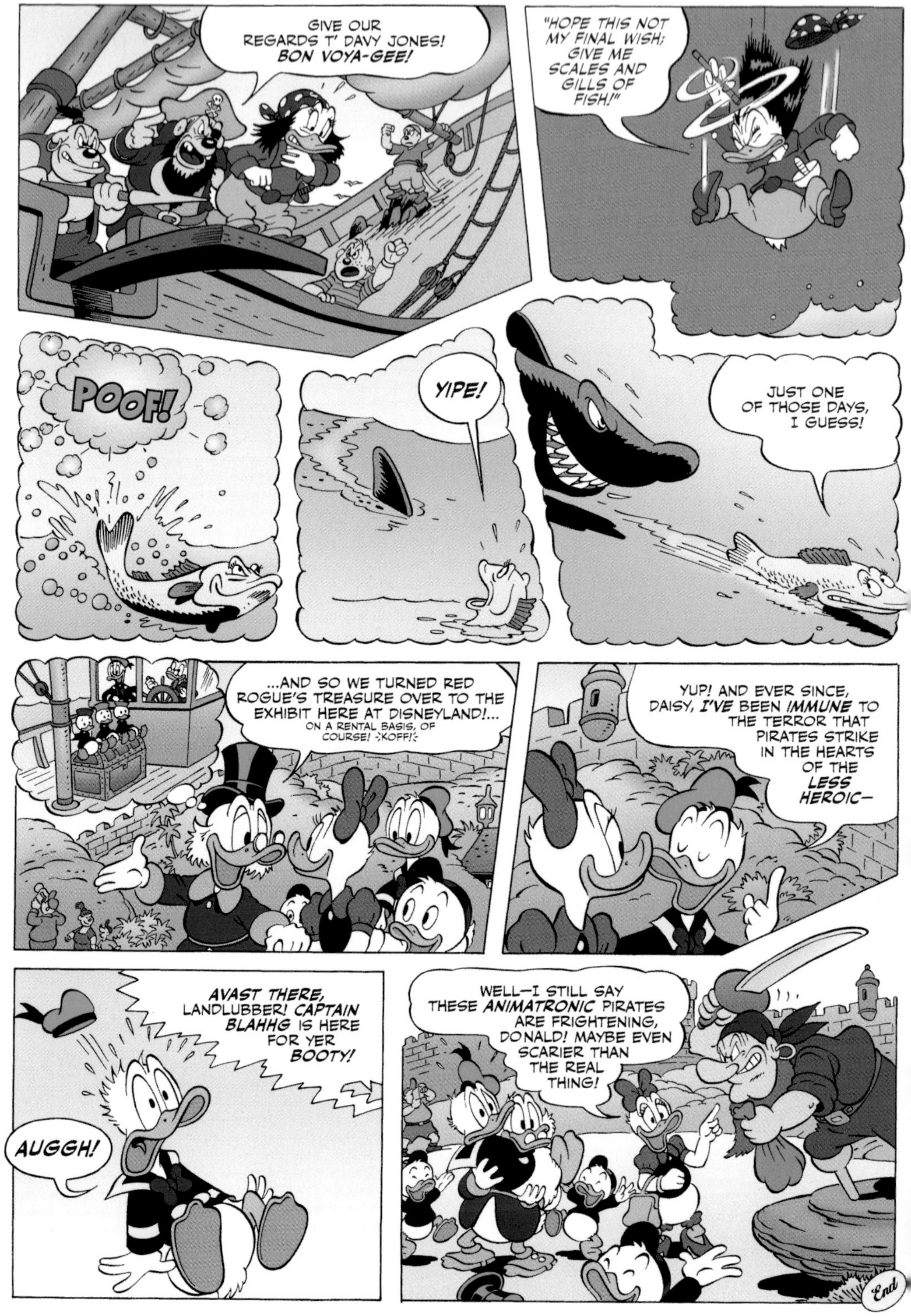
GIVE OUR REGARDS T' DAVY JONES! BON VOYA-GEE!
"HOPE THIS NOT MY FINAL WISH; GIVE ME SCALES AND GILLS OF FISH!"
POOF!
YIPE!
JUST ONE OF THOSE DAYS, I GUESS!
...AND SO WE TURNED RED ROGUE'S TREASURE OVER TO THE EXHIBIT HERE AT DISNEYLAND!... ON A RENTAL BASIS, OF COURSE! KOFF!
YUP! AND EVER SINCE, DAISY, I'VE BEEN IMMUNE TO THE TERROR THAT PIRATES STRIKE IN THE HEARTS OF THE LESS HEROIC—
AVAST THERE, LANDLUBBER! CAPTAIN BLAHHG IS HERE FOR YER BOOTY!
AUGGH!
WELL—I STILL SAY THESE ANIMATRONIC PIRATES ARE FRIGHTENING, DONALD! MAYBE EVEN SCARIER THAN THE REAL THING!
End

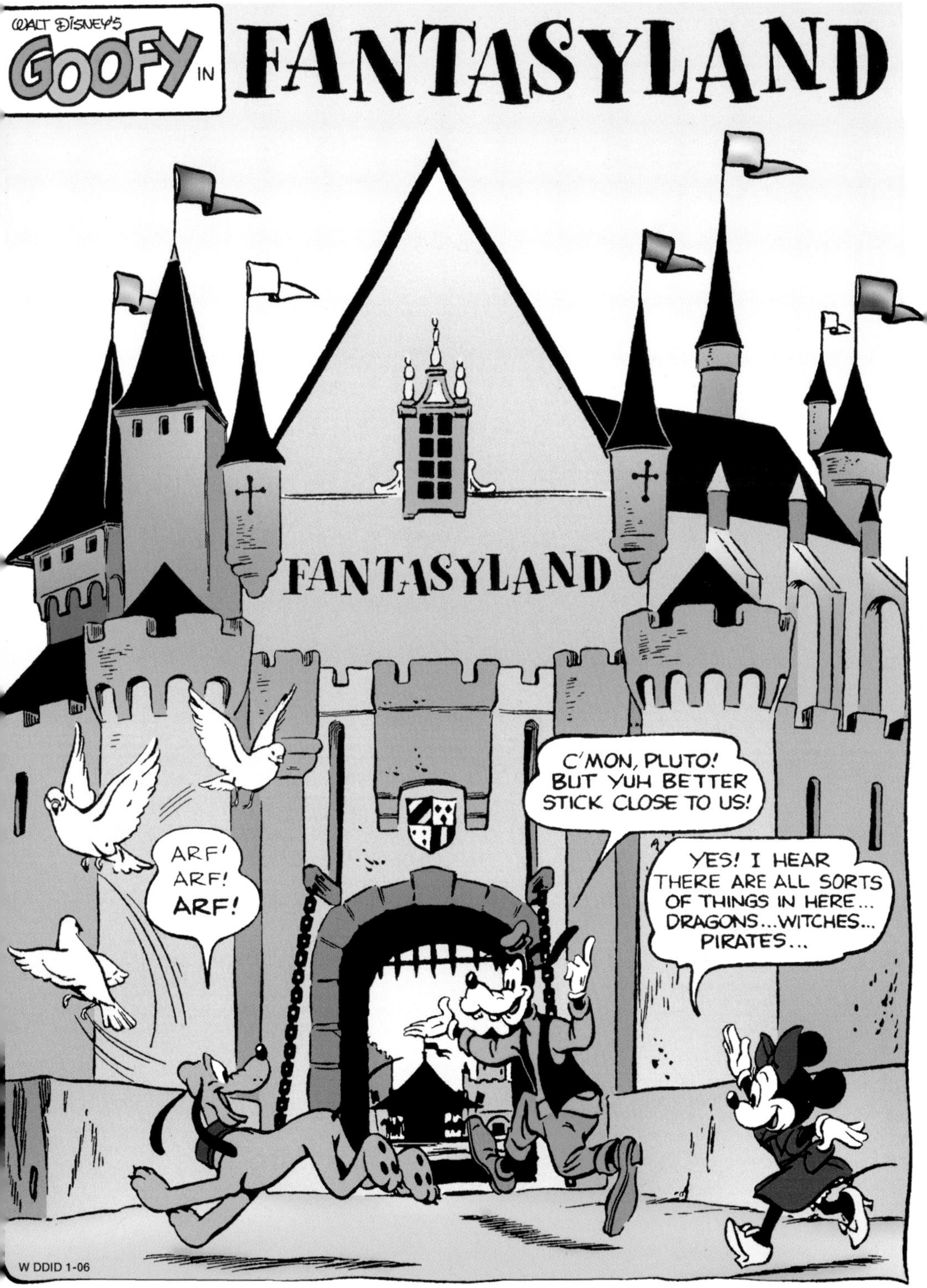
WALT DISNEY'S
GOOFY IN
FANTASYLAND
FANTASYLAND
C'MON, PLUTO! BUT YUH BETTER STICK CLOSE TO US!
ARF! ARF! ARF!
YES! I HEAR THERE ARE ALL SORTS OF THINGS IN HERE... DRAGONS...WITCHES... PIRATES...
W DDID 1-06

Originally published in *Donald Duck in Disneyland* #1 (USA, 1955)

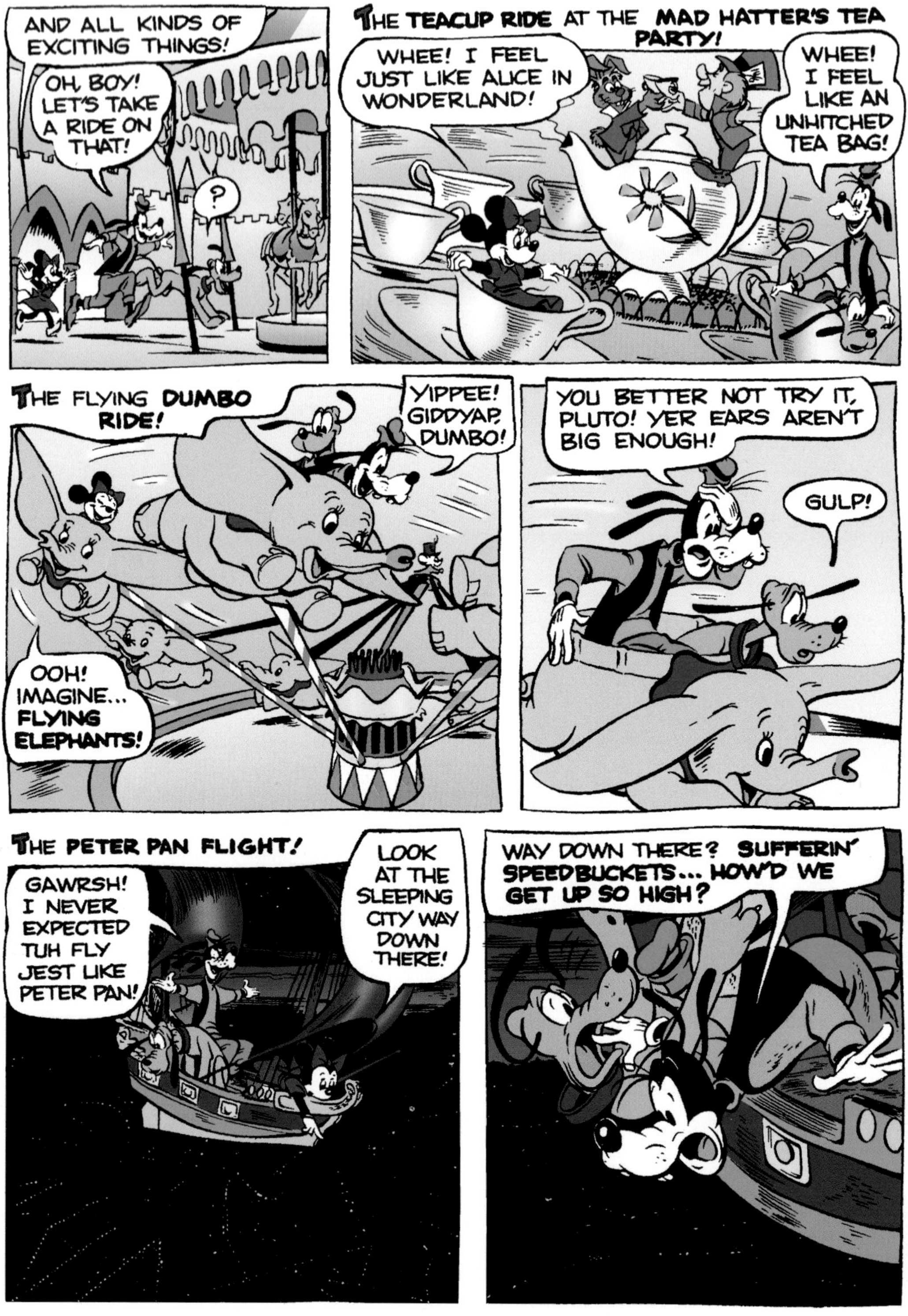
AND ALL KINDS OF EXCITING THINGS!
OH, BOY! LET'S TAKE A RIDE ON THAT!
?
THE TEACUP RIDE AT THE MAD HATTER'S TEA PARTY!
WHEE! I FEEL JUST LIKE ALICE IN WONDERLAND!
WHEE! I FEEL LIKE AN UNHITCHED TEA BAG!
THE FLYING DUMBO RIDE!
YIPPEE! GIDDYAP, DUMBO!
OOH! IMAGINE... FLYING ELEPHANTS!
YOU BETTER NOT TRY IT, PLUTO! YER EARS AREN'T BIG ENOUGH!
GULP!
THE PETER PAN FLIGHT!
GAWRSH! I NEVER EXPECTED TUH FLY JEST LIKE PETER PAN!
LOOK AT THE SLEEPING CITY WAY DOWN THERE!
WAY DOWN THERE? SUFFERIN' SPEEDBUCKETS... HOW'D WE GET UP SO HIGH?

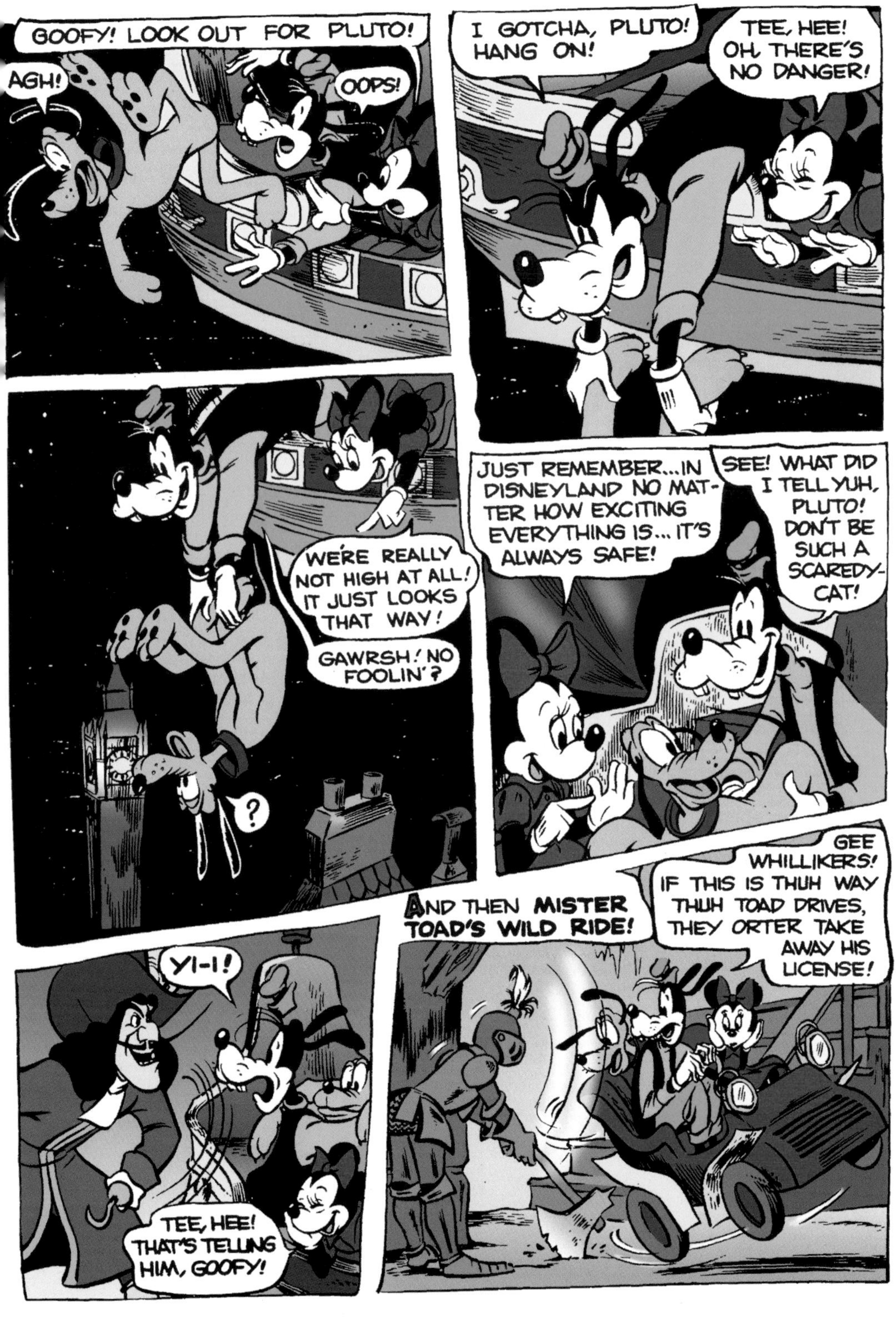
GOOFY! LOOK OUT FOR PLUTO!
AGH!
OOPS!
I GOTCHA, PLUTO! HANG ON!
TEE, HEE! OH, THERE'S NO DANGER!
WE'RE REALLY NOT HIGH AT ALL! IT JUST LOOKS THAT WAY!
GAWRSH! NO FOOLIN'?
?
JUST REMEMBER...IN DISNEYLAND NO MATTER HOW EXCITING EVERYTHING IS... IT'S ALWAYS SAFE!
SEE! WHAT DID I TELL YUH, PLUTO! DON'T BE SUCH A SCAREDY-CAT!
YI-I!
TEE, HEE! THAT'S TELLING HIM, GOOFY!
AND THEN MISTER TOAD'S WILD RIDE!
GEE WHILLIKERS! IF THIS IS THUH WAY THUH TOAD DRIVES, THEY ORTER TAKE AWAY HIS LICENSE!

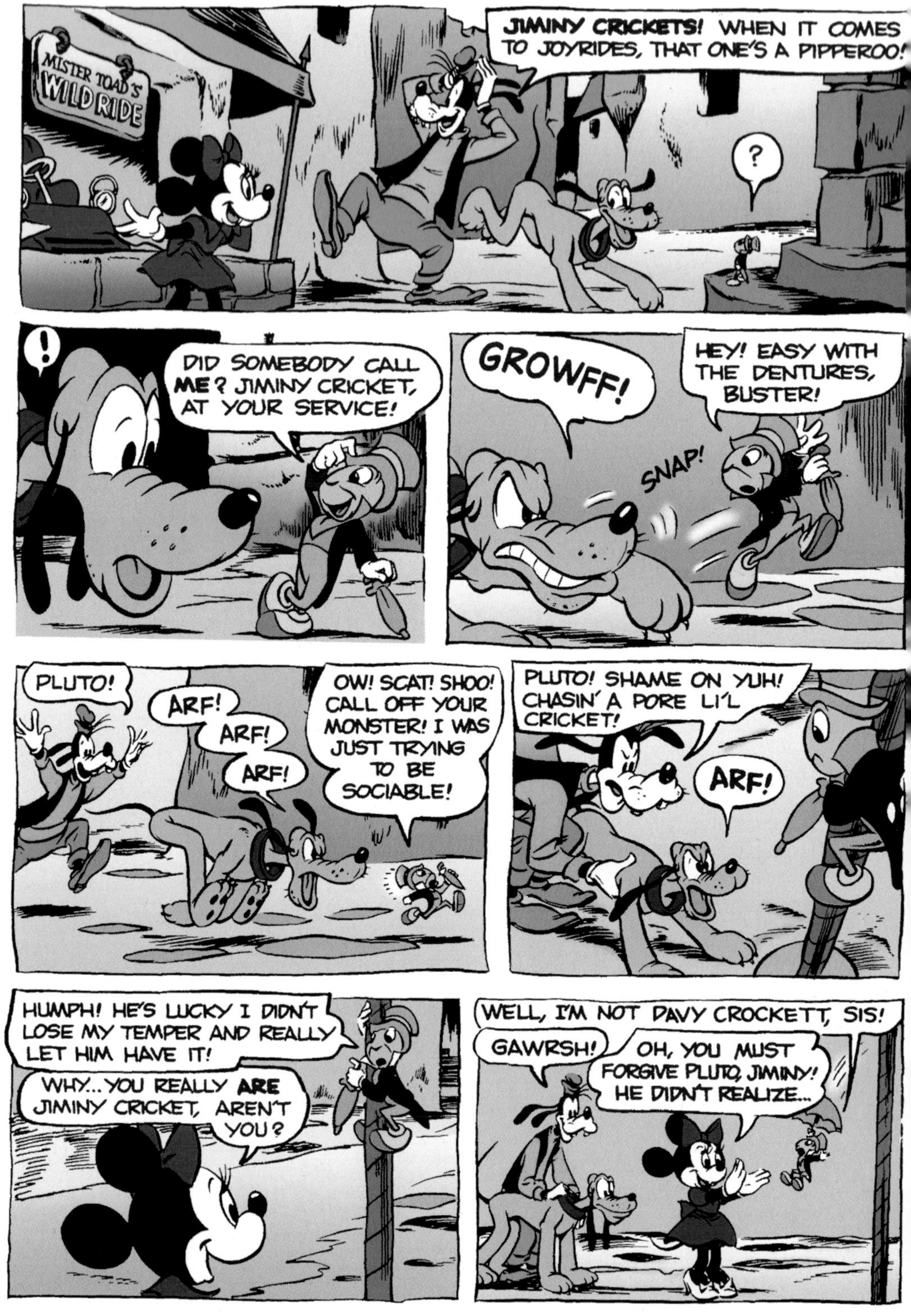
MISTER TOAD'S WILD RIDE
JIMINY CRICKETS! WHEN IT COMES TO JOYRIDES, THAT ONE'S A PIPPEROO!
?
!
DID SOMEBODY CALL ME? JIMINY CRICKET, AT YOUR SERVICE!
GROWFF!
HEY! EASY WITH THE DENTURES, BUSTER!
SNAP!
PLUTO!
ARF!
ARF!
ARF!
OW! SCAT! SHOO! CALL OFF YOUR MONSTER! I WAS JUST TRYING TO BE SOCIABLE!
PLUTO! SHAME ON YUH! CHASIN' A PORE LI'L CRICKET!
ARF!
HUMPH! HE'S LUCKY I DIDN'T LOSE MY TEMPER AND REALLY LET HIM HAVE IT!
WHY... YOU REALLY ARE JIMINY CRICKET, AREN'T YOU?
WELL, I'M NOT DAVY CROCKETT, SIS!
GAWRSH!
OH, YOU MUST FORGIVE PLUTO, JIMINY! HE DIDN'T REALIZE...

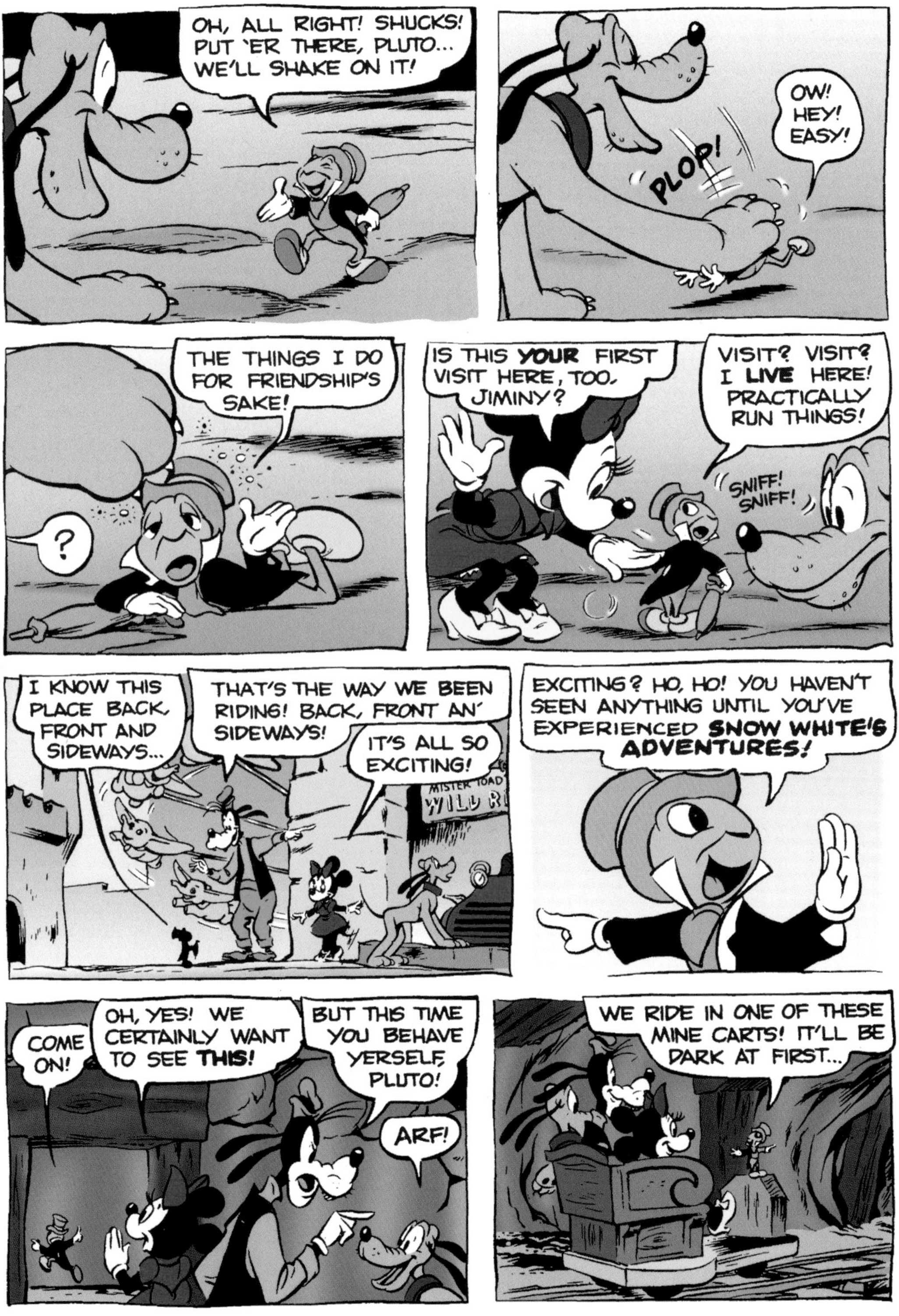

OH, ALL RIGHT! SHUCKS! PUT 'ER THERE, PLUTO... WE'LL SHAKE ON IT!
PLOP!
OW! HEY! EASY!
THE THINGS I DO FOR FRIENDSHIP'S SAKE!
?
IS THIS YOUR FIRST VISIT HERE, TOO, JIMINY?
VISIT? VISIT? I LIVE HERE! PRACTICALLY RUN THINGS!
SNIFF! SNIFF!
I KNOW THIS PLACE BACK, FRONT AND SIDEWAYS...
THAT'S THE WAY WE BEEN RIDING! BACK, FRONT AN' SIDEWAYS!
IT'S ALL SO EXCITING!
MISTER TOAD'S WILD RI
EXCITING? HO, HO! YOU HAVEN'T SEEN ANYTHING UNTIL YOU'VE EXPERIENCED SNOW WHITE'S ADVENTURES!
COME ON!
OH, YES! WE CERTAINLY WANT TO SEE THIS!
BUT THIS TIME YOU BEHAVE YERSELF, PLUTO!
ARF!
WE RIDE IN ONE OF THESE MINE CARTS! IT'LL BE DARK AT FIRST...

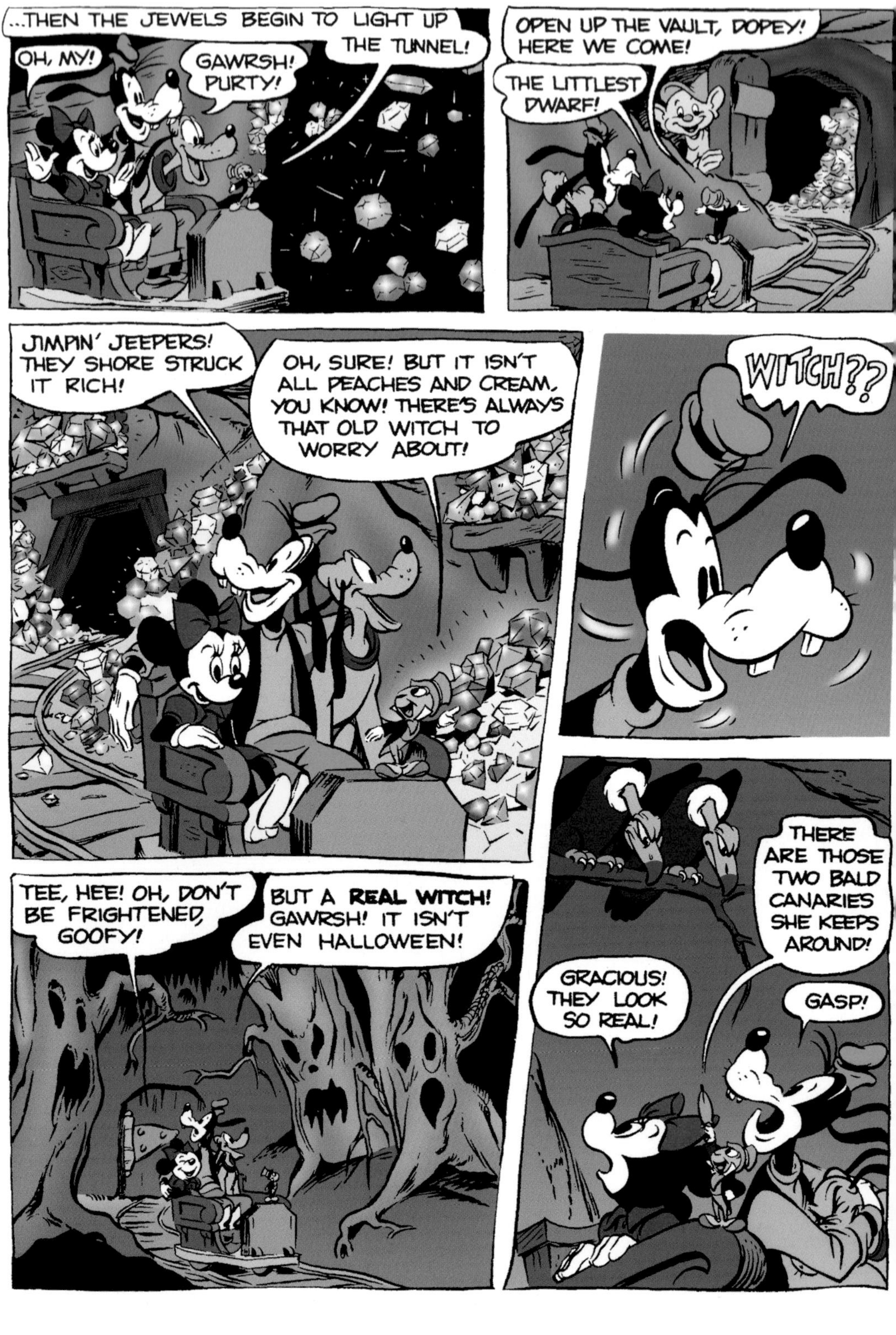
...THEN THE JEWELS BEGIN TO LIGHT UP THE TUNNEL!
OH, MY!
GAWRSH! PURTY!
OPEN UP THE VAULT, DOPEY! HERE WE COME!
THE LITTLEST DWARF!
JIMPIN' JEEPERS! THEY SHORE STRUCK IT RICH!
OH, SURE! BUT IT ISN'T ALL PEACHES AND CREAM, YOU KNOW! THERE'S ALWAYS THAT OLD WITCH TO WORRY ABOUT!
WITCH??
TEE, HEE! OH, DON'T BE FRIGHTENED, GOOFY!
BUT A **REAL WITCH**! GAWRSH! IT ISN'T EVEN HALLOWEEN!
THERE ARE THOSE TWO BALD CANARIES SHE KEEPS AROUND!
GRACIOUS! THEY LOOK SO REAL!
GASP!

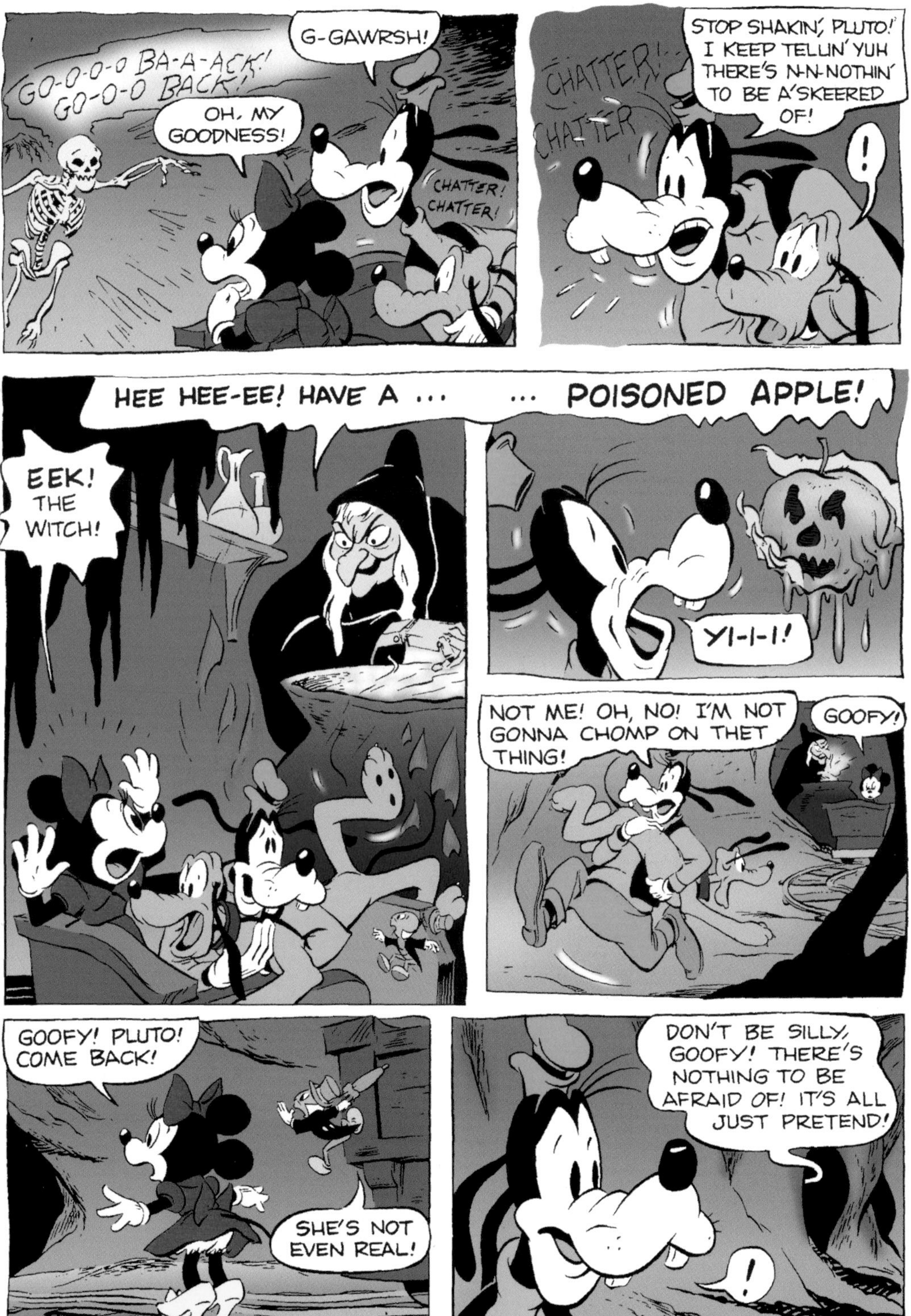
GO-O-O-O BA-A-ACK! GO-O-O BACK!
G-GAWRSH!
OH, MY GOODNESS!
CHATTER! CHATTER!
CHATTER! CHATTER
STOP SHAKIN', PLUTO! I KEEP TELLIN' YUH THERE'S N-N-NOTHIN' TO BE A'SKEERED OF!
!
HEE HEE-EE! HAVE A ... ... POISONED APPLE!
EEK! THE WITCH!
YI-I-I!
NOT ME! OH, NO! I'M NOT GONNA CHOMP ON THET THING!
GOOFY!
GOOFY! PLUTO! COME BACK!
SHE'S NOT EVEN REAL!
DON'T BE SILLY, GOOFY! THERE'S NOTHING TO BE AFRAID OF! IT'S ALL JUST PRETEND!
!

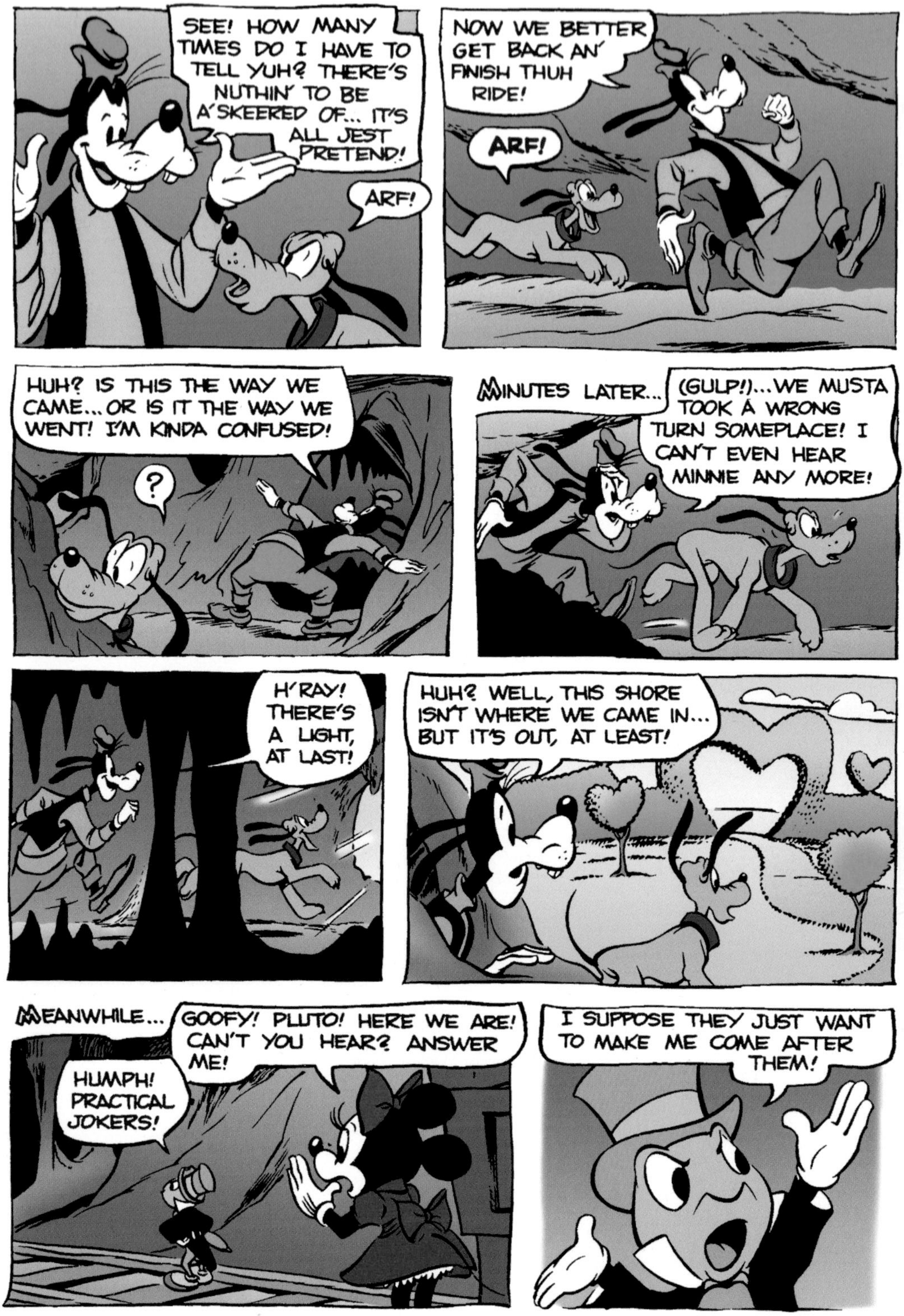
SEE! HOW MANY TIMES DO I HAVE TO TELL YUH? THERE'S NUTHIN' TO BE A'SKEERED OF... IT'S ALL JEST PRETEND!
ARF!
NOW WE BETTER GET BACK AN' FINISH THUH RIDE!
ARF!
HUH? IS THIS THE WAY WE CAME...OR IS IT THE WAY WE WENT! I'M KINDA CONFUSED!
?
MINUTES LATER...
(GULP!)...WE MUSTA TOOK A WRONG TURN SOMEPLACE! I CAN'T EVEN HEAR MINNIE ANY MORE!
H'RAY! THERE'S A LIGHT, AT LAST!
HUH? WELL, THIS SHORE ISN'T WHERE WE CAME IN... BUT IT'S OUT, AT LEAST!
MEANWHILE...
GOOFY! PLUTO! HERE WE ARE! CAN'T YOU HEAR? ANSWER ME!
HUMPH! PRACTICAL JOKERS!
I SUPPOSE THEY JUST WANT TO MAKE ME COME AFTER THEM!

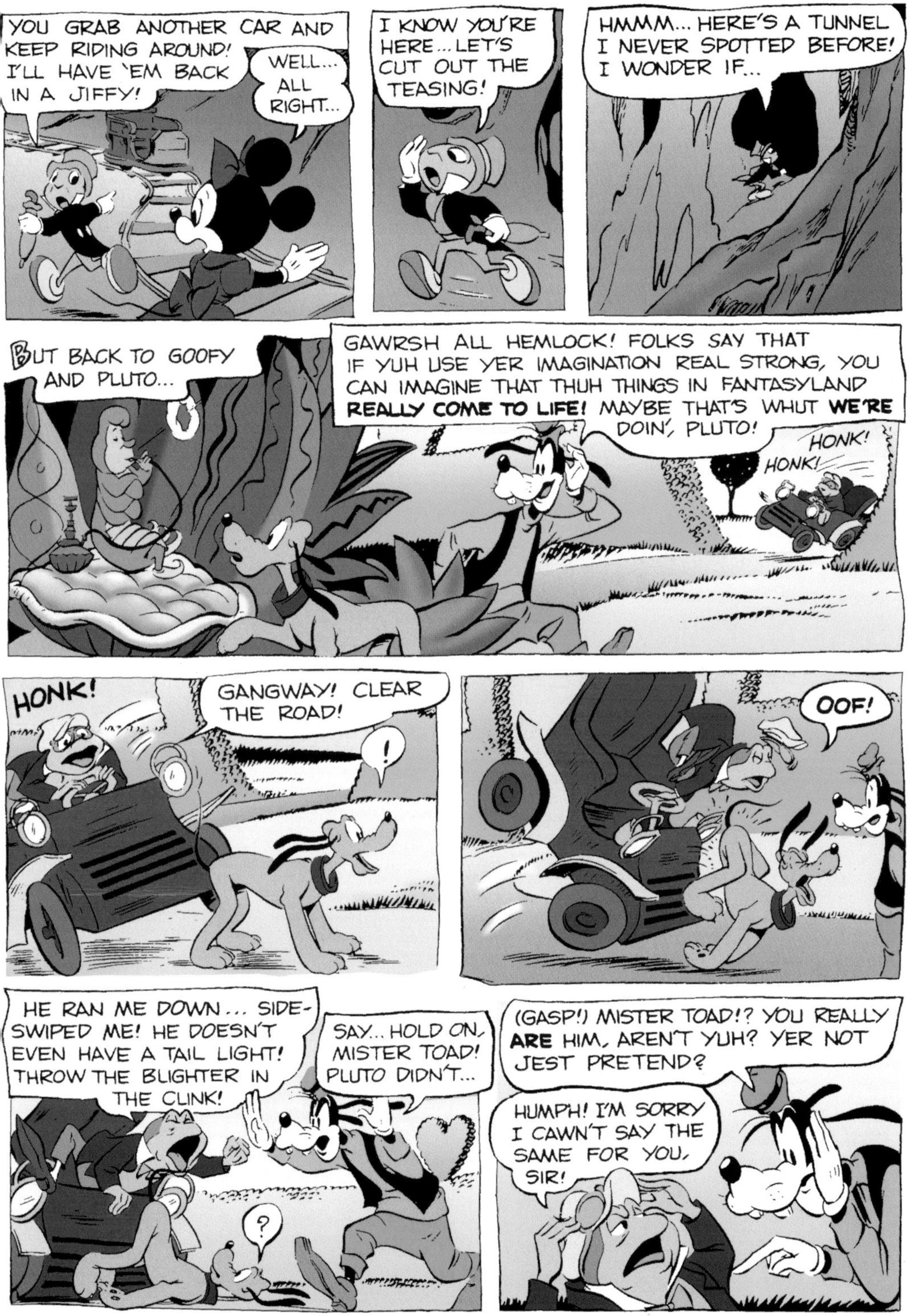

YOU GRAB ANOTHER CAR AND KEEP RIDING AROUND! I'LL HAVE 'EM BACK IN A JIFFY!
WELL... ALL RIGHT...
I KNOW YOU'RE HERE... LET'S CUT OUT THE TEASING!
HMMM... HERE'S A TUNNEL I NEVER SPOTTED BEFORE! I WONDER IF...
BUT BACK TO GOOFY AND PLUTO...
GAWRSH ALL HEMLOCK! FOLKS SAY THAT IF YUH USE YER IMAGINATION REAL STRONG, YOU CAN IMAGINE THAT THUH THINGS IN FANTASYLAND **REALLY COME TO LIFE!** MAYBE THAT'S WHUT **WE'RE** DOIN', PLUTO!
HONK! HONK!
HONK!
GANGWAY! CLEAR THE ROAD!
!
OOF!
HE RAN ME DOWN... SIDE-SWIPED ME! HE DOESN'T EVEN HAVE A TAIL LIGHT! THROW THE BLIGHTER IN THE CLINK!
SAY... HOLD ON, MISTER TOAD! PLUTO DIDN'T...
?
(GASP!) MISTER TOAD!? YOU REALLY **ARE** HIM, AREN'T YUH? YER NOT JEST PRETEND?
HUMPH! I'M SORRY I CAWN'T SAY THE SAME FOR YOU, SIR!

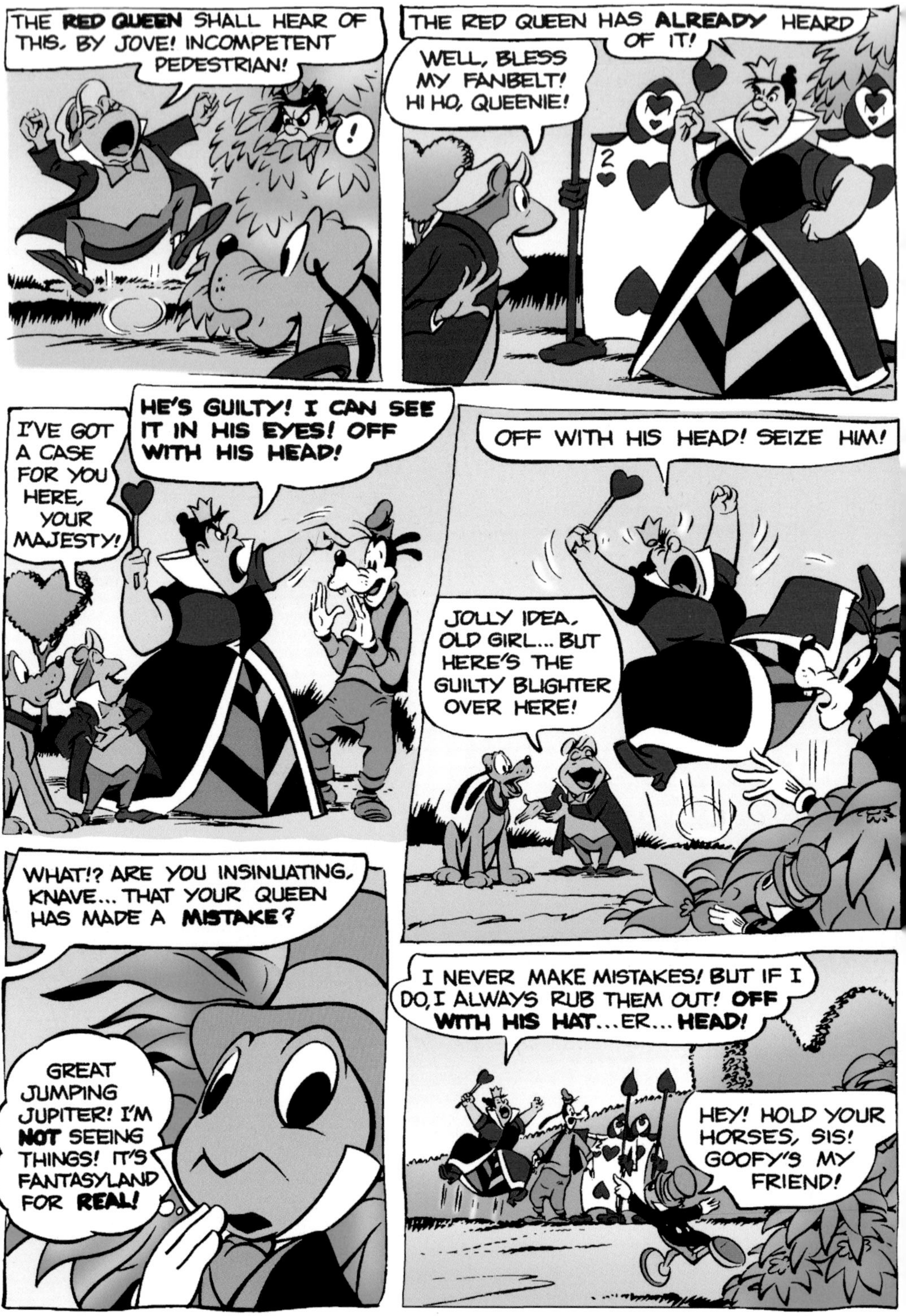
THE RED QUEEN SHALL HEAR OF THIS. BY JOVE! INCOMPETENT PEDESTRIAN!
!
THE RED QUEEN HAS ALREADY HEARD OF IT!
WELL, BLESS MY FANBELT! HI HO, QUEENIE!
I'VE GOT A CASE FOR YOU HERE, YOUR MAJESTY!
HE'S GUILTY! I CAN SEE IT IN HIS EYES! OFF WITH HIS HEAD!
OFF WITH HIS HEAD! SEIZE HIM!
JOLLY IDEA, OLD GIRL... BUT HERE'S THE GUILTY BLIGHTER OVER HERE!
WHAT!? ARE YOU INSINUATING, KNAVE... THAT YOUR QUEEN HAS MADE A MISTAKE?
GREAT JUMPING JUPITER! I'M NOT SEEING THINGS! IT'S FANTASYLAND FOR REAL!
I NEVER MAKE MISTAKES! BUT IF I DO, I ALWAYS RUB THEM OUT! OFF WITH HIS HAT...ER... HEAD!
HEY! HOLD YOUR HORSES, SIS! GOOFY'S MY FRIEND!

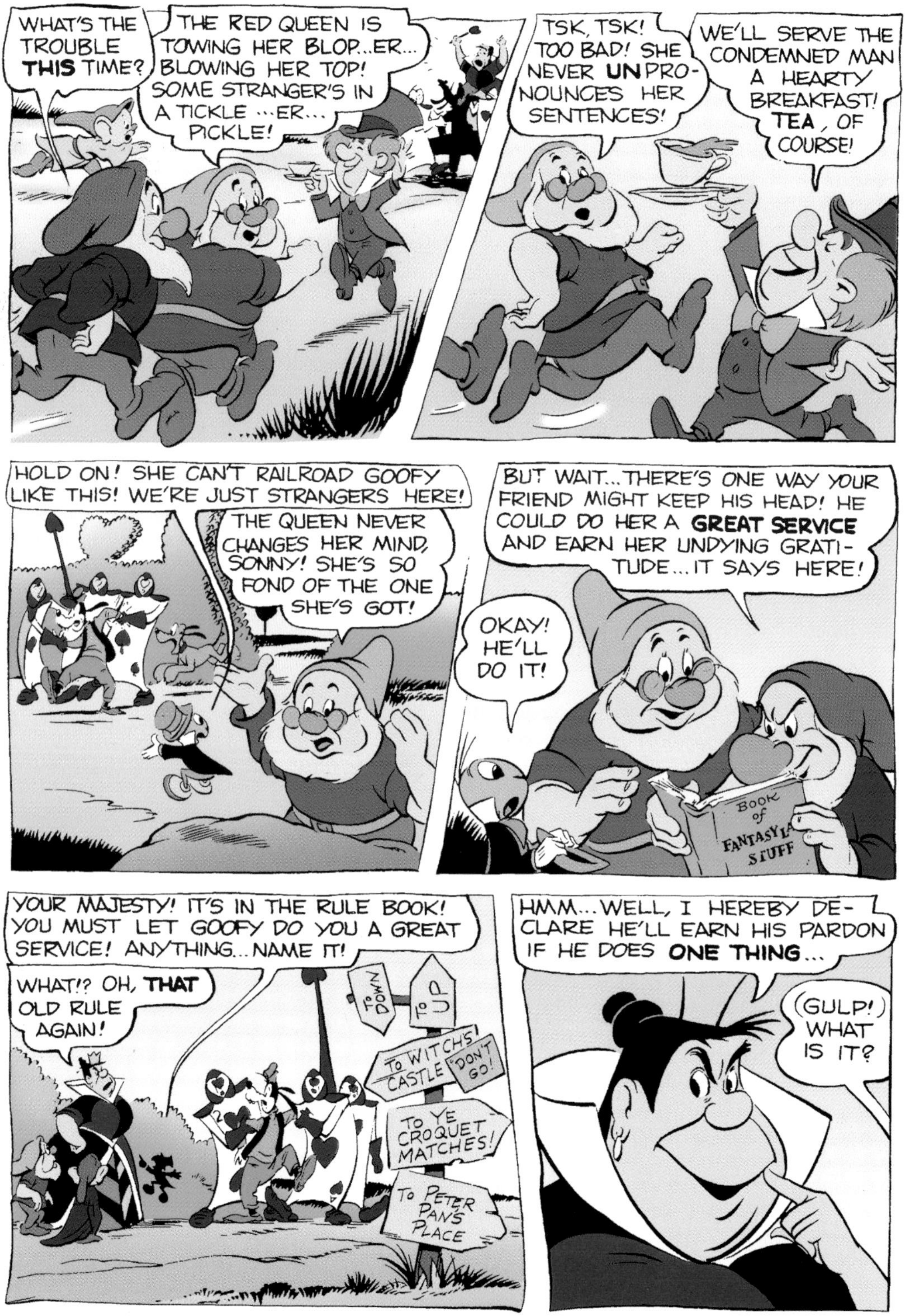

WHAT'S THE TROUBLE THIS TIME?
THE RED QUEEN IS TOWING HER BLOP...ER... BLOWING HER TOP! SOME STRANGER'S IN A TICKLE ...ER... PICKLE!
TSK, TSK! TOO BAD! SHE NEVER UNPRONOUNCES HER SENTENCES!
WE'LL SERVE THE CONDEMNED MAN A HEARTY BREAKFAST! TEA, OF COURSE!
HOLD ON! SHE CAN'T RAILROAD GOOFY LIKE THIS! WE'RE JUST STRANGERS HERE!
THE QUEEN NEVER CHANGES HER MIND, SONNY! SHE'S SO FOND OF THE ONE SHE'S GOT!
BUT WAIT...THERE'S ONE WAY YOUR FRIEND MIGHT KEEP HIS HEAD! HE COULD DO HER A GREAT SERVICE AND EARN HER UNDYING GRATITUDE...IT SAYS HERE!
OKAY! HE'LL DO IT!
BOOK of FANTASYLA STUFF
YOUR MAJESTY! IT'S IN THE RULE BOOK! YOU MUST LET GOOFY DO YOU A GREAT SERVICE! ANYTHING...NAME IT!
WHAT!? OH, THAT OLD RULE AGAIN!
TO DOWN
TO UP
TO WITCH'S CASTLE
DON'T GO!
TO YE CROQUET MATCHES!
TO PETER PAN'S PLACE
HMM...WELL, I HEREBY DECLARE HE'LL EARN HIS PARDON IF HE DOES ONE THING...
(GULP!) WHAT IS IT?

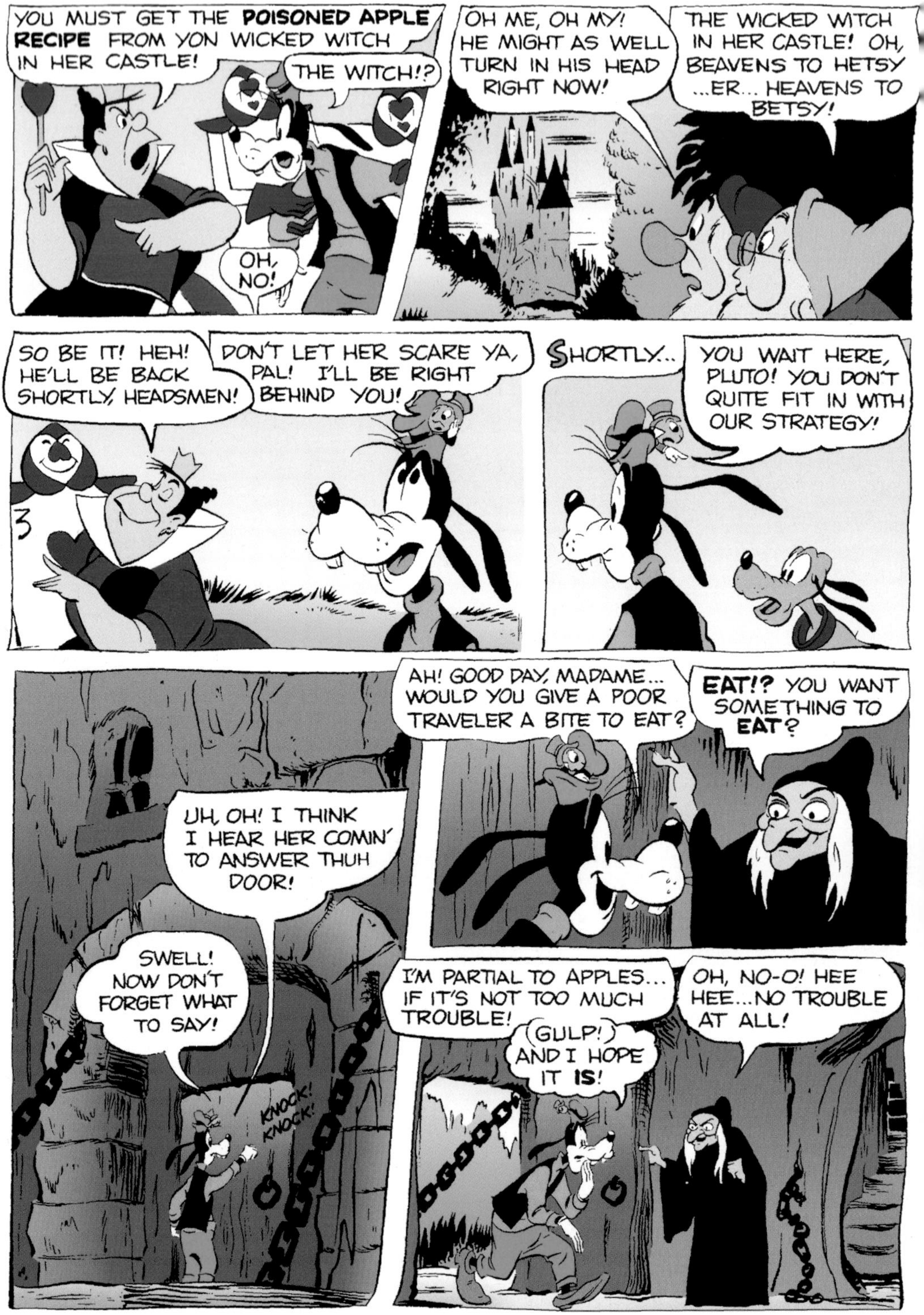
YOU MUST GET THE **POISONED APPLE RECIPE** FROM YON WICKED WITCH IN HER CASTLE!
THE WITCH!?
OH, NO!
OH ME, OH MY! HE MIGHT AS WELL TURN IN HIS HEAD RIGHT NOW!
THE WICKED WITCH IN HER CASTLE! OH, BEAVENS TO HETSY ...ER... HEAVENS TO BETSY!
SO BE IT! HEH! HE'LL BE BACK SHORTLY, HEADSMEN!
DON'T LET HER SCARE YA, PAL! I'LL BE RIGHT BEHIND YOU!
SHORTLY...
YOU WAIT HERE, PLUTO! YOU DON'T QUITE FIT IN WITH OUR STRATEGY!
UH, OH! I THINK I HEAR HER COMIN' TO ANSWER THUH DOOR!
SWELL! NOW DON'T FORGET WHAT TO SAY!
KNOCK! KNOCK!
AH! GOOD DAY, MADAME... WOULD YOU GIVE A POOR TRAVELER A BITE TO EAT?
EAT!? YOU WANT SOMETHING TO **EAT**?
I'M PARTIAL TO APPLES... IF IT'S NOT TOO MUCH TROUBLE!
(GULP!) AND I HOPE IT **IS**!
OH, NO-O! HEE HEE...NO TROUBLE AT ALL!

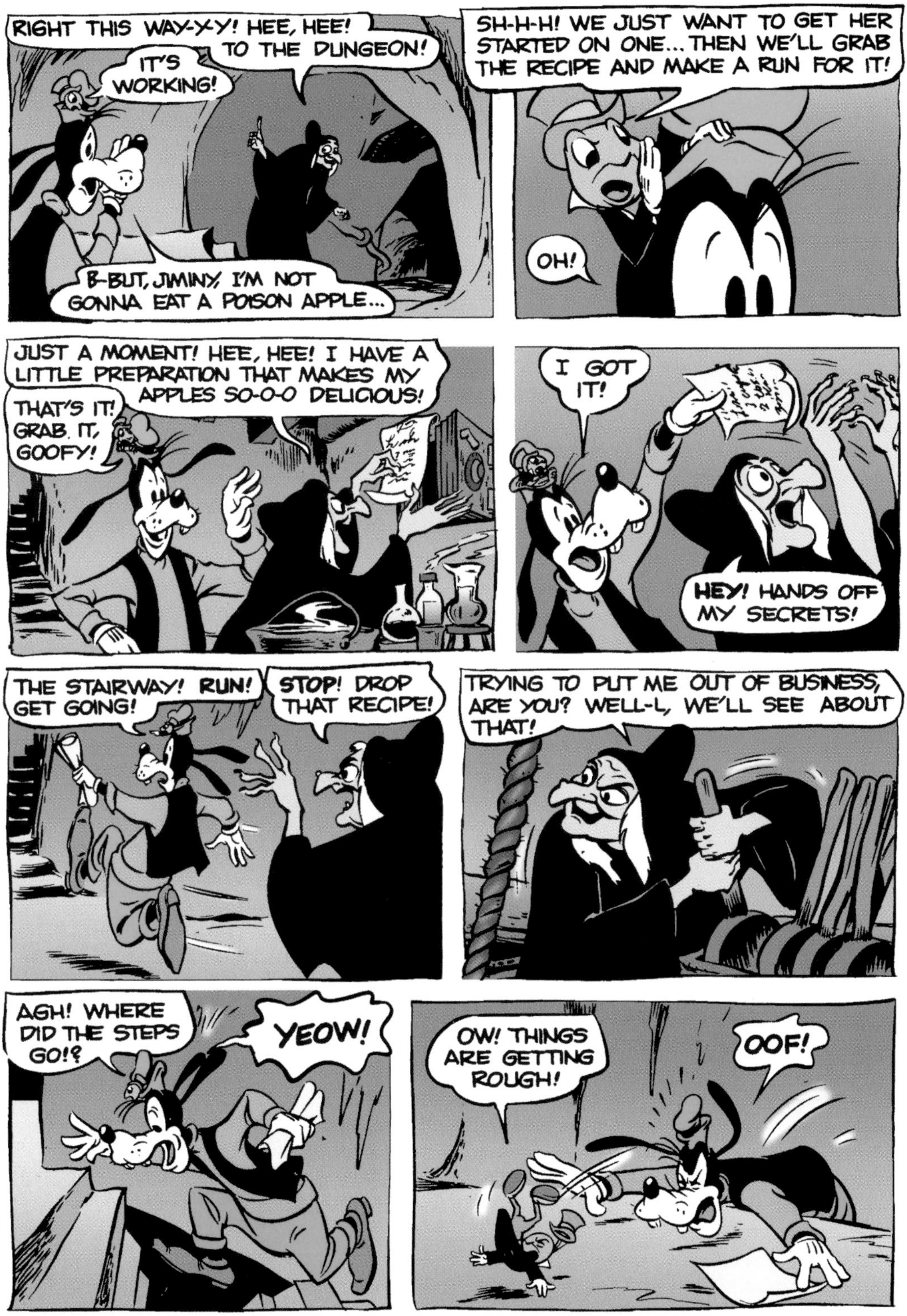
RIGHT THIS WAY-Y-Y! HEE, HEE! TO THE DUNGEON!
IT'S WORKING!
B-BUT, JIMINY, I'M NOT GONNA EAT A POISON APPLE...
SH-H-H! WE JUST WANT TO GET HER STARTED ON ONE... THEN WE'LL GRAB THE RECIPE AND MAKE A RUN FOR IT!
OH!
JUST A MOMENT! HEE, HEE! I HAVE A LITTLE PREPARATION THAT MAKES MY APPLES SO-O-O DELICIOUS!
THAT'S IT! GRAB IT, GOOFY!
I GOT IT!
HEY! HANDS OFF MY SECRETS!
THE STAIRWAY! RUN! GET GOING!
STOP! DROP THAT RECIPE!
TRYING TO PUT ME OUT OF BUSINESS, ARE YOU? WELL-L, WE'LL SEE ABOUT THAT!
AGH! WHERE DID THE STEPS GO!?
YEOW!
OW! THINGS ARE GETTING ROUGH!
OOF!

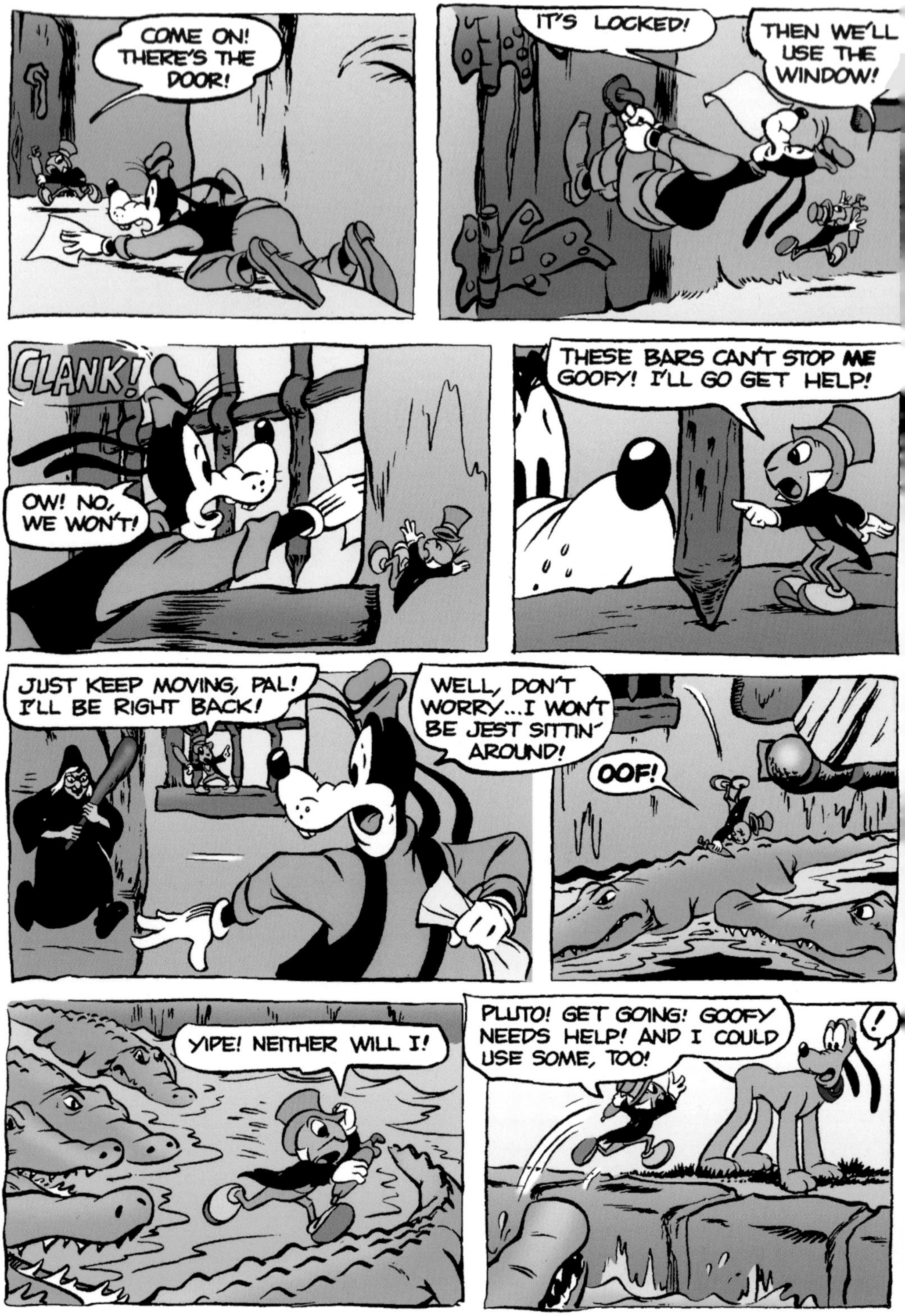
COME ON! THERE'S THE DOOR!
IT'S LOCKED!
THEN WE'LL USE THE WINDOW!
CLANK!
OW! NO, WE WON'T!
THESE BARS CAN'T STOP ME GOOFY! I'LL GO GET HELP!
JUST KEEP MOVING, PAL! I'LL BE RIGHT BACK!
WELL, DON'T WORRY...I WON'T BE JEST SITTIN' AROUND!
OOF!
YIPE! NEITHER WILL I!
PLUTO! GET GOING! GOOFY NEEDS HELP! AND I COULD USE SOME, TOO!
!

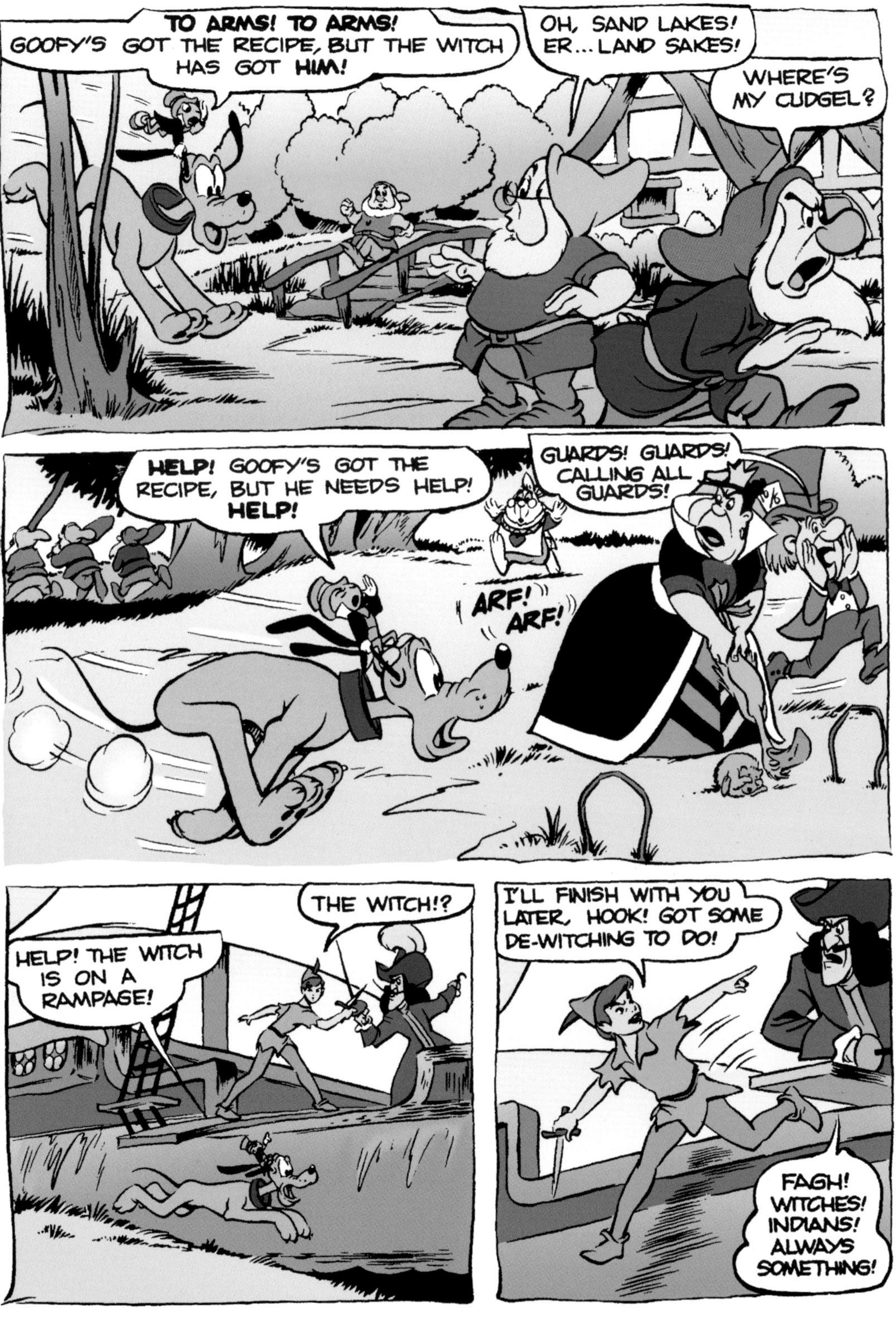
TO ARMS! TO ARMS! GOOFY'S GOT THE RECIPE, BUT THE WITCH HAS GOT HIM!
OH, SAND LAKES! ER... LAND SAKES!
WHERE'S MY CUDGEL?
HELP! GOOFY'S GOT THE RECIPE, BUT HE NEEDS HELP! HELP!
GUARDS! GUARDS! CALLING ALL GUARDS!
ARF! ARF!
THE WITCH!?
HELP! THE WITCH IS ON A RAMPAGE!
I'LL FINISH WITH YOU LATER, HOOK! GOT SOME DE-WITCHING TO DO!
FAGH! WITCHES! INDIANS! ALWAYS SOMETHING!

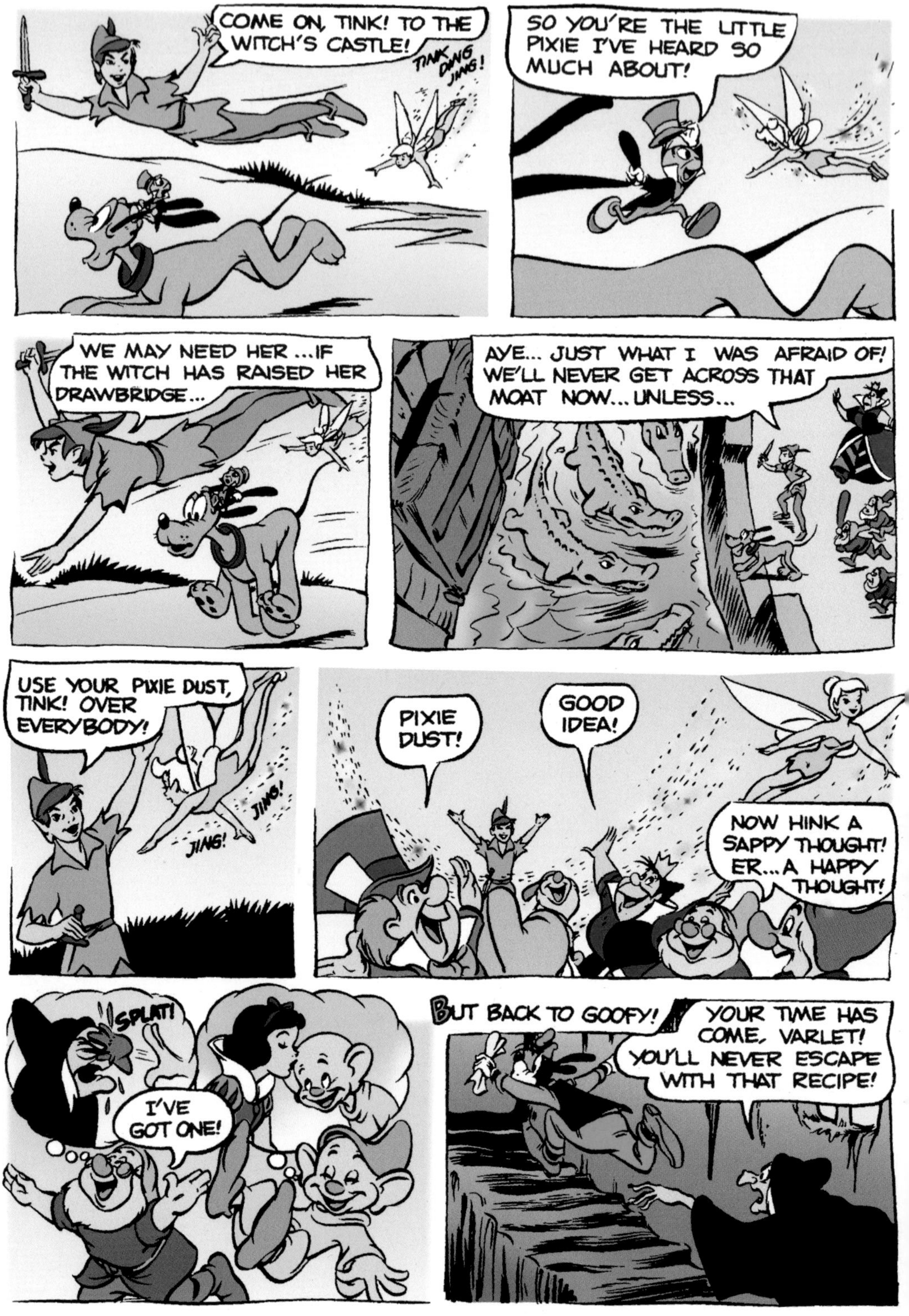
COME ON, TINK! TO THE WITCH'S CASTLE!
TINK DING JING!
SO YOU'RE THE LITTLE PIXIE I'VE HEARD SO MUCH ABOUT!
WE MAY NEED HER ...IF THE WITCH HAS RAISED HER DRAWBRIDGE...
AYE... JUST WHAT I WAS AFRAID OF! WE'LL NEVER GET ACROSS THAT MOAT NOW...UNLESS...
USE YOUR PIXIE DUST, TINK! OVER EVERYBODY!
JING!
JING!
PIXIE DUST!
GOOD IDEA!
NOW HINK A SAPPY THOUGHT! ER...A HAPPY THOUGHT!
SPLAT!
I'VE GOT ONE!
BUT BACK TO GOOFY!
YOUR TIME HAS COME, VARLET! YOU'LL NEVER ESCAPE WITH THAT RECIPE!

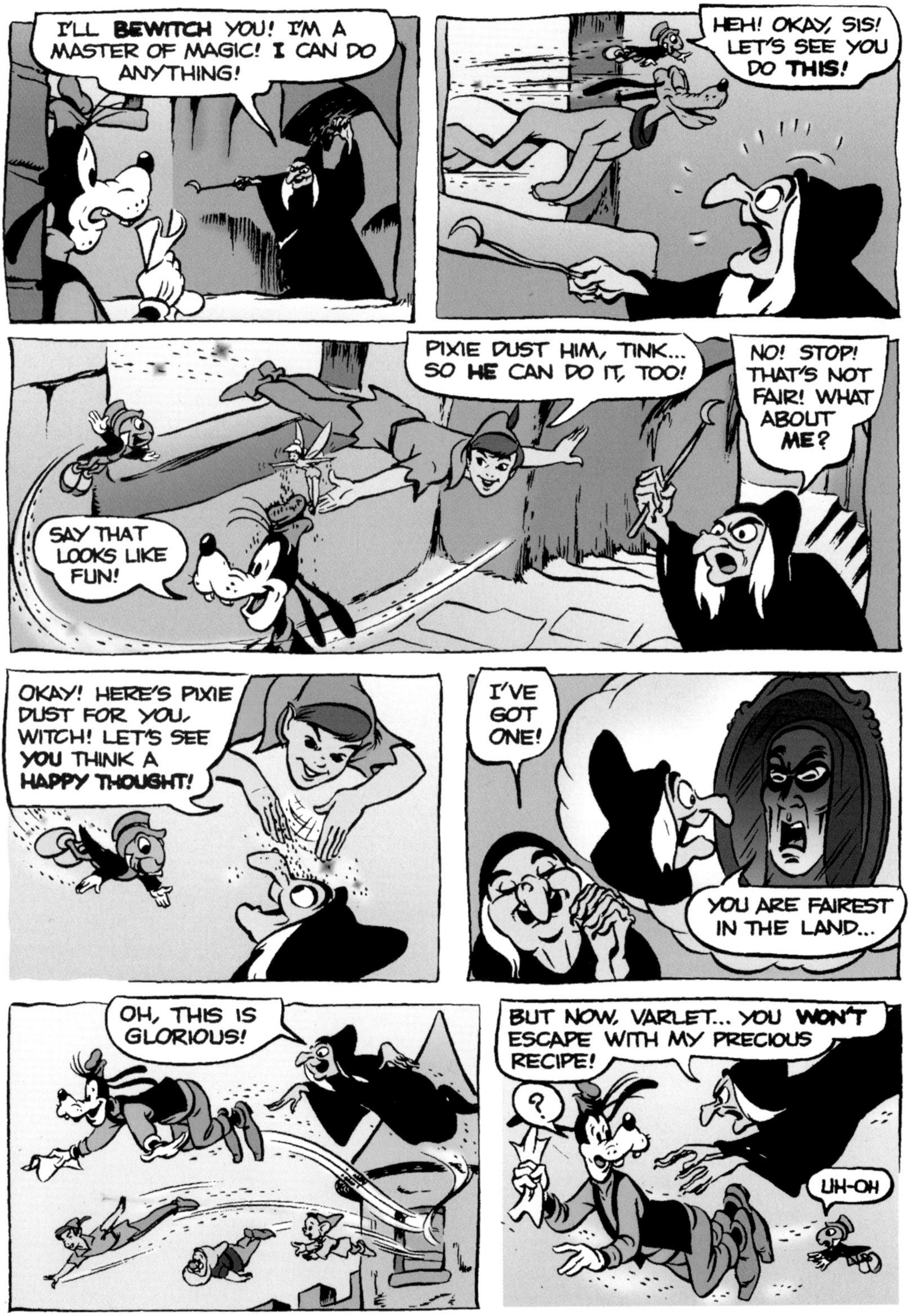
I'LL BEWITCH YOU! I'M A MASTER OF MAGIC! I CAN DO ANYTHING!
HEH! OKAY, SIS! LET'S SEE YOU DO THIS!
PIXIE DUST HIM, TINK... SO HE CAN DO IT, TOO!
NO! STOP! THAT'S NOT FAIR! WHAT ABOUT ME?
SAY THAT LOOKS LIKE FUN!
OKAY! HERE'S PIXIE DUST FOR YOU, WITCH! LET'S SEE YOU THINK A HAPPY THOUGHT!
I'VE GOT ONE!
YOU ARE FAIREST IN THE LAND...
OH, THIS IS GLORIOUS!
BUT NOW, VARLET... YOU WON'T ESCAPE WITH MY PRECIOUS RECIPE!
?
UH-OH

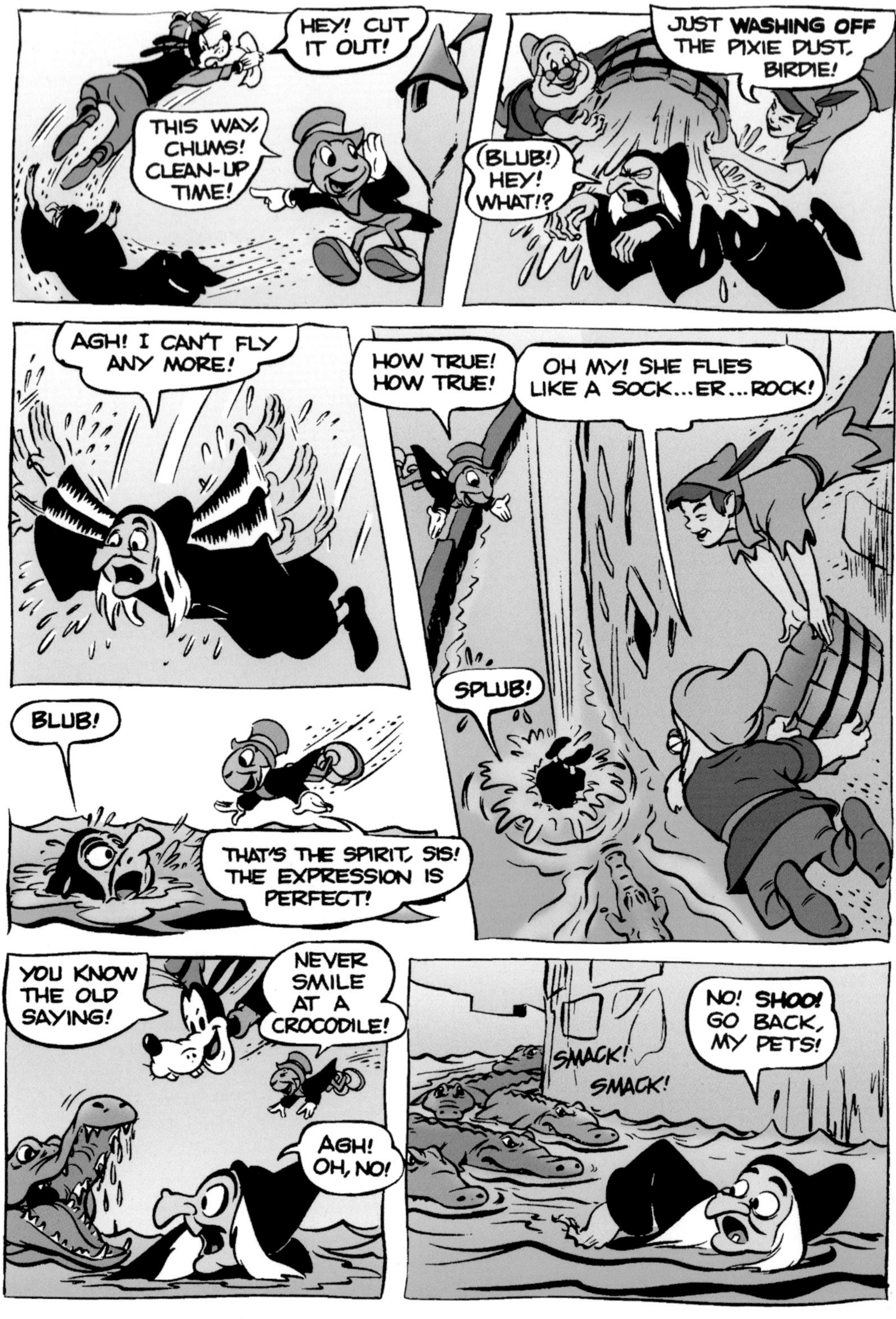

HEY! CUT IT OUT!
THIS WAY, CHUMS! CLEAN-UP TIME!
JUST WASHING OFF THE PIXIE DUST, BIRDIE!
(BLUB!) HEY! WHAT!?
AGH! I CAN'T FLY ANY MORE!
HOW TRUE! HOW TRUE!
OH MY! SHE FLIES LIKE A SOCK...ER...ROCK!
SPLUB!
BLUB!
THAT'S THE SPIRIT, SIS! THE EXPRESSION IS PERFECT!
YOU KNOW THE OLD SAYING!
NEVER SMILE AT A CROCODILE!
AGH! OH, NO!
NO! SHOO! GO BACK, MY PETS!
SMACK!
SMACK!

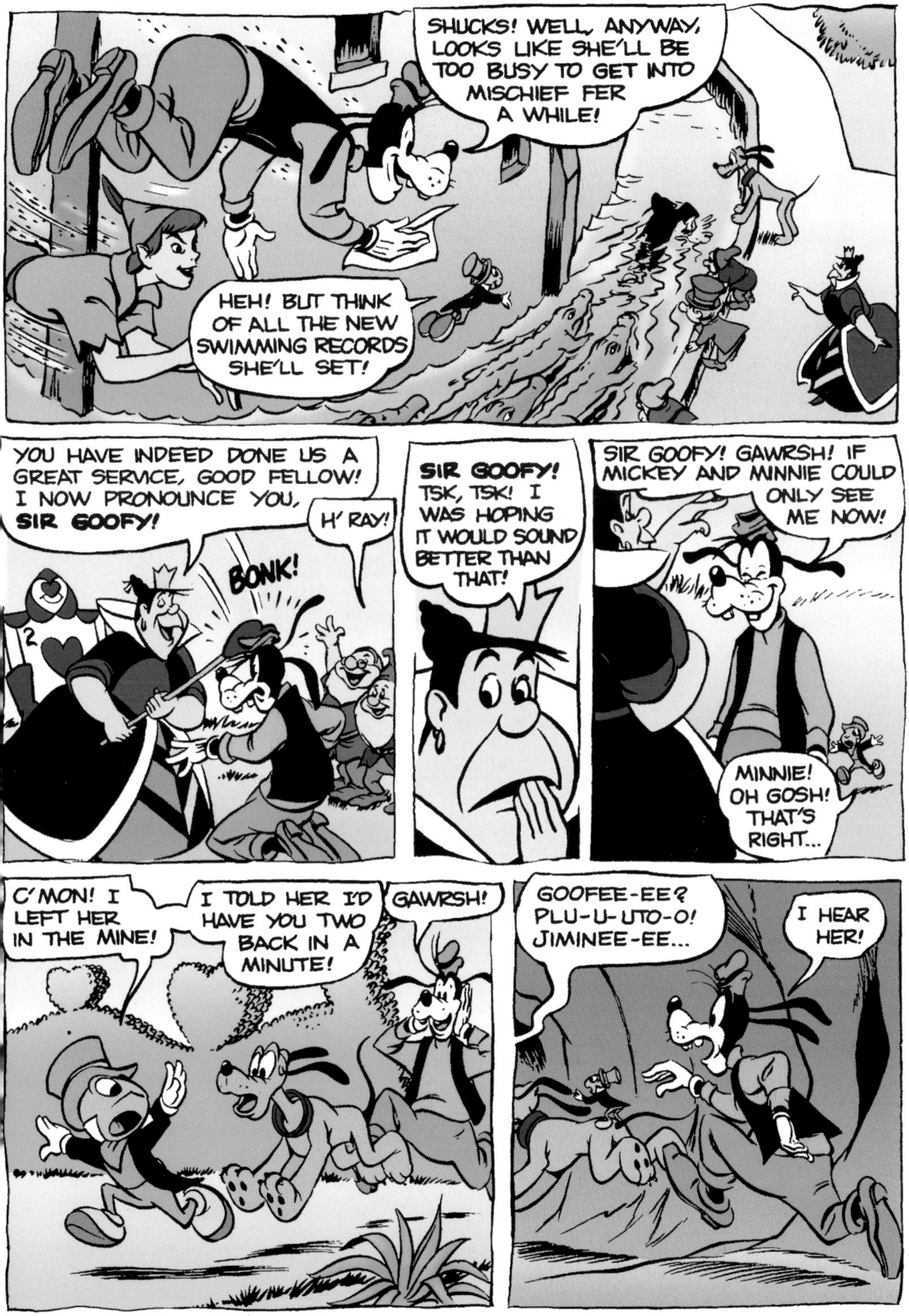
SHUCKS! WELL, ANYWAY, LOOKS LIKE SHE'LL BE TOO BUSY TO GET INTO MISCHIEF FER A WHILE!
HEH! BUT THINK OF ALL THE NEW SWIMMING RECORDS SHE'LL SET!
YOU HAVE INDEED DONE US A GREAT SERVICE, GOOD FELLOW! I NOW PRONOUNCE YOU, SIR GOOFY!
BONK!
H' RAY!
SIR GOOFY! TSK, TSK! I WAS HOPING IT WOULD SOUND BETTER THAN THAT!
SIR GOOFY! GAWRSH! IF MICKEY AND MINNIE COULD ONLY SEE ME NOW!
MINNIE! OH GOSH! THAT'S RIGHT...
C'MON! I LEFT HER IN THE MINE!
I TOLD HER I'D HAVE YOU TWO BACK IN A MINUTE!
GAWRSH!
GOOFEE-EE? PLU-U-UTO-O! JIMINEE-EE...
I HEAR HER!

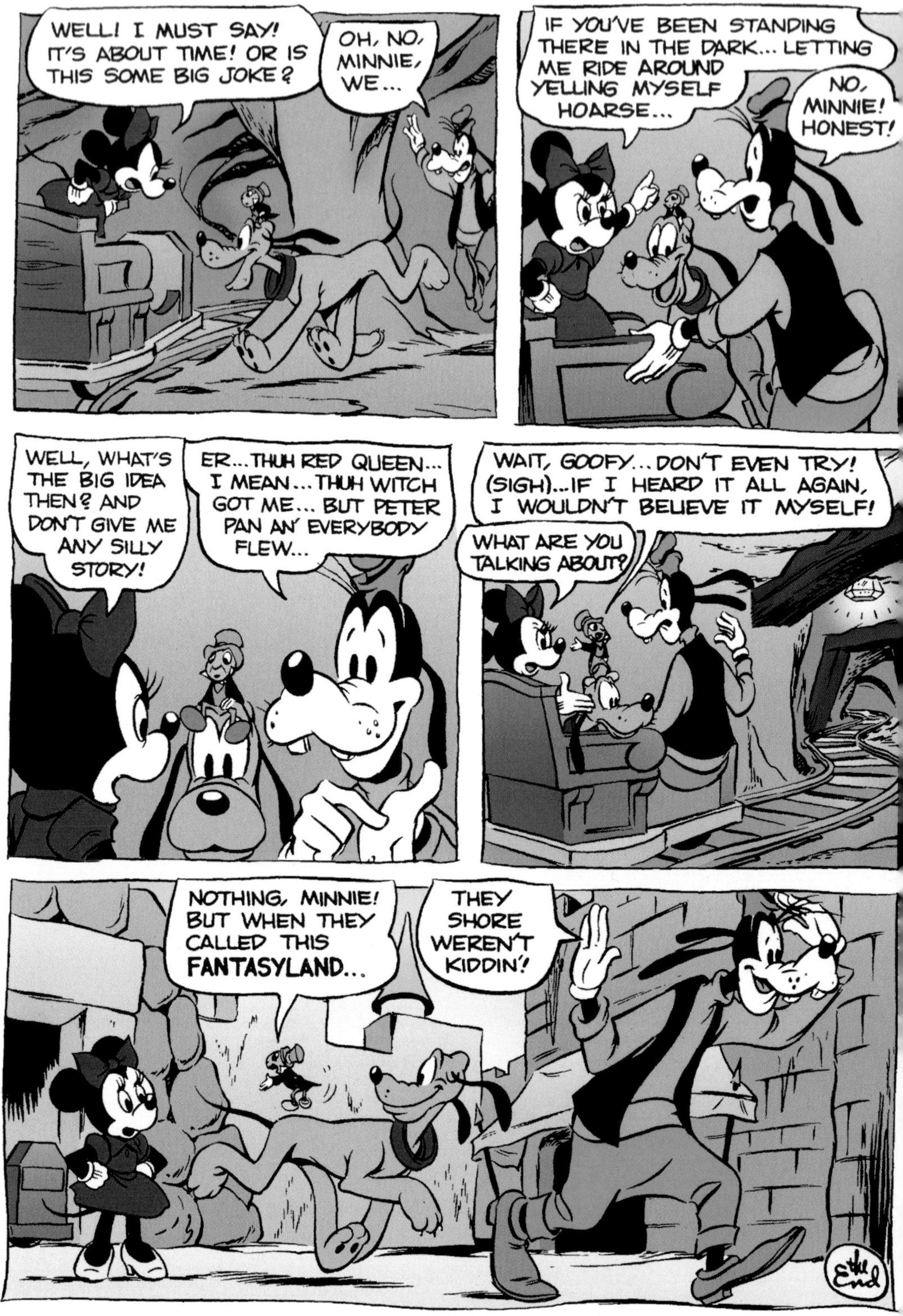
WELL! I MUST SAY! IT'S ABOUT TIME! OR IS THIS SOME BIG JOKE?
OH, NO, MINNIE, WE...
IF YOU'VE BEEN STANDING THERE IN THE DARK... LETTING ME RIDE AROUND YELLING MYSELF HOARSE...
NO, MINNIE! HONEST!
WELL, WHAT'S THE BIG IDEA THEN? AND DON'T GIVE ME ANY SILLY STORY!
ER...THUH RED QUEEN... I MEAN...THUH WITCH GOT ME... BUT PETER PAN AN' EVERYBODY FLEW...
WAIT, GOOFY...DON'T EVEN TRY! (SIGH)...IF I HEARD IT ALL AGAIN, I WOULDN'T BELIEVE IT MYSELF!
WHAT ARE YOU TALKING ABOUT?
NOTHING, MINNIE! BUT WHEN THEY CALLED THIS FANTASYLAND...
THEY SHORE WEREN'T KIDDIN'!
the End

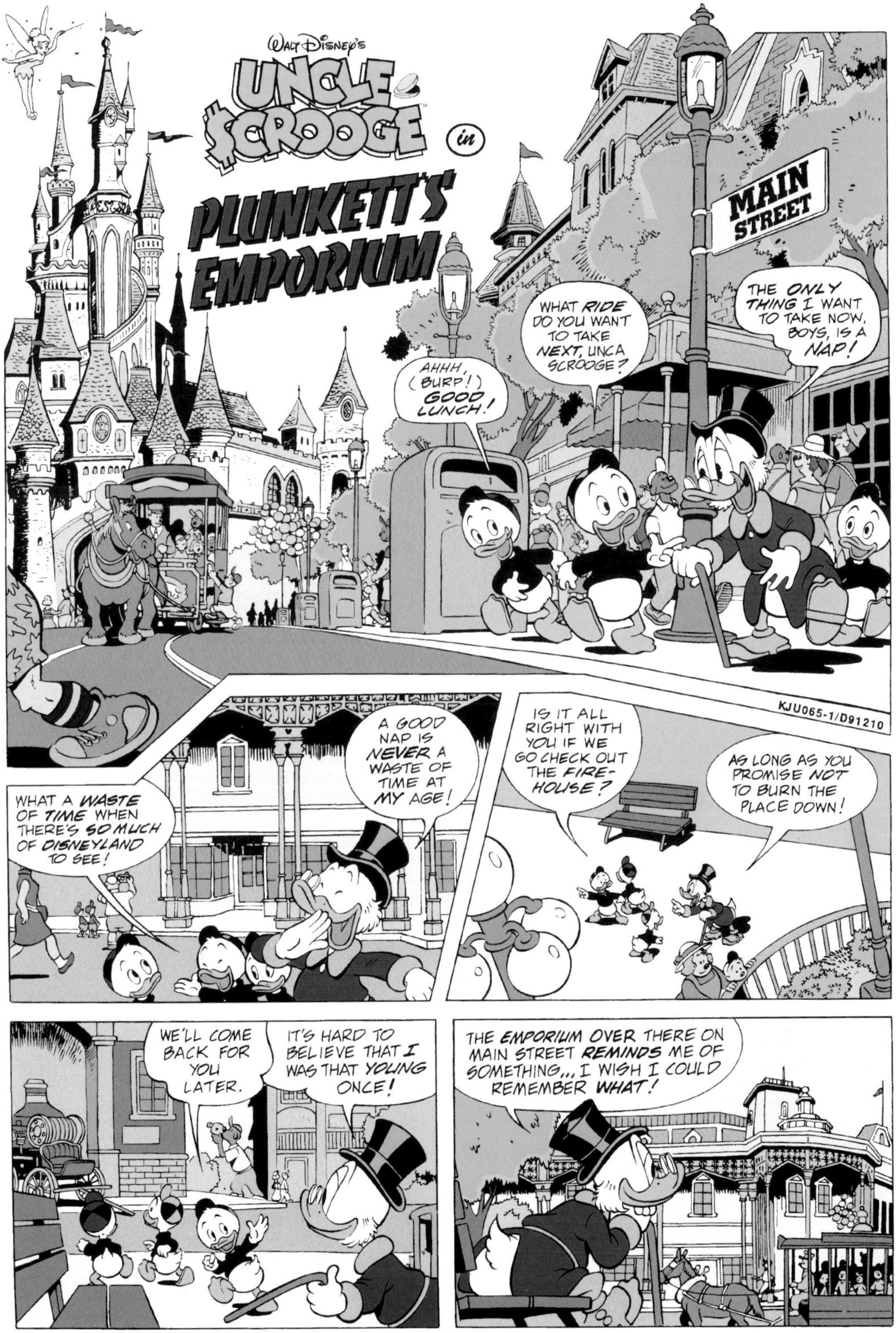
WALT DISNEY'S
UNCLE $CROOGE
in
PLUNKETT'S EMPORIUM
MAIN STREET
AHHH, (BURP!) GOOD LUNCH!
WHAT RIDE DO YOU WANT TO TAKE NEXT, UNCA SCROOGE?
THE ONLY THING I WANT TO TAKE NOW, BOYS, IS A NAP!
KJU065-1/D91210
WHAT A WASTE OF TIME WHEN THERE'S SO MUCH OF DISNEYLAND TO SEE!
A GOOD NAP IS NEVER A WASTE OF TIME AT MY AGE!
IS IT ALL RIGHT WITH YOU IF WE GO CHECK OUT THE FIRE-HOUSE?
AS LONG AS YOU PROMISE NOT TO BURN THE PLACE DOWN!
WE'LL COME BACK FOR YOU LATER.
IT'S HARD TO BELIEVE THAT I WAS THAT YOUNG ONCE!
THE EMPORIUM OVER THERE ON MAIN STREET REMINDS ME OF SOMETHING... I WISH I COULD REMEMBER WHAT!

Originally published in *Anders And & C:o* #21/1992 (Denmark, 1992)

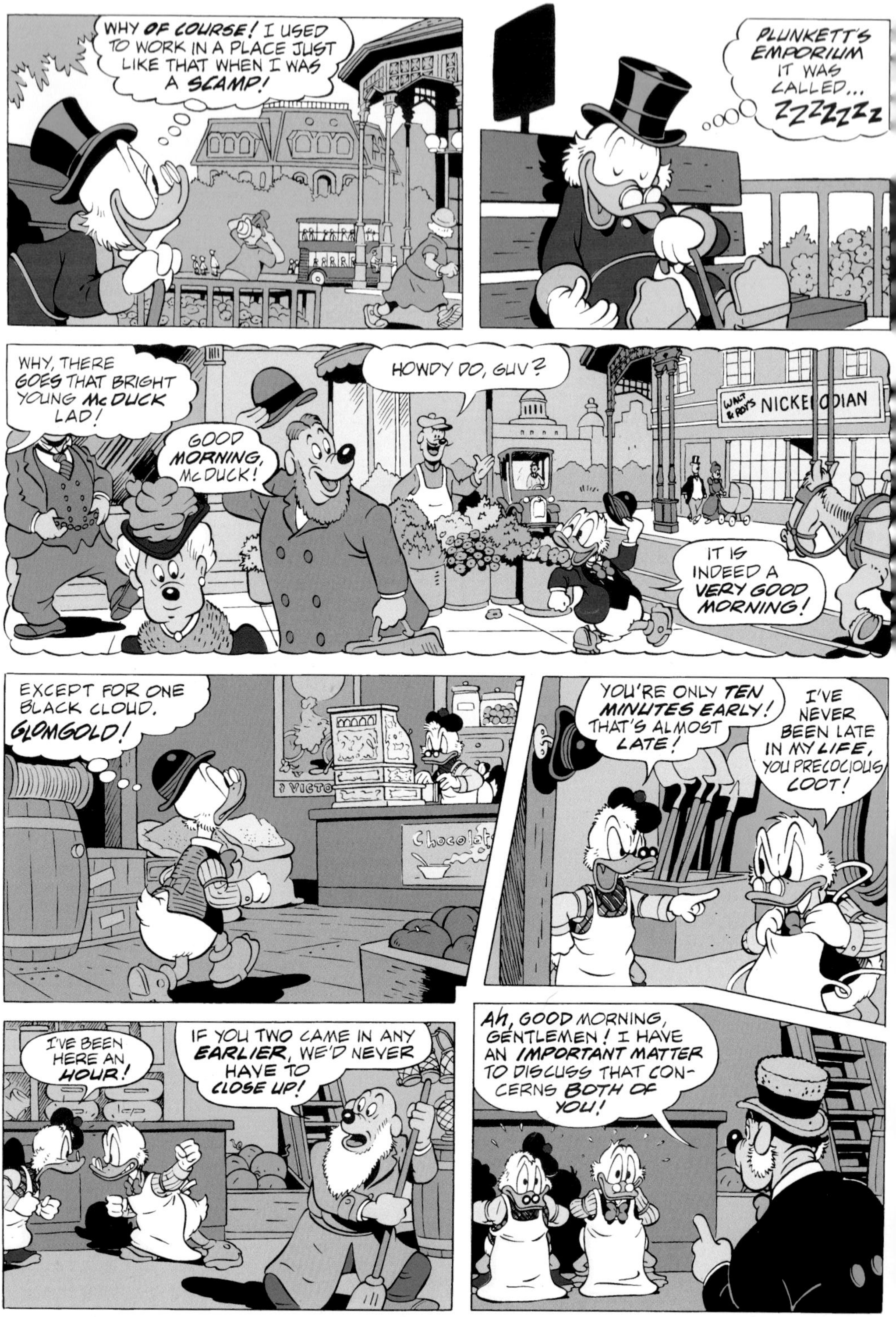

WHY OF COURSE! I USED TO WORK IN A PLACE JUST LIKE THAT WHEN I WAS A SCAMP!
PLUNKETT'S EMPORIUM IT WAS CALLED... ZZZZZZZ
WHY, THERE GOES THAT BRIGHT YOUNG McDUCK LAD!
HOWDY DO, GUV?
GOOD MORNING, McDUCK!
WALT & ROY'S NICKELODIAN
IT IS INDEED A VERY GOOD MORNING!
EXCEPT FOR ONE BLACK CLOUD. GLOMGOLD!
Chocolate
YOU'RE ONLY TEN MINUTES EARLY! THAT'S ALMOST LATE!
I'VE NEVER BEEN LATE IN MY LIFE, YOU PRECOCIOUS COOT!
I'VE BEEN HERE AN HOUR!
IF YOU TWO CAME IN ANY EARLIER, WE'D NEVER HAVE TO CLOSE UP!
Ah, GOOD MORNING, GENTLEMEN! I HAVE AN IMPORTANT MATTER TO DISCUSS THAT CONCERNS BOTH OF YOU!

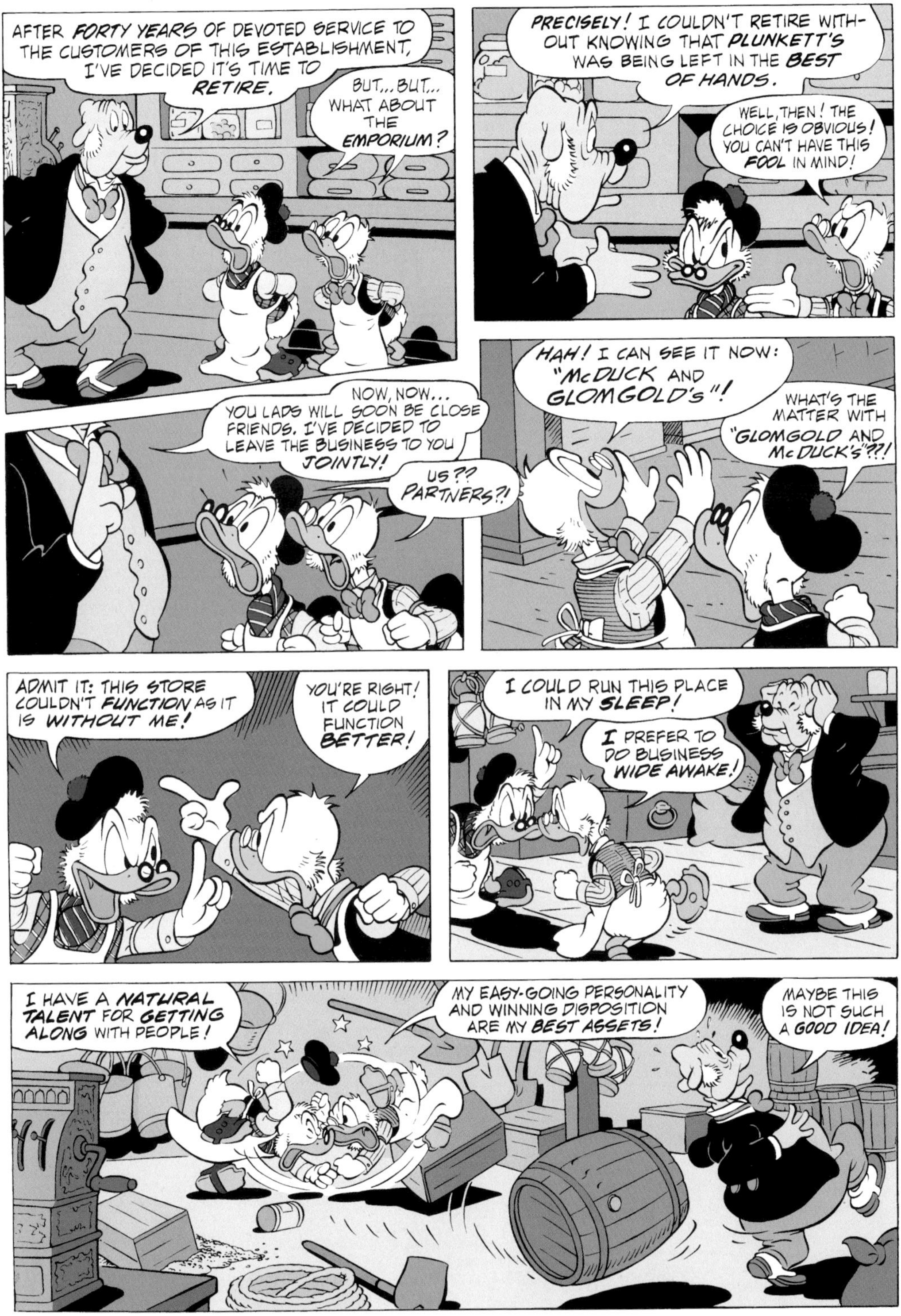
AFTER FORTY YEARS OF DEVOTED SERVICE TO THE CUSTOMERS OF THIS ESTABLISHMENT, I'VE DECIDED IT'S TIME TO RETIRE.
BUT... BUT... WHAT ABOUT THE EMPORIUM?
PRECISELY! I COULDN'T RETIRE WITHOUT KNOWING THAT PLUNKETT'S WAS BEING LEFT IN THE BEST OF HANDS.
WELL, THEN! THE CHOICE IS OBVIOUS! YOU CAN'T HAVE THIS FOOL IN MIND!
NOW, NOW... YOU LADS WILL SOON BE CLOSE FRIENDS. I'VE DECIDED TO LEAVE THE BUSINESS TO YOU JOINTLY!
US?? PARTNERS?!
HAH! I CAN SEE IT NOW: "McDUCK AND GLOMGOLD'S"!
WHAT'S THE MATTER WITH "GLOMGOLD AND McDUCK'S"?!
ADMIT IT: THIS STORE COULDN'T FUNCTION AS IT IS WITHOUT ME!
YOU'RE RIGHT! IT COULD FUNCTION BETTER!
I COULD RUN THIS PLACE IN MY SLEEP!
I PREFER TO DO BUSINESS WIDE AWAKE!
I HAVE A NATURAL TALENT FOR GETTING ALONG WITH PEOPLE!
MY EASY-GOING PERSONALITY AND WINNING DISPOSITION ARE MY BEST ASSETS!
MAYBE THIS IS NOT SUCH A GOOD IDEA!

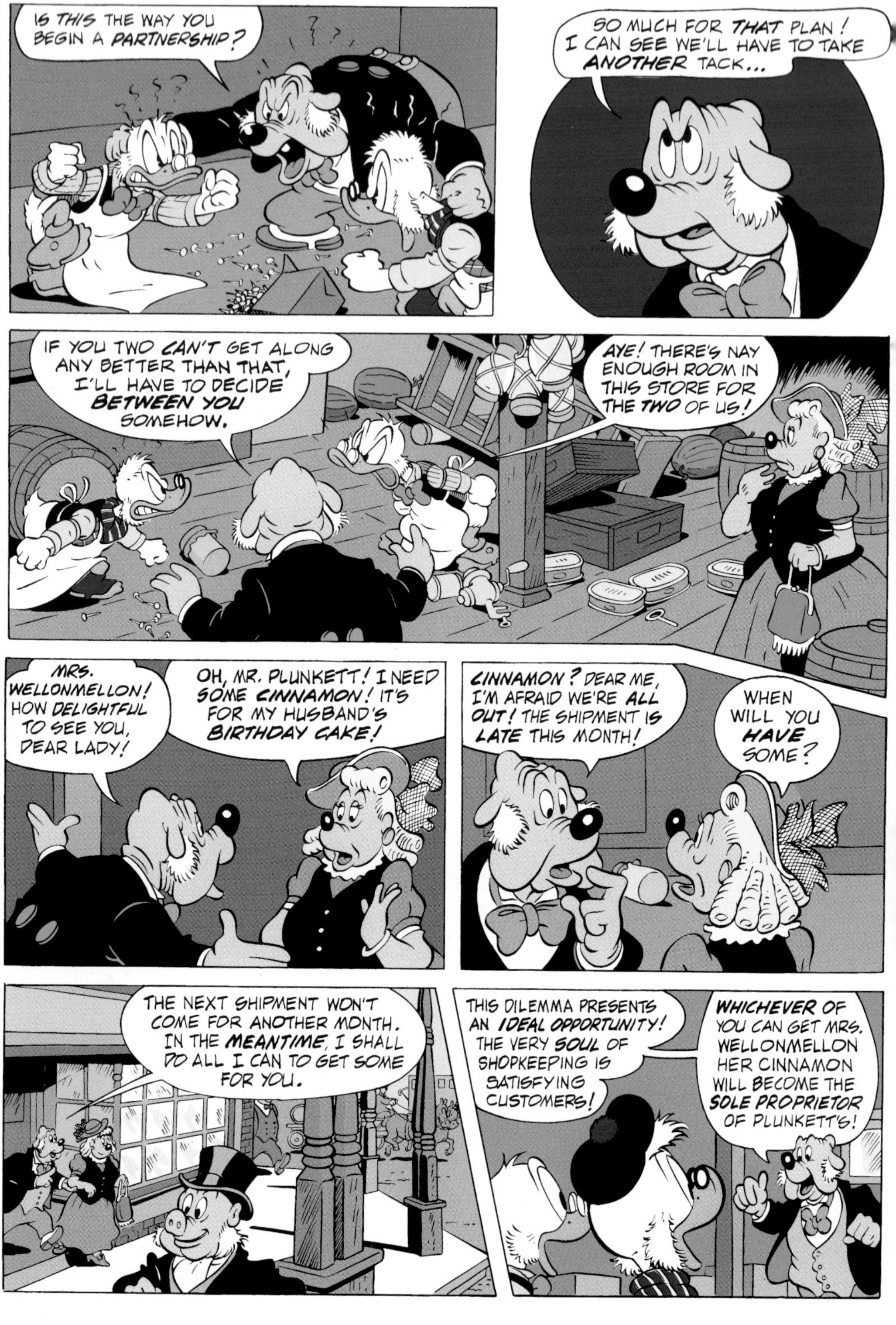
IS THIS THE WAY YOU BEGIN A PARTNERSHIP?
SO MUCH FOR THAT PLAN! I CAN SEE WE'LL HAVE TO TAKE ANOTHER TACK...
IF YOU TWO CAN'T GET ALONG ANY BETTER THAN THAT, I'LL HAVE TO DECIDE BETWEEN YOU SOMEHOW.
AYE! THERE'S NAY ENOUGH ROOM IN THIS STORE FOR THE TWO OF US!
MRS. WELLONMELLON! HOW DELIGHTFUL TO SEE YOU, DEAR LADY!
OH, MR. PLUNKETT! I NEED SOME CINNAMON! IT'S FOR MY HUSBAND'S BIRTHDAY CAKE!
CINNAMON? DEAR ME, I'M AFRAID WE'RE ALL OUT! THE SHIPMENT IS LATE THIS MONTH!
WHEN WILL YOU HAVE SOME?
THE NEXT SHIPMENT WON'T COME FOR ANOTHER MONTH. IN THE MEANTIME, I SHALL DO ALL I CAN TO GET SOME FOR YOU.
THIS DILEMMA PRESENTS AN IDEAL OPPORTUNITY! THE VERY SOUL OF SHOPKEEPING IS SATISFYING CUSTOMERS!
WHICHEVER OF YOU CAN GET MRS. WELLONMELLON HER CINNAMON WILL BECOME THE SOLE PROPRIETOR OF PLUNKETT'S!

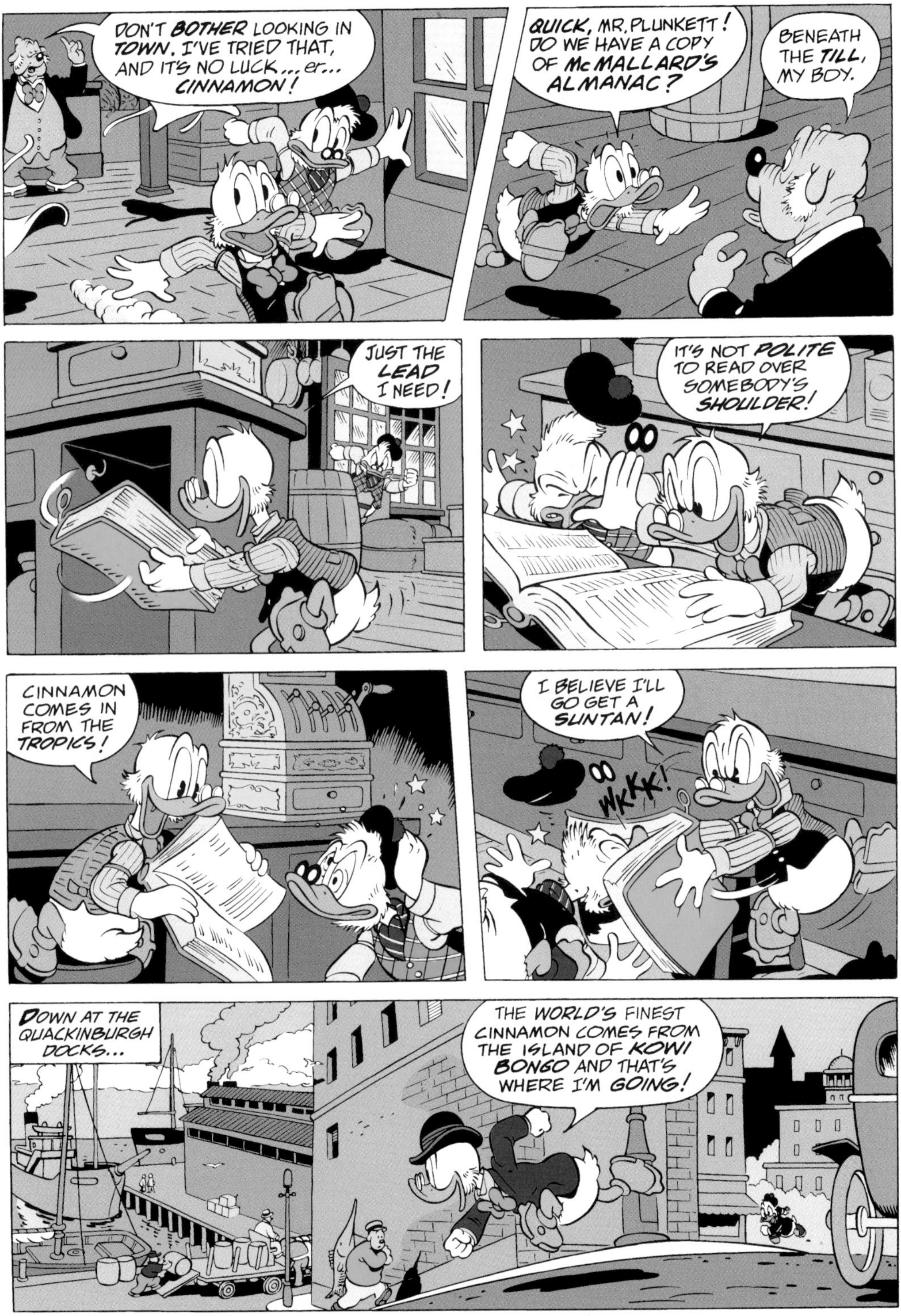
DON'T BOTHER LOOKING IN TOWN. I'VE TRIED THAT, AND IT'S NO LUCK... er... CINNAMON!
QUICK, MR. PLUNKETT! DO WE HAVE A COPY OF McMALLARD'S ALMANAC?
BENEATH THE TILL, MY BOY.
JUST THE LEAD I NEED!
IT'S NOT POLITE TO READ OVER SOMEBODY'S SHOULDER!
CINNAMON COMES IN FROM THE TROPICS!
I BELIEVE I'LL GO GET A SUNTAN!
WKKK!
DOWN AT THE QUACKINBURGH DOCKS...
THE WORLD'S FINEST CINNAMON COMES FROM THE ISLAND OF KOWI BONGO AND THAT'S WHERE I'M GOING!

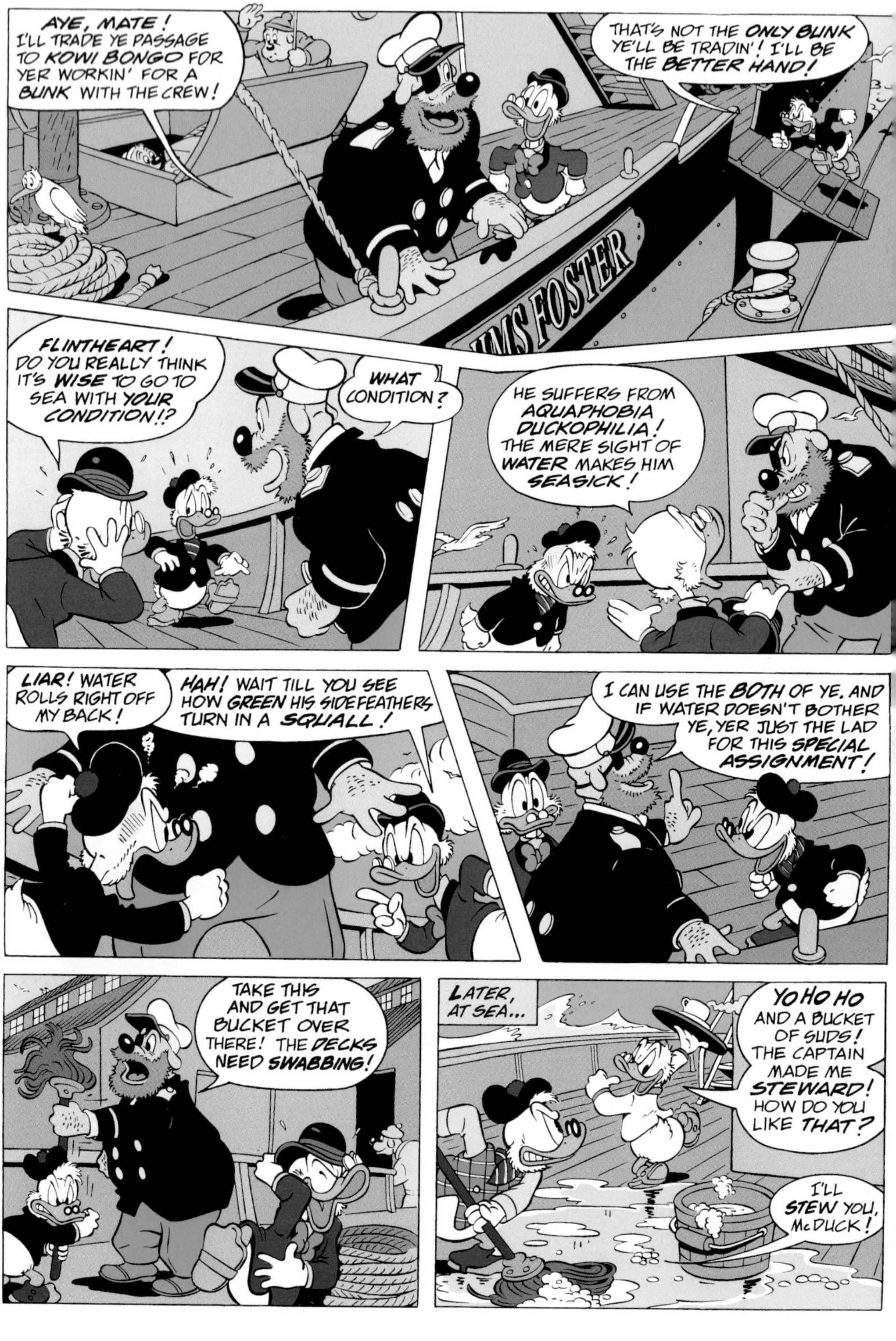
AYE, MATE! I'LL TRADE YE PASSAGE TO KOWI BONGO FOR YER WORKIN' FOR A BUNK WITH THE CREW!
THAT'S NOT THE ONLY BUNK YE'LL BE TRADIN'! I'LL BE THE BETTER HAND!
HMS FOSTER
FLINTHEART! DO YOU REALLY THINK IT'S WISE TO GO TO SEA WITH YOUR CONDITION!?
WHAT CONDITION?
HE SUFFERS FROM AQUAPHOBIA DUCKOPHILIA! THE MERE SIGHT OF WATER MAKES HIM SEASICK!
LIAR! WATER ROLLS RIGHT OFF MY BACK!
HAH! WAIT TILL YOU SEE HOW GREEN HIS SIDEFEATHERS TURN IN A SQUALL!
I CAN USE THE BOTH OF YE. AND IF WATER DOESN'T BOTHER YE, YER JUST THE LAD FOR THIS SPECIAL ASSIGNMENT!
TAKE THIS AND GET THAT BUCKET OVER THERE! THE DECKS NEED SWABBING!
LATER, AT SEA...
YO HO HO AND A BUCKET OF SUDS! THE CAPTAIN MADE ME STEWARD! HOW DO YOU LIKE THAT?
I'LL STEW YOU, McDUCK!

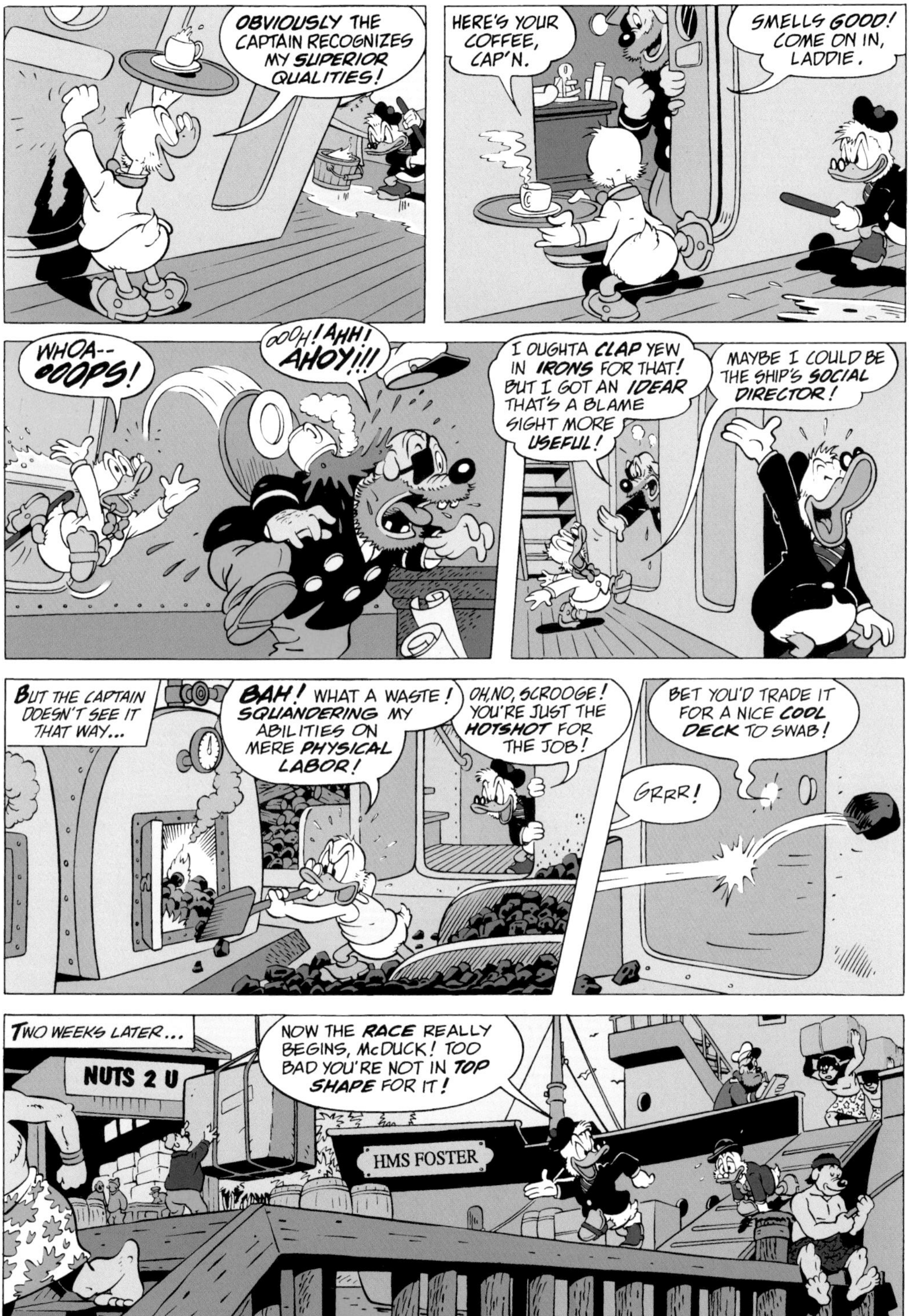
OBVIOUSLY THE CAPTAIN RECOGNIZES MY SUPERIOR QUALITIES!
HERE'S YOUR COFFEE, CAP'N.
SMELLS GOOD! COME ON IN, LADDIE.
WHOA-- OOOPS!
OOOH! AHH! AHOY!!!
I OUGHTA CLAP YEW IN IRONS FOR THAT! BUT I GOT AN IDEAR THAT'S A BLAME SIGHT MORE USEFUL!
MAYBE I COULD BE THE SHIP'S SOCIAL DIRECTOR!
BUT THE CAPTAIN DOESN'T SEE IT THAT WAY...
BAH! WHAT A WASTE! SQUANDERING MY ABILITIES ON MERE PHYSICAL LABOR!
OH, NO, SCROOGE! YOU'RE JUST THE HOTSHOT FOR THE JOB!
BET YOU'D TRADE IT FOR A NICE COOL DECK TO SWAB!
GRRR!
TWO WEEKS LATER...
NOW THE RACE REALLY BEGINS, McDUCK! TOO BAD YOU'RE NOT IN TOP SHAPE FOR IT!
NUTS 2 U
HMS FOSTER

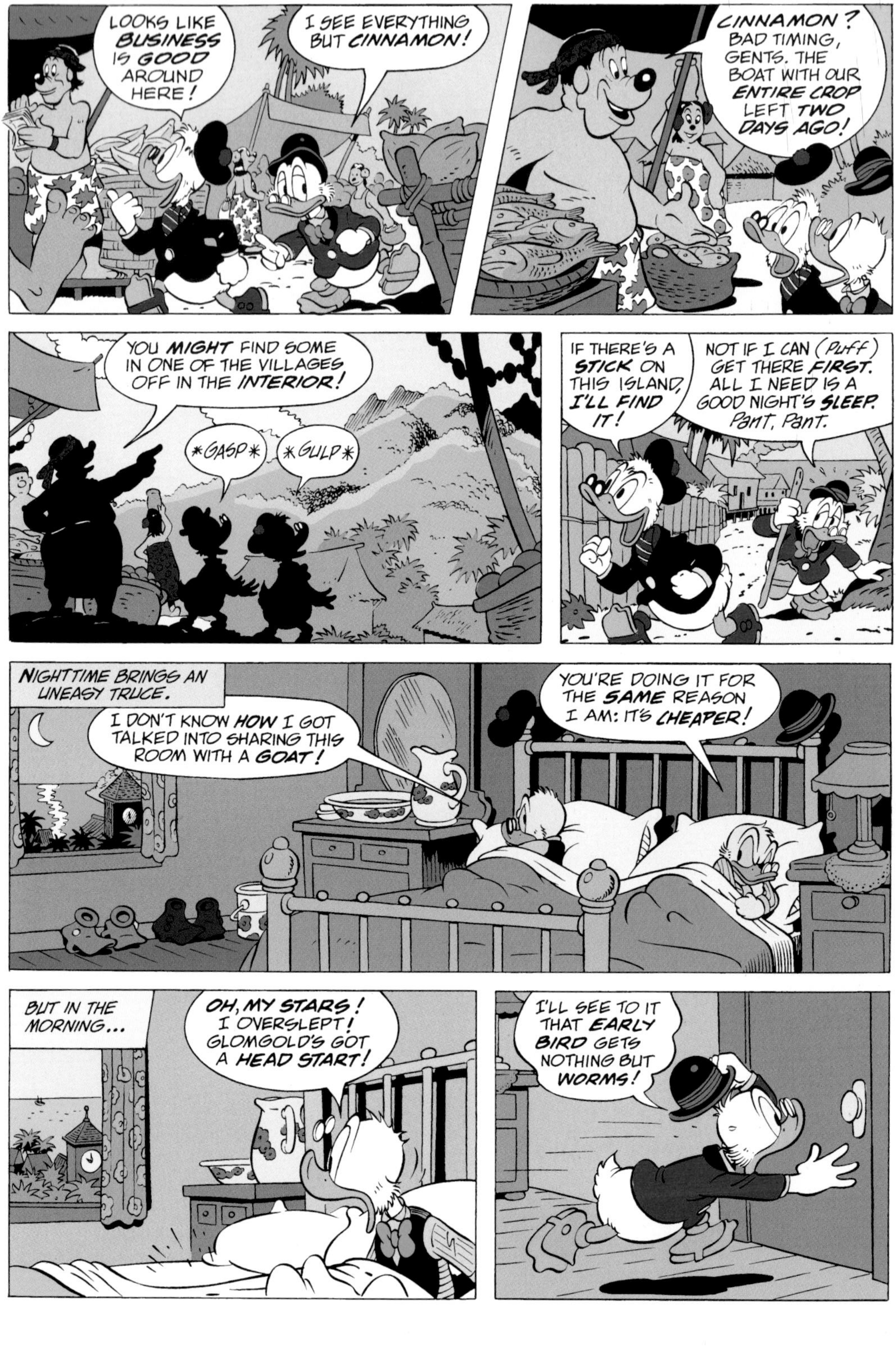
LOOKS LIKE BUSINESS IS GOOD AROUND HERE!
I SEE EVERYTHING BUT CINNAMON!
CINNAMON? BAD TIMING, GENTS. THE BOAT WITH OUR ENTIRE CROP LEFT TWO DAYS AGO!
YOU MIGHT FIND SOME IN ONE OF THE VILLAGES OFF IN THE INTERIOR!
GASP
GULP
IF THERE'S A STICK ON THIS ISLAND, I'LL FIND IT!
NOT IF I CAN (Puff) GET THERE FIRST. ALL I NEED IS A GOOD NIGHT'S SLEEP. Pant, Pant.
NIGHTTIME BRINGS AN UNEASY TRUCE.
I DON'T KNOW HOW I GOT TALKED INTO SHARING THIS ROOM WITH A GOAT!
YOU'RE DOING IT FOR THE SAME REASON I AM: IT'S CHEAPER!
BUT IN THE MORNING...
OH, MY STARS! I OVERSLEPT! GLOMGOLD'S GOT A HEAD START!
I'LL SEE TO IT THAT EARLY BIRD GETS NOTHING BUT WORMS!

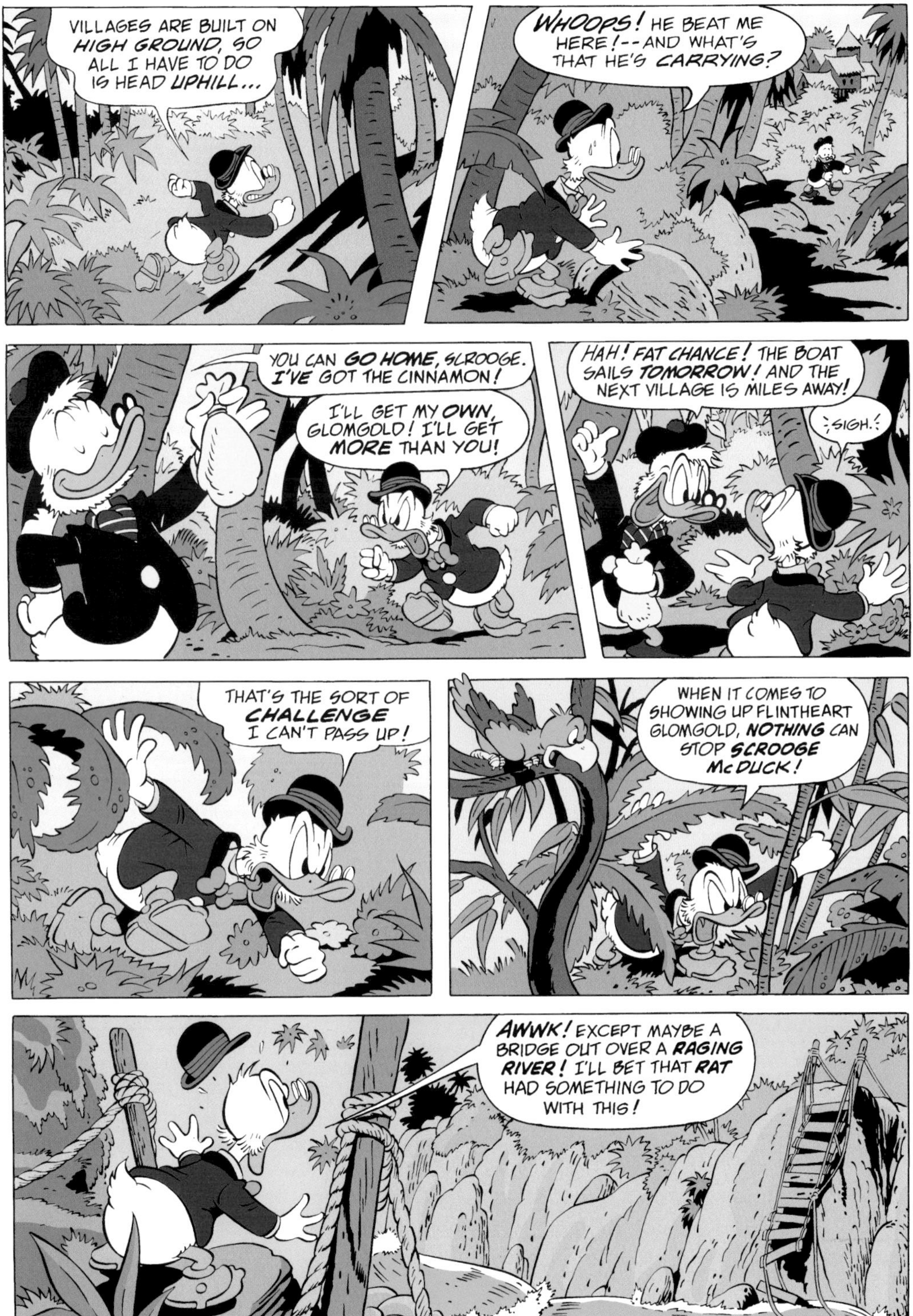
VILLAGES ARE BUILT ON HIGH GROUND, SO ALL I HAVE TO DO IS HEAD UPHILL...
WHOOPS! HE BEAT ME HERE!--AND WHAT'S THAT HE'S CARRYING?
YOU CAN GO HOME, SCROOGE. I'VE GOT THE CINNAMON!
I'LL GET MY OWN, GLOMGOLD! I'LL GET MORE THAN YOU!
HAH! FAT CHANCE! THE BOAT SAILS TOMORROW! AND THE NEXT VILLAGE IS MILES AWAY!
SIGH.
THAT'S THE SORT OF CHALLENGE I CAN'T PASS UP!
WHEN IT COMES TO SHOWING UP FLINTHEART GLOMGOLD, NOTHING CAN STOP SCROOGE McDUCK!
AWWK! EXCEPT MAYBE A BRIDGE OUT OVER A RAGING RIVER! I'LL BET THAT RAT HAD SOMETHING TO DO WITH THIS!

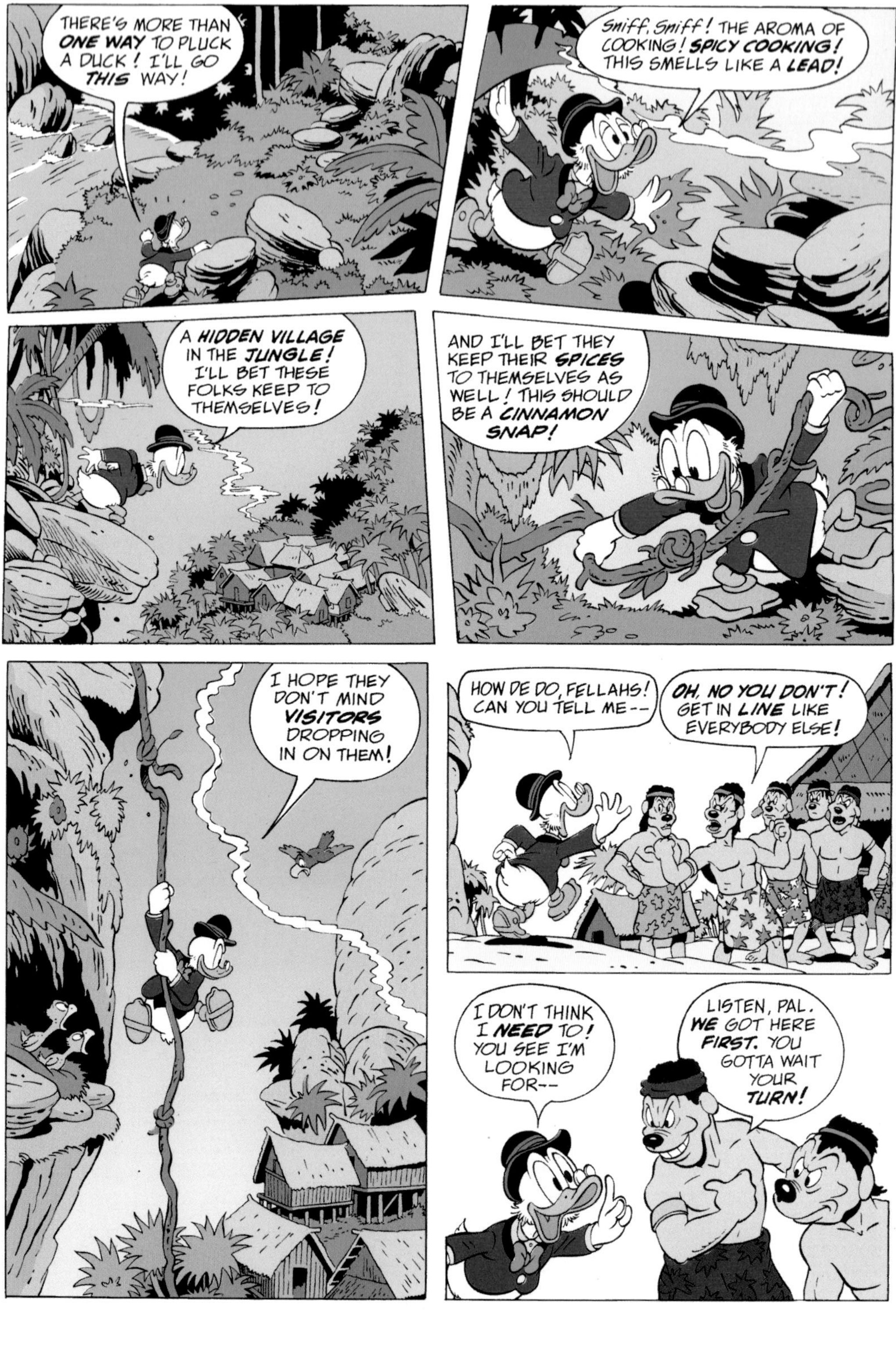
THERE'S MORE THAN ONE WAY TO PLUCK A DUCK! I'LL GO THIS WAY!
Sniff, Sniff! THE AROMA OF COOKING! SPICY COOKING! THIS SMELLS LIKE A LEAD!
A HIDDEN VILLAGE IN THE JUNGLE! I'LL BET THESE FOLKS KEEP TO THEMSELVES!
AND I'LL BET THEY KEEP THEIR SPICES TO THEMSELVES AS WELL! THIS SHOULD BE A CINNAMON SNAP!
I HOPE THEY DON'T MIND VISITORS DROPPING IN ON THEM!
HOW DE DO, FELLAHS! CAN YOU TELL ME--
OH, NO YOU DON'T! GET IN LINE LIKE EVERYBODY ELSE!
I DON'T THINK I NEED TO! YOU SEE I'M LOOKING FOR--
LISTEN, PAL. WE GOT HERE FIRST. YOU GOTTA WAIT YOUR TURN!

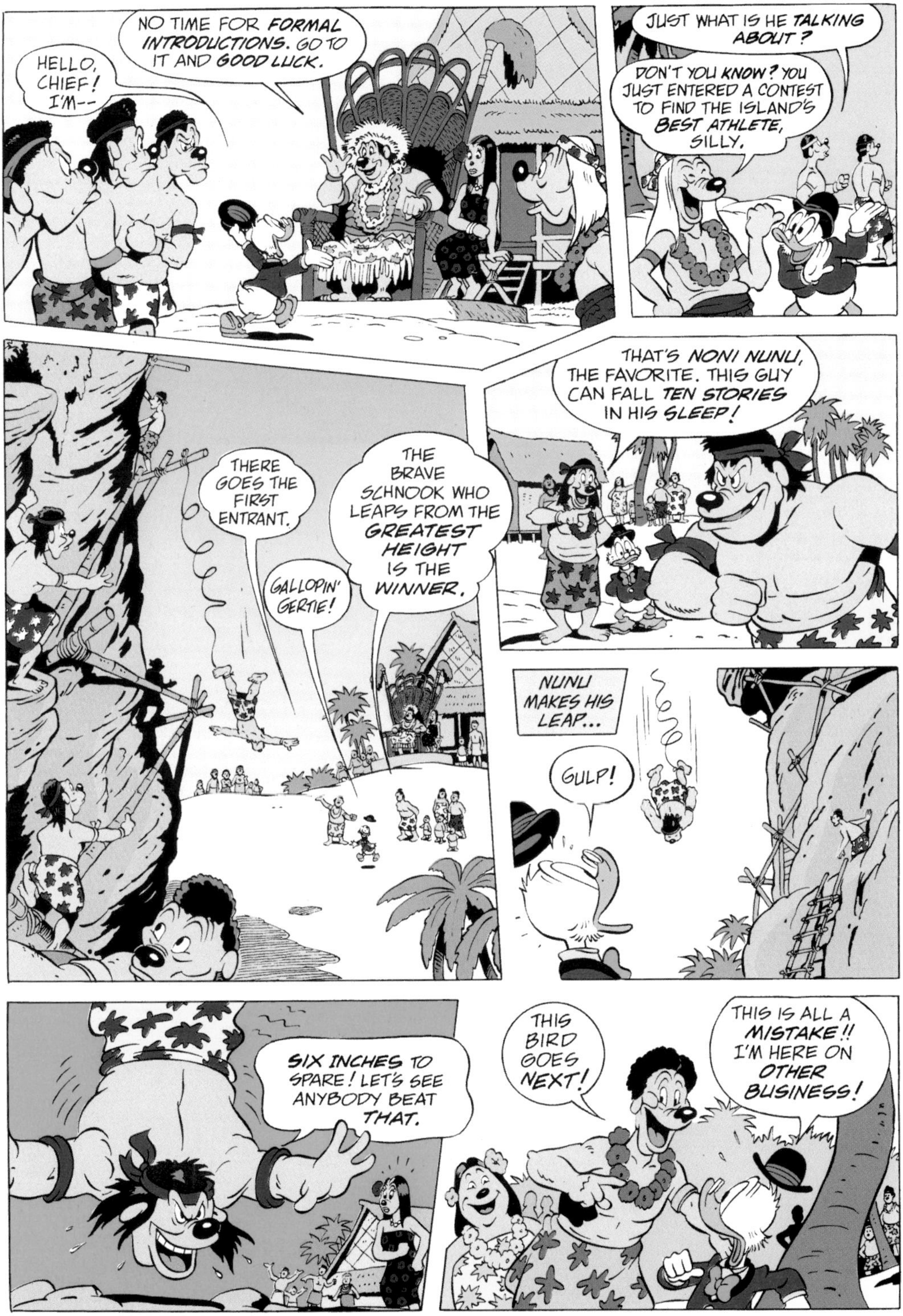
HELLO, CHIEF! I'M--
NO TIME FOR FORMAL INTRODUCTIONS. GO TO IT AND GOOD LUCK.
JUST WHAT IS HE TALKING ABOUT?
DON'T YOU KNOW? YOU JUST ENTERED A CONTEST TO FIND THE ISLAND'S BEST ATHLETE, SILLY.
THERE GOES THE FIRST ENTRANT.
GALLOPIN' GERTIE!
THE BRAVE SCHNOOK WHO LEAPS FROM THE GREATEST HEIGHT IS THE WINNER.
THAT'S NONI NUNU, THE FAVORITE. THIS GUY CAN FALL TEN STORIES IN HIS SLEEP!
NUNU MAKES HIS LEAP...
GULP!
SIX INCHES TO SPARE! LET'S SEE ANYBODY BEAT THAT.
THIS BIRD GOES NEXT!
THIS IS ALL A MISTAKE!! I'M HERE ON OTHER BUSINESS!

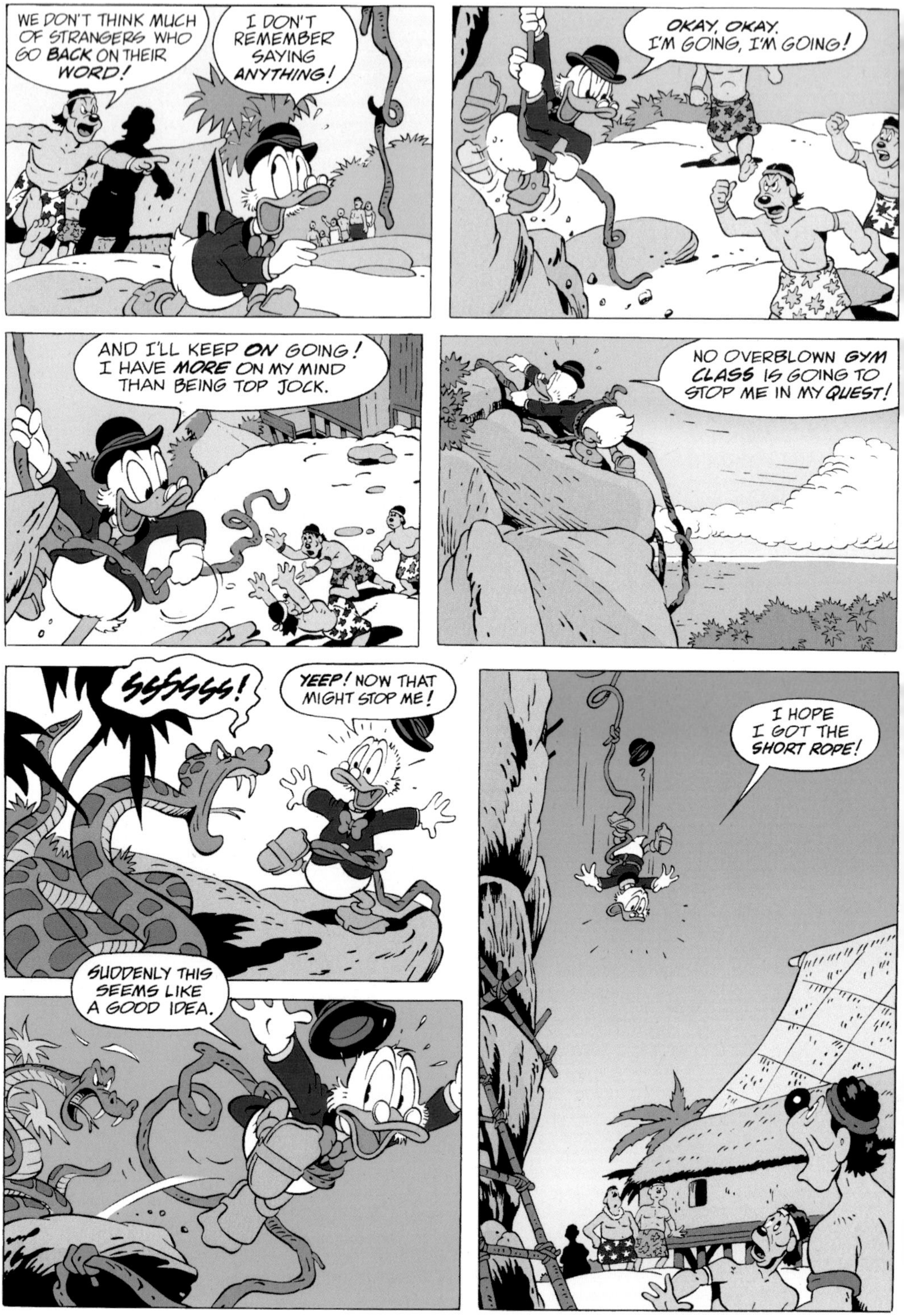
WE DON'T THINK MUCH OF STRANGERS WHO GO BACK ON THEIR WORD!
I DON'T REMEMBER SAYING ANYTHING!
OKAY, OKAY. I'M GOING, I'M GOING!
AND I'LL KEEP ON GOING! I HAVE MORE ON MY MIND THAN BEING TOP JOCK.
NO OVERBLOWN GYM CLASS IS GOING TO STOP ME IN MY QUEST!
SSSSSS!
YEEP! NOW THAT MIGHT STOP ME!
SUDDENLY THIS SEEMS LIKE A GOOD IDEA.
I HOPE I GOT THE SHORT ROPE!

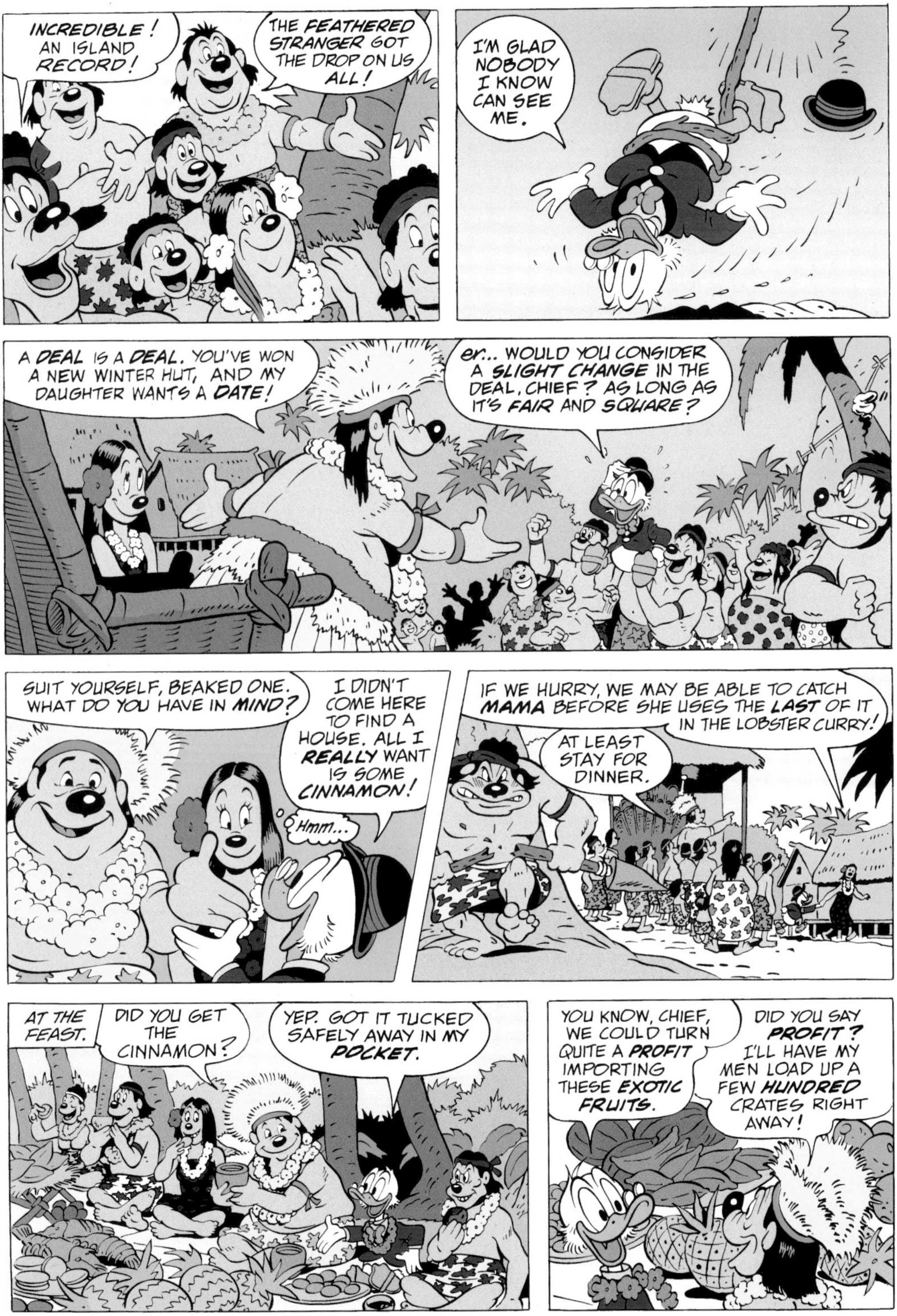
INCREDIBLE! AN ISLAND RECORD!
THE FEATHERED STRANGER GOT THE DROP ON US ALL!
I'M GLAD NOBODY I KNOW CAN SEE ME.
A DEAL IS A DEAL. YOU'VE WON A NEW WINTER HUT, AND MY DAUGHTER WANTS A DATE!
er... WOULD YOU CONSIDER A SLIGHT CHANGE IN THE DEAL, CHIEF? AS LONG AS IT'S FAIR AND SQUARE?
SUIT YOURSELF, BEAKED ONE. WHAT DO YOU HAVE IN MIND?
I DIDN'T COME HERE TO FIND A HOUSE. ALL I REALLY WANT IS SOME CINNAMON!
Hmm...
IF WE HURRY, WE MAY BE ABLE TO CATCH MAMA BEFORE SHE USES THE LAST OF IT IN THE LOBSTER CURRY!
AT LEAST STAY FOR DINNER.
AT THE FEAST.
DID YOU GET THE CINNAMON?
YEP. GOT IT TUCKED SAFELY AWAY IN MY POCKET.
YOU KNOW, CHIEF, WE COULD TURN QUITE A PROFIT IMPORTING THESE EXOTIC FRUITS.
DID YOU SAY PROFIT? I'LL HAVE MY MEN LOAD UP A FEW HUNDRED CRATES RIGHT AWAY!

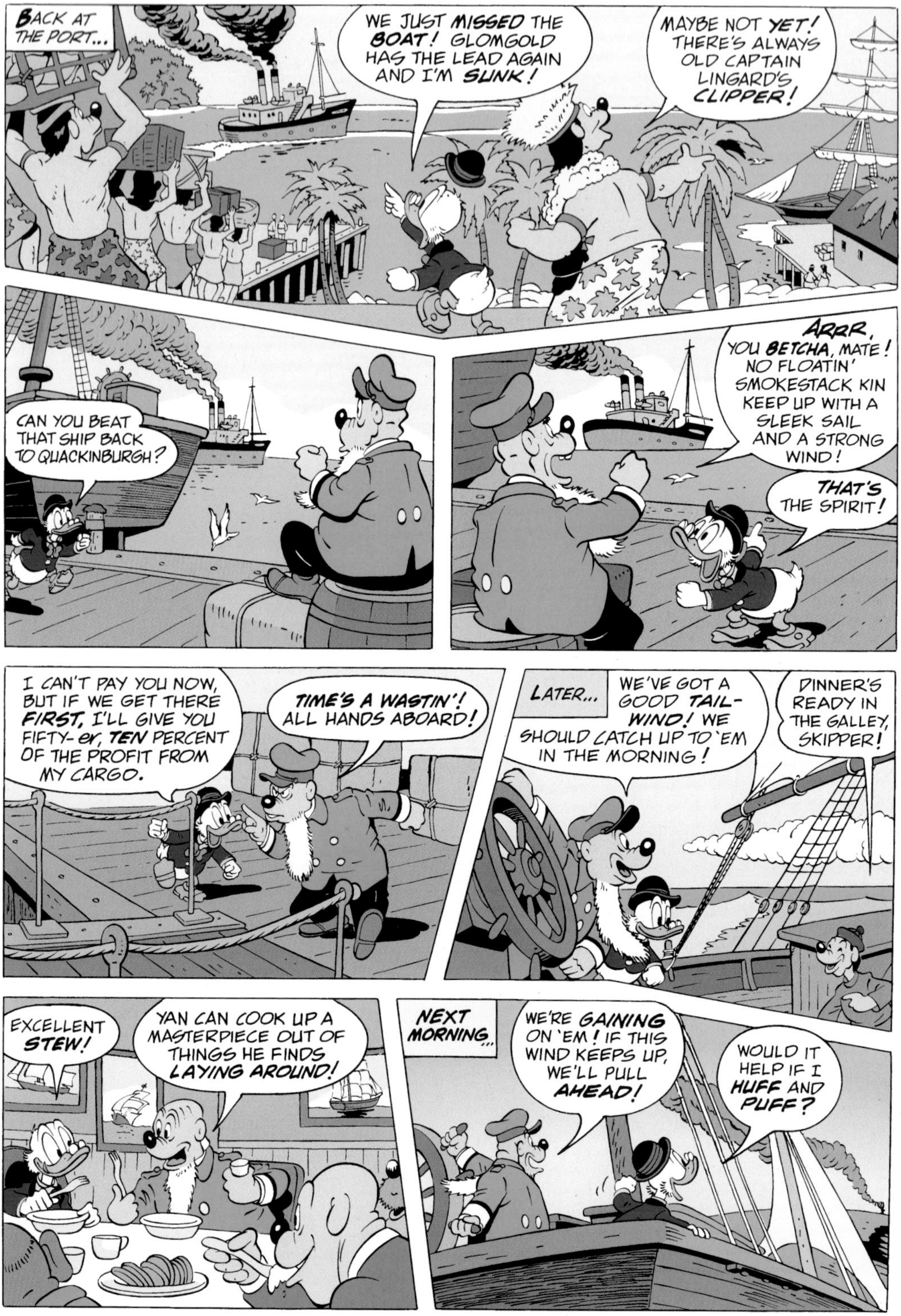

BACK AT THE PORT...
WE JUST MISSED THE BOAT! GLOMGOLD HAS THE LEAD AGAIN AND I'M SUNK!
MAYBE NOT YET! THERE'S ALWAYS OLD CAPTAIN LINGARD'S CLIPPER!
CAN YOU BEAT THAT SHIP BACK TO QUACKINBURGH?
ARRR, YOU BETCHA, MATE! NO FLOATIN' SMOKESTACK KIN KEEP UP WITH A SLEEK SAIL AND A STRONG WIND!
THAT'S THE SPIRIT!
I CAN'T PAY YOU NOW, BUT IF WE GET THERE FIRST, I'LL GIVE YOU FIFTY- er, TEN PERCENT OF THE PROFIT FROM MY CARGO.
TIME'S A WASTIN'! ALL HANDS ABOARD!
LATER...
WE'VE GOT A GOOD TAIL-WIND! WE SHOULD CATCH UP TO 'EM IN THE MORNING!
DINNER'S READY IN THE GALLEY, SKIPPER!
EXCELLENT STEW!
YAN CAN COOK UP A MASTERPIECE OUT OF THINGS HE FINDS LAYING AROUND!
NEXT MORNING...
WE'RE GAINING ON 'EM! IF THIS WIND KEEPS UP, WE'LL PULL AHEAD!
WOULD IT HELP IF I HUFF AND PUFF?

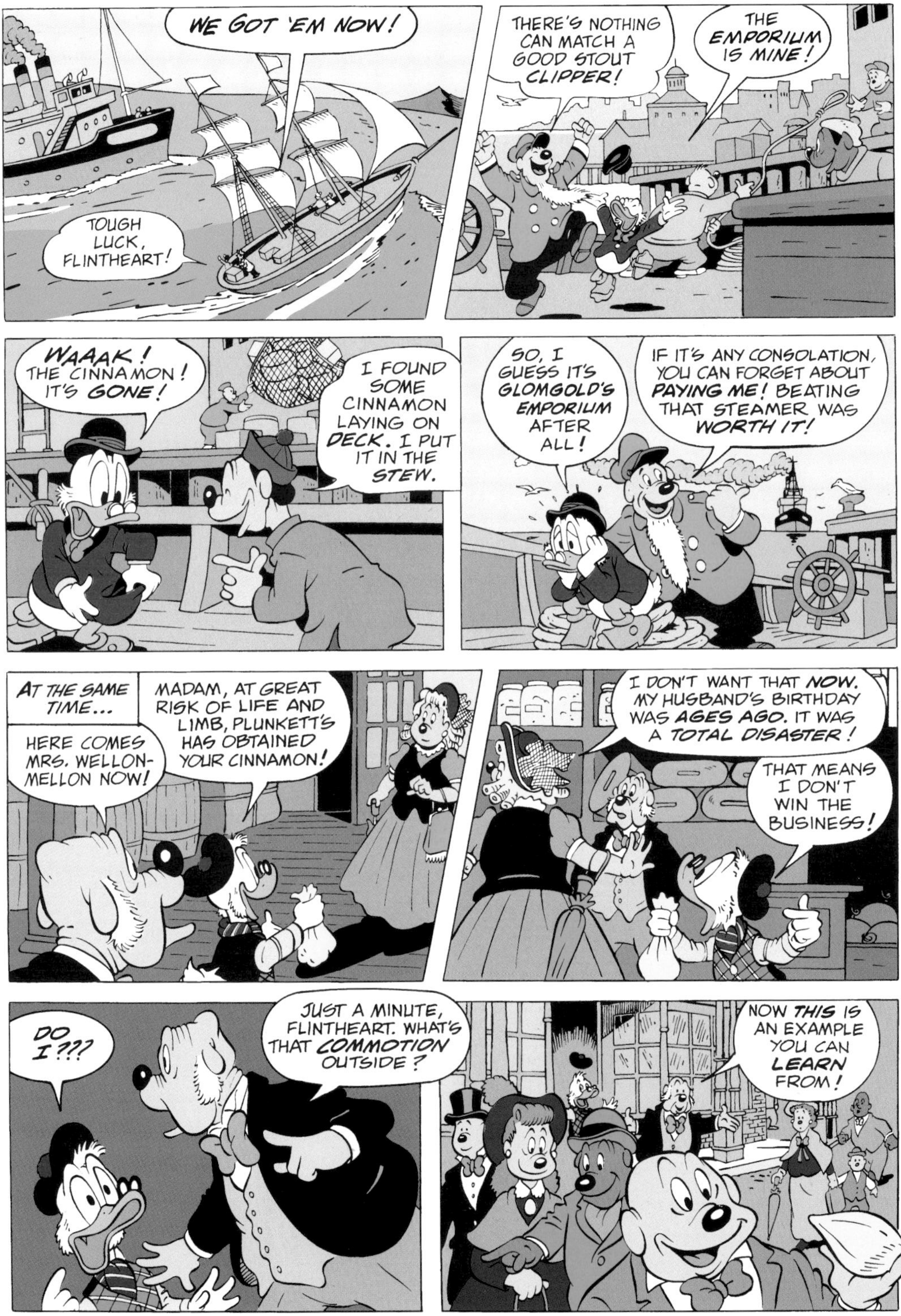
WE GOT 'EM NOW!
TOUGH LUCK, FLINTHEART!
THERE'S NOTHING CAN MATCH A GOOD STOUT CLIPPER!
THE EMPORIUM IS MINE!
WAAAK! THE CINNAMON! IT'S GONE!
I FOUND SOME CINNAMON LAYING ON DECK. I PUT IT IN THE STEW.
SO, I GUESS IT'S GLOMGOLD'S EMPORIUM AFTER ALL!
IF IT'S ANY CONSOLATION, YOU CAN FORGET ABOUT PAYING ME! BEATING THAT STEAMER WAS WORTH IT!
AT THE SAME TIME...
HERE COMES MRS. WELLON-MELLON NOW!
MADAM, AT GREAT RISK OF LIFE AND LIMB, PLUNKETT'S HAS OBTAINED YOUR CINNAMON!
I DON'T WANT THAT NOW. MY HUSBAND'S BIRTHDAY WAS AGES AGO. IT WAS A TOTAL DISASTER!
THAT MEANS I DON'T WIN THE BUSINESS!
DO I???
JUST A MINUTE, FLINTHEART. WHAT'S THAT COMMOTION OUTSIDE?
NOW THIS IS AN EXAMPLE YOU CAN LEARN FROM!

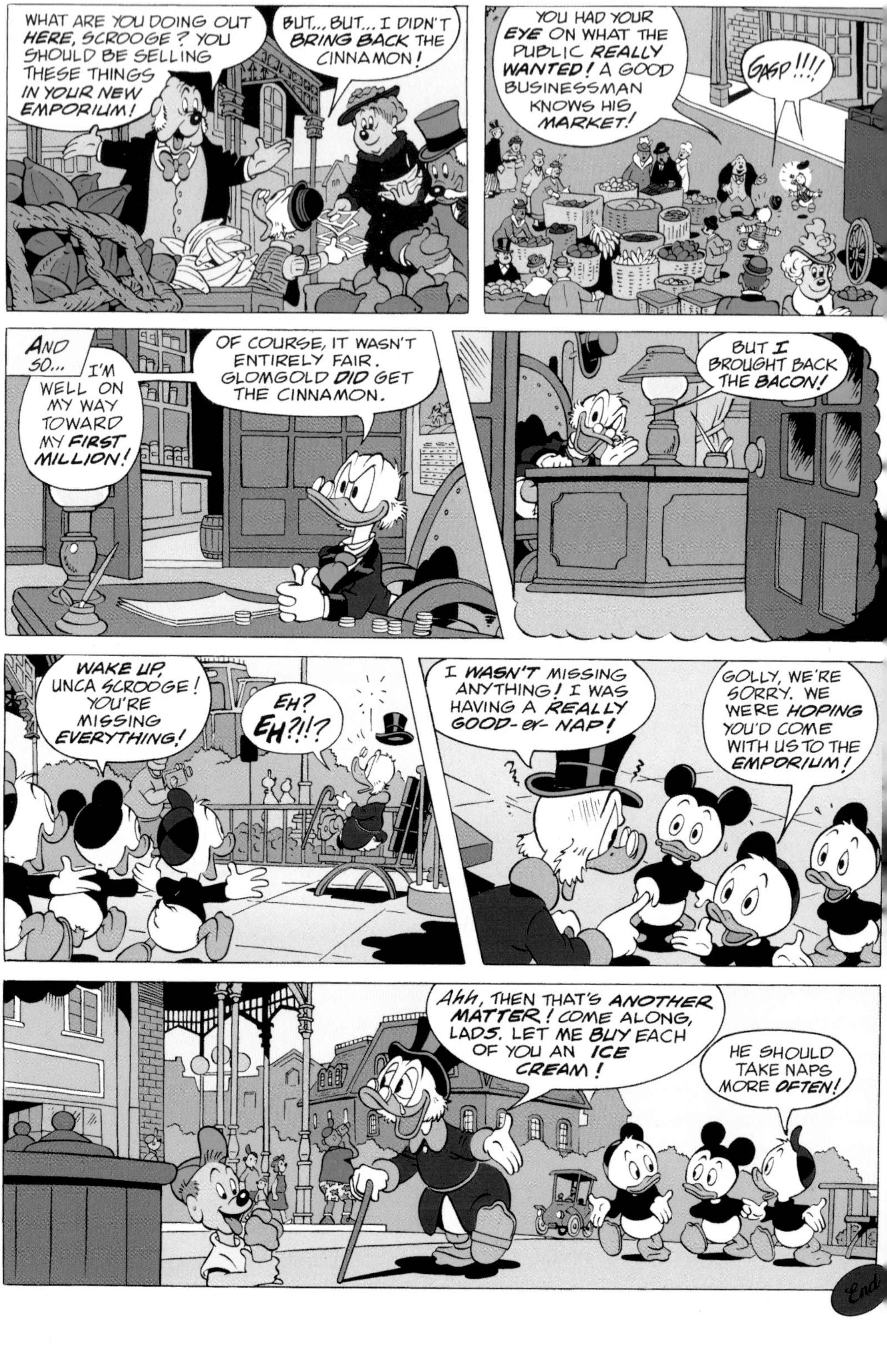

WHAT ARE YOU DOING OUT HERE, SCROOGE? YOU SHOULD BE SELLING THESE THINGS IN YOUR NEW EMPORIUM!
BUT... BUT... I DIDN'T BRING BACK THE CINNAMON!
YOU HAD YOUR EYE ON WHAT THE PUBLIC REALLY WANTED! A GOOD BUSINESSMAN KNOWS HIS MARKET!
GASP!!!!
AND SO...
I'M WELL ON MY WAY TOWARD MY FIRST MILLION!
OF COURSE, IT WASN'T ENTIRELY FAIR. GLOMGOLD DID GET THE CINNAMON.
BUT I BROUGHT BACK THE BACON!
WAKE UP, UNCA SCROOGE! YOU'RE MISSING EVERYTHING!
EH? EH?!!?
I WASN'T MISSING ANYTHING! I WAS HAVING A REALLY GOOD-er-NAP!
GOLLY, WE'RE SORRY. WE WERE HOPING YOU'D COME WITH US TO THE EMPORIUM!
Ahh, THEN THAT'S ANOTHER MATTER! COME ALONG, LADS. LET ME BUY EACH OF YOU AN ICE CREAM!
HE SHOULD TAKE NAPS MORE OFTEN!
End

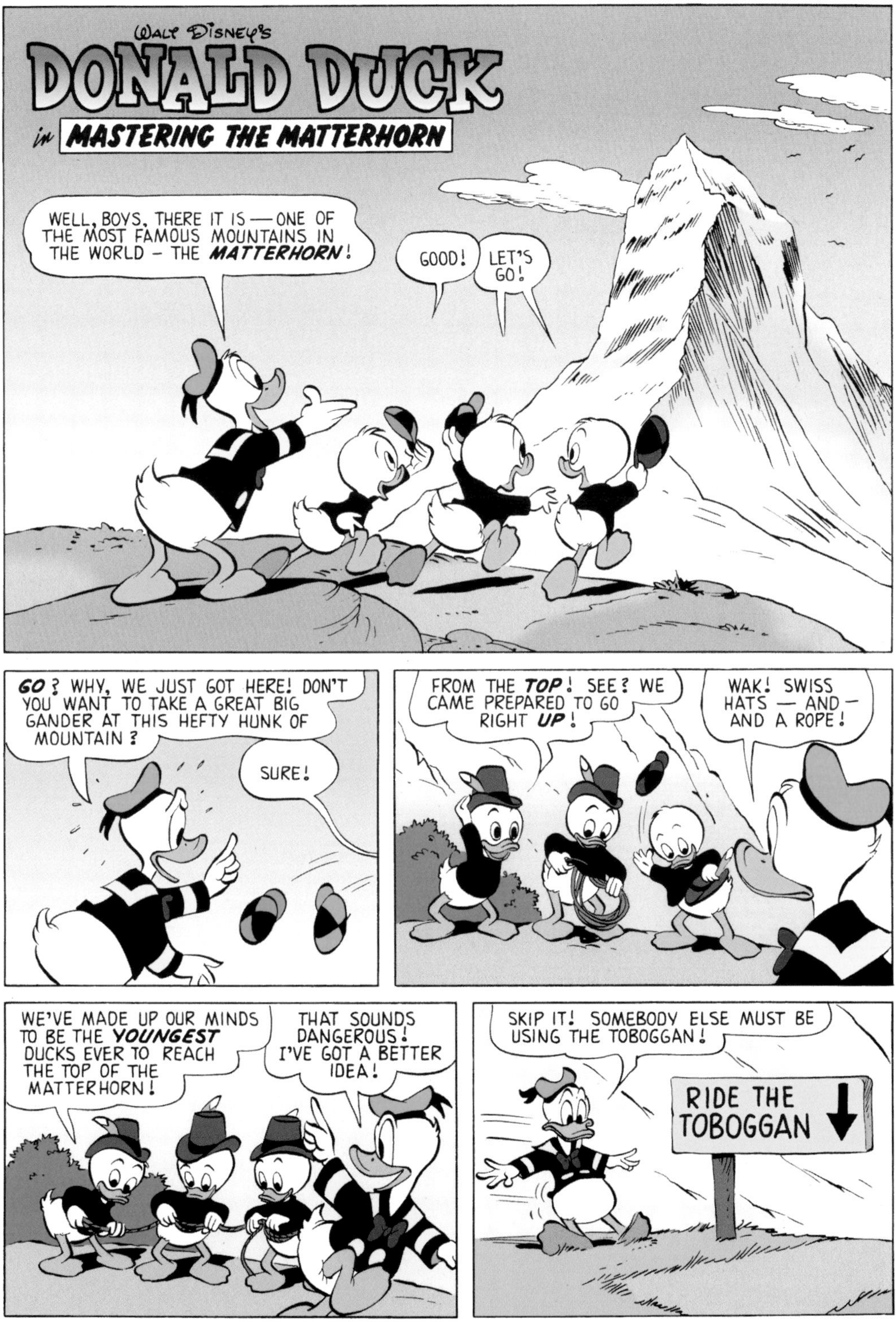
WALT DISNEY'S
DONALD DUCK
in MASTERING THE MATTERHORN
WELL, BOYS, THERE IT IS — ONE OF THE MOST FAMOUS MOUNTAINS IN THE WORLD - THE MATTERHORN!
GOOD!
LET'S GO!
GO? WHY, WE JUST GOT HERE! DON'T YOU WANT TO TAKE A GREAT BIG GANDER AT THIS HEFTY HUNK OF MOUNTAIN?
SURE!
FROM THE TOP! SEE? WE CAME PREPARED TO GO RIGHT UP!
WAK! SWISS HATS — AND — AND A ROPE!
WE'VE MADE UP OUR MINDS TO BE THE YOUNGEST DUCKS EVER TO REACH THE TOP OF THE MATTERHORN!
THAT SOUNDS DANGEROUS! I'VE GOT A BETTER IDEA!
SKIP IT! SOMEBODY ELSE MUST BE USING THE TOBOGGAN!
RIDE THE TOBOGGAN

Originally published in "Vacation in Disneyland" *Four Color* #1025 (USA, 1959)

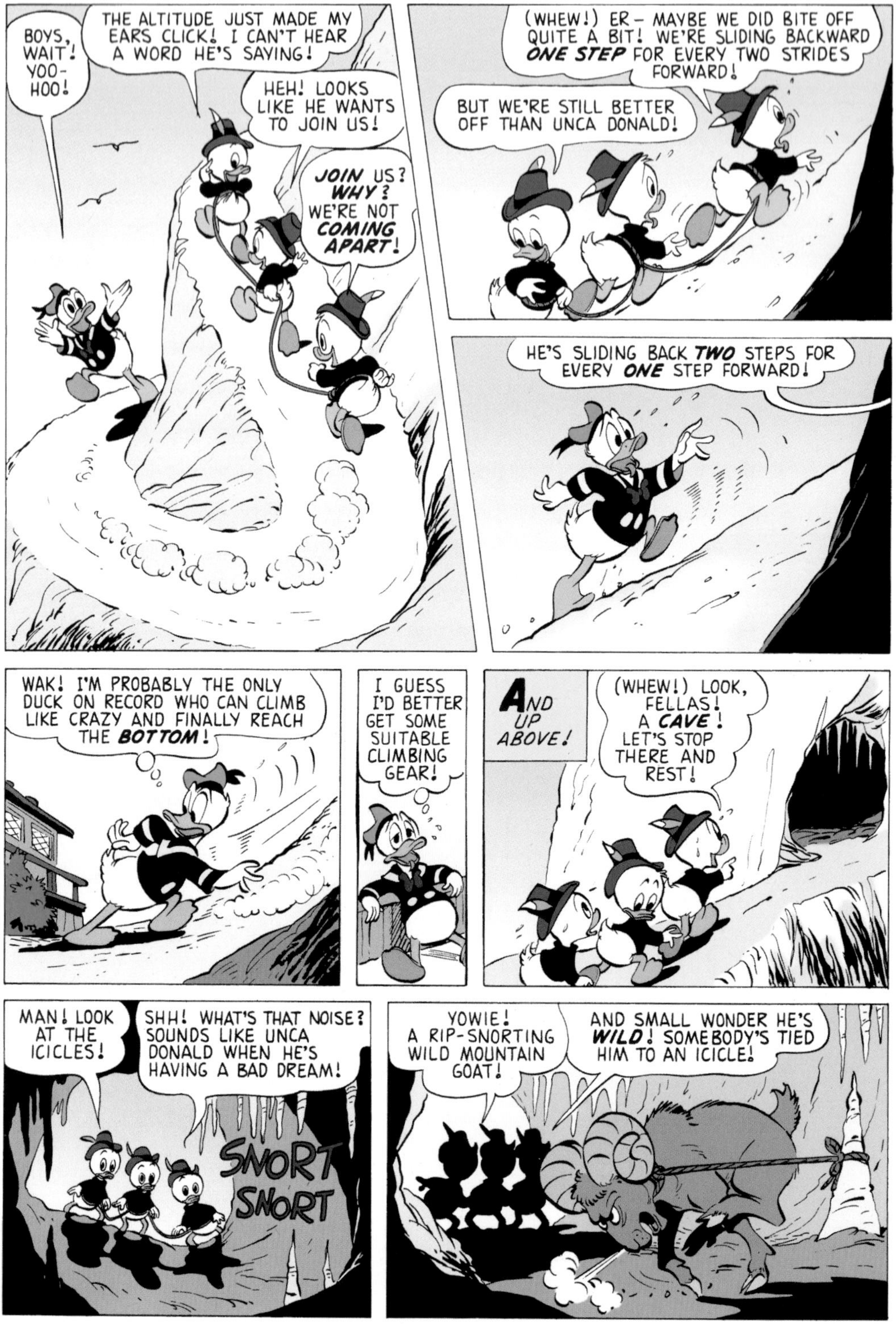
BOYS, WAIT! YOO-HOO!
THE ALTITUDE JUST MADE MY EARS CLICK! I CAN'T HEAR A WORD HE'S SAYING!
HEH! LOOKS LIKE HE WANTS TO JOIN US!
JOIN US? WHY? WE'RE NOT COMING APART!
(WHEW!) ER– MAYBE WE DID BITE OFF QUITE A BIT! WE'RE SLIDING BACKWARD ONE STEP FOR EVERY TWO STRIDES FORWARD!
BUT WE'RE STILL BETTER OFF THAN UNCA DONALD!
HE'S SLIDING BACK TWO STEPS FOR EVERY ONE STEP FORWARD!
WAK! I'M PROBABLY THE ONLY DUCK ON RECORD WHO CAN CLIMB LIKE CRAZY AND FINALLY REACH THE BOTTOM!
I GUESS I'D BETTER GET SOME SUITABLE CLIMBING GEAR!
AND UP ABOVE!
(WHEW!) LOOK, FELLAS! A CAVE! LET'S STOP THERE AND REST!
MAN! LOOK AT THE ICICLES!
SHH! WHAT'S THAT NOISE? SOUNDS LIKE UNCA DONALD WHEN HE'S HAVING A BAD DREAM!
SNORT SNORT
YOWIE! A RIP-SNORTING WILD MOUNTAIN GOAT!
AND SMALL WONDER HE'S WILD! SOMEBODY'S TIED HIM TO AN ICICLE!

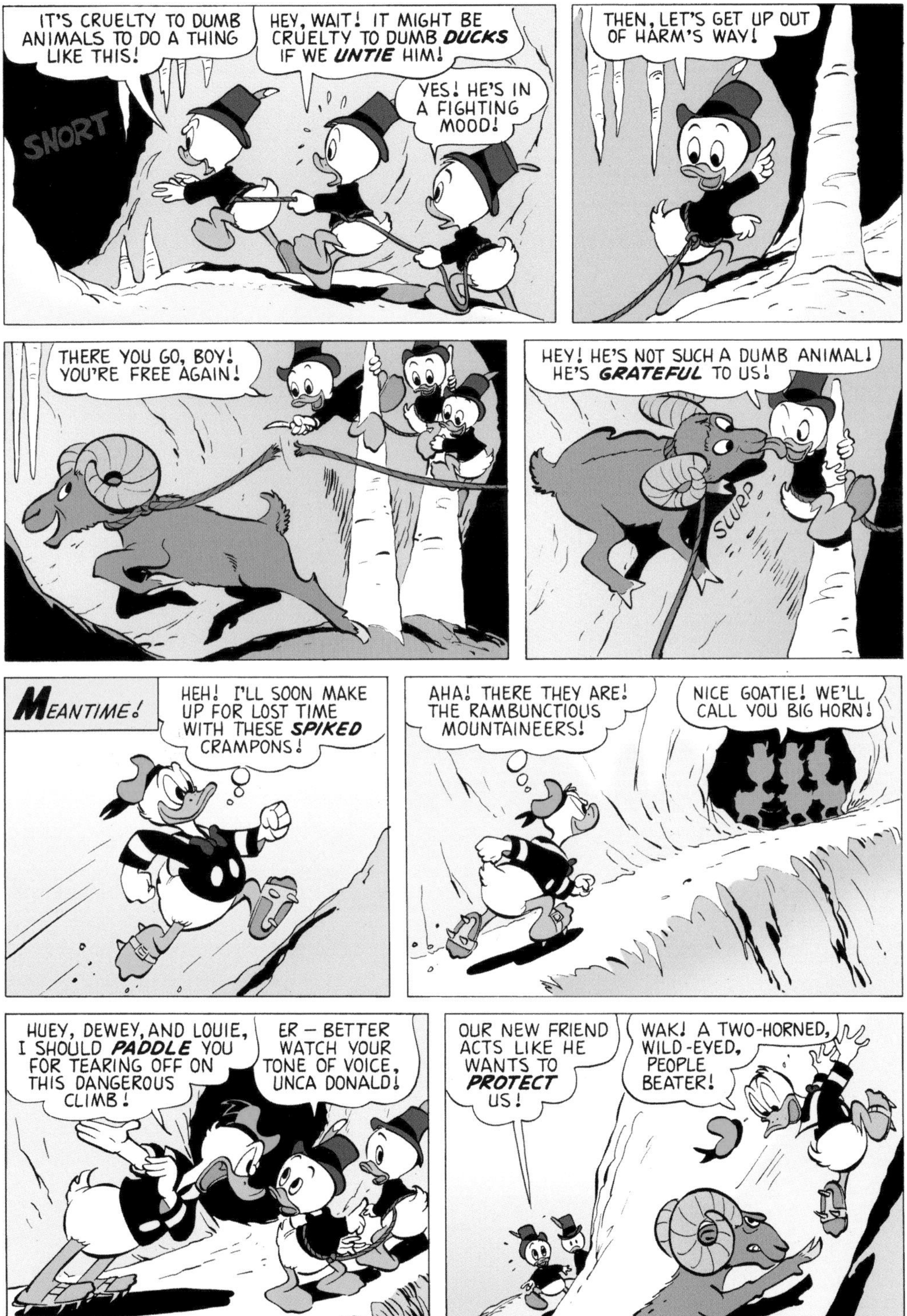

IT'S CRUELTY TO DUMB ANIMALS TO DO A THING LIKE THIS!
SNORT
HEY, WAIT! IT MIGHT BE CRUELTY TO DUMB DUCKS IF WE UNTIE HIM!
YES! HE'S IN A FIGHTING MOOD!
THEN, LET'S GET UP OUT OF HARM'S WAY!
THERE YOU GO, BOY! YOU'RE FREE AGAIN!
HEY! HE'S NOT SUCH A DUMB ANIMAL! HE'S GRATEFUL TO US!
SLURP
MEANTIME!
HEH! I'LL SOON MAKE UP FOR LOST TIME WITH THESE SPIKED CRAMPONS!
AHA! THERE THEY ARE! THE RAMBUNCTIOUS MOUNTAINEERS!
NICE GOATIE! WE'LL CALL YOU BIG HORN!
HUEY, DEWEY, AND LOUIE, I SHOULD PADDLE YOU FOR TEARING OFF ON THIS DANGEROUS CLIMB!
ER — BETTER WATCH YOUR TONE OF VOICE, UNCA DONALD!
OUR NEW FRIEND ACTS LIKE HE WANTS TO PROTECT US!
WAK! A TWO-HORNED, WILD-EYED, PEOPLE BEATER!

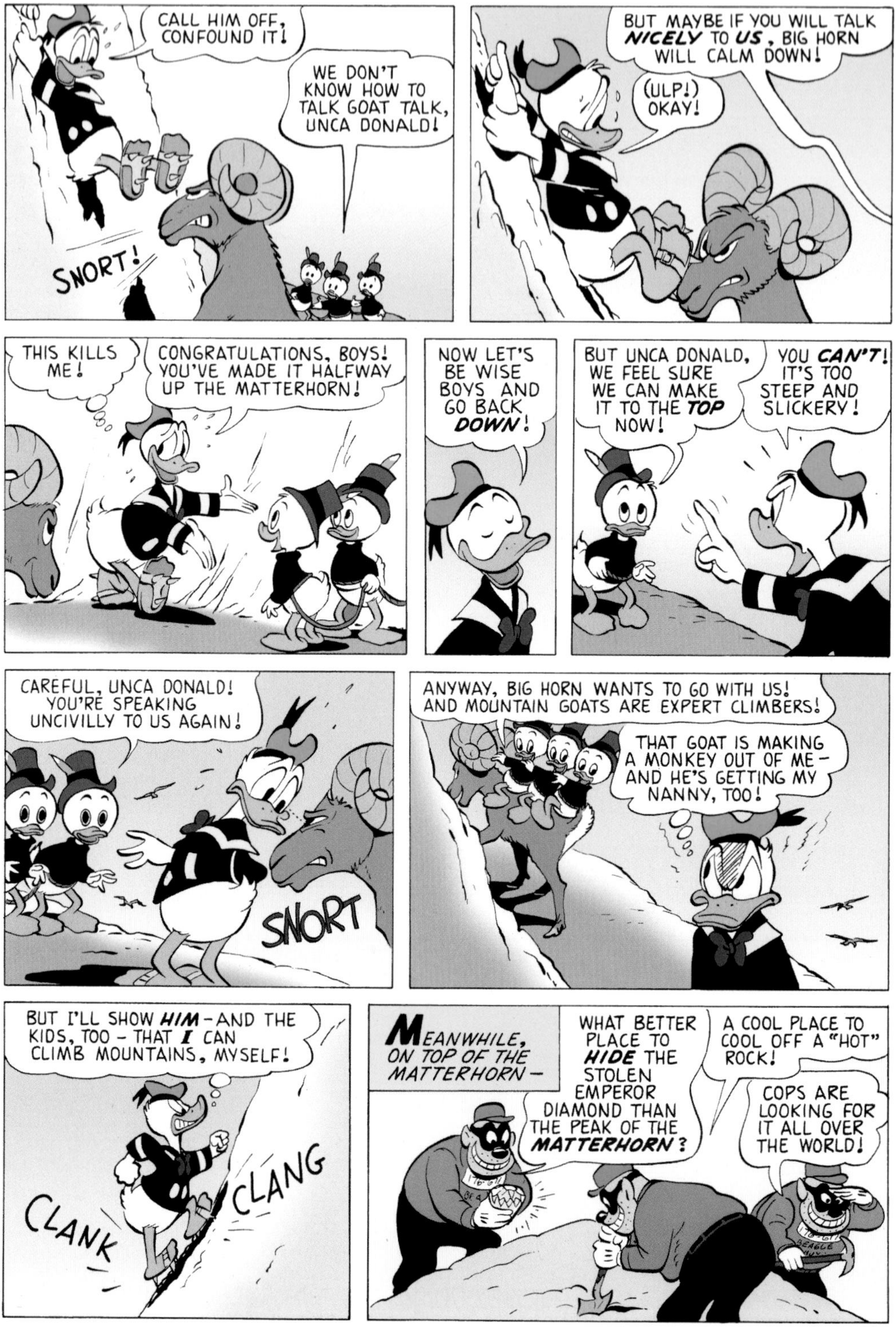
CALL HIM OFF, CONFOUND IT!
WE DON'T KNOW HOW TO TALK GOAT TALK, UNCA DONALD!
SNORT!
BUT MAYBE IF YOU WILL TALK NICELY TO US, BIG HORN WILL CALM DOWN!
(ULP!) OKAY!
THIS KILLS ME!
CONGRATULATIONS, BOYS! YOU'VE MADE IT HALFWAY UP THE MATTERHORN!
NOW LET'S BE WISE BOYS AND GO BACK DOWN!
BUT UNCA DONALD, WE FEEL SURE WE CAN MAKE IT TO THE TOP NOW!
YOU CAN'T! IT'S TOO STEEP AND SLICKERY!
CAREFUL, UNCA DONALD! YOU'RE SPEAKING UNCIVILLY TO US AGAIN!
SNORT
ANYWAY, BIG HORN WANTS TO GO WITH US! AND MOUNTAIN GOATS ARE EXPERT CLIMBERS!
THAT GOAT IS MAKING A MONKEY OUT OF ME— AND HE'S GETTING MY NANNY, TOO!
BUT I'LL SHOW HIM—AND THE KIDS, TOO—THAT I CAN CLIMB MOUNTAINS, MYSELF!
CLANK
CLANG
MEANWHILE, ON TOP OF THE MATTERHORN—
WHAT BETTER PLACE TO HIDE THE STOLEN EMPEROR DIAMOND THAN THE PEAK OF THE MATTERHORN?
A COOL PLACE TO COOL OFF A "HOT" ROCK!
COPS ARE LOOKING FOR IT ALL OVER THE WORLD!

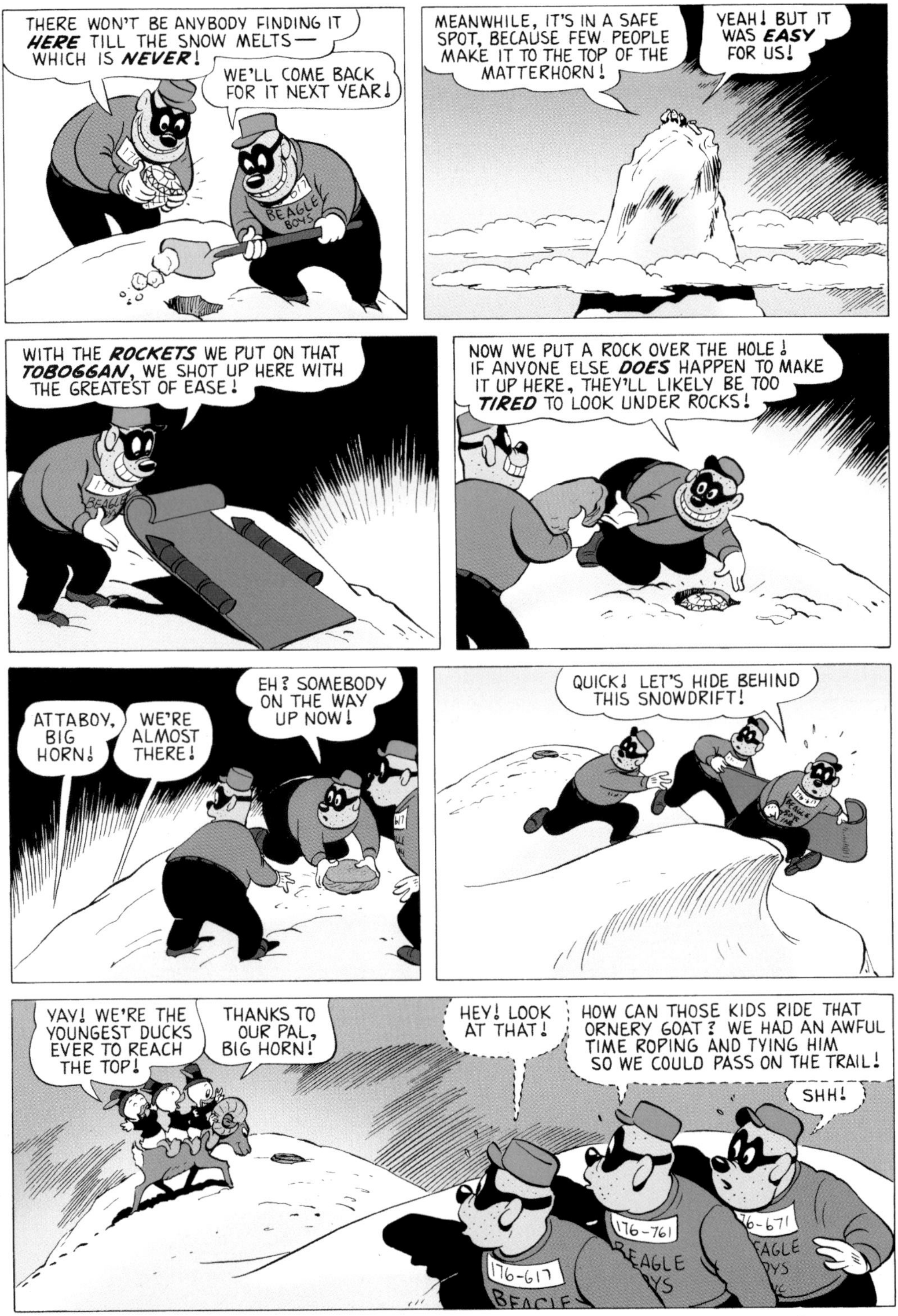
THERE WON'T BE ANYBODY FINDING IT HERE TILL THE SNOW MELTS— WHICH IS NEVER!
WE'LL COME BACK FOR IT NEXT YEAR!
BEAGLE BOYS
MEANWHILE, IT'S IN A SAFE SPOT, BECAUSE FEW PEOPLE MAKE IT TO THE TOP OF THE MATTERHORN!
YEAH! BUT IT WAS EASY FOR US!
WITH THE ROCKETS WE PUT ON THAT TOBOGGAN, WE SHOT UP HERE WITH THE GREATEST OF EASE!
NOW WE PUT A ROCK OVER THE HOLE! IF ANYONE ELSE DOES HAPPEN TO MAKE IT UP HERE, THEY'LL LIKELY BE TOO TIRED TO LOOK UNDER ROCKS!
ATTABOY, BIG HORN!
WE'RE ALMOST THERE!
EH? SOMEBODY ON THE WAY UP NOW!
QUICK! LET'S HIDE BEHIND THIS SNOWDRIFT!
YAY! WE'RE THE YOUNGEST DUCKS EVER TO REACH THE TOP!
THANKS TO OUR PAL, BIG HORN!
HEY! LOOK AT THAT!
HOW CAN THOSE KIDS RIDE THAT ORNERY GOAT? WE HAD AN AWFUL TIME ROPING AND TYING HIM SO WE COULD PASS ON THE TRAIL!
SHH!
176-617
176-761

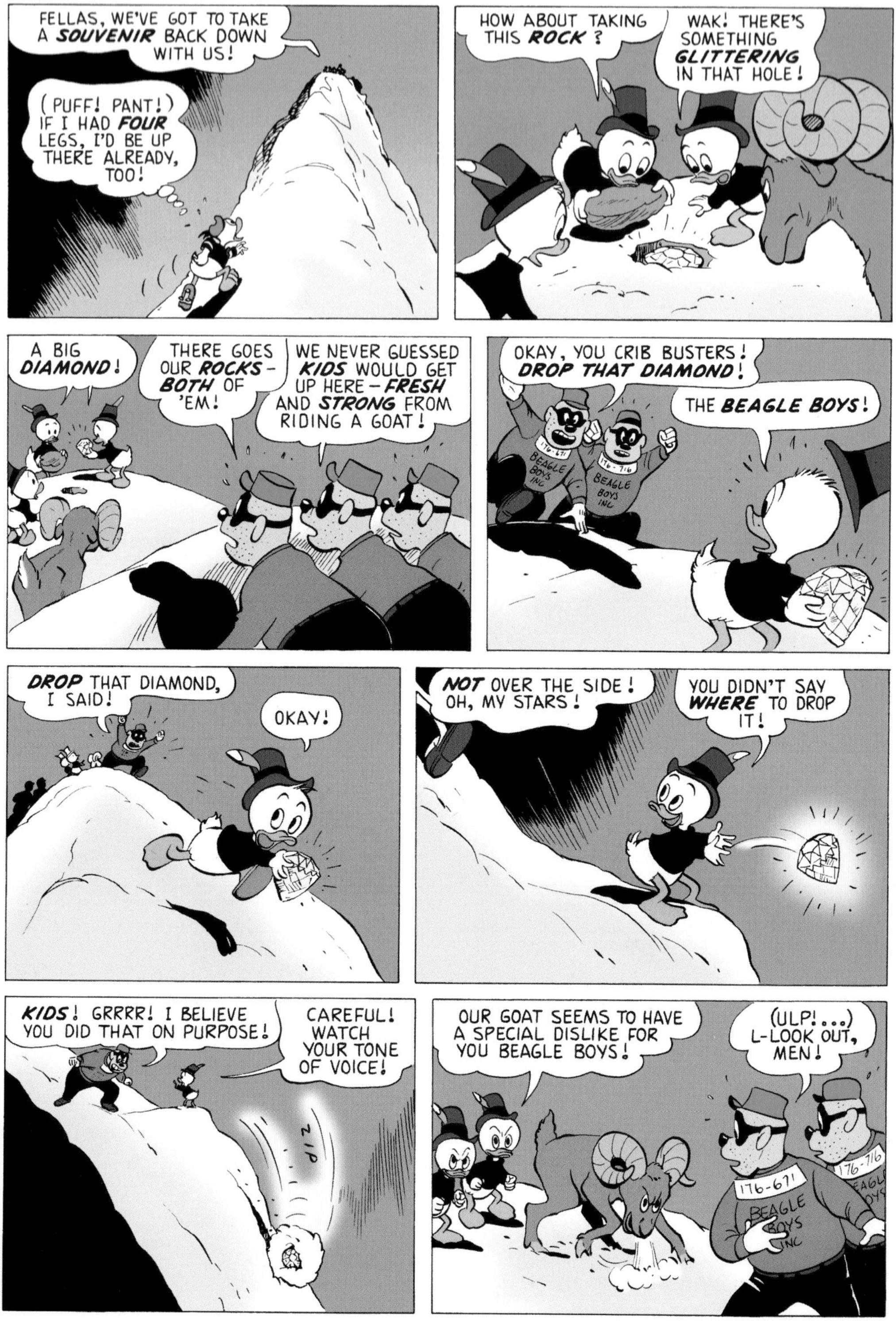
FELLAS, WE'VE GOT TO TAKE A SOUVENIR BACK DOWN WITH US!
(PUFF! PANT!) IF I HAD FOUR LEGS, I'D BE UP THERE ALREADY, TOO!
HOW ABOUT TAKING THIS ROCK?
WAK! THERE'S SOMETHING GLITTERING IN THAT HOLE!
A BIG DIAMOND!
THERE GOES OUR ROCKS- BOTH OF 'EM!
WE NEVER GUESSED KIDS WOULD GET UP HERE-FRESH AND STRONG FROM RIDING A GOAT!
OKAY, YOU CRIB BUSTERS! DROP THAT DIAMOND!
176-671 BEAGLE BOYS INC
176-716 BEAGLE BOYS INC
THE BEAGLE BOYS!
DROP THAT DIAMOND, I SAID!
OKAY!
NOT OVER THE SIDE! OH, MY STARS!
YOU DIDN'T SAY WHERE TO DROP IT!
KIDS! GRRRR! I BELIEVE YOU DID THAT ON PURPOSE!
CAREFUL! WATCH YOUR TONE OF VOICE!
ZIP
OUR GOAT SEEMS TO HAVE A SPECIAL DISLIKE FOR YOU BEAGLE BOYS!
(ULP!...) L-LOOK OUT, MEN!
176-671 BEAGLE BOYS INC
176-716

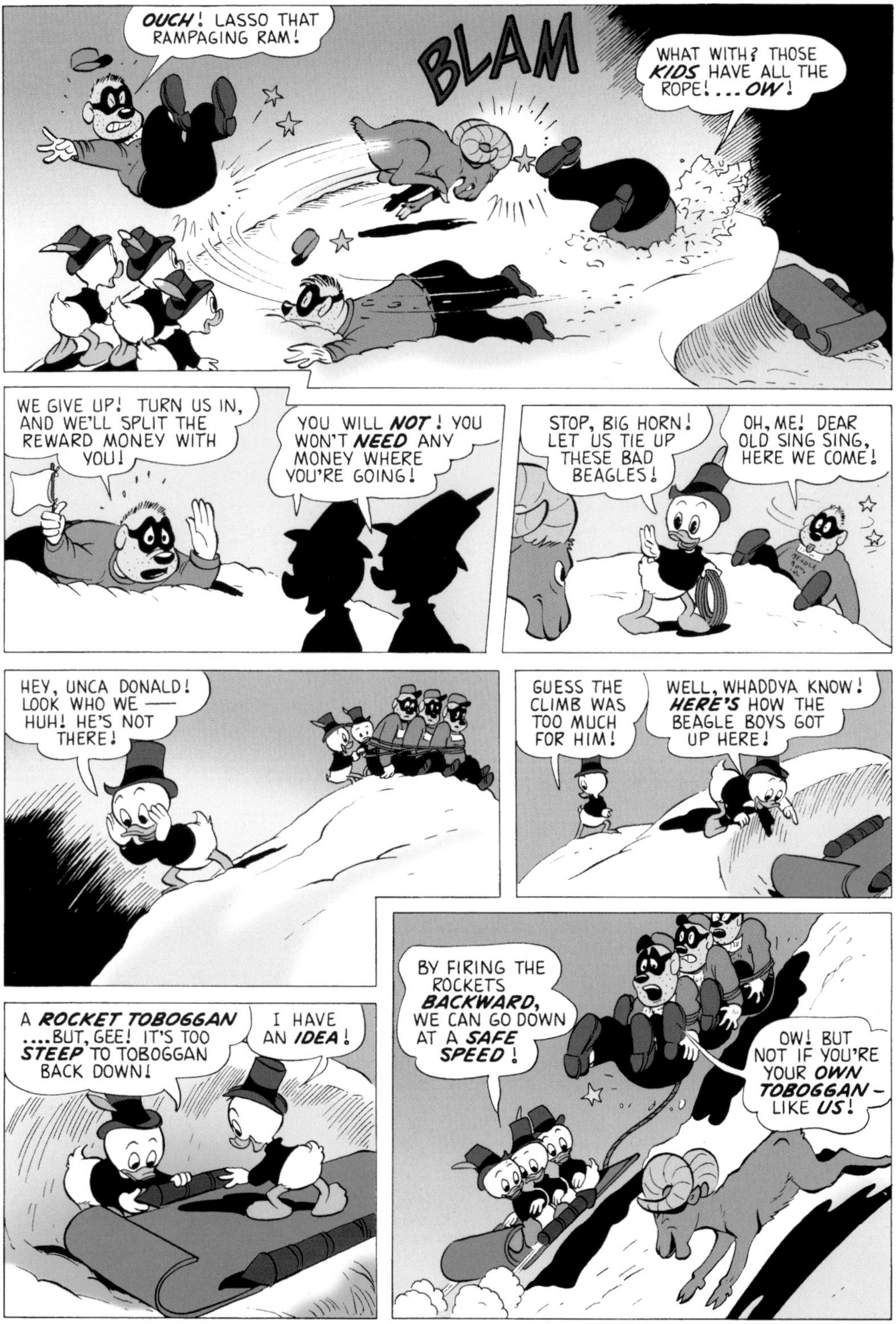
OUCH! LASSO THAT RAMPAGING RAM!
BLAM
WHAT WITH? THOSE KIDS HAVE ALL THE ROPE! ...OW!
WE GIVE UP! TURN US IN, AND WE'LL SPLIT THE REWARD MONEY WITH YOU!
YOU WILL NOT! YOU WON'T NEED ANY MONEY WHERE YOU'RE GOING!
STOP, BIG HORN! LET US TIE UP THESE BAD BEAGLES!
OH, ME! DEAR OLD SING SING, HERE WE COME!
HEY, UNCA DONALD! LOOK WHO WE — HUH! HE'S NOT THERE!
GUESS THE CLIMB WAS TOO MUCH FOR HIM!
WELL, WHADDYA KNOW! HERE'S HOW THE BEAGLE BOYS GOT UP HERE!
A ROCKET TOBOGGAN ....BUT, GEE! IT'S TOO STEEP TO TOBOGGAN BACK DOWN!
I HAVE AN IDEA!
BY FIRING THE ROCKETS BACKWARD, WE CAN GO DOWN AT A SAFE SPEED!
OW! BUT NOT IF YOU'RE YOUR OWN TOBOGGAN — LIKE US!

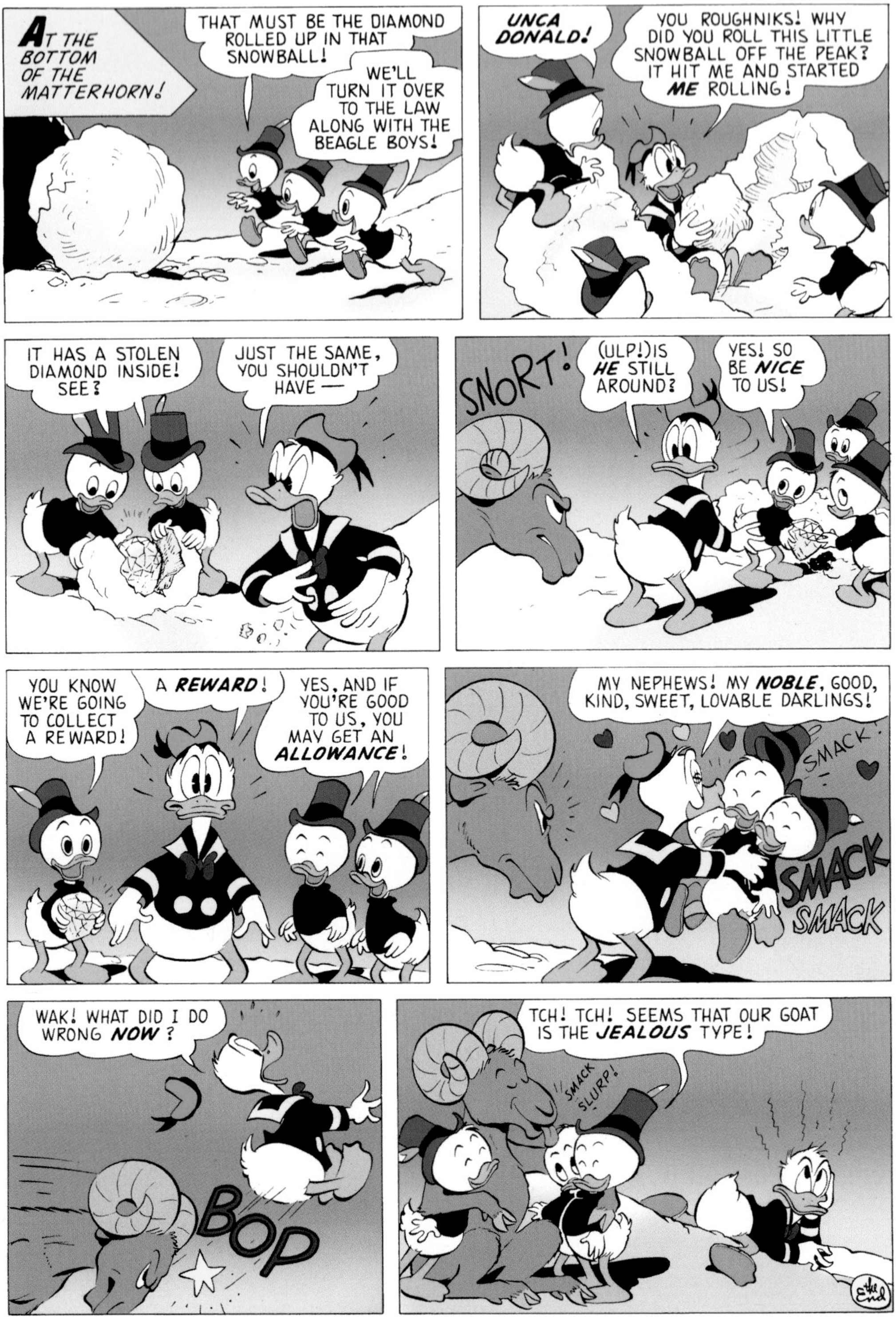
AT THE BOTTOM OF THE MATTERHORN!
THAT MUST BE THE DIAMOND ROLLED UP IN THAT SNOWBALL!
WE'LL TURN IT OVER TO THE LAW ALONG WITH THE BEAGLE BOYS!
UNCA DONALD!
YOU ROUGHNIKS! WHY DID YOU ROLL THIS LITTLE SNOWBALL OFF THE PEAK? IT HIT ME AND STARTED ME ROLLING!
IT HAS A STOLEN DIAMOND INSIDE! SEE?
JUST THE SAME, YOU SHOULDN'T HAVE —
SNORT!
(ULP!) IS HE STILL AROUND?
YES! SO BE NICE TO US!
YOU KNOW WE'RE GOING TO COLLECT A REWARD!
A REWARD!
YES, AND IF YOU'RE GOOD TO US, YOU MAY GET AN ALLOWANCE!
MY NEPHEWS! MY NOBLE, GOOD, KIND, SWEET, LOVABLE DARLINGS!
SMACK
SMACK
SMACK
WAK! WHAT DID I DO WRONG NOW?
BOP
TCH! TCH! SEEMS THAT OUR GOAT IS THE JEALOUS TYPE!
SMACK
SLURP!
the End

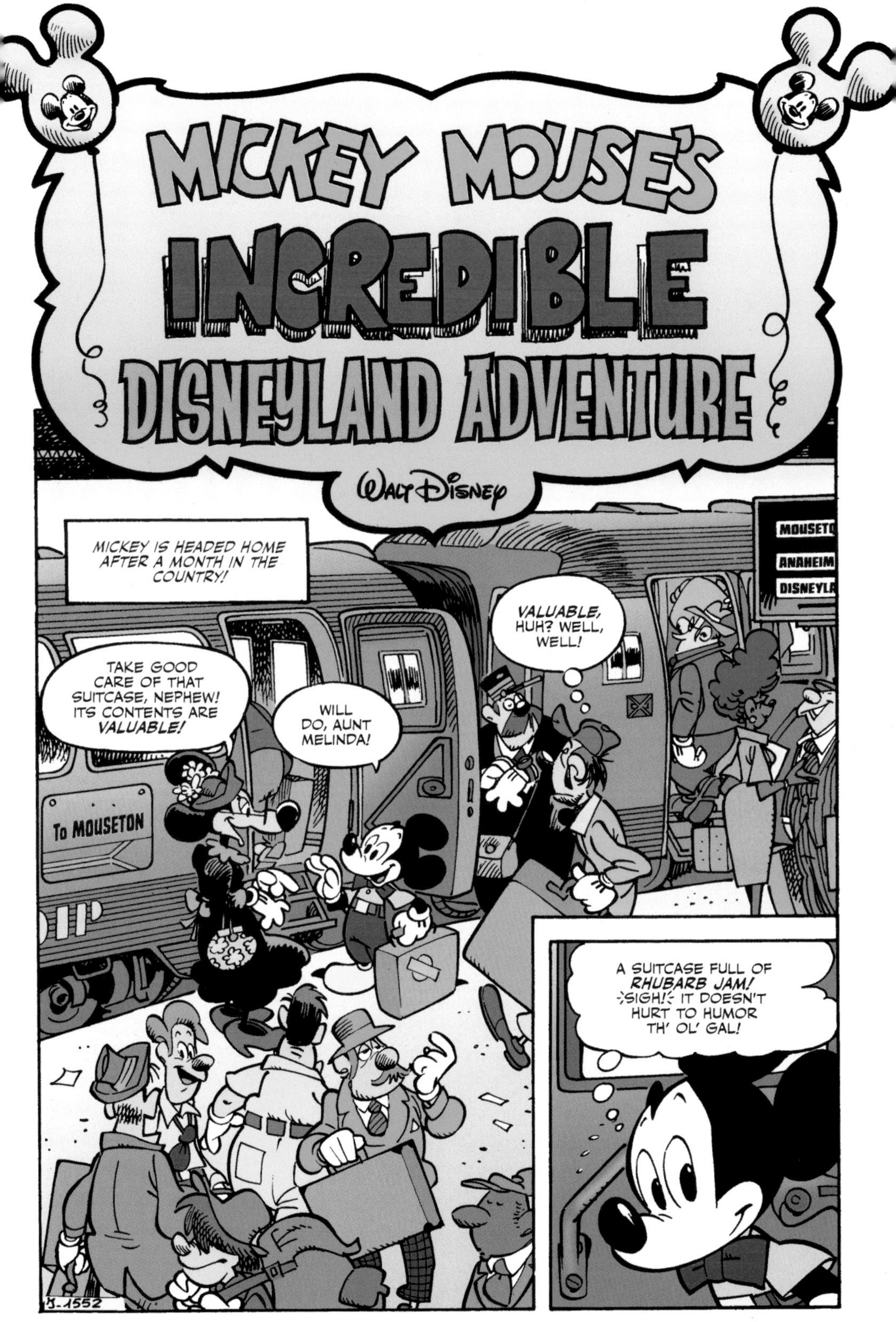
MICKEY MOUSE'S INCREDIBLE DISNEYLAND ADVENTURE
WALT DISNEY
MICKEY IS HEADED HOME AFTER A MONTH IN THE COUNTRY!
TAKE GOOD CARE OF THAT SUITCASE, NEPHEW! ITS CONTENTS ARE VALUABLE!
WILL DO, AUNT MELINDA!
VALUABLE, HUH? WELL, WELL!
MOUSETO
ANAHEIM
DISNEYLA
To MOUSETON
A SUITCASE FULL OF RHUBARB JAM! SIGH! IT DOESN'T HURT TO HUMOR TH' OL' GAL!
M-1552

Originally published in *Topolino* #1552 (Italy, 1985)

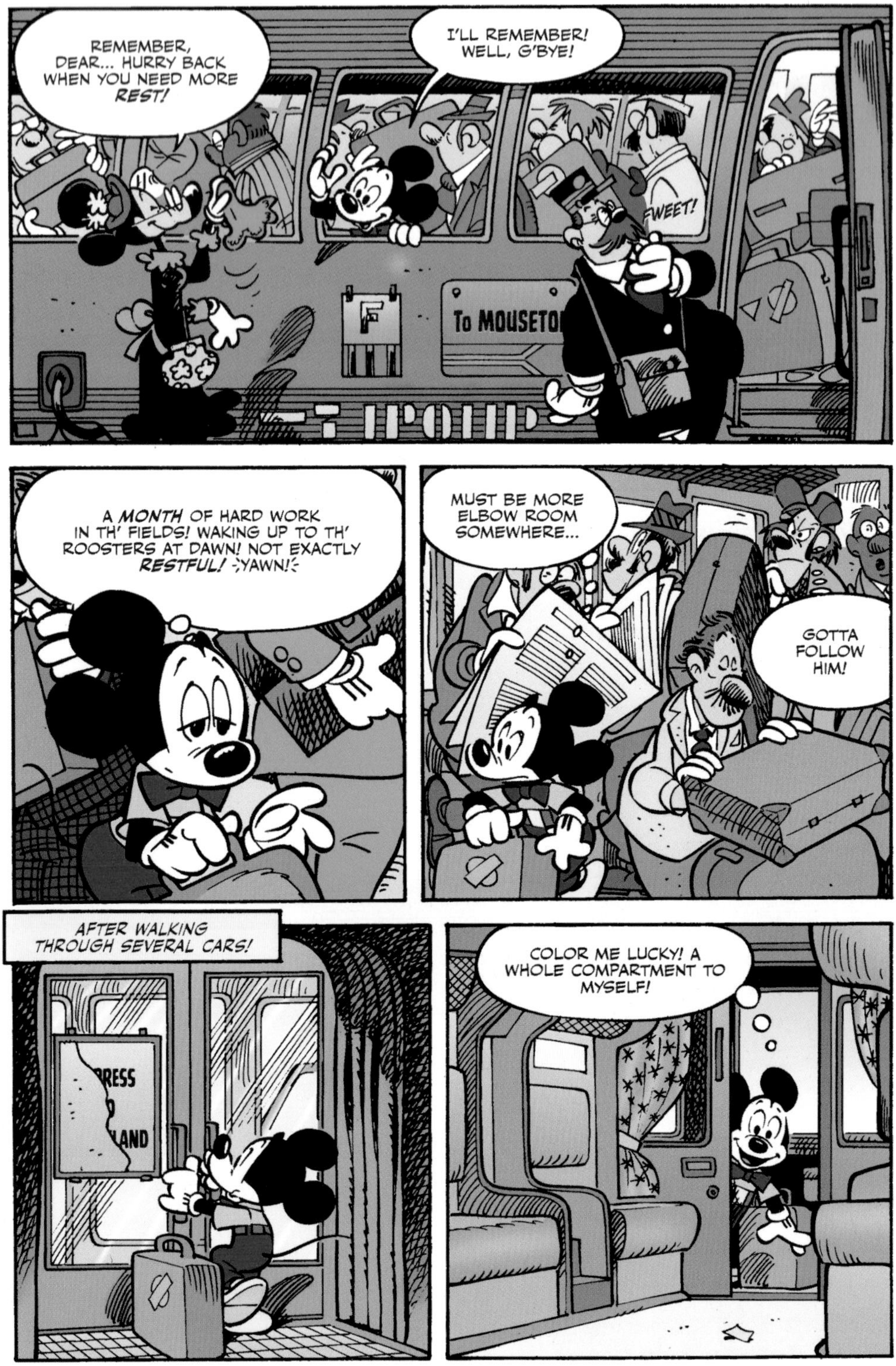
REMEMBER, DEAR... HURRY BACK WHEN YOU NEED MORE REST!
I'LL REMEMBER! WELL, G'BYE!
FWEET!
To MOUSETO
A MONTH OF HARD WORK IN TH' FIELDS! WAKING UP TO TH' ROOSTERS AT DAWN! NOT EXACTLY RESTFUL! YAWN!
MUST BE MORE ELBOW ROOM SOMEWHERE...
GOTTA FOLLOW HIM!
AFTER WALKING THROUGH SEVERAL CARS!
COLOR ME LUCKY! A WHOLE COMPARTMENT TO MYSELF!

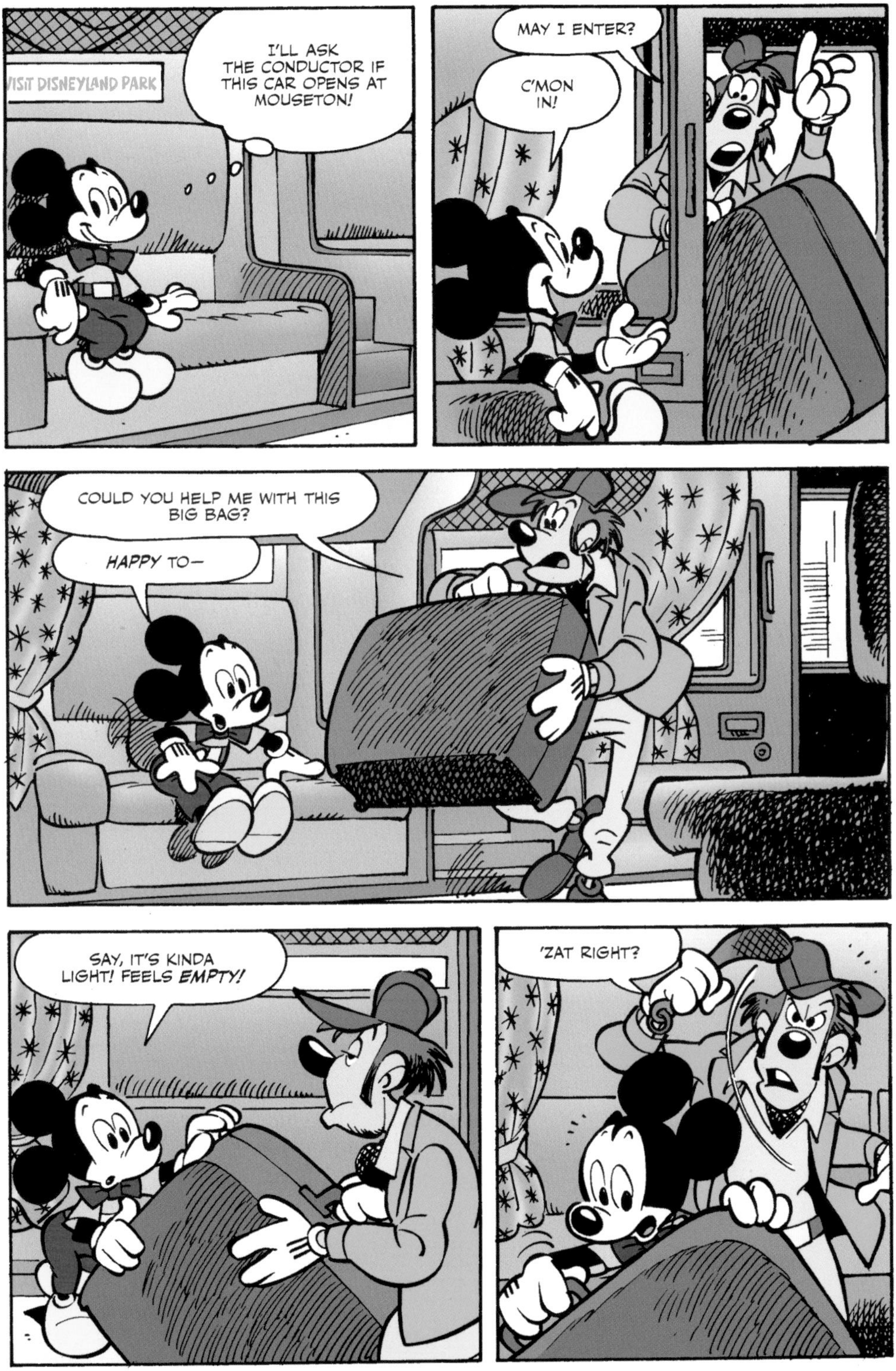
VISIT DISNEYLAND PARK
I'LL ASK THE CONDUCTOR IF THIS CAR OPENS AT MOUSETON!
MAY I ENTER?
C'MON IN!
COULD YOU HELP ME WITH THIS BIG BAG?
HAPPY TO—
SAY, IT'S KINDA LIGHT! FEELS EMPTY!
'ZAT RIGHT?

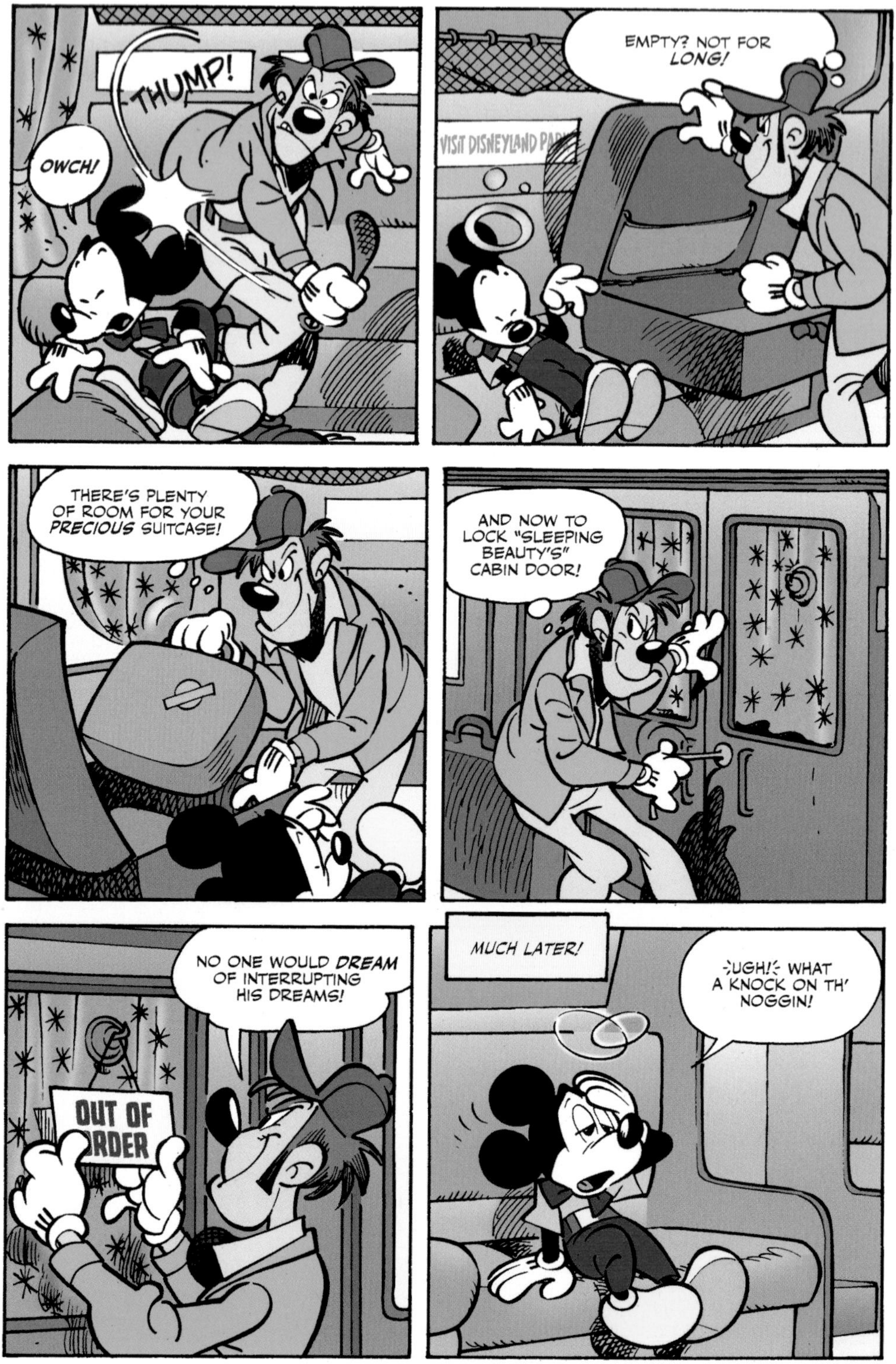
THUMP!
OWCH!
EMPTY? NOT FOR LONG!
VISIT DISNEYLAND PARK
THERE'S PLENTY OF ROOM FOR YOUR PRECIOUS SUITCASE!
AND NOW TO LOCK "SLEEPING BEAUTY'S" CABIN DOOR!
NO ONE WOULD DREAM OF INTERRUPTING HIS DREAMS!
OUT OF ORDER
MUCH LATER!
UGH! WHAT A KNOCK ON TH' NOGGIN!

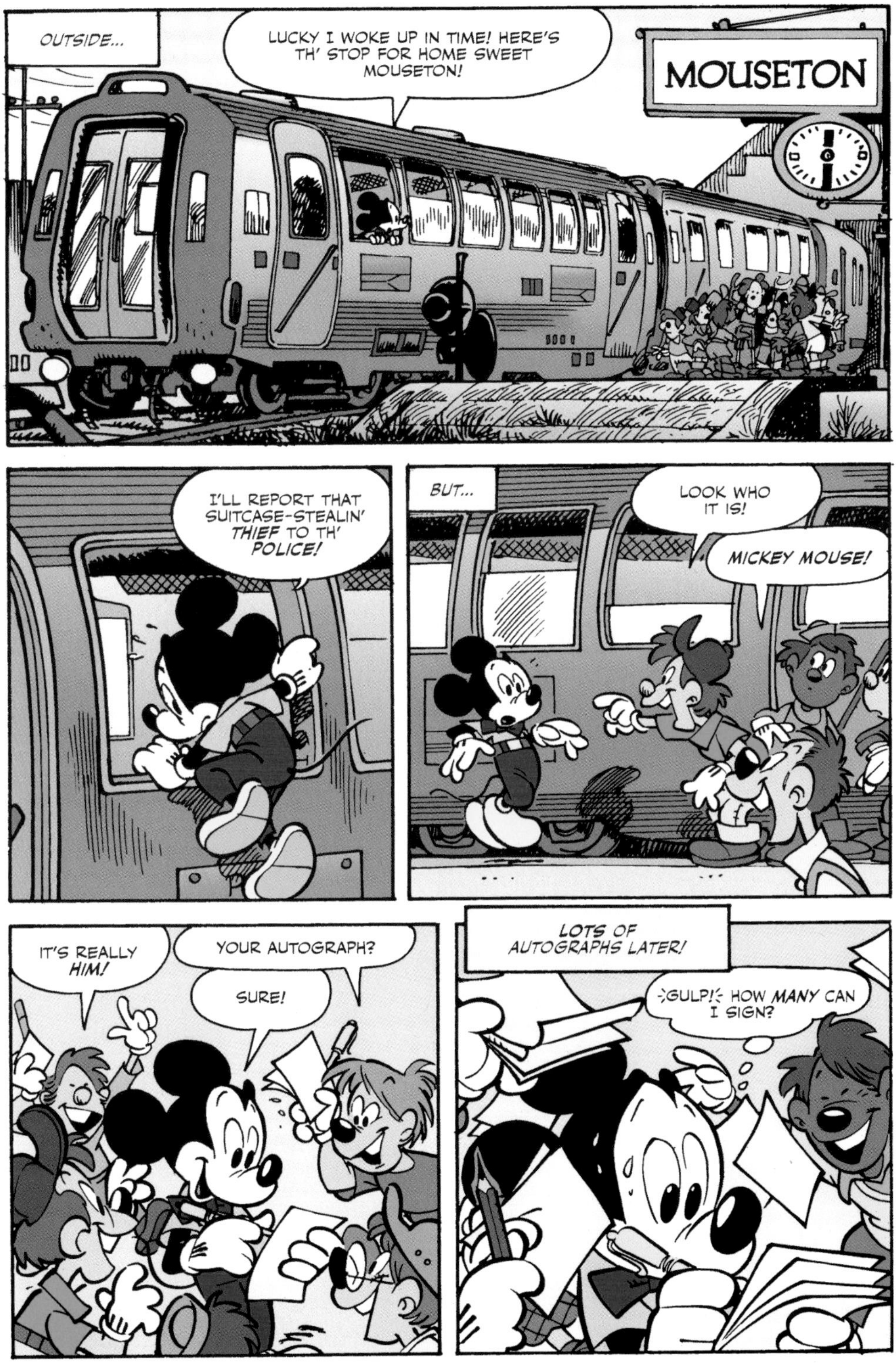
OUTSIDE...
LUCKY I WOKE UP IN TIME! HERE'S TH' STOP FOR HOME SWEET MOUSETON!
MOUSETON
I'LL REPORT THAT SUITCASE-STEALIN' THIEF TO TH' POLICE!
BUT...
LOOK WHO IT IS!
MICKEY MOUSE!
IT'S REALLY HIM!
YOUR AUTOGRAPH?
SURE!
LOTS OF AUTOGRAPHS LATER!
GULP! HOW MANY CAN I SIGN?

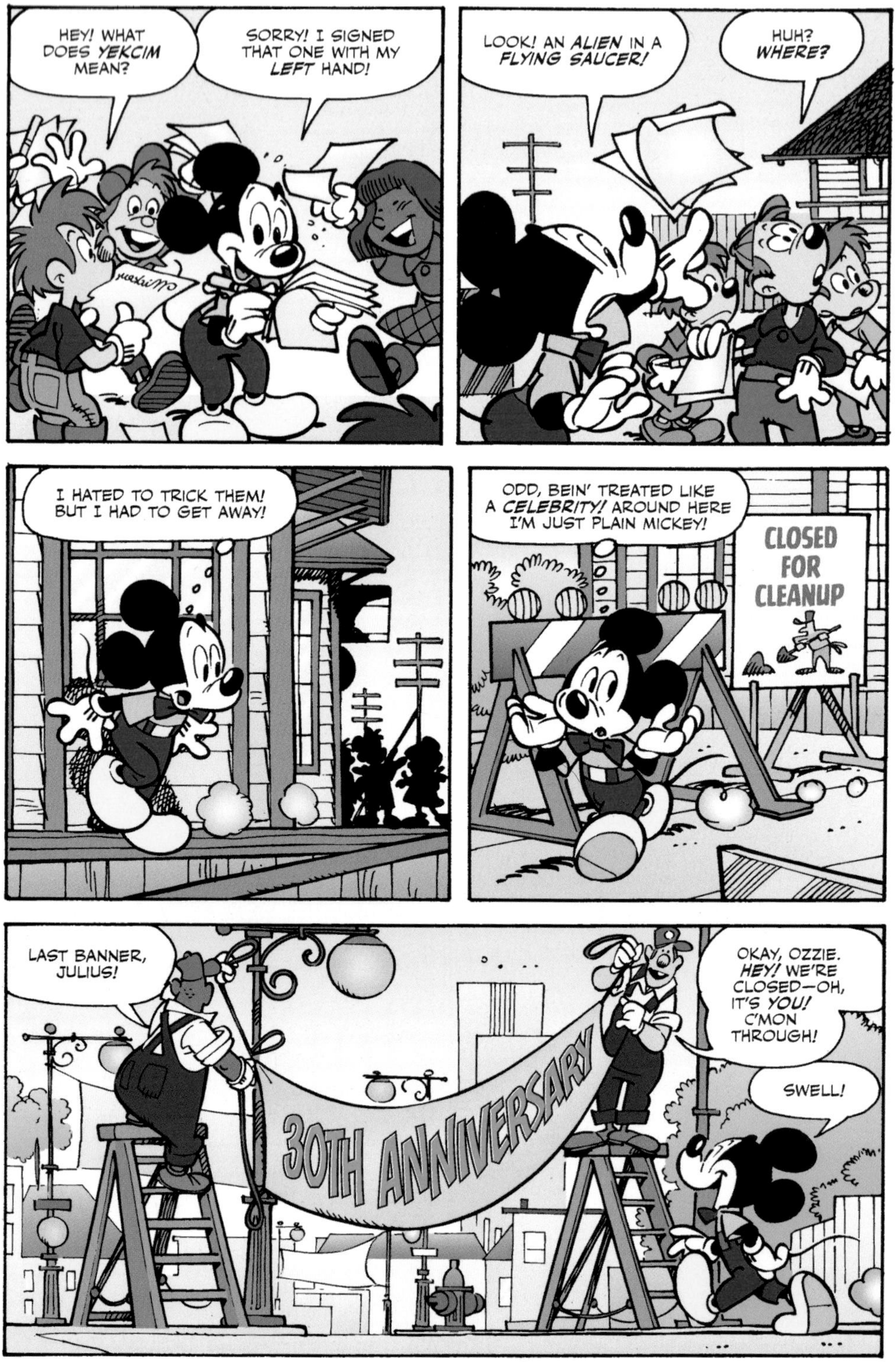
HEY! WHAT DOES YEKCIM MEAN?
SORRY! I SIGNED THAT ONE WITH MY LEFT HAND!
LOOK! AN ALIEN IN A FLYING SAUCER!
HUH? WHERE?
I HATED TO TRICK THEM! BUT I HAD TO GET AWAY!
ODD, BEIN' TREATED LIKE A CELEBRITY! AROUND HERE I'M JUST PLAIN MICKEY!
CLOSED FOR CLEANUP
LAST BANNER, JULIUS!
OKAY, OZZIE. HEY! WE'RE CLOSED—OH, IT'S YOU! C'MON THROUGH!
SWELL!
30TH ANNIVERSARY

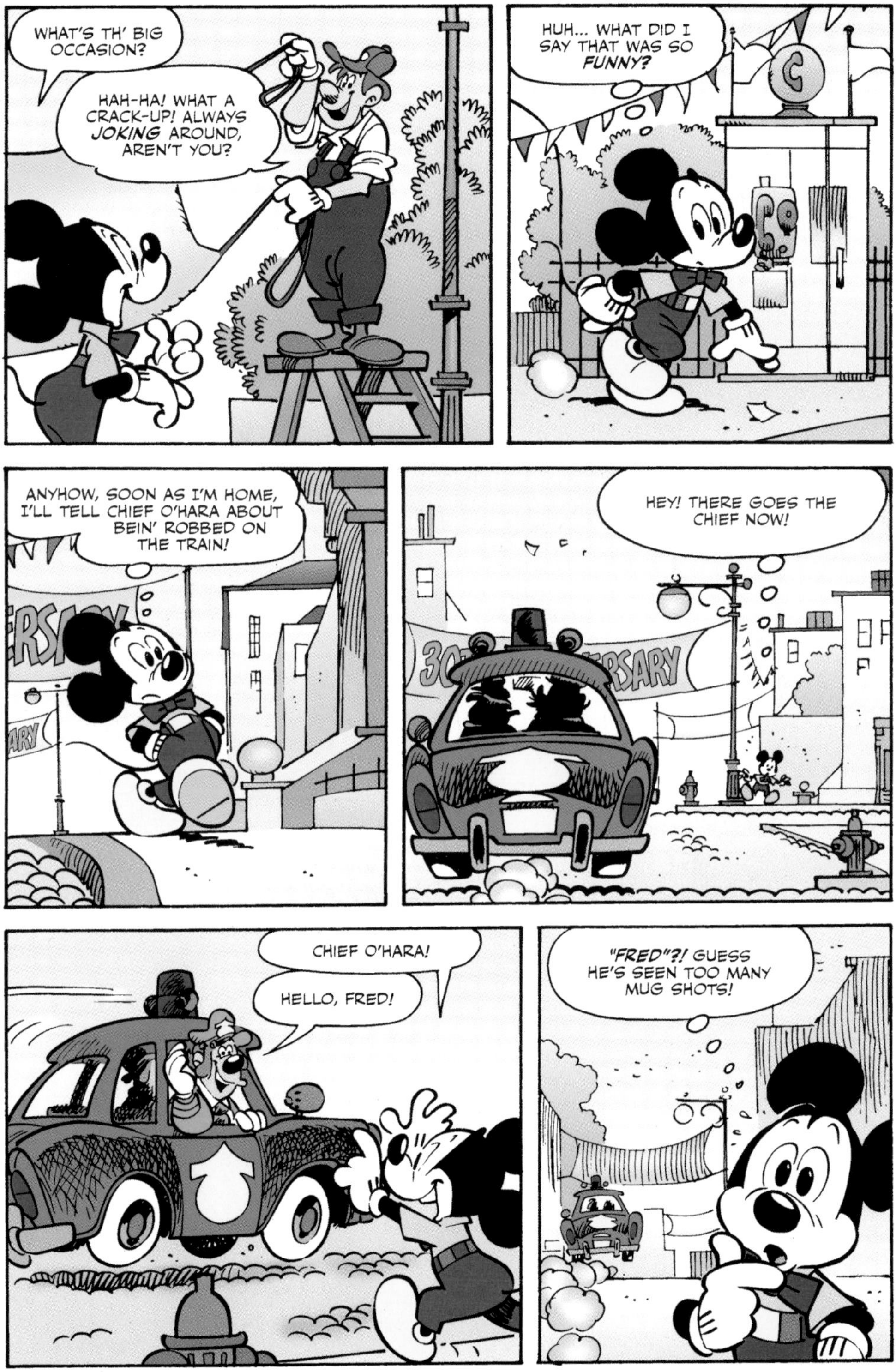
WHAT'S TH' BIG OCCASION?
HAH-HA! WHAT A CRACK-UP! ALWAYS *JOKING* AROUND, AREN'T YOU?
HUH... WHAT DID I SAY THAT WAS SO *FUNNY?*
ANYHOW, SOON AS I'M HOME, I'LL TELL CHIEF O'HARA ABOUT BEIN' ROBBED ON THE TRAIN!
HEY! THERE GOES THE CHIEF NOW!
CHIEF O'HARA!
HELLO, FRED!
"FRED"?! GUESS HE'S SEEN TOO MANY MUG SHOTS!

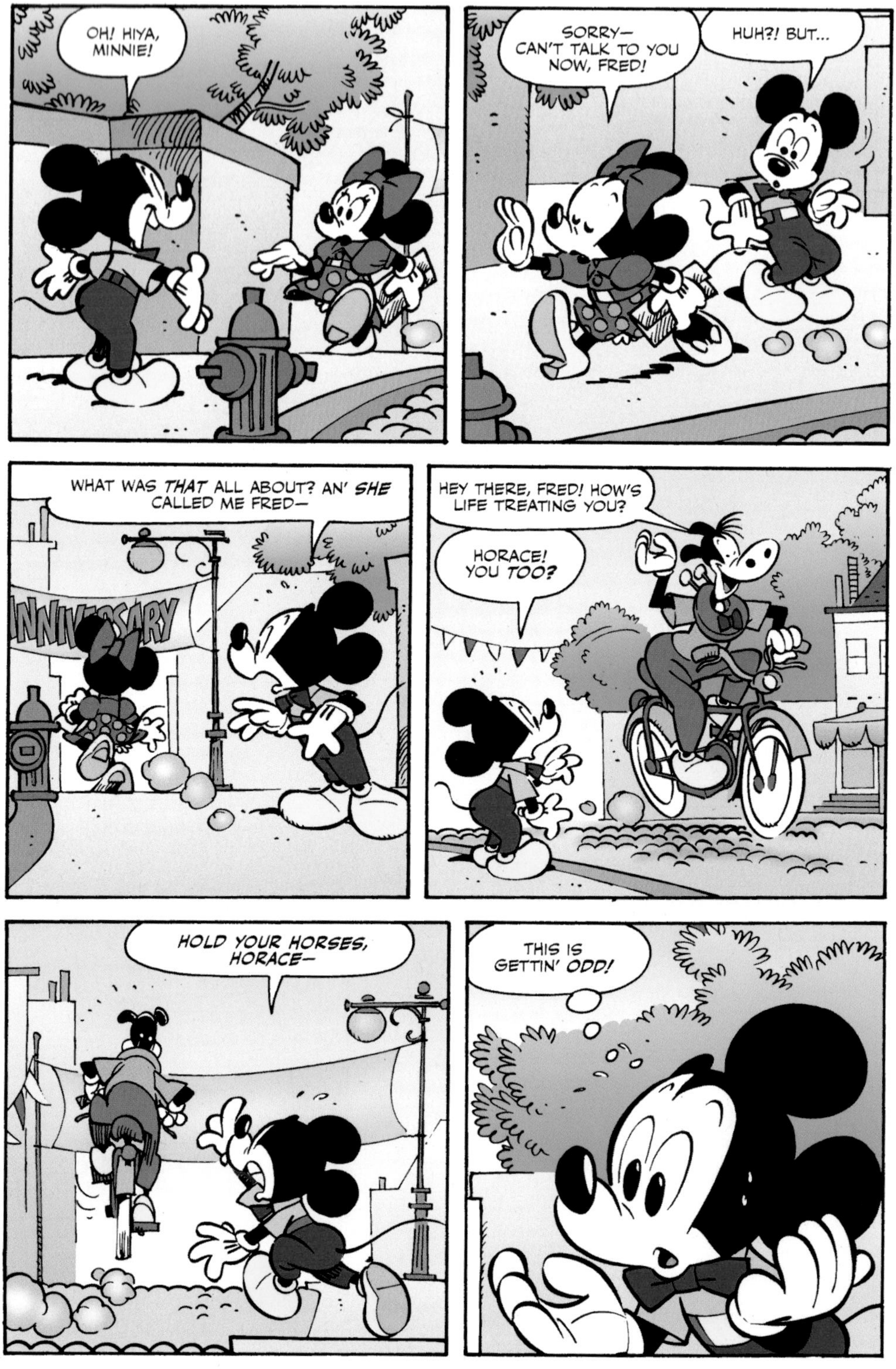
OH! HIYA, MINNIE!
SORRY— CAN'T TALK TO YOU NOW, FRED!
HUH?! BUT...
WHAT WAS *THAT* ALL ABOUT? AN' *SHE* CALLED ME FRED—
NNIVERSARY
HEY THERE, FRED! HOW'S LIFE TREATING YOU?
HORACE! YOU *TOO?*
HOLD YOUR HORSES, HORACE—
THIS IS GETTIN' *ODD!*

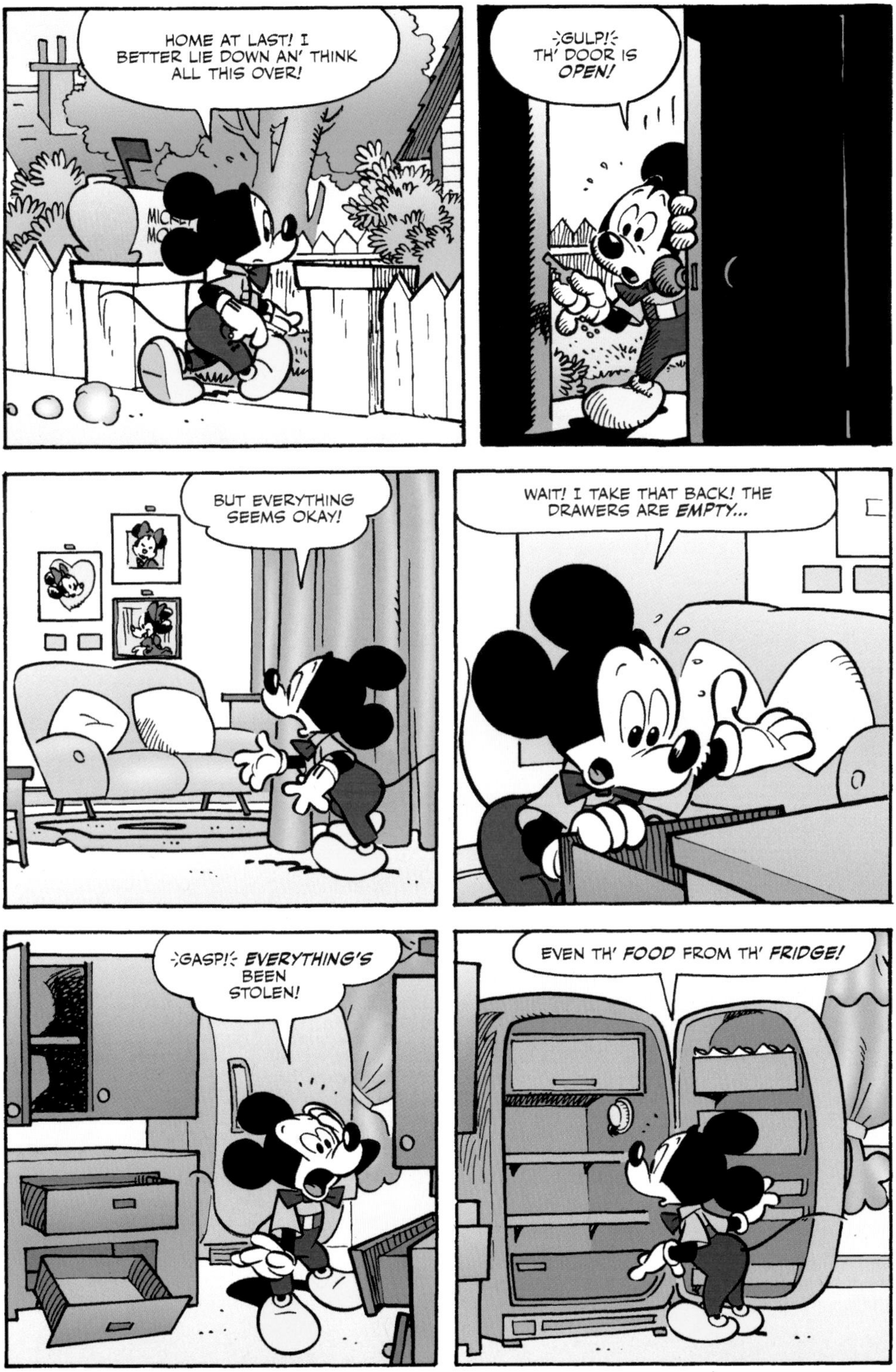
HOME AT LAST! I BETTER LIE DOWN AN' THINK ALL THIS OVER!
MICKEY MOUSE
GULP! TH' DOOR IS OPEN!
BUT EVERYTHING SEEMS OKAY!
WAIT! I TAKE THAT BACK! THE DRAWERS ARE EMPTY...
GASP! EVERYTHING'S BEEN STOLEN!
EVEN TH' FOOD FROM TH' FRIDGE!

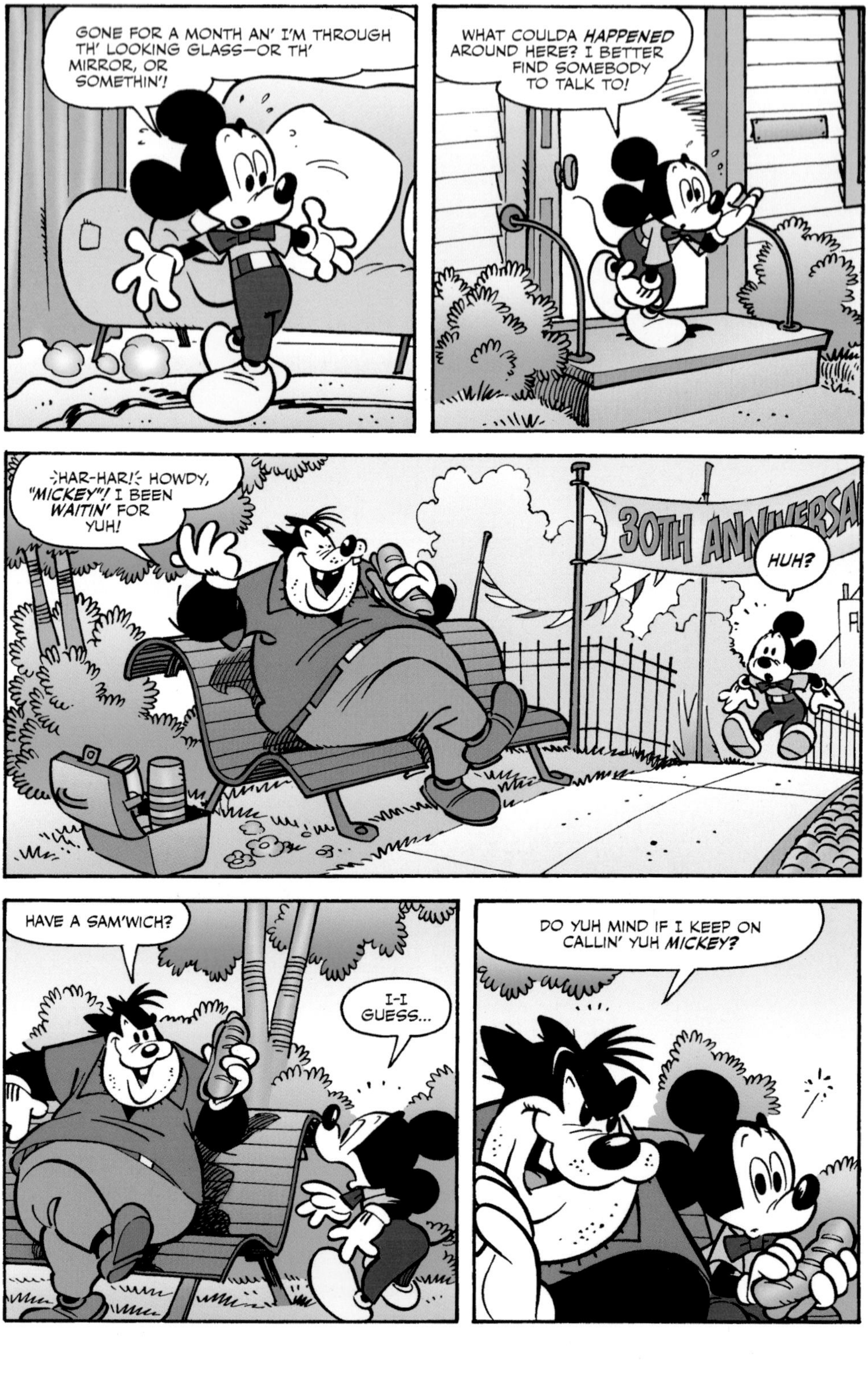
GONE FOR A MONTH AN' I'M THROUGH TH' LOOKING GLASS—OR TH' MIRROR, OR SOMETHIN'!
WHAT COULDA HAPPENED AROUND HERE? I BETTER FIND SOMEBODY TO TALK TO!
HAR-HAR! HOWDY, "MICKEY"! I BEEN WAITIN' FOR YUH!
30TH ANNIVERSA
HUH?
HAVE A SAM'WICH?
I-I GUESS...
DO YUH MIND IF I KEEP ON CALLIN' YUH MICKEY?

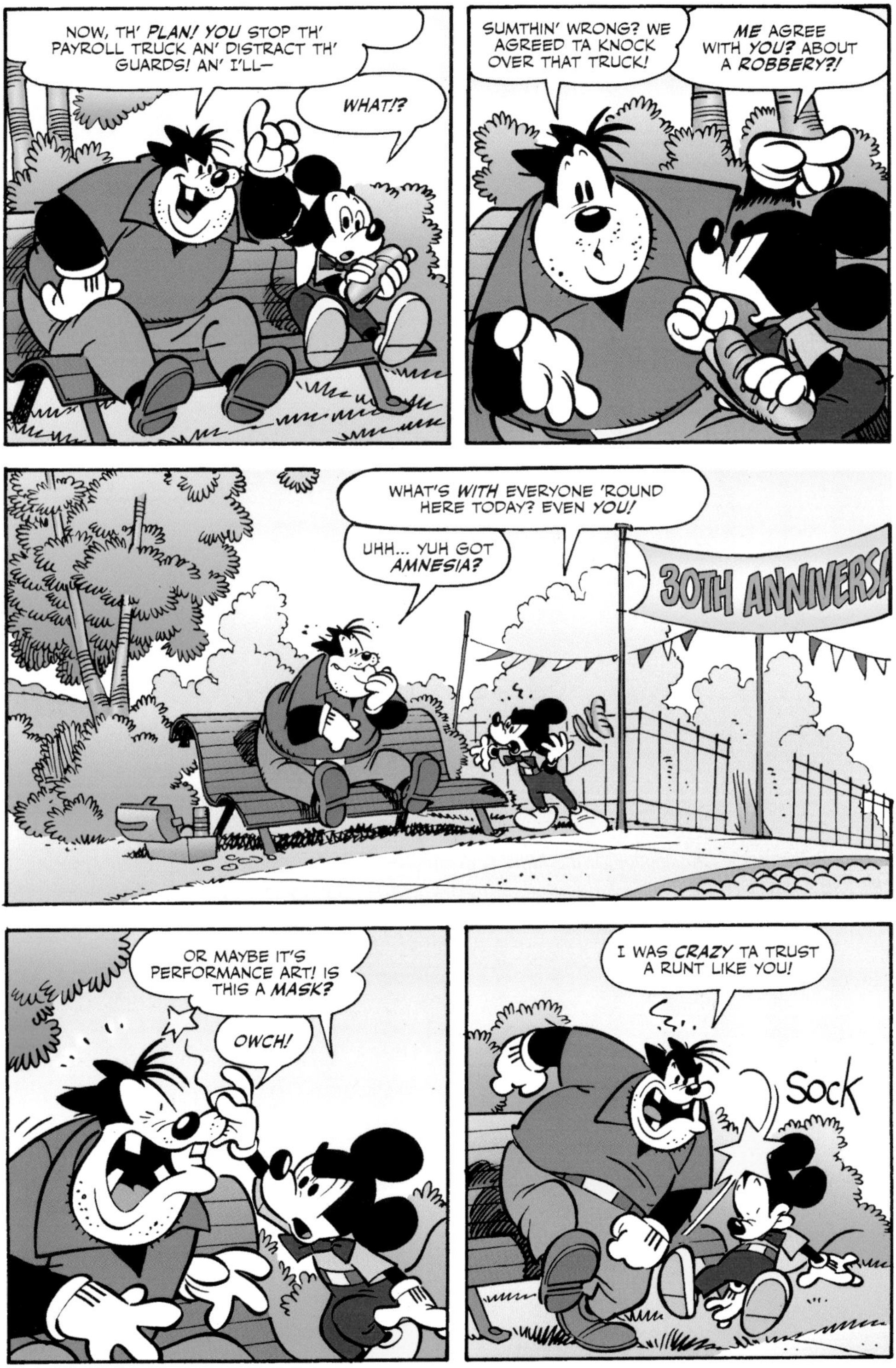

NOW, TH' PLAN! YOU STOP TH' PAYROLL TRUCK AN' DISTRACT TH' GUARDS! AN' I'LL—
WHAT!?
SUMTHIN' WRONG? WE AGREED TA KNOCK OVER THAT TRUCK!
ME AGREE WITH YOU? ABOUT A ROBBERY?!
WHAT'S WITH EVERYONE 'ROUND HERE TODAY? EVEN YOU!
UHH... YUH GOT AMNESIA?
30TH ANNIVERSA
OR MAYBE IT'S PERFORMANCE ART! IS THIS A MASK?
OWCH!
I WAS CRAZY TA TRUST A RUNT LIKE YOU!
SOCK

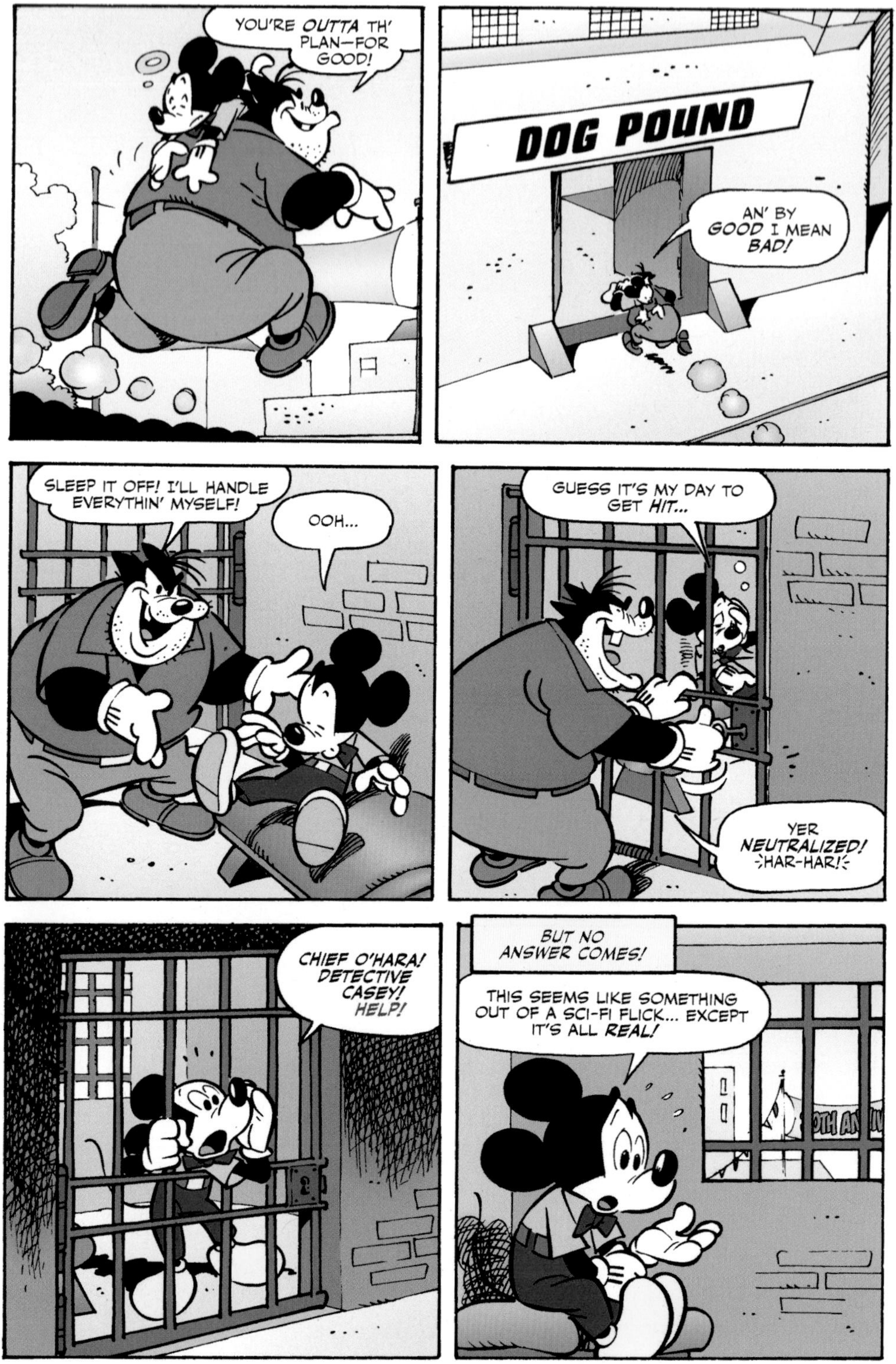
YOU'RE OUTTA TH' PLAN—FOR GOOD!
DOG POUND
AN' BY GOOD I MEAN BAD!
SLEEP IT OFF! I'LL HANDLE EVERYTHIN' MYSELF!
OOH...
GUESS IT'S MY DAY TO GET HIT...
YER NEUTRALIZED! HAR-HAR!
CHIEF O'HARA! DETECTIVE CASEY! HELP!
BUT NO ANSWER COMES!
THIS SEEMS LIKE SOMETHING OUT OF A SCI-FI FLICK... EXCEPT IT'S ALL REAL!

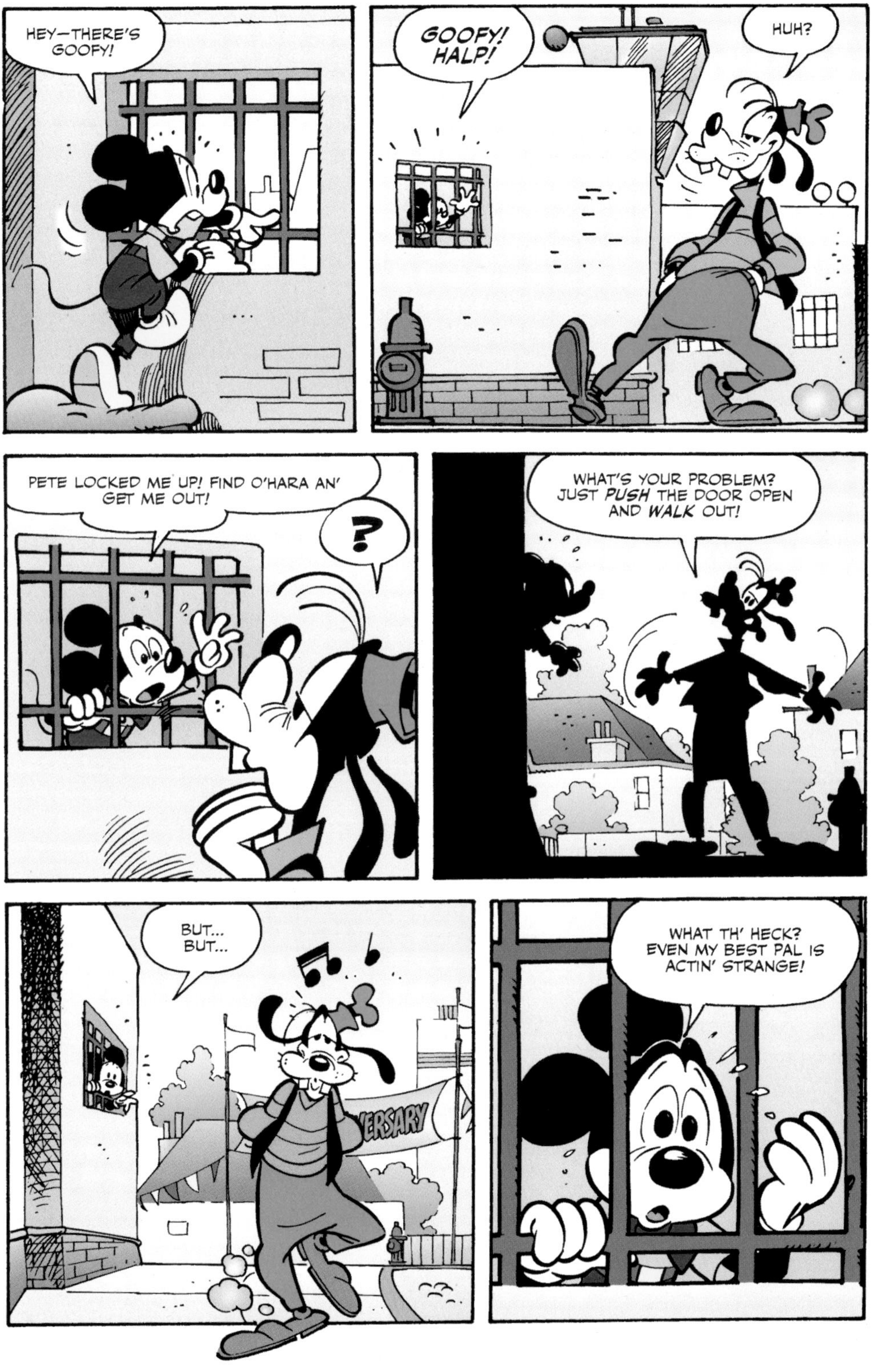
HEY—THERE'S GOOFY!
GOOFY! HALP!
HUH?
PETE LOCKED ME UP! FIND O'HARA AN' GET ME OUT!
?
WHAT'S YOUR PROBLEM? JUST PUSH THE DOOR OPEN AND WALK OUT!
BUT... BUT...
WHAT TH' HECK? EVEN MY BEST PAL IS ACTIN' STRANGE!

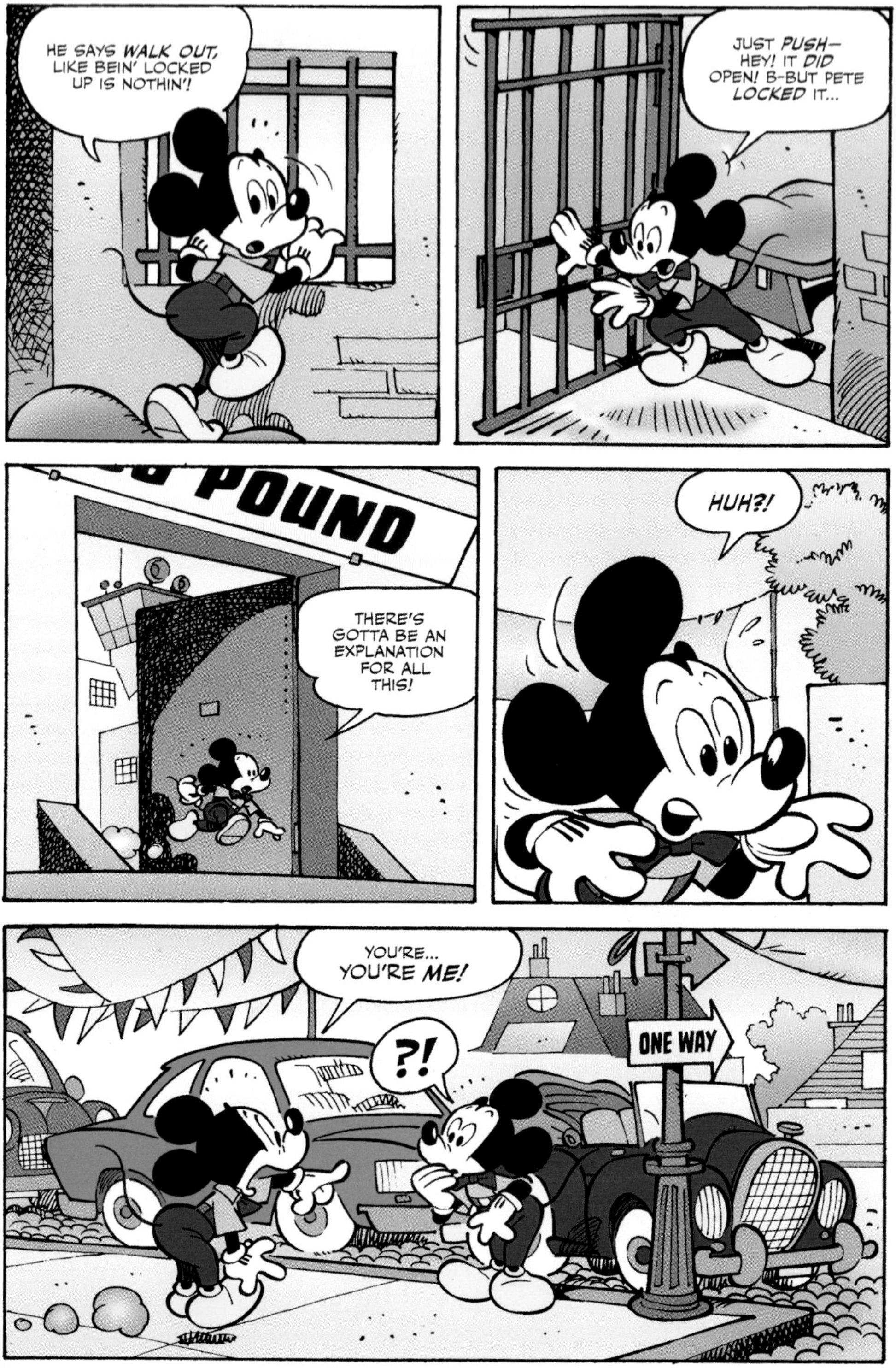
HE SAYS WALK OUT, LIKE BEIN' LOCKED UP IS NOTHIN'!
JUST PUSH— HEY! IT DID OPEN! B-BUT PETE LOCKED IT...
POUND
THERE'S GOTTA BE AN EXPLANATION FOR ALL THIS!
HUH?!
YOU'RE... YOU'RE ME!
?!
ONE WAY

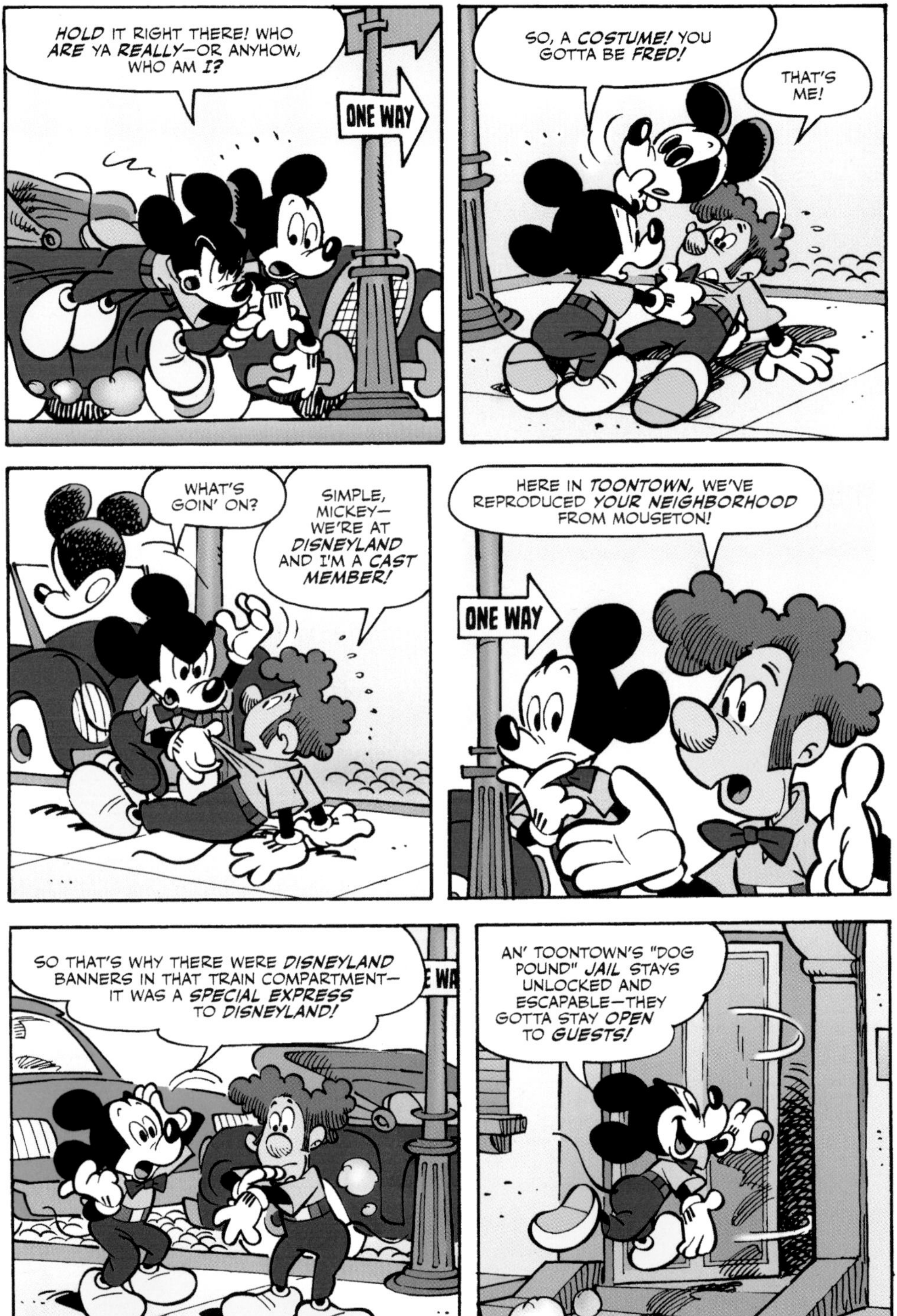
HOLD IT RIGHT THERE! WHO ARE YA REALLY—OR ANYHOW, WHO AM I?
ONE WAY
SO, A COSTUME! YOU GOTTA BE FRED!
THAT'S ME!
WHAT'S GOIN' ON?
SIMPLE, MICKEY—WE'RE AT DISNEYLAND AND I'M A CAST MEMBER!
HERE IN TOONTOWN, WE'VE REPRODUCED YOUR NEIGHBORHOOD FROM MOUSETON!
ONE WAY
SO THAT'S WHY THERE WERE DISNEYLAND BANNERS IN THAT TRAIN COMPARTMENT—IT WAS A SPECIAL EXPRESS TO DISNEYLAND!
AN' TOONTOWN'S "DOG POUND" JAIL STAYS UNLOCKED AND ESCAPABLE—THEY GOTTA STAY OPEN TO GUESTS!

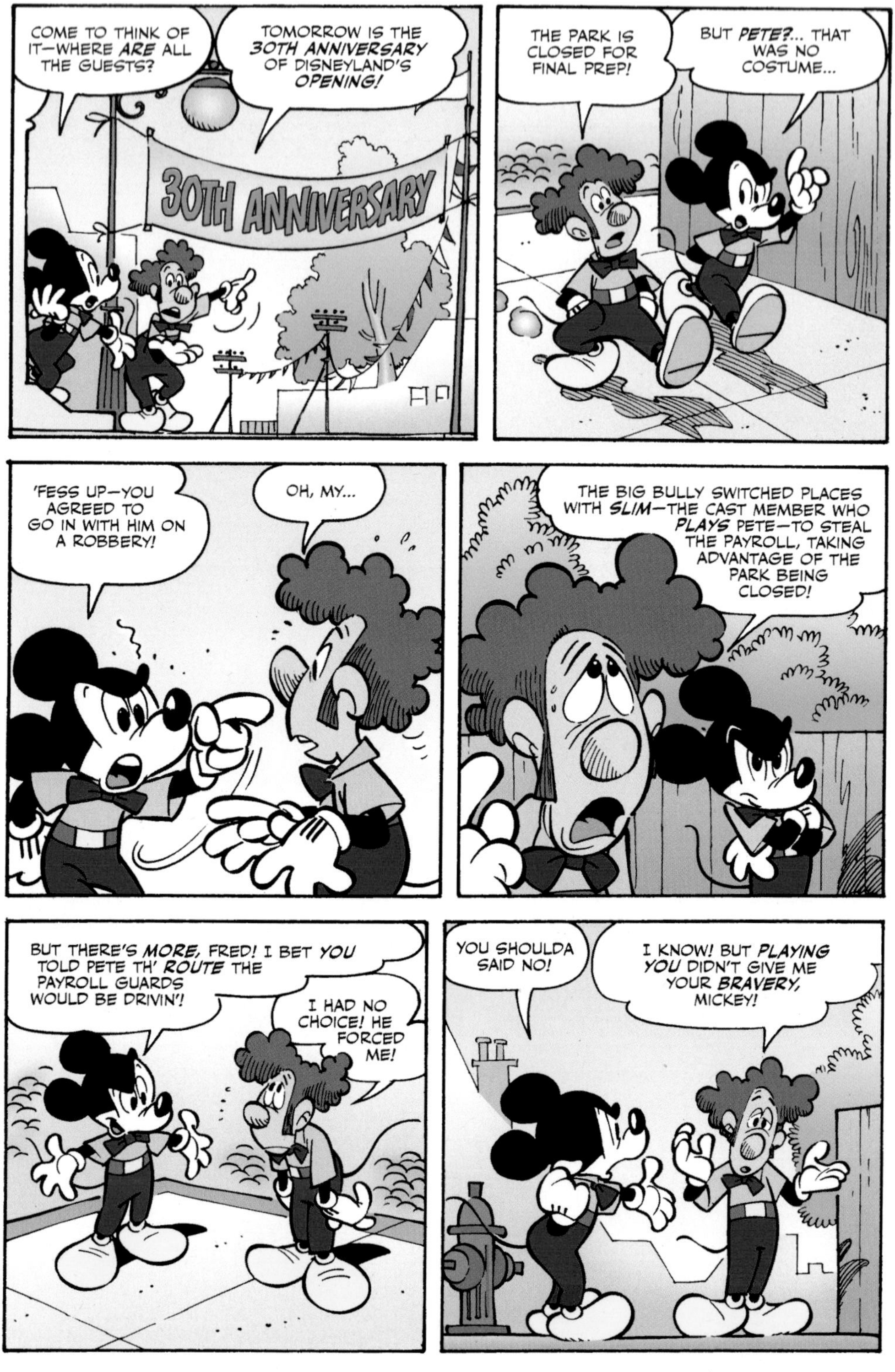
COME TO THINK OF IT—WHERE *ARE* ALL THE GUESTS?
TOMORROW IS THE *30TH ANNIVERSARY* OF DISNEYLAND'S *OPENING!*
30TH ANNIVERSARY
THE PARK IS CLOSED FOR FINAL PREP!
BUT *PETE?*... THAT WAS NO COSTUME...
'FESS UP—YOU AGREED TO GO IN WITH HIM ON A ROBBERY!
OH, MY...
THE BIG BULLY SWITCHED PLACES WITH *SLIM*—THE CAST MEMBER WHO *PLAYS* PETE—TO STEAL THE PAYROLL, TAKING ADVANTAGE OF THE PARK BEING CLOSED!
BUT THERE'S *MORE,* FRED! I BET *YOU* TOLD PETE TH' *ROUTE* THE PAYROLL GUARDS WOULD BE DRIVIN'!
I HAD NO CHOICE! HE FORCED ME!
YOU SHOULDA SAID NO!
I KNOW! BUT *PLAYING YOU* DIDN'T GIVE ME YOUR *BRAVERY,* MICKEY!

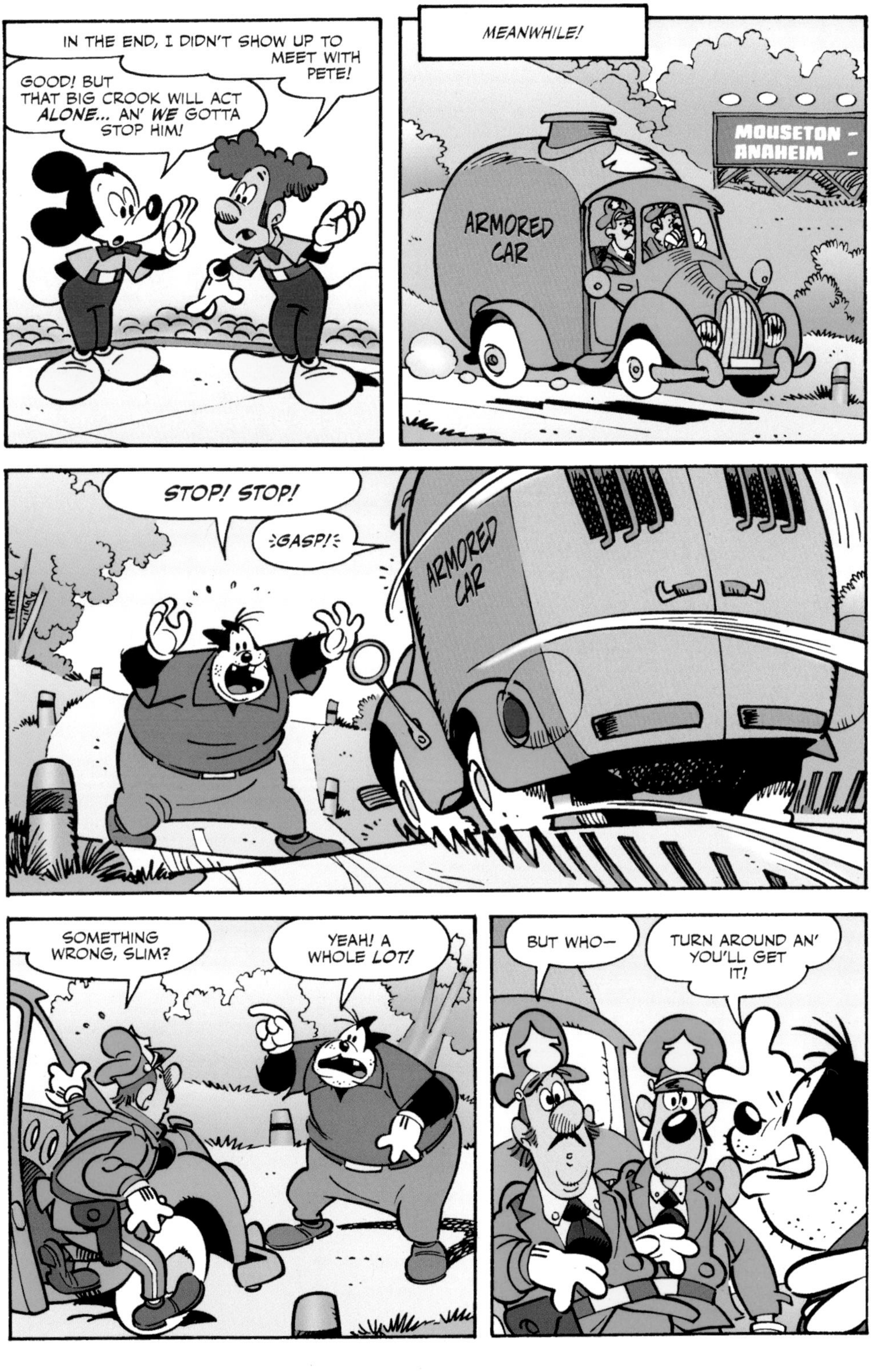
IN THE END, I DIDN'T SHOW UP TO MEET WITH PETE!
GOOD! BUT THAT BIG CROOK WILL ACT *ALONE*... AN' *WE* GOTTA STOP HIM!
MEANWHILE!
MOUSETON -
ANAHEIM -
ARMORED CAR
STOP! STOP!
GASP!
ARMORED CAR
SOMETHING WRONG, SLIM?
YEAH! A WHOLE *LOT!*
BUT WHO—
TURN AROUND AN' YOU'LL GET IT!

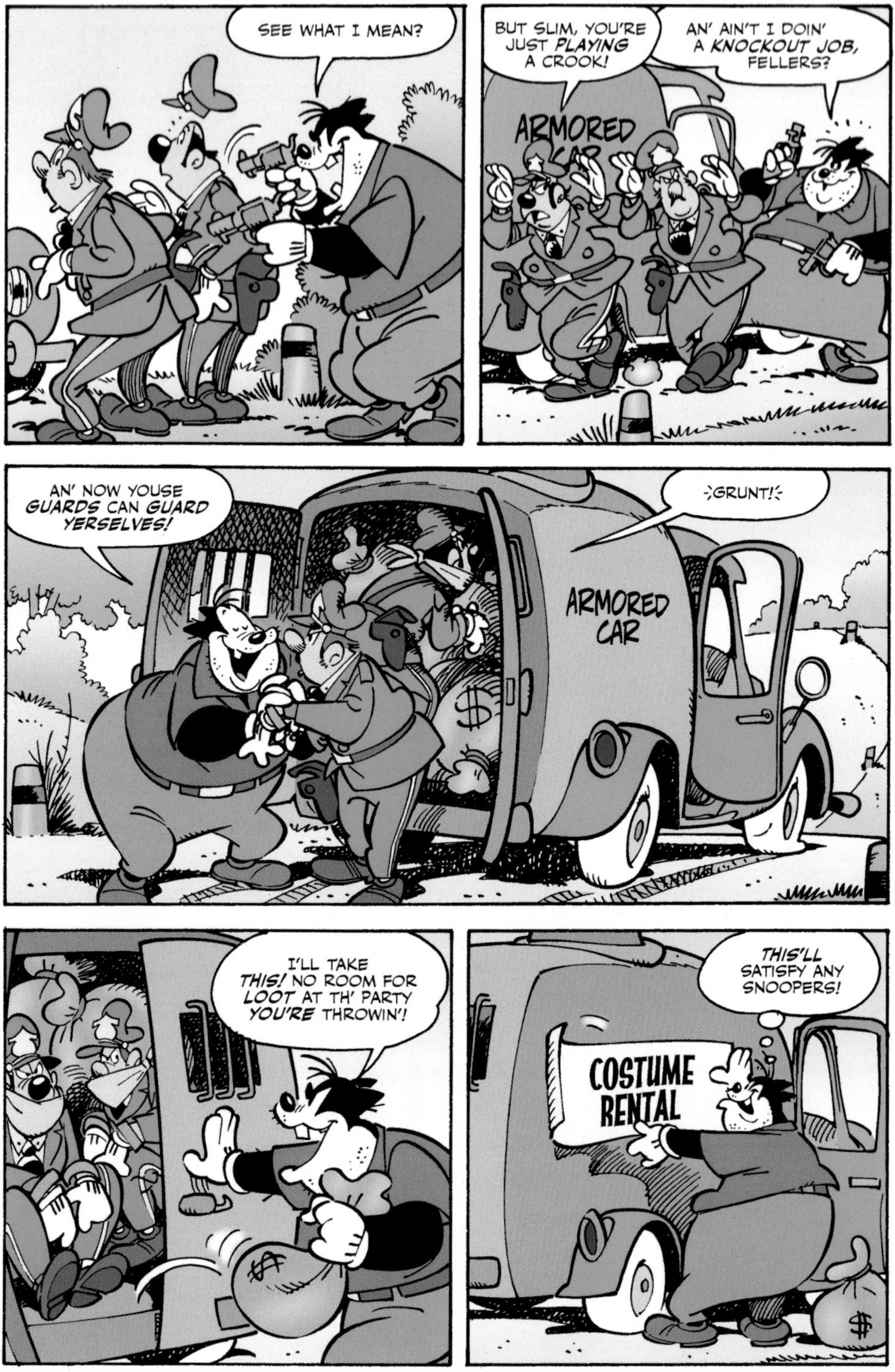
SEE WHAT I MEAN?
BUT SLIM, YOU'RE JUST PLAYING A CROOK!
AN' AIN'T I DOIN' A KNOCKOUT JOB, FELLERS?
ARMORED CAR
AN' NOW YOUSE GUARDS CAN GUARD YERSELVES!
GRUNT!
ARMORED CAR
I'LL TAKE THIS! NO ROOM FOR LOOT AT TH' PARTY YOU'RE THROWIN'!
THIS'LL SATISFY ANY SNOOPERS!
COSTUME RENTAL

NOW "SLIM" WILL SCRAM! ÷HAR! HAR!÷

OMIGOSH! PETE HAS *ALREADY* GRABBED TH' PAYROLL!

ISN'T THERE SOME KIND O' *SHORTCUT?*

HERE! I CAN DRAW A MAP OF DISNEYLAND!

AND FRED SKETCHES QUICKLY A SIMPLE BUT CLEAR PLAN...

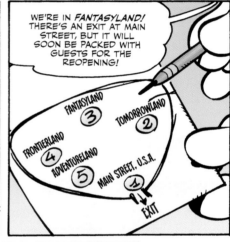

WE'RE IN *FANTASYLAND!* THERE'S AN EXIT AT MAIN STREET, BUT IT WILL SOON BE PACKED WITH GUESTS FOR THE REOPENING!

FANTASYLAND 3
TOMORROWLAND 2
FRONTIERLAND 4
ADVENTURELAND 5
MAIN STREET, U.S.A. 1
EXIT

SO PETE IS HEADING FOR THE TOMORROWLAND MONORAIL!

SWELL! WE'LL MAKE SURE WE'RE THERE!

MEANWHILE, IN SNOW WHITE'S FOREST!

I'M *HUNGRY!* EVEN THOUGH IT'S NOT IN THE *SCRIPT...*

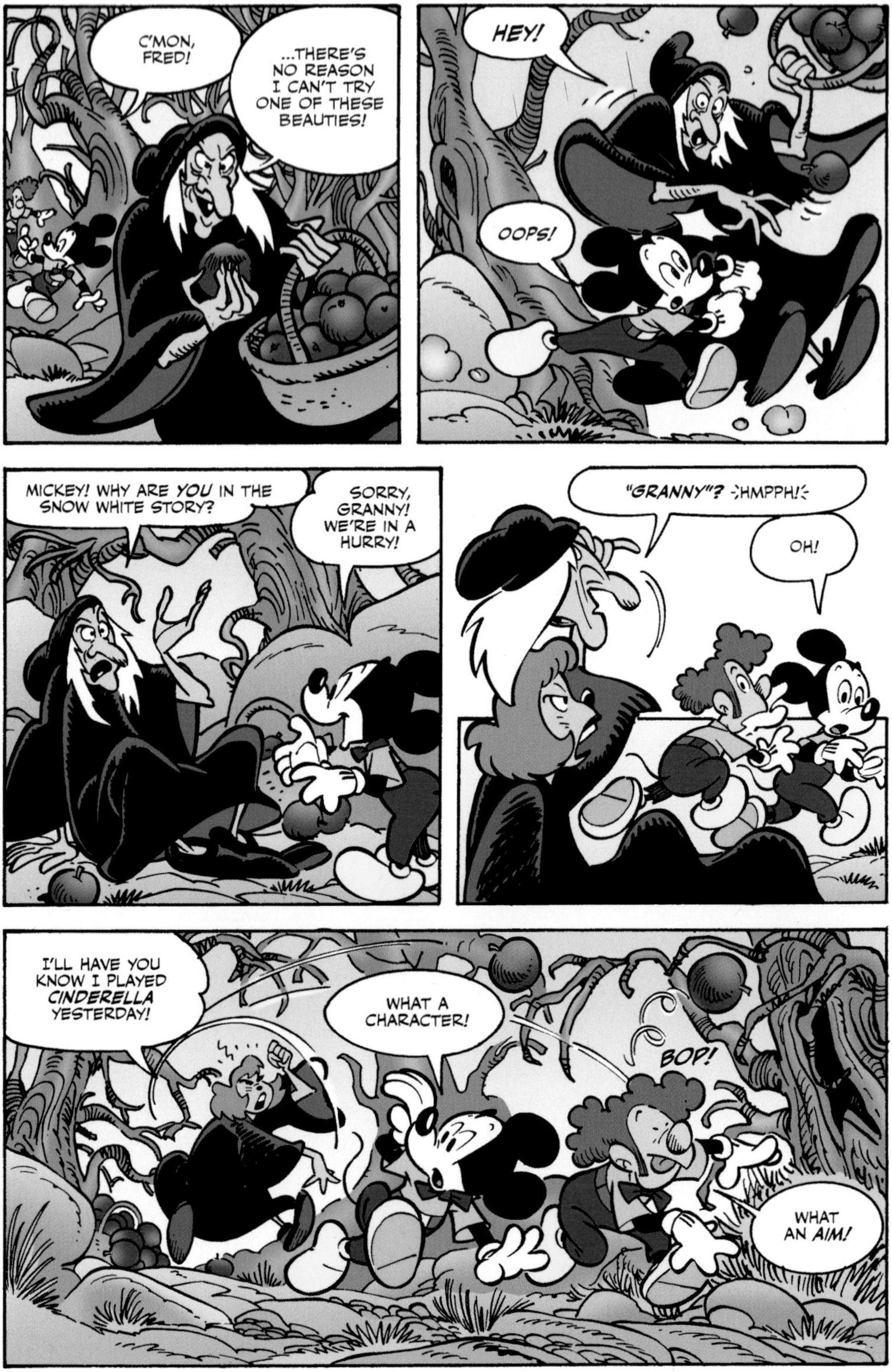
C'MON, FRED!
...THERE'S NO REASON I CAN'T TRY ONE OF THESE BEAUTIES!
HEY!
OOPS!
MICKEY! WHY ARE *YOU* IN THE SNOW WHITE STORY?
SORRY, GRANNY! WE'RE IN A HURRY!
"GRANNY"? HMPPH!
OH!
I'LL HAVE YOU KNOW I PLAYED *CINDERELLA* YESTERDAY!
WHAT A CHARACTER!
BOP!
WHAT AN *AIM!*

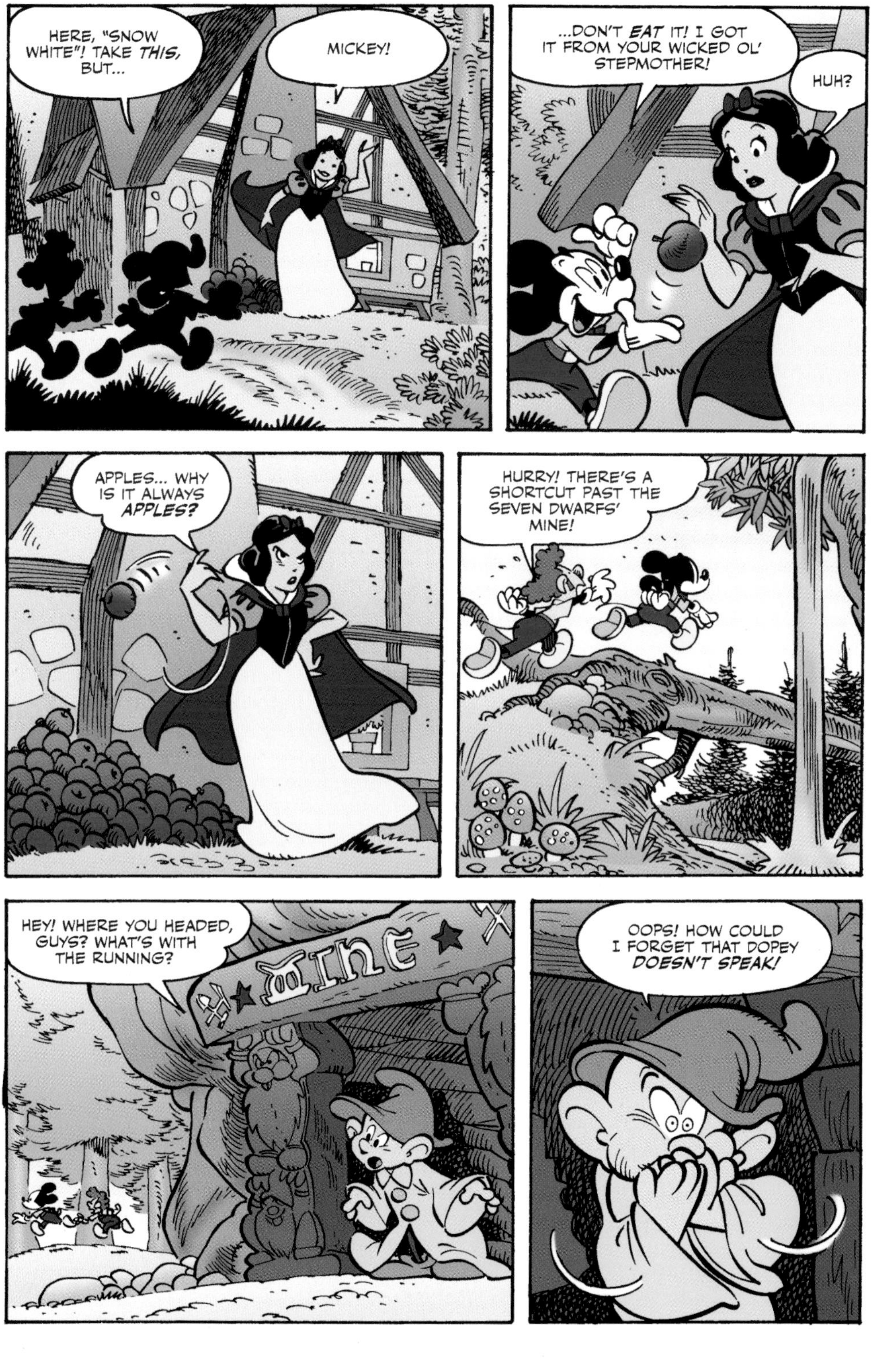
HERE, "SNOW WHITE"! TAKE THIS, BUT...
MICKEY!
...DON'T EAT IT! I GOT IT FROM YOUR WICKED OL' STEPMOTHER!
HUH?
APPLES... WHY IS IT ALWAYS APPLES?
HURRY! THERE'S A SHORTCUT PAST THE SEVEN DWARFS' MINE!
HEY! WHERE YOU HEADED, GUYS? WHAT'S WITH THE RUNNING?
MINE
OOPS! HOW COULD I FORGET THAT DOPEY DOESN'T SPEAK!

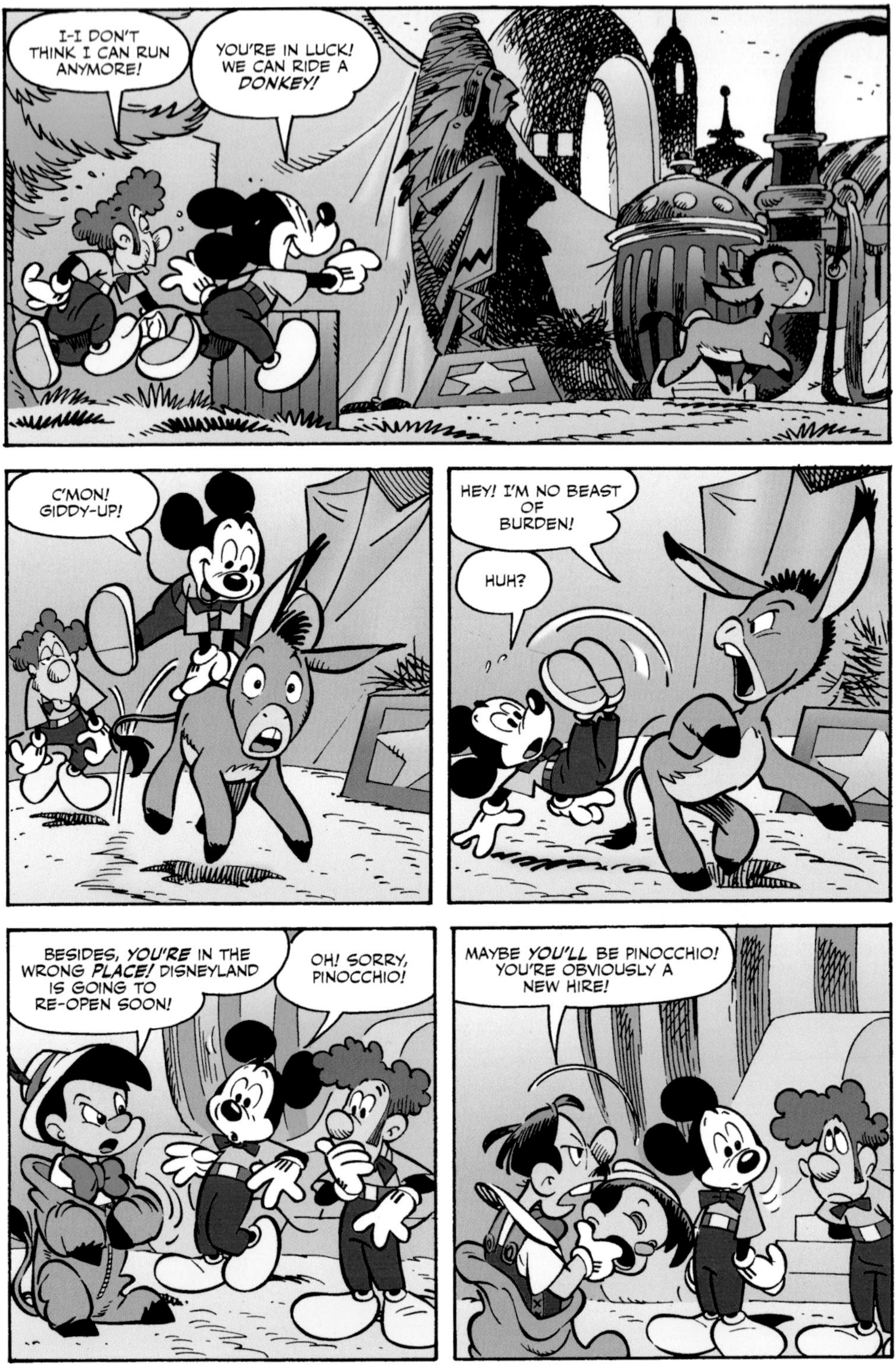
I-I DON'T THINK I CAN RUN ANYMORE!
YOU'RE IN LUCK! WE CAN RIDE A DONKEY!
C'MON! GIDDY-UP!
HEY! I'M NO BEAST OF BURDEN!
HUH?
BESIDES, YOU'RE IN THE WRONG PLACE! DISNEYLAND IS GOING TO RE-OPEN SOON!
OH! SORRY, PINOCCHIO!
MAYBE YOU'LL BE PINOCCHIO! YOU'RE OBVIOUSLY A NEW HIRE!

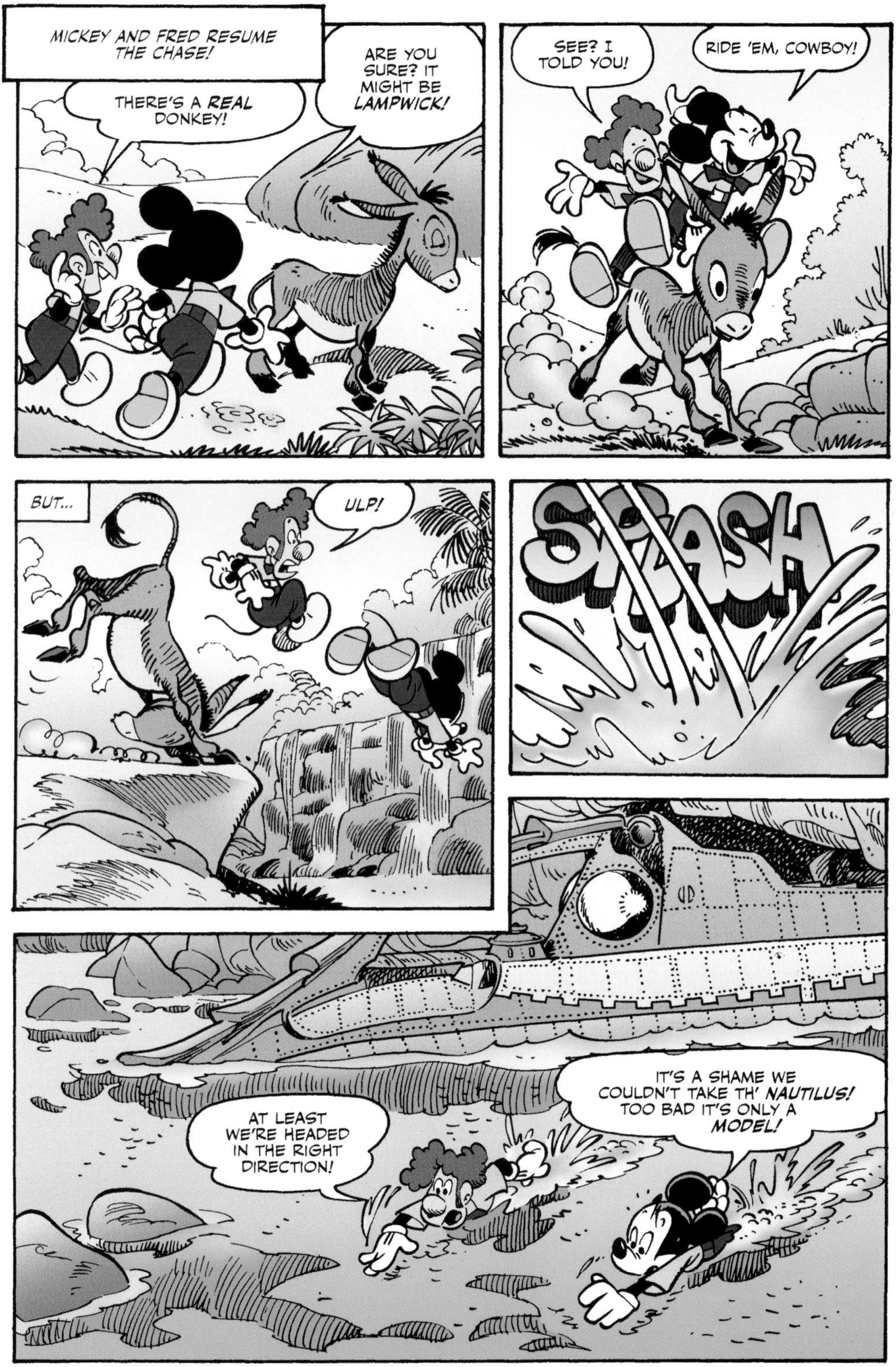
MICKEY AND FRED RESUME THE CHASE!
THERE'S A REAL DONKEY!
ARE YOU SURE? IT MIGHT BE LAMPWICK!
SEE? I TOLD YOU!
RIDE 'EM, COWBOY!
BUT...
ULP!
SPLASH
AT LEAST WE'RE HEADED IN THE RIGHT DIRECTION!
IT'S A SHAME WE COULDN'T TAKE TH' NAUTILUS! TOO BAD IT'S ONLY A MODEL!

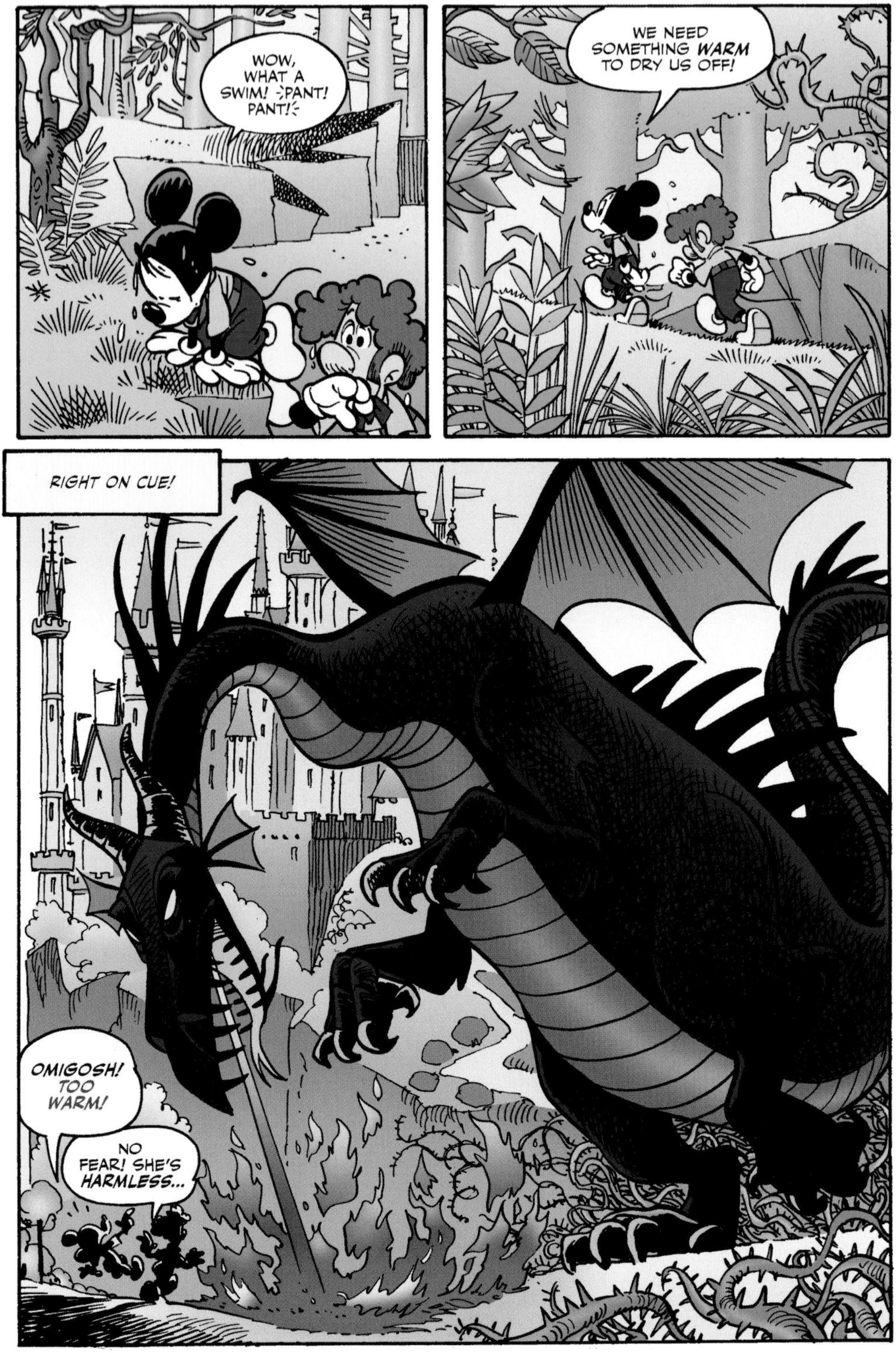

WOW, WHAT A SWIM! PANT! PANT!
WE NEED SOMETHING WARM TO DRY US OFF!
RIGHT ON CUE!
OMIGOSH! TOO WARM!
NO FEAR! SHE'S HARMLESS...

...AND REMOTE CONTROLLED!

˃WHEW!˂

I HEARD YOU TWO DEARS WANTED TO DRY OUT....

WHY, IT'S *SLEEPING BEAUTY!*

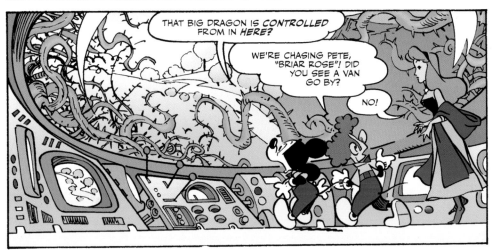

THAT BIG DRAGON IS *CONTROLLED* FROM IN *HERE?*

WE'RE CHASING PETE, "BRIAR ROSE"! DID YOU SEE A VAN GO BY?

NO!

THERE IT IS! WE'RE RIGHT ON TIME!

DISNEYLAND IS TH' HAPPIEST PLACE ON EARTH, ALL RIGHT—I'M PLENTY *HAPPY!*

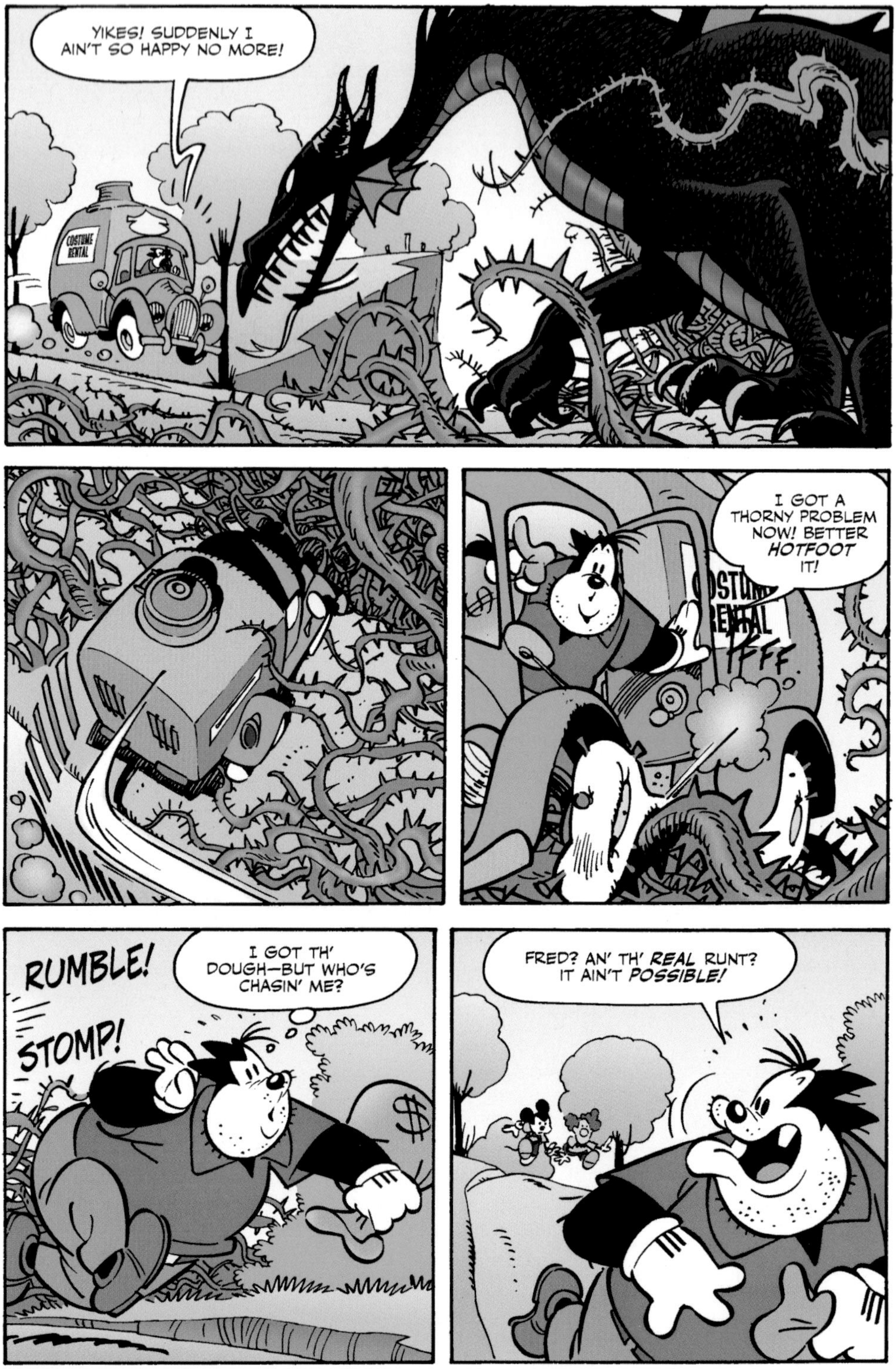
YIKES! SUDDENLY I AIN'T SO HAPPY NO MORE!
COSTUME RENTAL
I GOT A THORNY PROBLEM NOW! BETTER HOTFOOT IT!
COSTUME RENTAL
FFF
RUMBLE!
STOMP!
I GOT TH' DOUGH—BUT WHO'S CHASIN' ME?
FRED? AN' TH' REAL RUNT? IT AIN'T POSSIBLE!

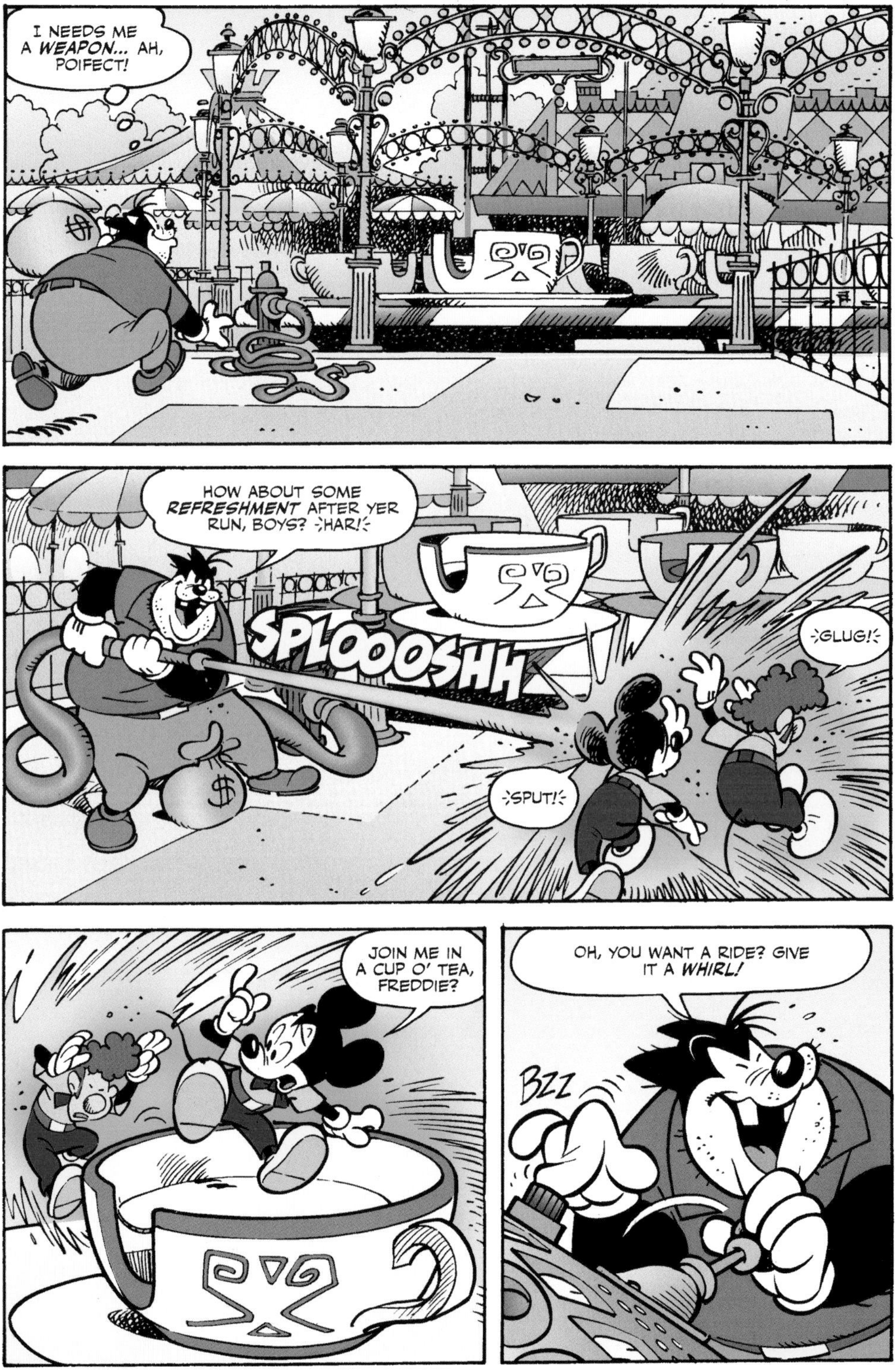
I NEEDS ME A WEAPON... AH, POIFECT!
HOW ABOUT SOME REFRESHMENT AFTER YER RUN, BOYS? HAR!
SPLOOOSHH
GLUG!
SPUT!
JOIN ME IN A CUP O' TEA, FREDDIE?
OH, YOU WANT A RIDE? GIVE IT A WHIRL!
BZZ

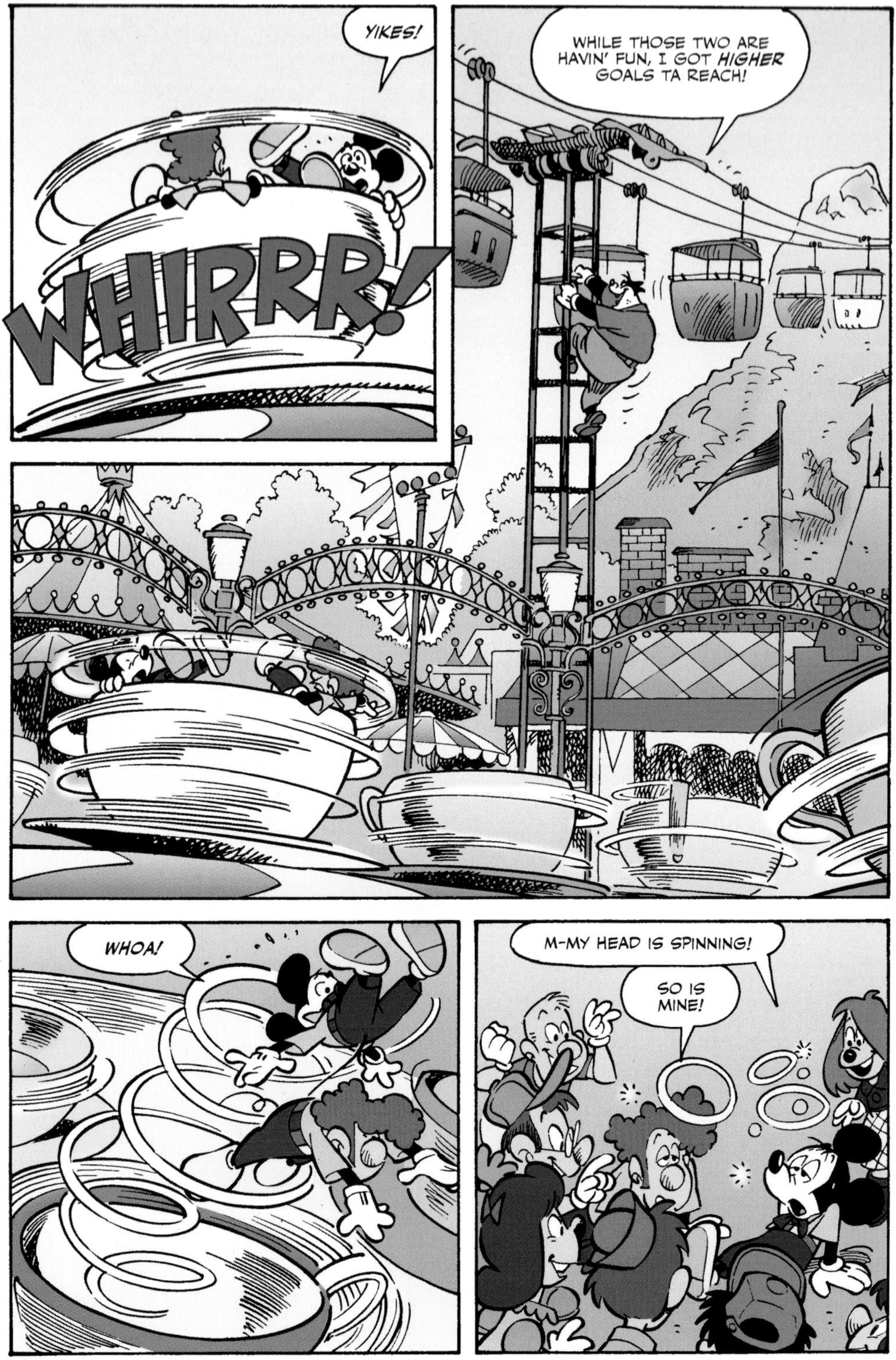
YIKES!
WHIRRR!
WHILE THOSE TWO ARE HAVIN' FUN, I GOT HIGHER GOALS TA REACH!
WHOA!
M-MY HEAD IS SPINNING!
SO IS MINE!

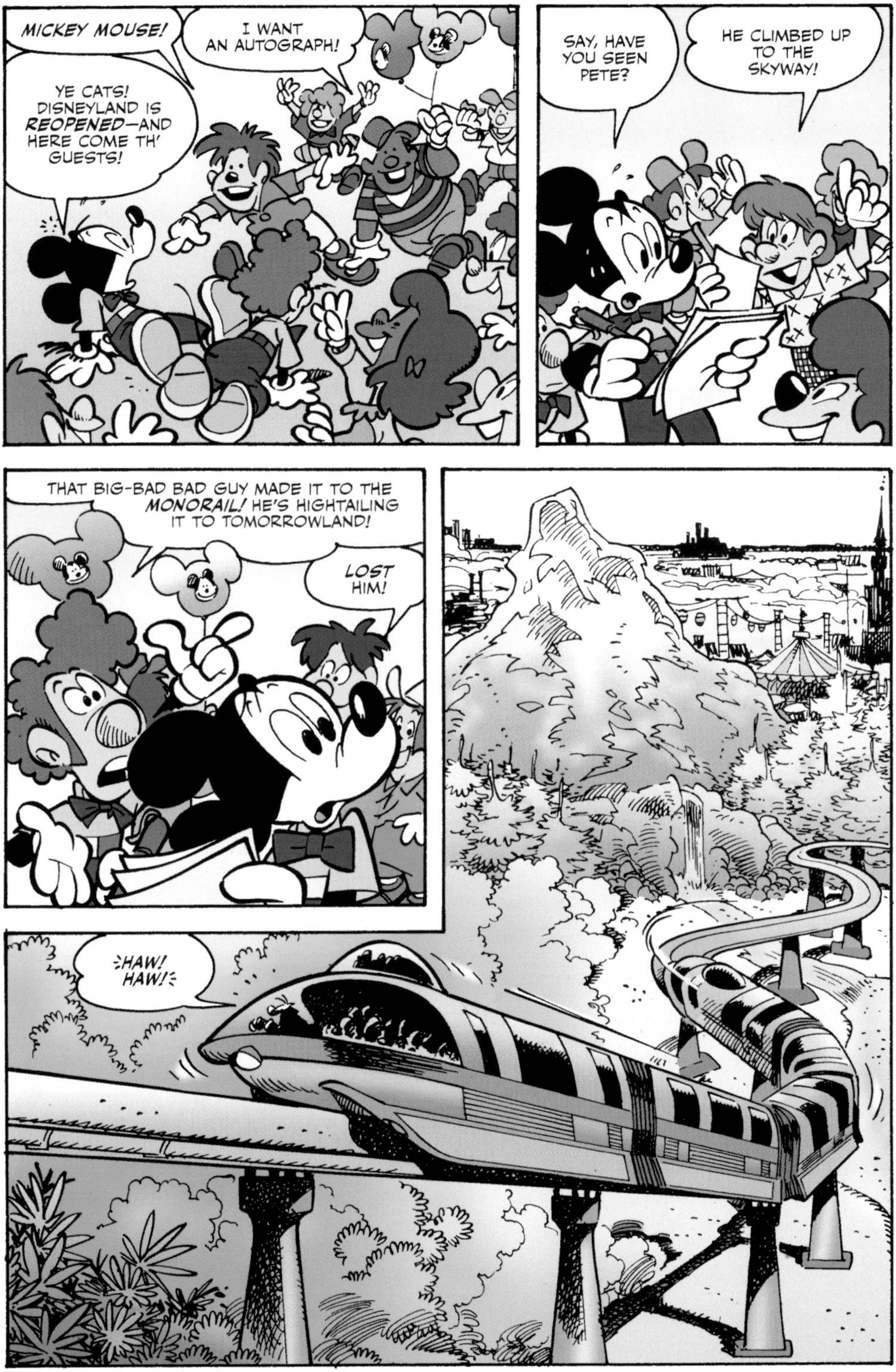

MICKEY MOUSE!
I WANT AN AUTOGRAPH!
YE CATS! DISNEYLAND IS REOPENED—AND HERE COME TH' GUESTS!
SAY, HAVE YOU SEEN PETE?
HE CLIMBED UP TO THE SKYWAY!
THAT BIG-BAD BAD GUY MADE IT TO THE MONORAIL! HE'S HIGHTAILING IT TO TOMORROWLAND!
LOST HIM!
HAW! HAW!

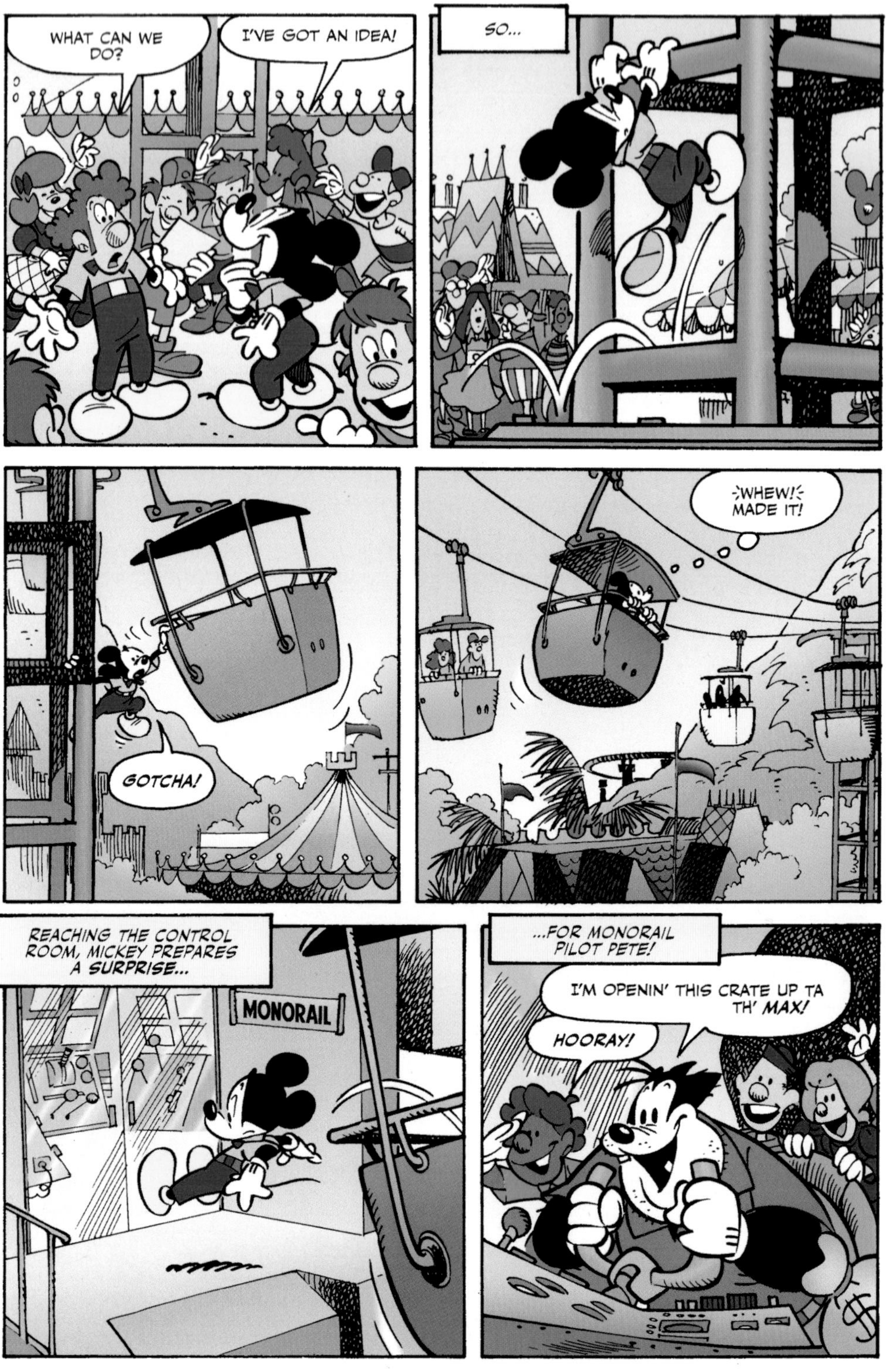
WHAT CAN WE DO?
I'VE GOT AN IDEA!
SO...
GOTCHA!
WHEW! MADE IT!
REACHING THE CONTROL ROOM, MICKEY PREPARES A SURPRISE...
MONORAIL
...FOR MONORAIL PILOT PETE!
I'M OPENIN' THIS CRATE UP TA TH' MAX!
HOORAY!

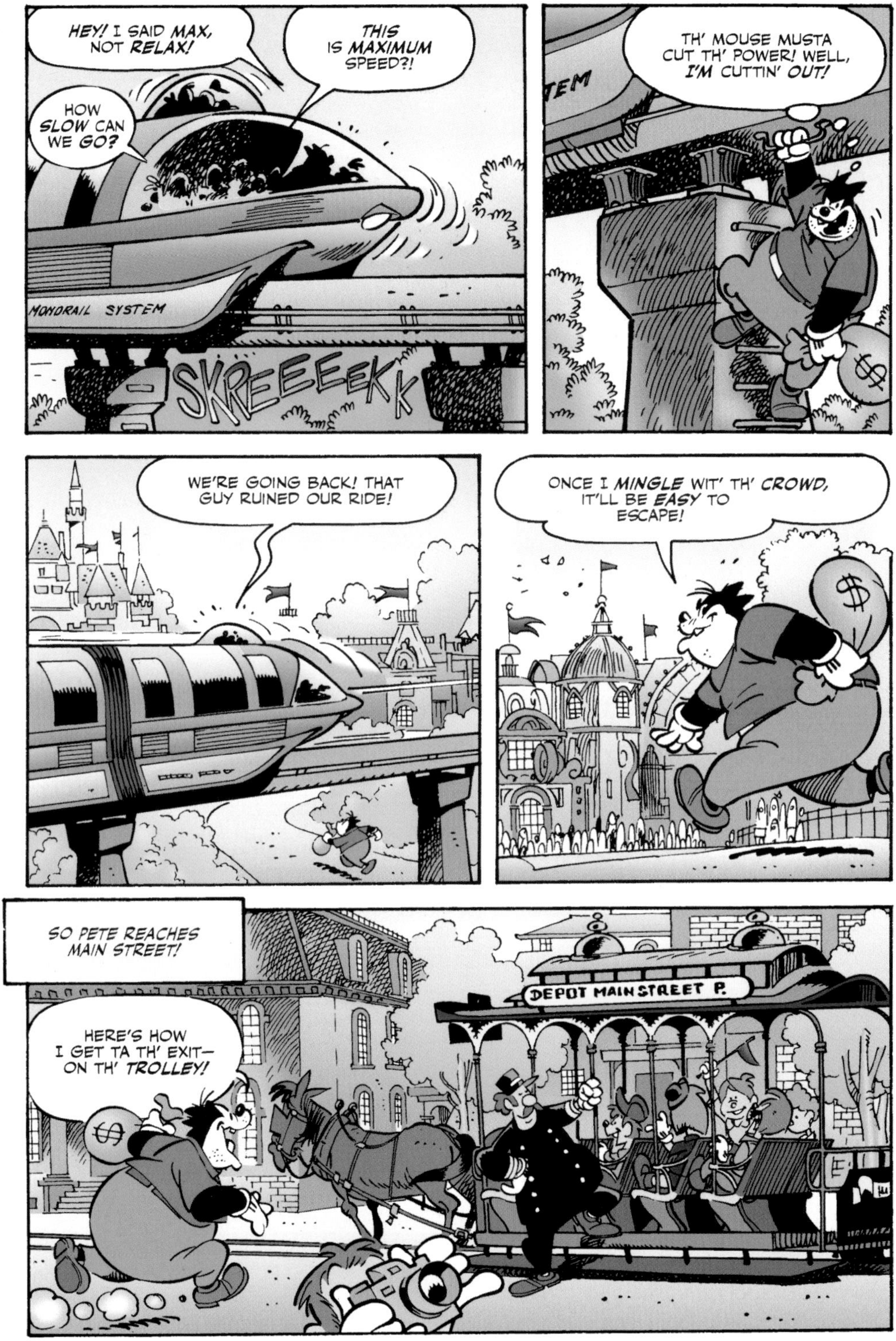
HEY! I SAID MAX, NOT RELAX!
THIS IS MAXIMUM SPEED?!
HOW SLOW CAN WE GO?
MONORAIL SYSTEM
SKREEEEEKK
TH' MOUSE MUSTA CUT TH' POWER! WELL, I'M CUTTIN' OUT!
WE'RE GOING BACK! THAT GUY RUINED OUR RIDE!
ONCE I MINGLE WIT' TH' CROWD, IT'LL BE EASY TO ESCAPE!
SO PETE REACHES MAIN STREET!
DEPOT MAIN STREET P.
HERE'S HOW I GET TA TH' EXIT— ON TH' TROLLEY!

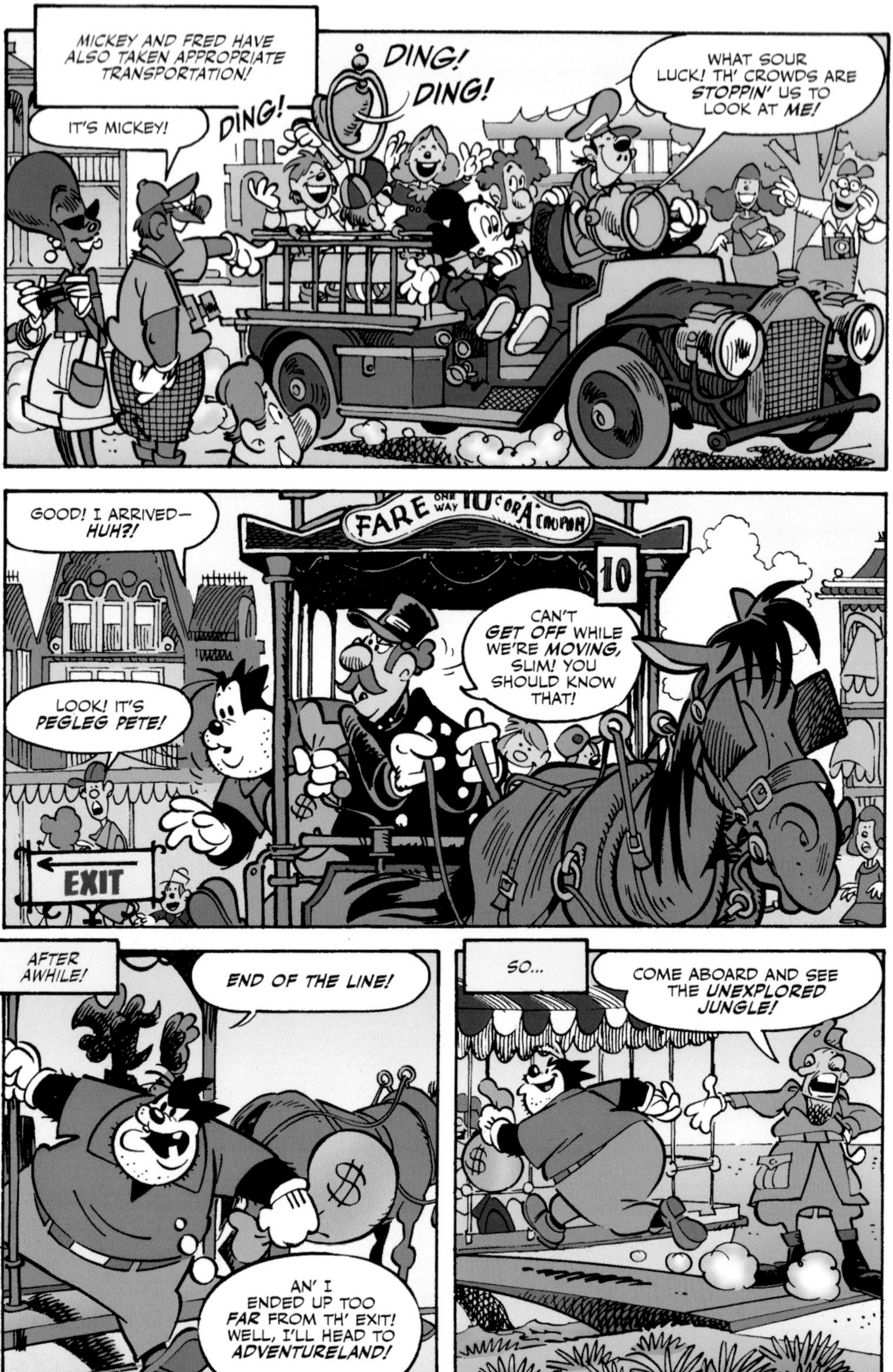
MICKEY AND FRED HAVE ALSO TAKEN APPROPRIATE TRANSPORTATION!
IT'S MICKEY!
DING!
DING!
DING!
WHAT SOUR LUCK! TH' CROWDS ARE STOPPIN' US TO LOOK AT ME!
GOOD! I ARRIVED— HUH?!
FARE ONE WAY 10¢ OR 'A' COUPON
10
LOOK! IT'S PEGLEG PETE!
CAN'T GET OFF WHILE WE'RE MOVING, SLIM! YOU SHOULD KNOW THAT!
EXIT
AFTER AWHILE!
END OF THE LINE!
AN' I ENDED UP TOO FAR FROM TH' EXIT! WELL, I'LL HEAD TO ADVENTURELAND!
SO...
COME ABOARD AND SEE THE UNEXPLORED JUNGLE!

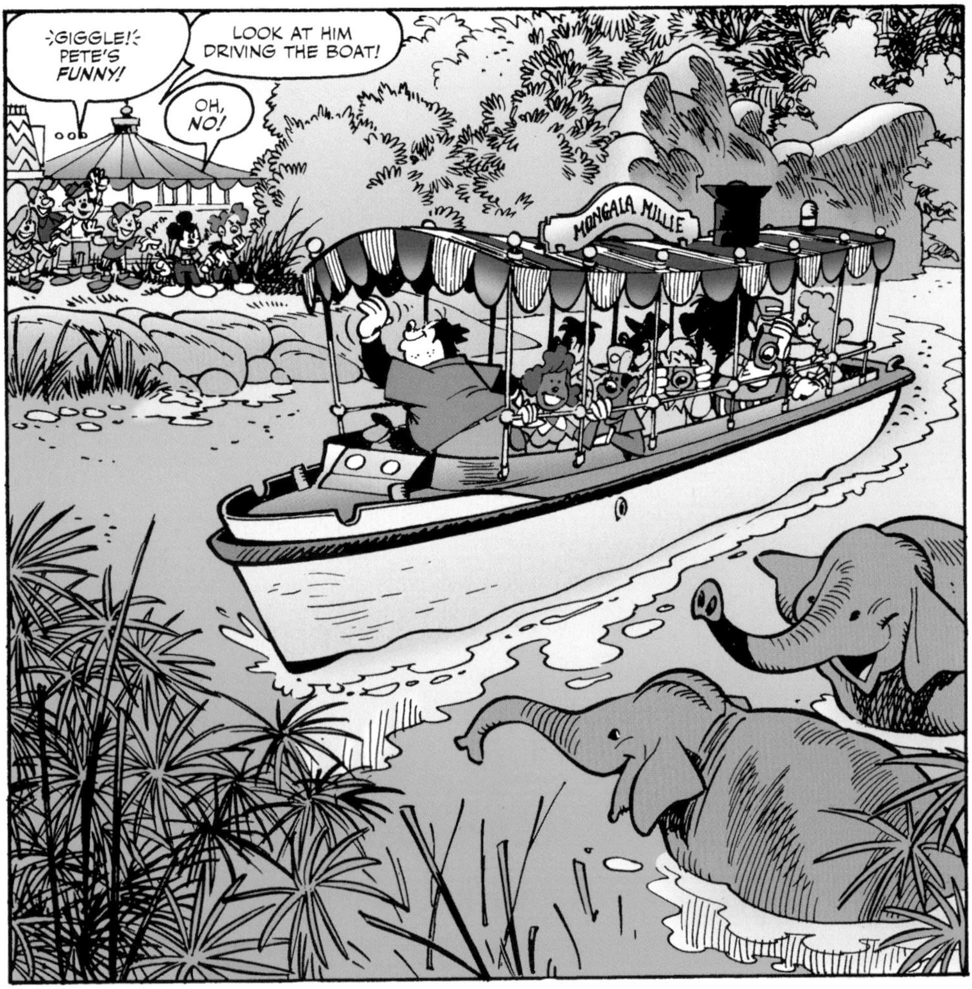

-GIGGLE!- PETE'S FUNNY!
LOOK AT HIM DRIVING THE BOAT!
OH, NO!
MONGALA MILLIE

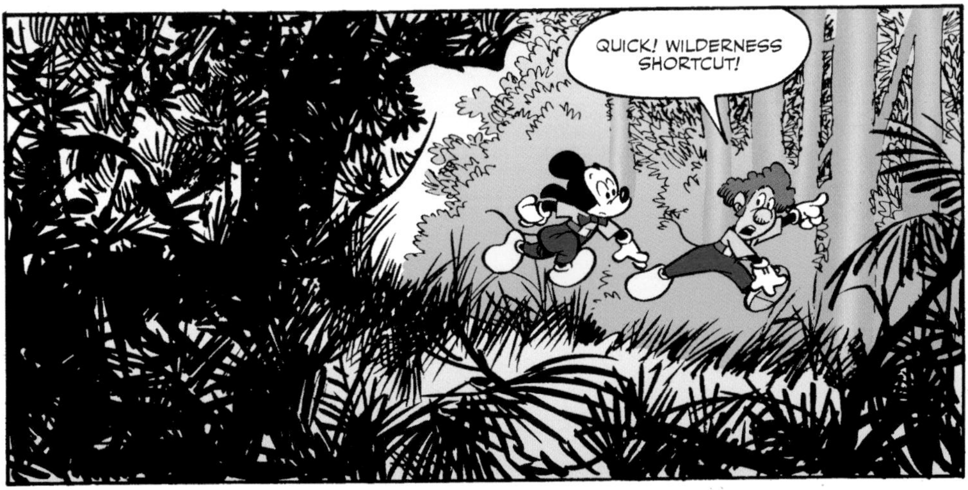

QUICK! WILDERNESS SHORTCUT!

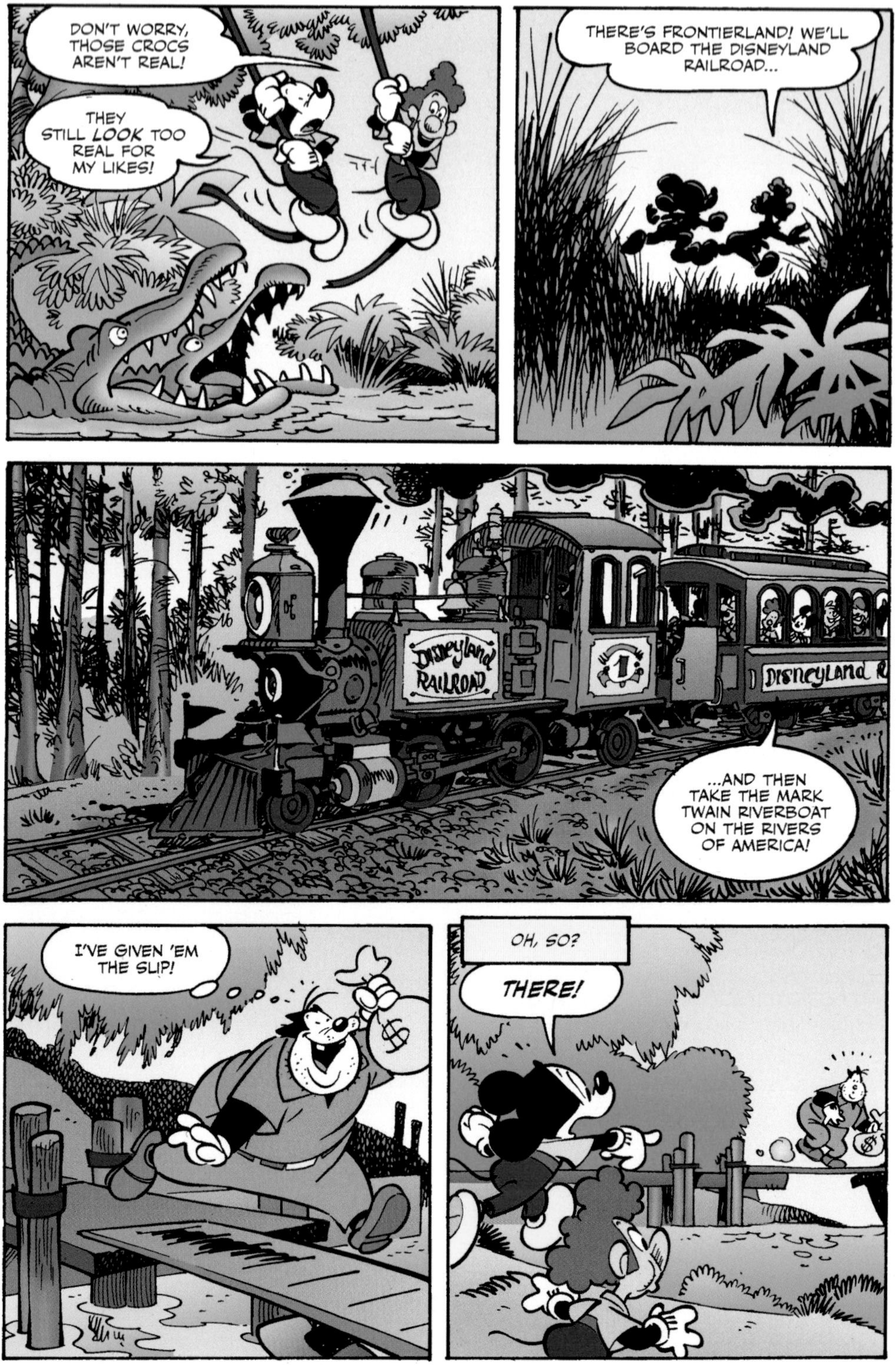
DON'T WORRY, THOSE CROCS AREN'T REAL!
THEY STILL LOOK TOO REAL FOR MY LIKES!
THERE'S FRONTIERLAND! WE'LL BOARD THE DISNEYLAND RAILROAD...
DISNEYLAND RAILROAD
1
DISNEYLAND
...AND THEN TAKE THE MARK TWAIN RIVERBOAT ON THE RIVERS OF AMERICA!
I'VE GIVEN 'EM THE SLIP!
$
OH, SO?
THERE!

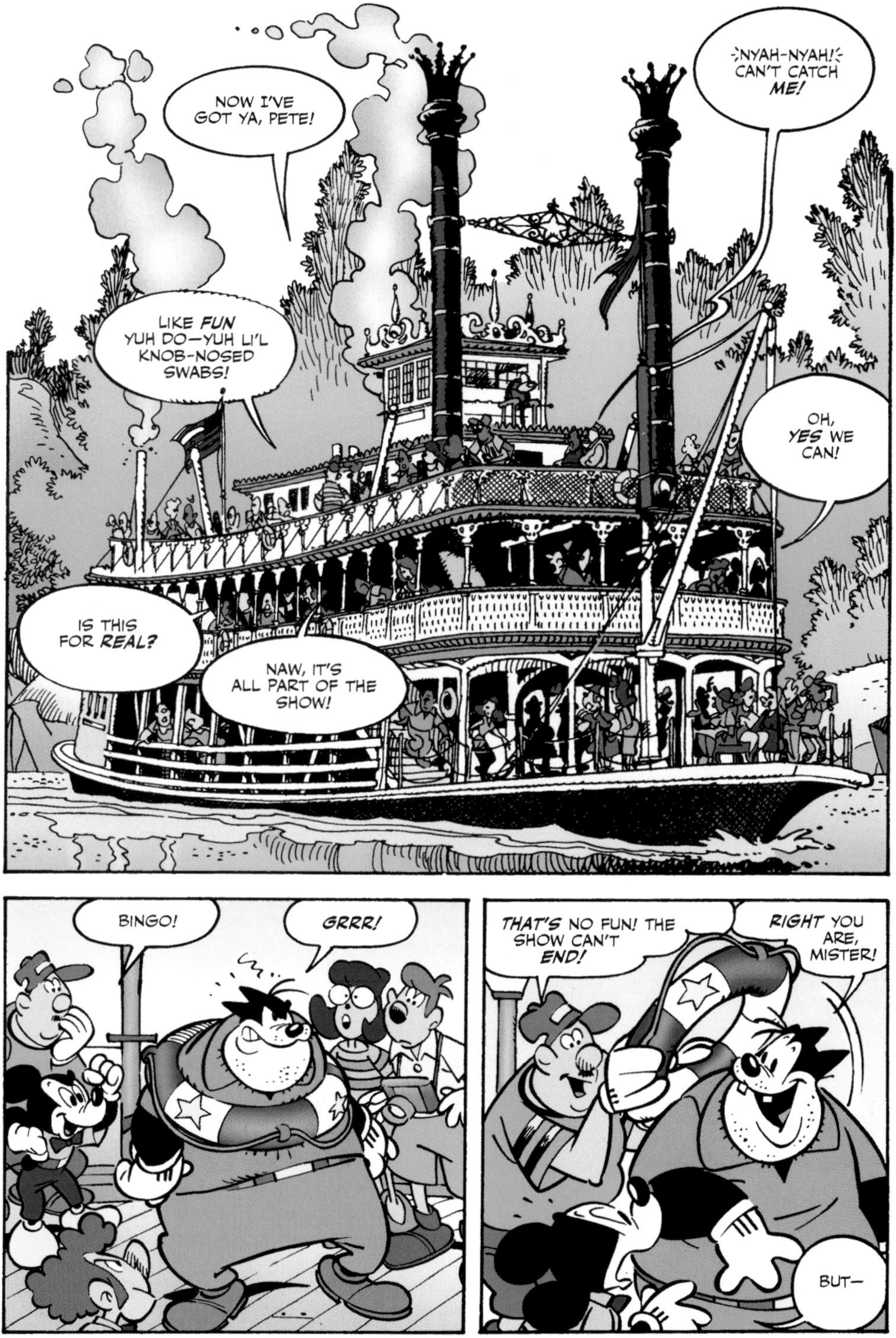
NOW I'VE GOT YA, PETE!
NYAH-NYAH! CAN'T CATCH ME!
LIKE FUN YUH DO—YUH LI'L KNOB-NOSED SWABS!
OH, YES WE CAN!
IS THIS FOR REAL?
NAW, IT'S ALL PART OF THE SHOW!
BINGO!
GRRR!
THAT'S NO FUN! THE SHOW CAN'T END!
RIGHT YOU ARE, MISTER!
BUT—

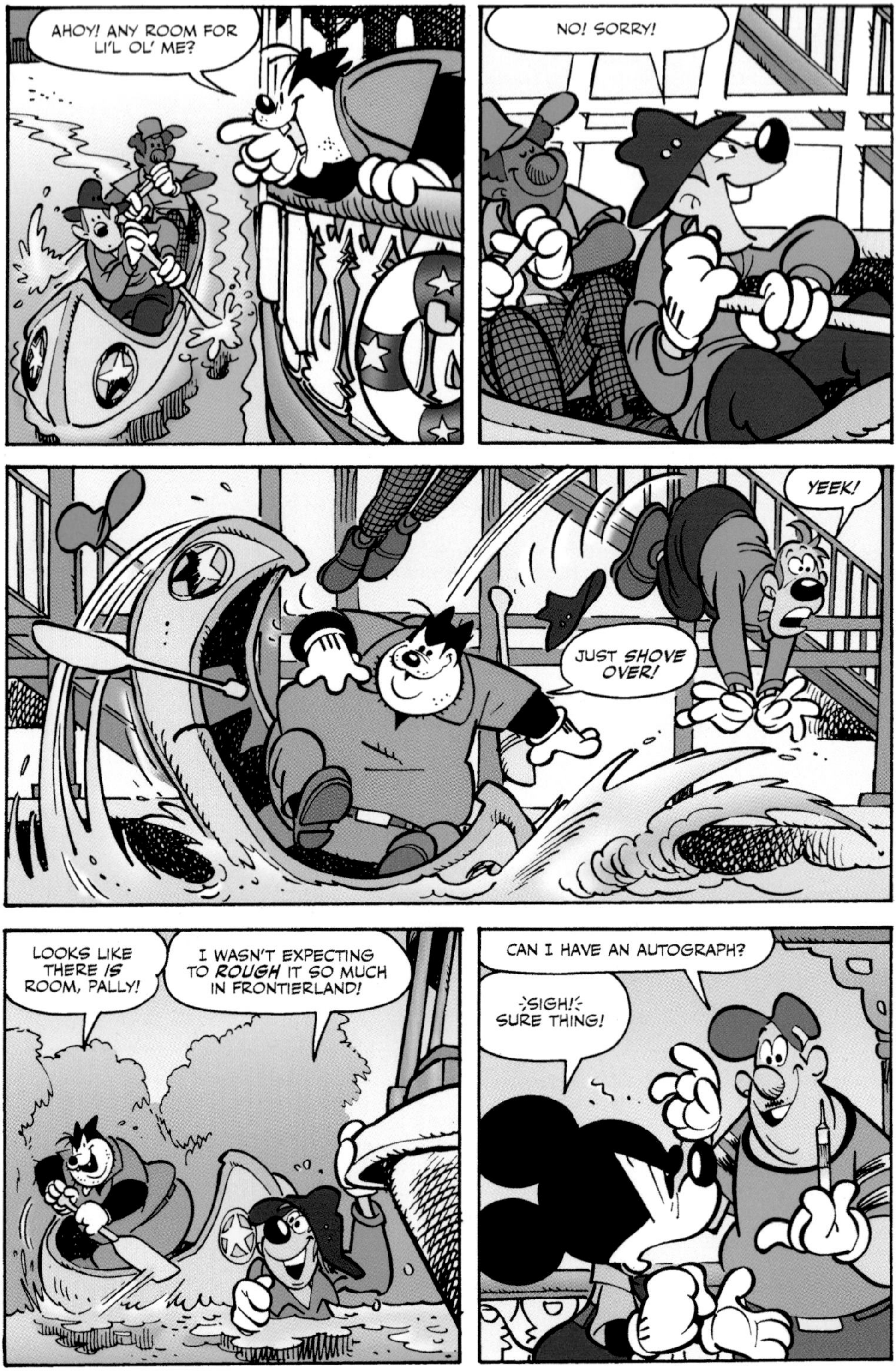

AHOY! ANY ROOM FOR LI'L OL' ME?
NO! SORRY!
YEEK!
JUST SHOVE OVER!
LOOKS LIKE THERE IS ROOM, PALLY!
I WASN'T EXPECTING TO ROUGH IT SO MUCH IN FRONTIERLAND!
CAN I HAVE AN AUTOGRAPH?
SIGH! SURE THING!

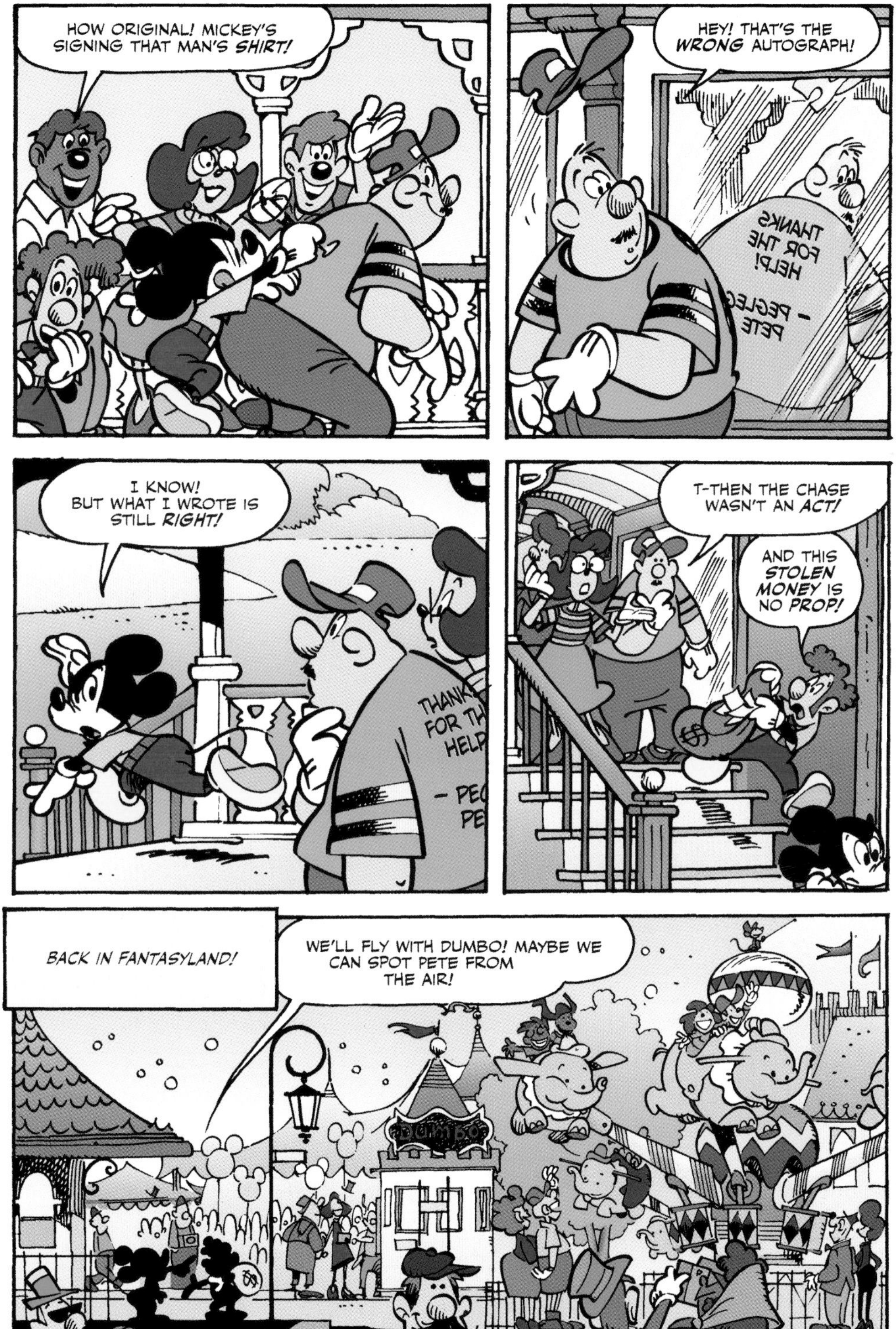
HOW ORIGINAL! MICKEY'S SIGNING THAT MAN'S *SHIRT!*
HEY! THAT'S THE *WRONG* AUTOGRAPH!
THANKS FOR THE HELP! – PEGLEG PETE
I KNOW! BUT WHAT I WROTE IS STILL *RIGHT!*
T-THEN THE CHASE WASN'T AN *ACT!*
AND THIS *STOLEN MONEY* IS NO *PROP!*
BACK IN FANTASYLAND!
WE'LL FLY WITH DUMBO! MAYBE WE CAN SPOT PETE FROM THE AIR!

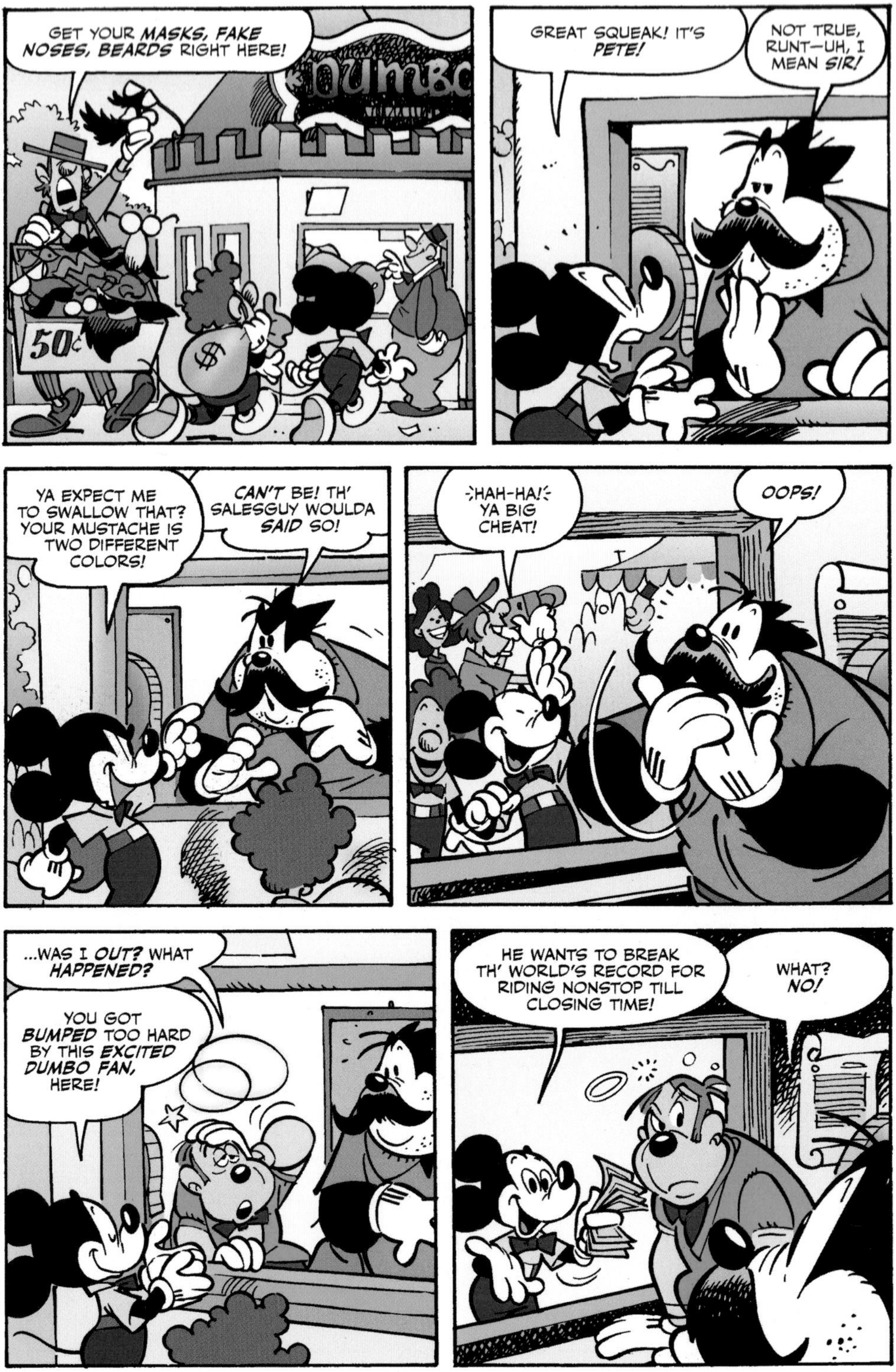
GET YOUR MASKS, FAKE NOSES, BEARDS RIGHT HERE!
DUMBO
50¢
GREAT SQUEAK! IT'S PETE!
NOT TRUE, RUNT—UH, I MEAN SIR!
YA EXPECT ME TO SWALLOW THAT? YOUR MUSTACHE IS TWO DIFFERENT COLORS!
CAN'T BE! TH' SALESGUY WOULDA SAID SO!
HAH-HA! YA BIG CHEAT!
OOPS!
...WAS I OUT? WHAT HAPPENED?
YOU GOT BUMPED TOO HARD BY THIS EXCITED DUMBO FAN, HERE!
HE WANTS TO BREAK TH' WORLD'S RECORD FOR RIDING NONSTOP TILL CLOSING TIME!
WHAT? NO!

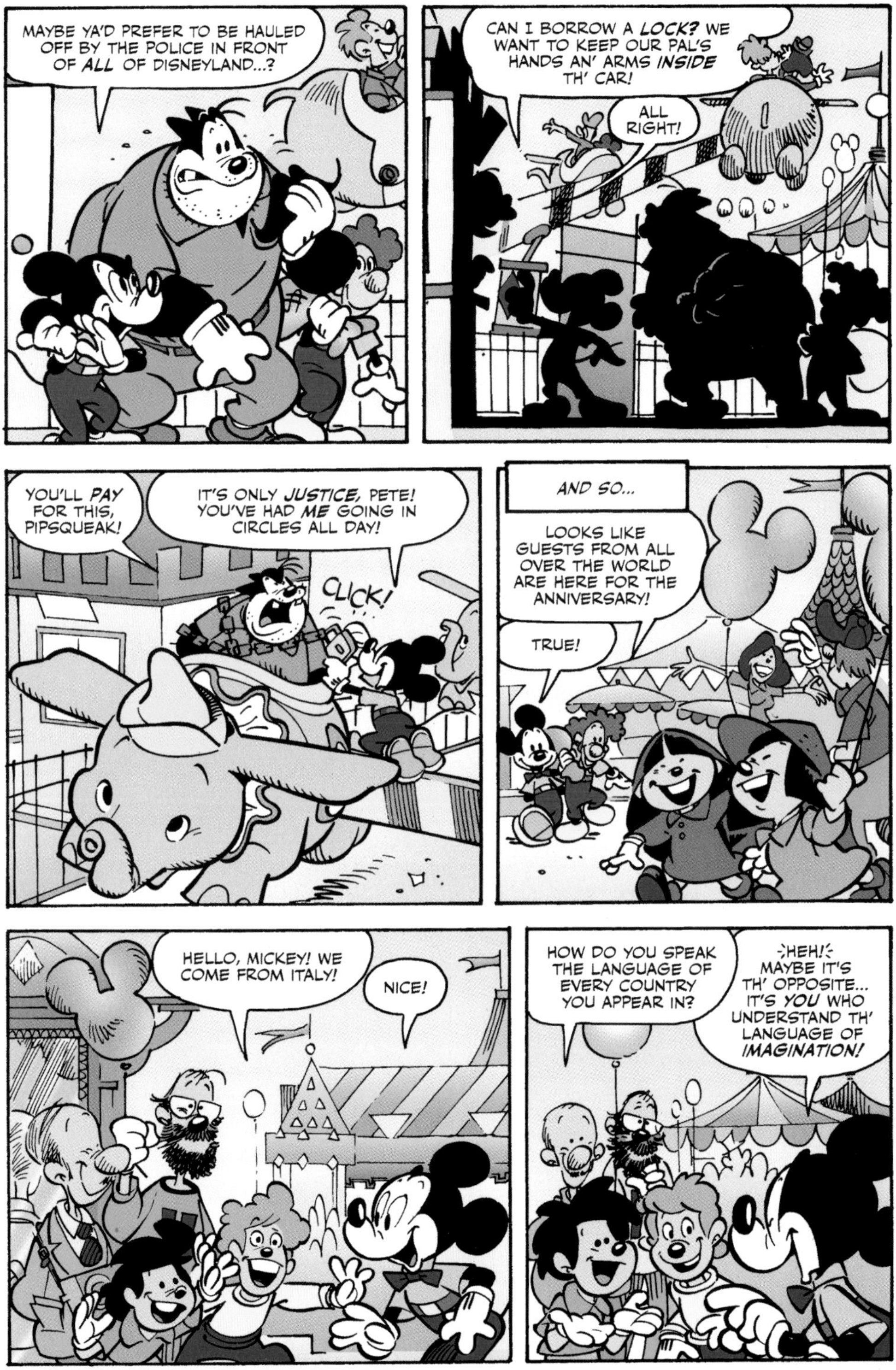
MAYBE YA'D PREFER TO BE HAULED OFF BY THE POLICE IN FRONT OF ALL OF DISNEYLAND...?
CAN I BORROW A LOCK? WE WANT TO KEEP OUR PAL'S HANDS AN' ARMS INSIDE TH' CAR!
ALL RIGHT!
YOU'LL PAY FOR THIS, PIPSQUEAK!
IT'S ONLY JUSTICE, PETE! YOU'VE HAD ME GOING IN CIRCLES ALL DAY!
CLICK!
AND SO...
LOOKS LIKE GUESTS FROM ALL OVER THE WORLD ARE HERE FOR THE ANNIVERSARY!
TRUE!
HELLO, MICKEY! WE COME FROM ITALY!
NICE!
HOW DO YOU SPEAK THE LANGUAGE OF EVERY COUNTRY YOU APPEAR IN?
HEH! MAYBE IT'S TH' OPPOSITE... IT'S YOU WHO UNDERSTAND TH' LANGUAGE OF IMAGINATION!

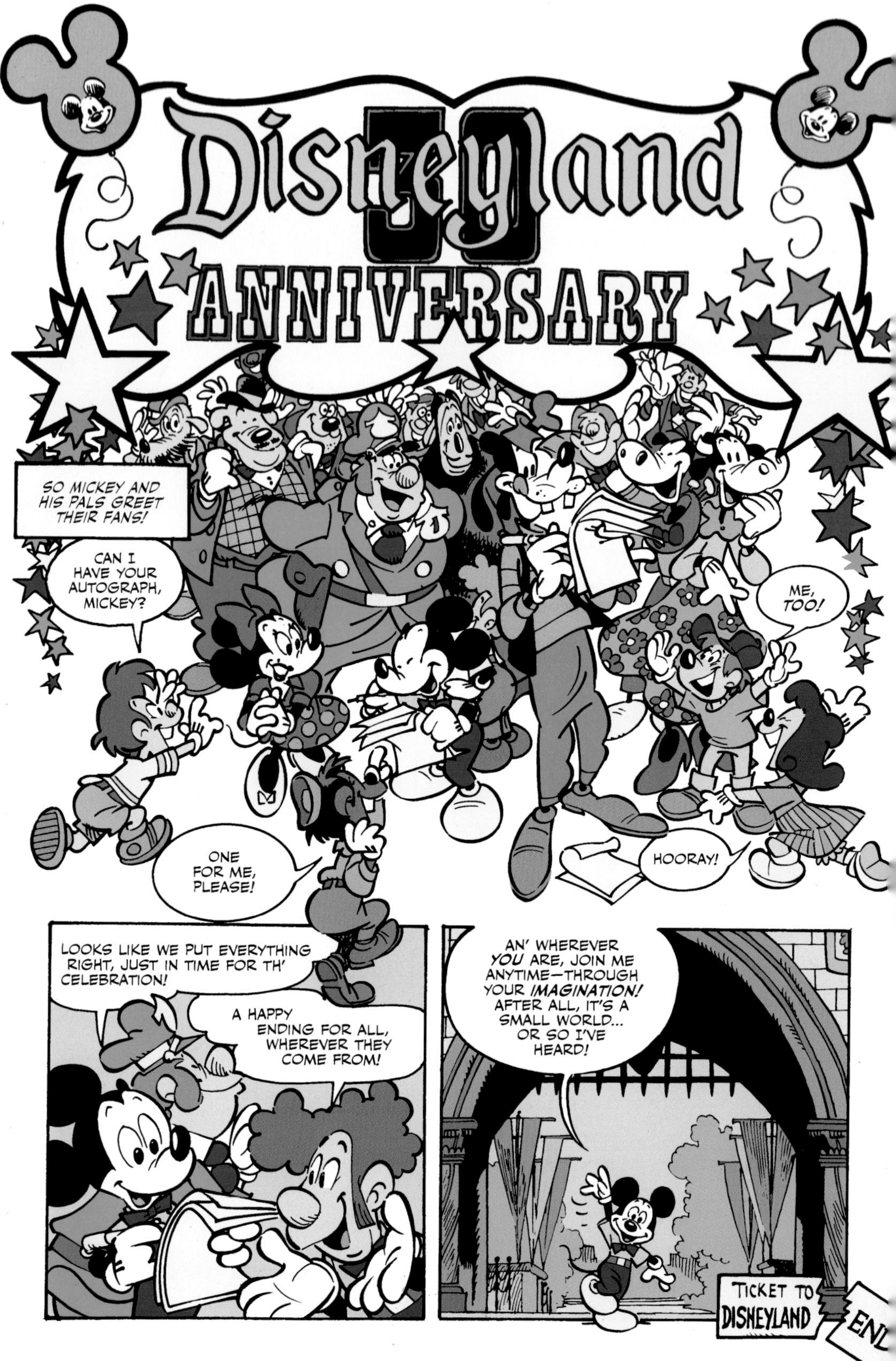
Disneyland
ANNIVERSARY
SO MICKEY AND HIS PALS GREET THEIR FANS!
CAN I HAVE YOUR AUTOGRAPH, MICKEY?
ME, TOO!
ONE FOR ME, PLEASE!
HOORAY!
LOOKS LIKE WE PUT EVERYTHING RIGHT, JUST IN TIME FOR TH' CELEBRATION!
A HAPPY ENDING FOR ALL, WHEREVER THEY COME FROM!
AN' WHEREVER YOU ARE, JOIN ME ANYTIME—THROUGH YOUR IMAGINATION! AFTER ALL, IT'S A SMALL WORLD... OR SO I'VE HEARD!
TICKET TO DISNEYLAND
END

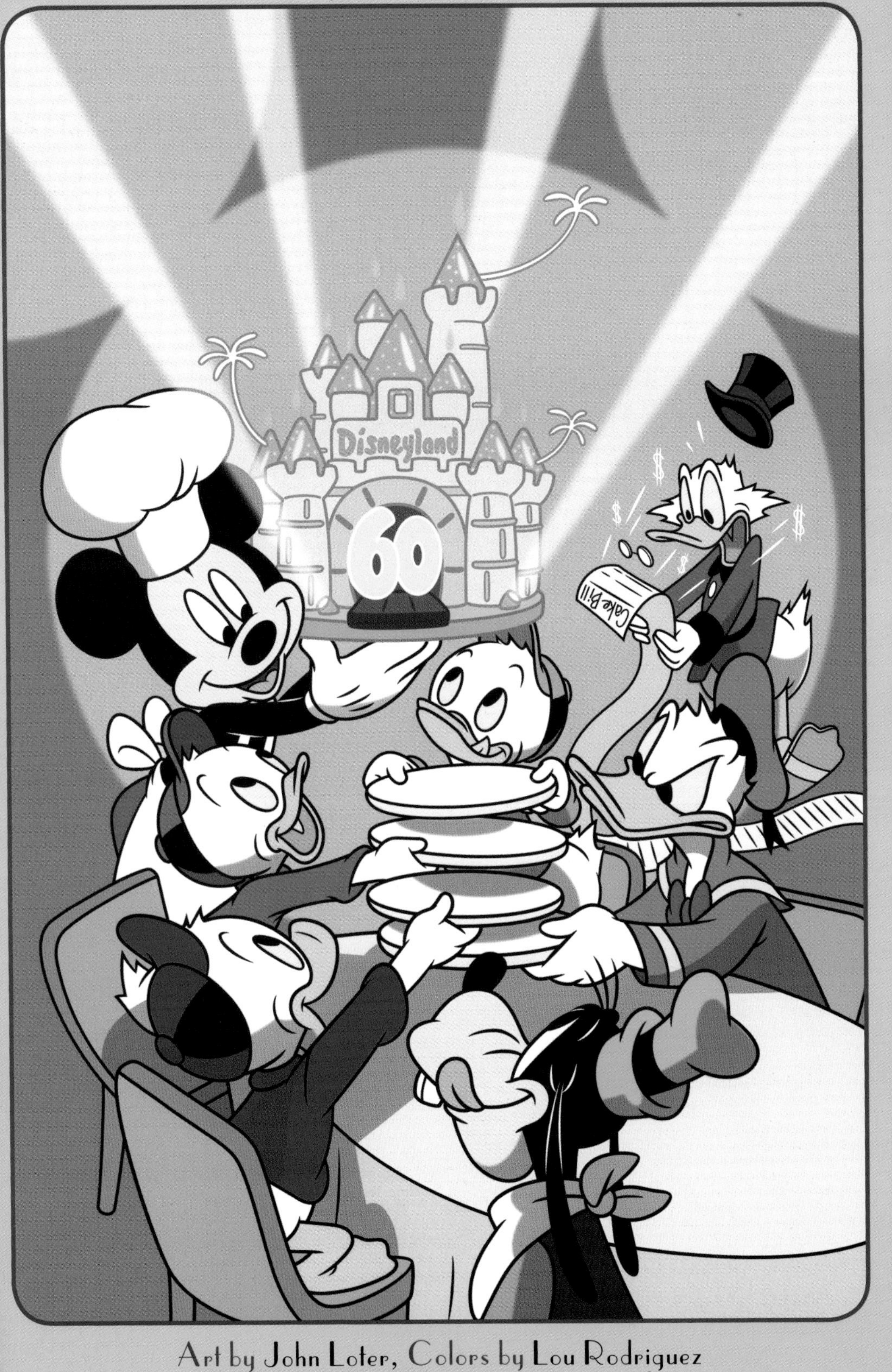

Disneyland
60
Cake Bill

Art by John Loter, Colors by Lou Rodriguez

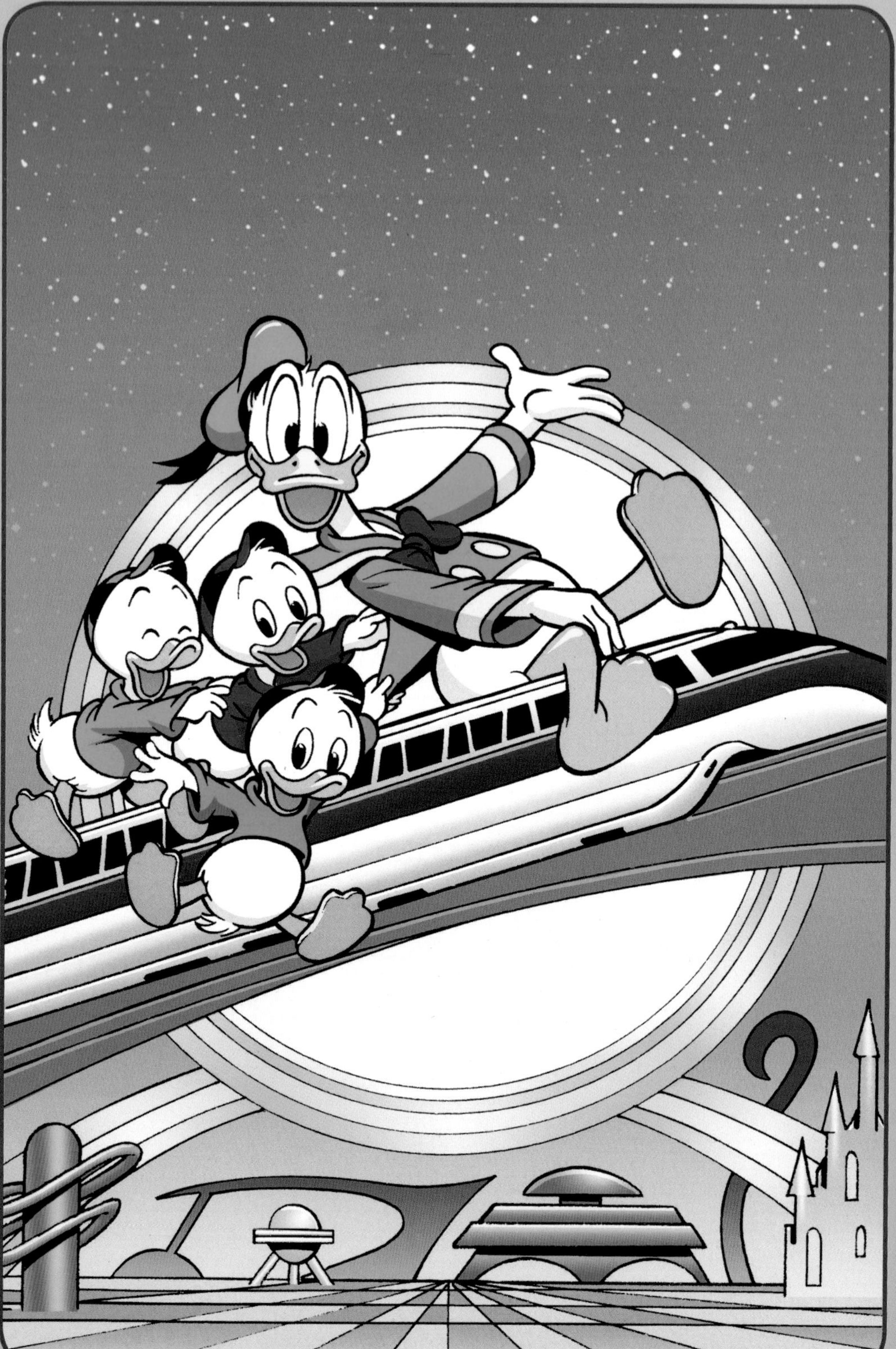

Art by Marco Rota, Colors by Ronda Pattison